PRAISE FOR THE GIFT

The Gift is not just for fans of science fiction or fantasy. It's for readers who want to feel the clash of fear and hope, who enjoy sci-fi stories where survival is as important as destiny, and where the heart matters as much as the universe. I would recommend it to anyone who likes their adventure raw and relatable, layered with both cosmic wonder and everyday struggle.

The writing surprised me. It has a dreamlike quality in places, flowing almost like waves, then suddenly crashing into moments of raw grit and pain.

— LITERARY TITAN

THE GIFT

EVA BARBER

To the love of my life
To my husband, Michael
Thank you
For restoring my courage
For giving me wings

✿ Formatted with Vellum

1

THE VOID

E mery! Emery! Where are you? It's your mother! Say something!" Olesya's voice cut through the darkness and reached Emery in silvery waves as the dark shapes dragged her to a destination only they knew. Despite not having heard her mother's voice for ten years, Emery recognized it immediately. Her mother had been here, waiting for her all these years. Emery now knew that she had made the right decision to plunge into this ghostly abyss, after all. Well, with Zoe's persuasive help.

When she heard her mother calling her, Emery felt a jolt of energy and her resolve returned. Until now, she had let the dark shapes pull her along, resigning to their will while silently weeping over losing Peter.

"Mother! Is that you? Where are you?" Emery cried out in response and noticed with astonishment that the sounds leaving her dark, shapeless body that was speckled with golden dots, formed silvery waves and dispersed, flowing away as if they knew where to go. She gathered these waves were her voice, swiftly crossing the darkness as if transmitting her message. Emery imagined they were responding to her mother's voice, rushing to unite with it and guide her mother toward her. She watched as they floated away, wishing she could move her nebulous body as quickly and easily as they moved, and longing to follow them.

Meanwhile, the dark shapes guided her somewhere. When they had first found her and silently surrounded her in a tight, dark circle, she had thought their intentions were vile. But as she watched their ever-shifting dark arms move slowly and deliberately toward her despite their apparent haste, she sensed this was to avoid frightening her. They circled her to guide and protect, not harm, as they purposefully and zealously herded her to a destination of their choosing. Despite their unnerving haste and their silence, their gentleness and the way they bowed their heads suggested peacefulness and even a certain reverence. As her mother's voice echoed, Emery grew apprehensive and impatient with being dragged to an unknown destination. She had to find her mother, but watching the waves drift away, she believed they were not moving in the direction from where her mother was calling.

As they glided through the endless grayness, Emery tried to engage her companions in a conversation, asking where they were taking her. They didn't answer but waved their shapeless arms, pointing into the distance.

Maybe they can't talk, she wondered. They look slightly different from me. They lack the golden dots.

"Where are you taking me? I need to find my mother. Are you taking me to her?" she asked.

Their heads blurred as they shook them in response.

When her mother's voice calling her name reached her again, Emery concentrated and stopped moving. The shapes watched her but did not force her to move. She tried to touch one of her dark guides, but the being scurried away to avoid her touch.

"I'm here to find and save my mother. I heard her voice, so I know she's here. Are you taking me to my mother?"

The dark shapes surrounded her in a tighter circle. Then she saw it. They shared a vision of a giant black hole. A vision so clear and powerful that she felt the intense pull of the chasm. The black giant was building up, amassing its dark energy by pulling and swallowing all matter in its vicinity. There was only a limited time for her to pass through it before it imploded, while its energy was at its peak, which was critical to pulling her through and into the past. Emery's possession of both the gold and black elements enabled her to get through the black hole and release the black shards (dark matter locked in the past by a dark energy implosion) to save the world and offer humanity the greatest gift—immortality, or near immortality, and health. She was destined to play the heroine. Fated to protect the world from imploding and give people something very few deserved, and many didn't want.

After its collapse, the black hole would remain in unparalleled stillness for thousands of years before it started rebuilding itself. This unbalanced universe couldn't wait that long. The shapes showed entire cities collapsing and disappearing while parents, screaming in terror, gathered their children, looking around frantically for a place to hide, trying to protect them. But the ground vanished from underneath their feet. And so did the oceans and the mountains and everything else.

"I understand. But I'm not going anywhere without my mother ... I have to find her and take her with me."

The shapes shook their heads and pointed the way, urging her to move.

But Emery wouldn't budge. "No, not without my mother. I can't leave her in this forsaken darkness."

The shapes showed her another vision. Her mother and her brother, Alexander, being pulled into a bright light, and then they floated through it.

"What does it mean? Why are you showing me this? Is it a way out of here?"

The shapes nodded.

"Where would she go? Tell me what will happen to my mother. Will she be saved? I'm not moving until you tell me."

One shape engaged in a staring match with Emery, who stood her ground, not moving.

Finally, the shape spoke. "Nobody knows where she'll end up.

She'll be reborn into a different dimension and a different life. It may be similar, it may be entirely different, but it probably won't be like the one she came from. Where she'll end up is a matter of chance and her ... destiny. We don't know her destiny, but we know your mother can't pass through the singularity with you. She'd be stuck in there forever, becoming part of its fabric and imploding with it." As the shape spoke, his voice's silvery waves danced around Emery, almost touching her dark body as if teasing her.

"We must go, Emery," the shadow added, seeing her hesitation. "If you want to save your mother and everyone else, you must go now."

"Who are you? Do you have a name?" Emery asked.

They didn't respond but nudged her forward. The deep sorrow in their voice and their quiet resignation moved her, and yet she questioned their motivations. Why were they helping her? What would they gain from helping her? They were not part of the universe she was about to save. They were stuck in this dark world. So why would they care?

"What will become of you when I go through the black hole?"

They ignored her question, pressing forward.

Emery grew suspicious. She stopped. "You don't know, or you don't want to tell me?"

"We'll disintegrate. We'll disappear."

"So why go with me? Why help me? By helping me, you are destroying yourselves. Why don't you just point me the way?"

"We must see you go through it. This is our destiny. If you succeed, there will be no more of us. We'll suffer no more."

"No more of you? What are you saying? Who are you?"

"We are the unborn. We've been wandering the dark dimension in this form since this universe's creation, but we can't get through the light or pass through the black giant. Many have tried, only to be scattered by the light or be stuck in the black hell," the shadow said and paused.

Emery waited patiently, sensing he would continue. And as he spoke, the silvery waves surrounded him in a shroud. "One of the reasons the universe is unbalanced is because of us. We exist in this form, unable to be born and add our dark matter to the growing world. And that's why we're helping you. If you succeed, instead of wandering the world aimlessly, we could be born in an alternative universe. So we believe and hope."

"But how do you know about me? How did you find out I was here and needed help? You've been here forever, you said." Emery asked.

"We've always known. This knowledge has been with us since our creation. Some of us stopped believing you'd come. They are now in there, in the black torment, silently crying for help. We are helping not only you—we are helping ourselves. We'll gladly disappear into the black hole, knowing you went through it safely."

The sincerity and pain in their silvery voices swayed Emery into believing them. Why would they deceive her?

"Mother! Can you hear me?"

Emery saw the faint silvery wave proceeding toward her. Getting closer. "I'm coming, Emery."

"Don't! Can you hear me? Don't follow me! Please! Listen to me! I will be okay. I know what to do now. I love you. Find your brother!"

She let her dark guides steer her through the dark space, drifting silently the rest of the way.

She asked one more question. "How certain are you I'll be able to go back in time?"

"That's what we've believed throughout our existence. When the black hole is at its maximum energy, all matter rotates faster than the speed of light, warping space-time and bending it back on itself, forming loops ... time-like curves. You can jump a loop and end up back at the beginnings of time."

"I don't want to go back to the beginning of time. I want to go where I need to go to unlock the dark matter."

"We believe you will get where you need to be."

"How certain are you I'll even be able to get through, much less end up where I'm supposed to?"

"We believe you will."

"You believe, but you have no certainty," Emery grumbled, and for a moment, considered escaping and making her own way through the darkness to find her mother and lead her to the light (if there was such a thing). But she couldn't refute the sincerity in their voices. They believed that what they were telling her was the truth. "Fine," Emery said and followed them. *I'll see where they take me. If they are lying, I can always dodge them later.*

2

THE BLACK HOLE

The darkness became even darker and denser, like molasses. Emery felt its heaviness pressing on her from all sides, but to her surprise, she still moved as fast and effortlessly as before. Her companions, though, slowed down, and eventually stopped moving altogether. She couldn't see them anymore, only sensed they were by her side by the slight undulations of the dense matrix until one spoke his last words to her.

"We can't go any further with you. You must move forward by yourself."

"How will I know I've arrived?"

"We don't know. This is as far as we can go. You'll probably know. After all, this is your destiny. Thank you, Emery. Thank you for making this sacrifice for everyone else."

Probably? I will probably know where to go? Am I really doing this? Going through the black hole?

Emery moved forward through the ever-thickening darkness. Never in her life had she been more uncertain about how much time had passed. As if it didn't exist—in one moment it felt like months; in another, it felt like years had gone by; and yet another, like minutes.

Confusion clouded her thoughts, and at times, she doubted whether she was moving at all.

To keep her mind off the oppressive darkness, she started thinking about Peter. She imagined his blue eyes staring at her, reassuring her she'd be okay. She imagined his soothing smile. The memory calmed her down, and she started getting used to the monotonous drifting and gradually resigned herself to her fate. Until she started hearing sounds. At first, they were distant, faint, and unrecognizable; then they sounded increasingly like human cries for help. As she drifted, they became louder, clearer, and unbearable. Sounds of crying, sobbing, screaming in pain, and hysterical laughter of women, men, and children, increasing in volume and intensity as she drifted through the blackness.

The unsettling sounds passed through her cloudy body in throbbing beats as she drifted, threatening to overwhelm her. She was about to join their cries out of frustration, to drown out the sounds of the others, when the wailings ended abruptly. Then the pain began.

She was stunned that she could feel pain without a body full of nerves and blood, skin, and muscles. But she did. Pain so excruciating and deep, she was certain she had been cut with a million blades and burned to her bones. It hurt so badly that she wanted to die. At one point, she realized she no longer had a body. Her shadowy being was no more, cut into a million pieces, spinning all around her. Each one hurt even more.

Suddenly, a black spinning tunnel opened, pulling all the pieces into a vortex. She was aware of its speed defying gravity as she felt the pieces of her colliding as they spun and the pain morphing into an escalating pressure. As the tiny pieces slammed into each other, her body coalesced back into an aching, dark blob. She wished it'd stop and just kill her, astonished she wasn't dead by now.

The pain eased when the lights started appearing in the distance. Blue lights. Many shades of blue. From pale and almost white to almost black. They came at her from the left and right at high velocities, producing blinding flashes when crossing paths and colliding with each other. When they started coming straight at her, she panicked, thinking they would run into her, and impulsively swerved to avoid them.

She quickly discovered she couldn't avoid them, but also that they were not harmful. They passed through her without causing pain, but not without affecting her. When they passed through her, they left physical marks on her: tiny blue spots all over her dark being. As they marked her body with more spots, she felt a gentle tingling, as if the lights were gently caressing her body, changing it, and morphing it into something different. She became a blue light herself, and her speed increased. Emery was traversing through the black hole at the speed of this mesmerizing cerulean light. Carried by it ever so gently, and with the pain completely gone, she felt more alive and blissful—she could stay like this forever.

But her blue-light period did not last forever. Emery felt a pull and plunged. For what felt like an eternity, she fell into blue darkness. As she fell, the lights disappeared from around her and from her body. She felt different now, as if the lights had left something inside of her—heavier. And she could feel her limbs and her body, just like before she went into the capsule. While inspecting her slightly bluish body, admiring the newly formed fingers and toes, she remembered her mother and Sara talking about how light could hold memories and information. Normally, she didn't pay attention to what they talked about while working, but this one had struck her as magical. After hearing this, she'd never looked the same way at the sun, wondering what secrets it held.

Then, her attention shifted to what was happening around her. As she drifted, images emerged from the darkness. Faint and incomplete at first, the mirages morphed into different worlds or dimensions. She lacked the words to describe them because most were so different from Earth. They unfolded before her as she whizzed by them. Some worlds were dense purple jungles, some entirely blue and pink deserts, and some looked like mountains she'd seen on Earth. Others looked like mountains or oceans, but they were inverted—red oceans floated in space while violet mountains, with peaks bent in ways that mocked the laws of physics, disappeared into the abyss below.

When she drifted through worlds full of futuristic skyscrapers with objects flying through them, she wished she had time to explore. Some looked like towns from the past. Others were indescribable, as she had seen nothing like them before. They vaguely resembled cities; some looked more like giant beehives, some resembled see-through labyrinths. She tried to stop and admire the mesmerizing worlds that exchanged striking colors and shapes with each other, flowing as if they were part of something bigger, like an enormous, colorful ocean or sky. Some worlds were empty ... or maybe they were not worlds at all, but empty voids and spaces between.

A few realms halted her breath and stopped her heart momentarily. Dark and sharply defined structures, with silvery creatures slithering between them. She instinctively veered away from them. But in one instant, she drifted too close to one and suddenly saw a flash of something zooming toward her faster than she was moving. As the silvery, snake-like shape approached, three oval eyes opened. The yellowish whites of the eyes emitted a pulsating glow while the black pupils spun. She stopped moving and then felt herself pulled by the creature's eyes. Its long body shifted, transformed, and grew, and she saw three long tentacles moving toward her, trying to reach her. It attempted to take her into its world. One tentacle reached her, and she felt a sharp pain that spread through her entire body from where it touched her. The pain and fear she felt morphed into a fury. Emery thrust her hands at the creature, turned, and pulled away. She didn't waste time checking whether her powers had worked. She moved away with all the strength her body possessed.

It was a while before she dared to look back. The dark world had vanished, replaced by others, some even more disturbing, and some more bizarre. Now, she had to do something equally terrifying—find the right one. This world-saving mission didn't come with instructions, and the dark shapes were not helpful. How would she find her way? Her desperation grew as she watched the worlds float and rotate around her. She even considered jumping into a random one, letting fate decide for her. But she didn't. She couldn't risk it. She had to be certain.

Think, Emery, think. What would Mom do? Where would she go? She'd researched it, so she must have had an idea.

Emery shut her eyes and imagined her mother. Smiling, her mother appeared before her. Then she drifted away, revealing a world behind her. It looked like Earth—it had valleys, mountains, forests, and deserts. And the colors were right. The deserts were golden; the forests were green, and the sky was blue.

I don't remember seeing this one yet, Emery thought. I hope I didn't miss it.

Emery opened her eyes and searched for the one she had seen in her mind. For a very long time—or so it seemed to her—she had searched but had not seen the one her mother had revealed to her.

Be patient. Wait.

Being patient wasn't easy. Not knowing how much time had elapsed since she entered the black hole, she felt a heaviness in her blue chest when she imagined the universe ending because she couldn't select the right world in time. Resisting the urge to jump into any realm, Emery waited, and the world her mother had shown her finally unfolded before her slowly, like a slow-motion movie. Emery sighed with relief, smiled, and stepped into that world.

"Thank you, Mom."

3

WHERE AM I?

Expecting to walk into the world as if she were stepping through a door, Emery lost her balance, plummeting from a considerable height. She fell onto a tree, scraping the skin on her hands and legs on her way down while attempting to grab the branches to slow the fall. But she missed them and fell, hitting the ground with a thump and a groan. She rested, looking up at the tree she'd just fallen through. From behind the tree, the blue, cloudless sky provided a backdrop for a blinding sun that poked its big yellow head through the branches, welcoming her to this new world with its warmth.

To her surprise and dismay, there was no hole in the sky where she had come from. Nothing pointed to a passage, as if it had never existed. The tree didn't look familiar—it looked nothing like the trees that grew in Washington state, where she was from. She retained very little knowledge from her college biology classes of anything green and growing. She could distinguish evergreens from deciduous. Palms from conifers. This tree looked neither. Scraggly and bent in ways trees shouldn't bend, the tree spread its tangled branches far from its bulbous trunk and resembled a witch's broom.

I should've paid more attention to botany instead of flirting with Nathan.

Emery looked around, squinting. This lonely tree was the only tree within her view in a dry, desert landscape as flat as a pancake and devoid of vegetation except for an occasional scraggly shrub rising from the golden sand. The entangled branches and the long, soft leaves of the lone tree saved her from serious injuries by slowing her fall. She ended up with a few minor scrapes and bruises on her skin, which, to her relief, was back to its normal golden state. Stretched tightly over her muscular body, her skin glowed with health.

Was it pure luck that I fell on the only tree in the area? The only tree? Emery marveled. After what she'd been through, she should have believed in fairies, trolls, and astrology, but the skeptic gene she'd inherited from her mother made her search for a more ordinary or scientific explanation.

With a grunt, she rose to her feet and spat out the sand that had somehow found its way into her mouth. It was already warm, even though the sun was still low on the horizon. Emery glanced at the hot yellow ball of heat, guessing it would get much hotter as the day progressed. When she examined her bruised and scratched body, she discovered she was only wearing her cotton underwear and a cotton tank top—what she'd worn under her clothes when she entered the capsule. Her other clothes were gone.

Emery tried to remember what else she'd worn that day. *Synthetic —the rest of my clothes were synthetic, and they are all gone! They didn't survive the black hole. Interesting.*

Shoeless and nearly naked, Emery had walked toward the hills she saw in the distance, hoping to escape the heat and find water. The hills were the only visible feature in an otherwise desert-like land-scape. She tried to recall her limited knowledge of geography, remembering states or countries with sizable desert areas. She gave that up quickly as she came up with too many.

I guess I'll find out soon enough.

The sand and the rocks under her feet grew warmer as the sun rose further from the horizon. She took off her tank top and wrapped it around her head. Walking topless under the scorching sun, she was certain she'd get burned before reaching a higher elevation, but she opted to protect her head, knowing it would hurt more than sunburned skin would. Wincing and hissing in pain at the sharp rocks stabbing her feet as she walked through the desert, she focused her eyes on the sand in front of her. With no shade or water in sight, Emery worried she might not make it before her feet were completely bloodied and burned. She seemed no closer to the hills than she had been hours ago.

To get all the way here through the dark world and the black hole only to die in the desert would be so pathetic and so wrong. *Oh, just shut up and keep going. Stop being a baby. You haven't even walked a whole day yet.*

Emery continued moving, glancing at the hills, knowing they would offer shade, water, and shelter for the night. And the night was approaching fast—the sun was already low on the horizon. The lack of water and her aching feet screaming for rest and attention irritated her. She walked as fast as she could, yet didn't seem to get any closer. It was as if she were staying in one place or even going backwards.

Maybe they are a mirage? No, they look too real for a mirage. And how do you know that? Have you ever seen one? Just keep walking.

Alternating between pep talks and scolding herself, Emery kept walking with her eyes to the ground, occasionally glancing into the distance. At last, the sun was low enough on the horizon to allow the sand to cool down. She could walk faster now, but the hills still appeared far away and beyond reach. The air cooled rapidly as the sun was setting. She put her top back on, but the thin sleeveless shirt hardly eased the cold, which now felt like ice pricks on her burned torso. She sped up to keep herself warm, realizing she'd have to keep up a brisk pace all night not to freeze to death. Like most other deserts, this one would experience a significant drop in temperature during the night. She worried hypothermia might set in quickly for someone wearing only a pole-dancing outfit.

When it became dark, Emery slowed down, unable to see her

own feet and afraid to step on something sharp or venomous. The dim stars provided little light, and the moon was nonexistent. *Perhaps I am not on Earth? Maybe it's a planet just like Earth, but moonless.* She agonized over the unfamiliarity with her surroundings, incessantly second-guessing her decision to jump down into this world. And just as her mind wandered off, and she lost focus, she stumbled and fell, tripping over something hard. Her toe, already sore from hitting the rocks all day, was on fire now. "Son of a bitch!" she shouted and slumped to the sand, now cool to the touch.

Cursing, thinking she'd broken her toe, she sat and inspected it with her fingers and was relieved, finding no open wound or bones sticking out. After a few minutes, the sharp pain subsided, and only the painful but bearable throbbing remained; her pride hurt more. She inspected the ground with her hands, trying to find the thing she'd fallen over, and discovered it was a giant rock, and that more lay scattered ahead.

Finding the rocks elicited a burst of enthusiasm and hope. The abundance of rocks implied she was getting near the hills or at least a change of scenery from the hot and desolate desert. Excited, she got up and carefully stepped over the rock. As she stepped over the next rock, she lost her footing and her balance and fell for what felt like forever, but was merely seconds. She waved her arms frantically, grabbing desperately at the air. Her head hit something hard when she finally reached the ground, and she lost consciousness.

When she awoke, the sunlight felt good on her body, but her eyes hurt when she opened them and the intense light struck them. Her head felt as if someone were pounding it with a sledgehammer. After a while, she tried to open her eyes again, slower this time, but the light sent stabbing pains into her skull, and she squeezed her eyes shut.

Emery stayed motionless, afraid to move, imagining her body broken and bent in all directions. *Mom,* she cried silently. *Mom. Why me? Why couldn't someone else save the fucking world?*

Moments passed as Emery waited to move, suspended by her fear and self-pity, thinking about her childhood cut short when her mother left. She allowed the tears to escape her closed eyelids. As she cried out in despair and anger, her chest moved in spasms, her hands closed in tight fists, and her feet kicked the earth below, she realized her body wasn't broken. She sat up and wiped her tears with her hand, which was covered with scrapes and dirt. Then, she inspected her body for other injuries but found only more bruises and scrapes. When she touched the back of her head, she felt stickiness and assumed it was blood. Had she lost enough blood to be life-threatening? Knowing she had to get up and start walking again, she opened her eyes and held them open despite the throbbing, the red blotches, and the ringing in her ears. There was not much blood on the sand-covered stone below, and she let out a breath of relief. She'll live.

The red blotches eventually disappeared. Emery scrambled to her knees, unleashing a wave of nausea. She waited for it to subside, and then she stumbled to her feet and looked around. She gasped, realizing she had landed in a deep and steep-walled pit. It looked as if an enormous drill had pierced straight down through the rock. The hole extended deeper, forming a small cave. Curious, she walked deeper to explore it. The cave sloped dramatically just a few feet in and then cut off at a wall.

She was about to turn around when she noticed something lighter near the cave wall. She lifted it and carried it into the sunlight to inspect it. Her eyes were now adjusted to the light. In her hand, she held a shiny white stone, painstakingly chipped to form a shapely knife. She traced the chip marks with her fingers and turned the knife around; it fit nicely in her hand. Her heart raced when she realized she had found a prehistoric stone knife. She had either achieved her goal and landed back in time o,r she had stumbled onto an archeological site.

Excitement distracted her from the headache, and moving around eased the nausea. Having washed her misery and fear with tears, she felt more optimistic about her chance of survival and enthusiastic about exploring the past. Now, she just had to get out of the cave. *Easy-peasy*, she thought, but when she glanced at the vertical rock face, her face dropped as she noticed its steepness.

Emery had been rock climbing with friends, but she had never quite developed the skills or the desire to be a serious climber. Her fear of hurting herself and possibly losing her independence as a result, and respectful avoidance of heights, made her seek other, safer hobbies. Like dating.

Left with no choice but to climb up without help with her bare, sore feet and hands, she had to be smart about it. She inspected the sheer rock face with dismay. None of the walls was good for climbing. They were all steep and lacked good holds for her to pull herself up. But if she ever wanted to get out of here, she had to climb it. The crevices were so small she could barely fit her fingertips and toes in. She tried climbing up but felt pain in her toe when it touched the hard rock, and she lost confidence after a few moves and jumped down, breathing hard in panic. When she looked up at the height of the perpendicular wall, what was left of her confidence ebbed away.

There's no way in hell I could climb this without falling, she thought. No way!

What are you gonna do? Just stand here and be scared? Climb up. Otherwise, this entire endeavor was for nothing. Do you want to die here without even trying?

Emery sat down on the cave floor and concentrated, remembering what her friend Jackson had taught her about climbing and controlling her body to deceive gravity. "Don't stick your butt out!" he would shout at her. "It is a nice butt, but keep it on the wall, otherwise it will pull you down." She remembered Jack teaching her to hug the wall tightly with her body; keep it glued to the wall at all times; climb steadily and slowly; and never look down. She drew a deep breath and, with the knife held between her teeth, her eyes on the wall, she started climbing.

During the first few moves, her hands and legs trembled and her palms were sweaty, but she didn't stop. She moved her body up in tiny, imperceptible movements, her fingers and toes searching for the best crevices and protrusions before taking the next step. Suddenly, everything Jackson had ingrained in her about climbing came back with extraordinary clarity. Using the big muscles of her legs to do most of the work, she saved the strength of her fingers for the last pulls. Not once did she look down or up, but focusing on the rock, almost touching it with her face, she climbed. She didn't realize when her breathing had become steady and her movements efficient, smooth, and cat-like. Her hands were no longer shaking, but working like spider legs, clinging to the steep wall as if she were a spider woman. Jackson would be proud of her. He'd told her she could have been a natural climber if she'd only taken it seriously.

When she reached the top, the adrenaline wore off, her hands shook, and her legs turned into jelly. She stood just below the top for a moment, gathering her physical and mental strength to pull her body over the edge. When she finally pulled herself up, she stayed on the ground and laughed nervously.

"I did it, Jackson, I did it."

Her chest bobbed up and down in uneven, shallow breaths as she tried to calm herself while her forearms were on fire, and the tips of her fingers and toes screamed in pain. Emery was elated and so proud of herself; her eyes moistened.

You go, girl. You kicked butt. Mom would be so proud.

A few moments later, she got up and surveyed the surrounding area. She saw with relief that she had made more progress than she thought and had only a little way to go before reaching the hills. From up close and in broad daylight, the peaks looked like pointy dinosaur teeth. As she had expected, with the hills came the greenery. Scraggly shrubs and grasses grew in crevices and became more abundant and greener as she approached the pointy knolls.

The sun was already making its way up, and Emery realized she desperately needed to drink. She dared not draw deep breaths as her lungs seemed so dry; they hurt with even the tiniest breaths. Her breathing became uneven and shallow. Her dry mouth, cracked lips demanded water, with corners nicked by the knife she'd held in her teeth as she climbed. Emery knew dehydration would get her before anything else would. She had to find water. She weaved between rocks and scraggly brush that kept snagging the bare skin on her legs, and scrutinized the ground for signs of moisture. Periodically, she bent down when something sparkled between the rocks and scoured the ground with her hands in search of a water source but found none.

Emery had not lost hope, knowing the vegetation wouldn't survive without water, and continued searching. She ventured deeper into the green areas within the strange-looking, pointy rocks, expecting to find some kind of puddle at any time. She didn't take her eyes off the ground the entire time and was shocked when she finally looked up and realized she had stumbled upon a small basin surrounded by white rocky outcroppings and dried out trees covered in white film. For a moment she considered it was snow. But the air wasn't cold enough, and it had a chalky scent to it.

Emery's attention was drawn to a small lake ahead, sparkling in the sunlight. Her heart jumped with joy, and so did her legs. Her mind rang a tiny alarm at the whiteness of the lake and the trees, but Emery, desperate for a drink of water, shrugged it off and ran into the lake at full speed, immersing her entire body and taking big gulps. The moment she swallowed the first few gulps, she realized something was wrong, and she jumped out with her eyes wide and round as dollar coins. She spat vigorously, shaking her head, wiping her eyes and mouth, and blinking rapidly.

"It's not water! What is this?"

The water in the small lake turned out to be pure salt. Her eyes and her sore and bloody feet stung, and her mouth felt numb, as if she had eaten a barrel of salt. Through her stinging and watering eyes, she studied the lake, and when she saw no streams replenishing the freshwater, she understood. Water evaporated over the years, leaving a concentrated salt solution. A trap for thirsty fools.

You've seen how white it was! You can't just jump into anything you see, idiot!

Thirsty before, drinking the salty water had made it even worse, and Emery felt desperate, imagining she'd die or go crazy without finding water soon. Her mouth was so dry that it seemed glued together. In frustration and anger, she threw her hands at the ground. She stepped back, seeing a silvery ball escape her hands and strike the ground in a silvery wave laced with gold spots. The ground responded with a thundering sound, followed by a tremor, and a cloud of orange dust enveloped her and her surroundings. Frantically, Emery waved her arms around, trying to push the dust away from her mouth, eyes, and nostrils.

What was that? Did I just do that? As she looked at her hands as if she were seeing them for the very first time, the tremors stopped and the clouds dissipated, revealing a sight that stole her breath. Before her, the ground darkened as water sprang from underneath, carrying with it sand and rocks and puddled on the orange sand, darkening it and making it appear red, like blood.

"Can't be!"

I must be hallucinating.

As the puddle grew and its coldness licked her feet, Emery kneeled and filled her hands with it. It was water—cold and clear. She brought it closer to her face and smelled it. It didn't smell like anything, and it didn't sting her sore fingers, so she tried a sip. It tasted sweet and fresh, just like spring water. She sat in the puddle, gulping hungrily as the water gushed from below ground. Once she had satisfied her thirst, she poured it over her face, arms, and the rest of her body. As she splashed in the water, her body trembled, and she burst into laughter. As she laughed and cried interchangeably, the dust, salt, and blood sloughed off her body in brown streaks.

Then she sat by the spring, staring at the water. She must have struck an underground spring. She shivered, thinking about that luck again, and the uneasy suspicion that the events unfolding since she found the letter were not utterly under her control intensified. Emery cast a glance at the pool of water and saw her reflection. A little sunburned, but still the same heart-shaped face with blue eyes speckled with gold and black dots and full lips that were now curved in a grin.

It is still me, and I caused it. I still have it. My powers didn't disappear in the darkness. They came with me through the black hole.

It was only the second time in her life she had used her power because she had never known she had it before the encounter with

Zoe's thugs in Grossos. The first time she acted to save Peter and her own life, and now when she unintentionally split the ground open. When she tried her powers for the first time, she was certain they would not work, and she had closed her eyes, readying herself for death, and didn't see the silvery ball or the wave. This time, not expecting it, she only glimpsed it, but was still enthralled by it. Each time, just before it happened, she felt an intense force building deep inside, leaving her gasping for air. And each time, she was certain that if she didn't release it, it would suffocate and crush her.

Now, as she sat thinking about it, her trembling body was slowly calming down as she realized that this force was her strength. Since it was part of her, she shouldn't fear it but ought to embrace it and learn how to trigger and control it, ignoring the small, recalcitrant part of her still clinging to the idea of normalcy.

Face it, you're not normal. Emery inspected her hands again. Now clean but covered with abrasions and cuts, they looked like normal hands. *It's not your hands. It's your mind.*

"Right," she said and exhaled a frustrated sigh. I wish you'd taught me how to use my powers, Mother. You knew I would need them, and you knew you'd leave me. Why didn't you tell me?

After having read the letter, Emery oscillated between resenting her mother for leaving her clueless and believing she included them in the pages torn from the notebook that contained the letter. *Zoe must have done it. She didn't want me to know how to control my powers.*

Emery closed her eyes, concentrated, thought about Zoe, and immediately the anger stirred inside her, rushing through her veins like hot iron and settling heavily on her chest. She blinked, jumped up, and thrust her hands at a hefty boulder a few feet away. It shattered into several pieces with a loud crack and a swirl of golden dust. The weight lifted off, and she could breathe again. Wide-eyed, she stared at the pieces, and then, when it finally dawned on her she had broken it, a wide grin spread across her face. "I slayed it!"

Staring at the broken boulder, she suddenly remembered a scene from one of her camping trips with her mother. Her mother stood by a boulder that was smashed to smithereens, just like this one, smiling at her, telling her she was special. Was her mother trying to teach her? Emery pressed her palms against her eyes, hoping to induce her memories, but the harder she tried, the fainter the memory became. While she was forcing her mind to remember and wondering what else she could do with her powers, her stomach rumbled, reminding her of its existence. Hydrated and cleansed with water, her body now demanded nourishment.

I haven't eaten in a long time. Maybe centuries. Emery giggled at the thought.

Meanwhile, the sun was making its way up, warming the air and the ground. Emery took another sip of water, poured more on her head and arms, got up, soaked her shirt with it, and made her way toward the hills. Now that she knew she could protect herself, the vegetation looked greener than it had before. More trees grew on the slopes. The orange sandy ground gave way to darker soil and sparse grass, providing her feet some relief from the hot sand.

She came to a patch of purple berries and stood staring at them. Her mouth wanted them desperately, salivating. Her stomach continued growling, but her brain cautioned her not to touch them.

They might be poisonous. They don't look poisonous. Yeah? How would you know that? Well, there is only one way to find out.

Emery took one and popped it into her mouth. *Just a taste.* But as the berry exploded in her mouth, releasing its full, tangy, earthy flavor, she gave in and shoved a handful into her mouth.

They can't be bad, tasting so good. She was tempted to eat more, but prudence won over her hunger. Emery called on her willpower to stop herself and walk past the berries without eating more.

Drawing near to the green hills, she strove to walk faster, but her body refused. The berries had only stirred her hunger. Now, she felt full-blown hunger pains but kept walking, clutching her stomach. With the increasing stomach cramps came nausea and a headache. Emery realized these were not hunger pangs. She continued walking, albeit slower, until she reached a point when her stomach revolted and started spasming in pain. Emery flopped to the ground, put two fingers in her mouth, and made herself vomit. The purple spew stained the ground as she heaved. Soon, she was vomiting yellow liquid, and then nothing else came out, although she still was spasming as her body tried to get rid of the poison. A while later, exhausted and feverish, her knees gave out from under her and she collapsed, shedding tears of pain, fatigue, and misery.

I'm going to die out here because of some stupid berries. No, I'm being punished for sleeping with a man my mother loved? No, she didn't. She didn't even want him. And she left him, just as she left me. Stop it, stop it ...

The sobbing eventually subsided, and Emery fell unconscious, holding her stomach.

4

SAVED BY AN ANGEL

She dreamed of her mother, Olesya. They had just finished an arduous climb up a steep mountain trail, threw their backpacks on the nearby rocks, and flopped on the ground, tired but giggling with excitement, joy, and pride at their accomplishment. Emery inched closer to her mother and laid her head on her stomach, as she frequently did. Her mother gently stroked her head. She was startled when her mother started hitting her in the face, tugging at her shoulders, and shouting something unintelligible.

Emery woke up, but instead of seeing her mother's beautiful face, she saw big brown eyes the color of a ripe walnut shell in an unfamiliar young woman's face with the peachy complexion of a child staring at her, and asking questions in an unfamiliar language. Emery fought to stay immersed in the dream, pushing away the memory of the void, the black hole, and reality. She wanted to stay with her mother, even if it was just a dream. But the beautiful apparition wasn't giving up, shouting and shaking her.

Young and pretty, the woman—a girl really, maybe sixteen years old—spoke to Emery in a softer tone, seeing that her eyes had opened. The language was nothing Emery had ever heard before.

The deep-throated "h" in combination with softer whooshing sounds sounded mystical, reminiscent of a flowing stream or the rustling of leaves in the forest. Emery was so enthralled with this language, spoken in the girl's soft and pleasant voice, that she didn't react but lay still, staring at the lovely vision, doubting she was real. She was convinced she was dreaming again and refused to wake up.

But when the girl touched her forehead with something moist and cold, she jerked.

"Who are you? Where am I?" Emery asked, suspecting she would not get an answer in English.

Hearing Emery speak, the girl clapped her hands and smiled, showing a mouthful of pearly teeth. Next, she turned her head and shouted something in her mesmerizing language. The girl herself was mesmerizing. Her fine, light brown hair streaked with blonde sun smudges was braided in an intricate design and adorned with blue and orange wool strings that matched the designs on her white leather tunic. Her light-brown eyes shone with such brilliant intensity that for a second, Emery thought she had died and was now in heaven, cared for by an angel. But the enchanted moment was shattered by a harsher voice and an image of a man in his forties, staring at her. He had come to investigate, drawn by the girl's shouts.

He, too, asked Emery a question and, seeing she didn't understand him, said something to the girl. She shook her head vigorously and spoke fast. There was a plea in her voice. He shrugged, said something, and left. The girl smiled at Emery and asked a question. Emery sat up, shook her head, and shrugged, demonstrating she didn't understand her language. The young woman smiled and nodded in understanding.

"Visla." The girl repeated the word a few times, pressing her hand to her chest.

It must be her name. "I am Emery. Emery," Emery said, thumping her chest.

Visla grinned and repeated Emery's name flawlessly. She asked something, but then waved her hands and left, returning shortly with a wooden bowl, which she handed to Emery and gestured for her to drink. A whitish liquid filled the bowl to the brim. Its sweet aroma reached Emery's nostrils and eliminated her hesitation. She licked her dry lips and guzzled the contents of the bowl in no time. It was as good as it smelled. With the hint of flowers and berries and tasting tangy and sweet, the drink was both refreshing and filling. Visla, overjoyed at the empty bowl, patted her belly in round strokes, pointing at the bowl and then at the still-visible, reeking berry puke.

"You gave me medicine?"

The girl said something, nodded, and then gestured for Emery to follow her. Hesitantly, Emery got up, surprised at how good she felt, and followed her young nurse, sensing the girl's intentions were affable. They approached a small camp with fourteen adults—she quickly counted—all performing different tasks. Some were mixing something in wooden bowls, some were pounding wooden stakes into the ground with hammers made of wood and stone, and some yet carried water in leather sacks. Others were gutting and cleaning small game resembling wild rabbits. Their brown eyes sparked with slight curiosity when they saw Visla leading Emery into their camp, but they continued with their tasks.

The five women in the group wore leather sandals and short leather tunics with interwoven colorful wool strands. Their -brown hair as fine as Visla's was braided in a similar style to the girl's. The men also wore tunics, but theirs lacked embellishments. Instead, they had different-size pockets and belts that held stone and wooden tools. Six children, ranging from four to eight, she guessed, ran around chasing each other, shouting and laughing when one caught another. When they saw Emery, they stopped moving and goggled at her intently, dropping the rocks and sticks they had been playing with from their hands.

Visla called to the man who had first appraised Emery. He approached and assessed Emery a second time with a quick, assertive glance and then started laughing. Others in the group started laughing too, pointing at Emery's scant clothes. Visla didn't laugh and didn't seem to appreciate that they were making fun of Emery's outfit.

"That is okay. I don't mind it at all. I would make fun of myself if I were you, too. I must look ridiculous," Emery said to Visla, though the girl didn't hear her (not that she would have understood her), busy scolding the man. Wrinkling her forehead with a scowling grimace and a harsh tone, she rebuked him. He stopped laughing immediately, but his chin and lips still twitched as he stared at Emery.

You've never seen women's underwear?

He turned his head and left, but Emery could tell he was still laughing at her by the way his chest moved. Visla pointed at him, shaking her head in disapproval, and said, "Otshet."

Emery guessed he was her father, as they shared similar features. He had the same brown eyes that shone almost as bright as hers and full, red lips, which formed a perfect soft curve when extended into a smile.

Visla took Emery's hand and led her to a small leather tent stretched over wooden poles. She rummaged in the tent, found a leather tunic similar to the one she wore, and handed it to Emery. Emery took it in her hands and gasped, surprised at how soft it was. It felt more like silk than leather.

Visla smiled and nodded. Emery put it on. It was a little on the tight side, as Visla was smaller, but it covered her entire torso. It was not as long as Visla's tunic, only reaching her mid-thighs, but Emery was delighted to have a piece of clothing protecting her from the sun, the cold, and the laughing men.

On impulse, she kissed the girl on the cheek. "Thank you. Maybe now they won't make fun of me."

The girl graciously accepted her thanks, giving her a brilliant smile.

When two young women appeared from under the flap of the tent, every member of the group, including the children, glanced at Emery and nodded in approval. Visla led Emery to two women who were preparing a meal together, cutting a large green vegetable into chunks and throwing them onto a mat woven from thick-stemmed grass. A man approached and handed two cleaned and gutted rabbits to one woman. She took it while gawking at Emery, asking Visla something in an argumentative tone. In return, Visla shrugged and answered, sounding sure of herself, but the woman persisted, asking something, eyeing Emery. Her glance was not unfriendly, but wary of a stranger who looked remarkably different from them, spoke an unfamiliar language, and, worse yet, was wearing a bizarre, skimpy outfit. The girl stood her ground and kept talking, and it soon became apparent that she had a gift of persuasion and was wearing the woman down.

While Visla argued with her, the father approached and listened to them without interrupting. Finally, seeing his daughter getting more upset, he said something to the woman, and she instantly changed her tone, nodded, and made a dismissive hand gesture.

He must be important. Maybe he is the leader of this tribe.

Visla pointed to a wooden seat by the fire for Emery to sit while she helped the woman cut more green vegetables. Another woman was making cakes from ground-up seeds she scraped from inside giant green pods. The rabbits—skewered on wooden sticks—roasted over the fire. Emery's mouth watered as her stomach, now fully recovered from the berry fiasco, demanded food again in loud and angry growls. The woman looked up at her, and her small brown eyes squinted as she grinned at Emery.

"Omana," said Visla, pointing at the woman.

Once the food was cooked, everyone grabbed a piece of meat, a cake, and vegetables for themselves and the children, then sat by the fire and started eating. Emery, encouraged by Visla, took a piece of meat, several green chunks, and one of the cakes cooking on a hot rock. She sat back down and started eating.

The green stuff isn't as bad as it looks. Kind of like an earthy carrot. The rabbit and the cake are delish. Emery thought, licking her fingers and smacking her lips.

She finished quickly, but she didn't dare ask for more. Omana noticed the hunger in Emery's eyes and handed her another chunk of meat and more green vegetable pieces. Emery smiled gratefully and wolfed it down.

After they'd all eaten, the elders told stories, one after another. Each story was received with laughter and occasional shouts when opinions differed. Emery looked around discreetly, appraising the tribe. The nine men in the group ranged from two young men in their twenties, four in their thirties, one in his forties (Visla's father), and two older men in their sixties.

Soon, Emery's eyes decided it was bedtime and refused to stay open. She couldn't stop yawning. Visla noticed, got up, and walked toward her small tent, beckoning Emery to follow.

Visla made an inviting gesture toward the bed, which was a mat woven out of thick grass and wool. Emery lay on the mat, and Visla covered her with a blanket. Then the girl curled up beside her, with those curious brown eyes fixed on Emery, and smiled the type of smile one has after accomplishing something worthwhile. Soon her eyes—shaded by delicate, long eyelashes—closed, and her breath became even.

Despite Emery's tiredness, sleep didn't come right away. She lay on the bed, listening to the steady breathing of Visla by her side, thinking about everything that had happened to her. How fortunate it was that this group camped right next to where she collapsed after vomiting herself into unconsciousness. How lucky it was that Visla noticed her.

Was it just luck? This serendipity that kept happening to her?

Emery wondered what her mother would have thought of her journey so far. Would she be proud of her, or would she scorn her for being clumsy and falling into a hole in the ground and for being stupid and eating poisonous berries? She forced her eyes shut, and Peter's blue eyes materialized. The hard lump in her throat became even harder, and she felt even lonelier and more lost. *You must stop thinking about him.*

She sighed, thinking sleep wouldn't come, opened her eyes, and looked at Visla. In the dark tent, lit only by two silvery streaks that forced their way inside through the openings in the flap, Visla seemed even younger. Emery felt an instant affection for this girl, who was brave enough to help a stranger, quarrel with her elders on her behalf, and whose smile instantly assuaged her anxiety.

I never had a sister. I wonder how it feels. A sudden warmth dissolved the cold lump in her throat and filled her chest. And she felt less lonely in an instant.

5

VISLA

Emery decided her chance of determining her location would be better if she stayed with the tribe a while longer. Meanwhile, Emery's need to carry on her journey and fulfill her destiny continued to build and kept pressing on her heavily whenever she was alone or during sleepless nights. And during those nights, she prayed to her mother to give her a sign, just like she did in the black hole. But her mother was silent. Emery stayed, despite the guilt and the anguish she felt. Visla followed her like an amiable shadow, sensing her new friend needed company and a distraction from whatever was troubling her. They soon became inseparable, discovering they shared similar traits and attitudes. Emery, although popular at school, had never had many close girlfriends and was surprised at how quickly she grew fond of this girl.

Visla was overjoyed with Emery's presence, having only younger kids, women in their thirties and sixties, and men in the camp. Closer to her age and temperament, Visla perceived Emery as an older sister. Emery observed the girl amidst other women in the camp and, not seeing her interact with anyone with the closeness a mother and daughter would have, concluded that Visla's mother wasn't around.

Despite Visla's outward cheerfulness, Emery caught glimpses of melancholy in her brown eyes, especially during the evenings, after the daily activities had died down. Emery guessed she missed her mother and wondered if Visla's mother had abandoned her, just like her own mother had.

The very next day, after Emery had joined the tribe, Visla started teaching Emery her language and insisted she wanted to learn hers. Emery's only encounter with a foreign language was Spanish in high school, which she'd enjoyed enough but was convinced she lacked the aptitude for learning languages. But now she didn't have a choice. Visla insisted and continued to shower her with new words and then giggled, hearing her butcher them. Emery surrendered to the girl's wishes, believing learning her language could bring her closer to understanding where she was.

Emery was also hoping the tribe's nomadic living would lead to discovering where and when she'd ended up. Maybe then she'd figure out where to go next and what to do. The group stayed in one place for only a few days. Then they packed and moved to a different location, where they would hunt small game with spears outfitted with the thinnest stone points possible. The gossamer triangular ends were so thin they were almost translucent, and yet they were deadly weapons in the skilled hands of the hunters, who threw them at their prey with high precision and speed. The women collected edible berries and grains, dug for roots, stretched animal skins on wooden sticks, and processed them with rocks and plant extracts.

Omana picked plants and berries to make ointments and medicine for the tribe. One day, she solicited Emery's help in collecting plants and berries she needed, but as Emery soon discovered, she only wanted to make fun of her, pointing at the poisonous berries and laughing.

"Sure, laugh all you want. I could just see you making blunders in my world and running away, screaming, seeing a car," Emery murmured, but seeing the old woman's expression, she realized it was not meant to be spiteful.

She picked a handful of poisonous berries and pretended to shove them into her mouth. Omana opened her mouth in surprise and protested loudly. Emery grinned and dropped the berries from her hand. Omana eyeballed her, and her face wrinkled in a wide grin as she rocked her head in approval. The old woman had a sense of humor.

Emery watched with amazement how much work it took to grind grains on the stones and then make delicious and filling berry cakes and loaves. They also stuffed the small game with the brownish flour before cooking it over the fire, which they started with a flint.

The tribe had four sheep they took with them everywhere. Out of the sheep's milk, they made cheese and fermented milk, which tasted better than Emery thought it should have.

The women taught her how to gather and cook food, while Visla taught her the names of plants and animals and then badgered her about her poor pronunciation. It wasn't easy. Her tongue couldn't make the soft sounds Visla made, and the throaty sounds came out as coughing.

"No, not 'siloma.'" She laughed, wrinkling her nose. "It's 'seloma.'"

When she stopped laughing, she explained that "siloma" meant to puke, not to eat as "seloma" did.

"So what you just said was…'the cat…puked your cake,' not 'the cat ate your cake,'" she said and continued laughing. And Emery laughed with her. Emery continued to massacre words, but Visla stubbornly repeated them until Emery could say each one to her satisfaction. The grammar, as Emery found out, was very complex and sometimes made little sense, but Visla pushed her until she got it right.

Visla had a knack for languages and a voracious appetite for learning. Emery struggled with how to explain syntax or the countless exceptions to the rules, but Visla's intuition and ability to grasp the nuances of the English language were exceptional, and her hunger for learning was inspiring. Frequently, they used pantomime to learn verbs in each other's language. They would scratch their heads to convey "scratch," they would fake laugh to learn "laugh," and in doing so, they would explode in laughter. Emery's pronunciation progressively improved as she practiced. With her impeccable memory, once she had learned a word, she never forgot it. The learning process brought the two girls even closer together. In the presence of this passionate, curious girl, Emery felt young and carefree in between her bouts of anguish about not doing anything to fulfill her destiny.

Visla's father recognized how much she liked Emery's company and tolerated her. To each other, fathers and daughters, mothers and daughters seemed to be only slightly more affectionate than with the others. Mothers didn't shower their children with affection, and neither did the fathers. Emery presumed the harsh life kept everyone working all day, gathering, and processing what they found to survive, and had little left to give at the end, but she sometimes doubted her assumptions when she caught mothers' nervous glances at the sky when their children climbed on their laps, begging for closeness and attention. They would shun their children after giving them a quick, perfunctory hug. Emery followed their gaze at the sky, but saw nothing that could scare the mothers or anyone else. *Are they afraid of something?*

Visla was different. She made even the grumpiest of the old men smile and laughed more than her tribe members. She hugged and kissed the children when their mothers' attentions were somewhere else, and did the same to her father, who pretended not to like it, but Emery could see that he secretly loved and even expected the attention. It was apparent he adored his daughter, and she could do no wrong in his eyes. Emery soon found out that she was correct in her assumption that he was the tribe's leader.

"My father has been our leader for many years," Visla said with pride one day after the two younger men, Urus and Malek, approached her father, Lach, sitting nearby, with questions.

"How do you decide who will lead?"

"The tribe gathers to elect a new leader if he becomes unable to lead."

Each day, Emery and Visla learned more about each other as the basic verbs and nouns were replaced with more complex ones, leading to more insightful conversations. Visla described everyone in the camp with a perceptiveness that belied her age. Emery spoke to her about her mother and grandmother and how much she missed them.

Emery was stunned at the quick progress the girl had made in just a few months. Her curiosity had no limits, and she clung hungrily to every word when Emery was describing her world. Surprisingly enough, she didn't question the existence of cars or planes when Emery explained what they did and how they worked, but wanted to learn more about them.

Visla was enamored with Emery's blonde hair. She braided it frequently, adding her personal touches—colorful wool strands and colorful wooden beads. Emery braided her hair in return. She was not as skilled as Visla, and in the beginning, the braids looked more like messy, colorful dreadlocks. But Visla grinned and kept them as they were.

One day, Visla asked Emery if she looked like her mother or her father.

"I've been told that I look like my mother, but my blue eyes and blonde hair came from my father, I believe."

"You believe? You don't know your father?"

"No, I don't. I've never seen him in person. He died before I was born," Emery said, pursing her lips. "I used to think I didn't need him or a father. But sometimes I wish I knew him. Supposedly, he wasn't a good man, but..." Her words trailed off, and she finished her sentence in her head. *But I'm not quite so sure anymore.*

"I'm sorry," Visla said and hung her head. "My mother is dead, too."

"Oh, I'm so sorry. How did she die?"

"When I was born. I think about her all the time. Imagine how she'd look, how she'd smile and laugh."

Emery hugged the girl, who folded into her arms with ease. "I miss my mother, too. All the time." What Emery couldn't tell Visla was that she sometimes begrudged her mother for abandoning her. She believed once the words had left her lips, she could never untell them, and they would become a reality.

Sitting on a rock and stuffing her mouth with berry cakes, Emery and Visla enjoyed the afternoon breeze when Malek came running toward them. "Hide," he yelled. "The children spotted the birds."

Visla immediately jumped off the rock and waved at Emery, asking her to follow. The cake fell out of her hands.

"What's going on?"

"Come on, I'll tell you later."

Hiding in the shrubs, Visla told Emery about the birds.

"They are big and black and they are ... bad."

"Why are they bad?"

"They spy on us ..." Visla's words trailed off as Lach announced loudly that everyone needed to pack and leave. Emery tried to hide her grimace and asked no more questions about the birds, thinking secretly that it was some superstition. She promptly forgot about them, packed, and wondered where they were going next.

When she first joined the Paleolithic tribe, Emery had expected she'd be able to provide them with insightful information from the future and improve their lives. She quickly realized she couldn't teach them anything useful, while they taught her how to survive with practically nothing. Without her smartphone, she was not of much use to anyone. She didn't know how to extract metals, how to build better shelters, or how to make medicine. The tribe had no use for her powers. They knew how to find water and food. Traveling with them, she learned their simple way of life and humility.

Weeks passed and then months, and each day Emery felt increasingly like a member of the tribe, but the nagging feeling she needed to move on and fulfill her destiny grew in intensity. The guilt gnawed at her that the time was running out on the universe while she rested and enjoyed herself in Visla's company. *Mother*, she pleaded silently. *Give me a sign, please. Somebody, give me a sign. I don't know what to do.*

One day, Visla disappeared for most of the afternoon. Emery looked all over trying to find her friend. She finally found her sitting on a large rock, busy doing something, and she jerked as if trying to hide from Emery.

"What are you doing?"

Visla sighed. "Okay, you can come. I'm almost done. Come and sit by me."

Emery approached and settled on the rock next to Visla. The girl handed her a bracelet made of colorful small rocks and wooden beads. She must have been working on it for a while.

"I made two of them. I've tried to make them the same. One for you, one for me. Do you like it?" she asked shyly.

Emery was speechless for a timeless moment, fighting off tears. She swallowed hard and took the bracelet. "I absolutely love it. This is the most beautiful thing anyone has ever given me. And you made it yourself. Oh, Visla. Come here." Emery held the girl for a long, long moment while her tears soaked Visla's braids.

Emery thought the tribe didn't have a specific direction in mind when they traveled, but she soon found out she'd been wrong. Visla explained they traveled north and south, east, and west, staying ahead of changing seasons and following the resources they offered. They had just changed their course and were heading south. Emery asked Visla if she knew where they were going.

"Winter is coming. We follow the sun to be warm and to have food."

"What is south?"

Visla didn't respond immediately. Emery noticed a shadow crossing over the girl's face.

"Bad people are south," she finally said.

"Why are we going south if there are 'bad people' there?"

"For food. We are going further south this year because the elders said winter will be colder than usual, and food will be scarce. We know how to hide from 'bad people.' And they don't always come out. Without food, we'll die."

"Why are they bad?"

"They take young women and children and kill men and old women."

"That's horrible. How will you avoid them?"

"One man goes first and looks."

"Ah. You send out a scout."

"A scout," Visla repeated, happy to have learned a new word.

"What do they look like? The 'bad people?' Do they look like you, or are they different?"

"Different. They have black hair. They are tall."

"Black hair? Do they have black eyes too?"

"Yes. How did you know?"

A chilling shiver went down Emery's spine hearing Visla's depiction of the "bad people." Her mother and uncle, Zoe and her people, all had black hair and eyes—their defining features. Could they be like her mother or Zoe? Changed by the shards? Hearing about the "bad people," she had mixed feelings. This was her chance to discover the location of the black shards, and yet the thought of leaving the security and shelter of the tribe, and leaving Visla, petrified and saddened her. The very first time she saw Visla, she felt connected to her. When she looked into the girl's wise and warm brown eyes, she had an unexplainable feeling that she had known this girl, whom she had just met, all her life. Would she never stop losing loved ones?

What she had learned about the "bad people" stirred the need to continue on her path. She had to find them.

"Do they speak your language?"

38

Visla shrugged. "I don't know. Ask my father. He knows everything."

Emery smiled.

The next day, Emery asked Lach about the people from the south. Initially, he was unwilling to discuss them, but Emery insisted. He relented and invited her to sit with him by the fire. Her fluency in his language surprised him. This was the first time she'd had a meaningful one-on-one conversation with him. Until now, they had only exchanged a few words, and mostly about everyday chores. Although delighted she'd become close with his daughter, Lach had never tried to engage Emery in a conversation.

"What do you want to know?"

"Everything you know about them."

"Why do you want to know that?" Lach asked, and that was the only time she saw suspicion creep into his eyes. "What do you want with them?"

Emery hesitated, realizing she had to be careful with Lach. She could share anything with Visla, but she must be wary of her father, the tribe leader, the man entrusted with the clan's protection. The wrong answer could mean the end of her friendship with Visla.

"I think they kidnapped my mother," she said, wondering if he would believe her half-lie. After all, Zoe had pushed her mother into the capsule and was possibly one of them—the "bad people." Well, so was her mother in appearance, but he didn't need to know that.

From his sympathetic expression, Emery guessed she had made the right choice in telling him. Her voice, choked with emotion, sounded sincere when she spoke of her mother. He believed her.

"I know little about them. We avoid them to stay alive. We used to be a large tribe. Over time, they kidnapped many children and young women and killed the men who tried to defend them. Now, we barely have enough men to protect the women and children. They destroyed many other tribes."

"How did they ... kill people?"

Lach glared at her. "Why does it matter?"

Emery hesitated; she couldn't tell him about her powers.

"To know how to fight them."

"You want to fight them?" Lach's brown eyes glared at her with an incredulous expression. "They will kill you in an instant. They are powerful."

"Powerful how?"

"They have powerful weapons that can kill many at one time. You can't fight them. You can only run and hide in caves," Lach added, sighing and looking up at Emery. "Visla would be very sad if anything happened to you."

"Nothing will happen to me. I promise," Emery said earnestly and asked cautiously. "Is one of the old men your father?"

"I don't want you talking to him," he said, getting up.

"Why not?"

"I don't want you to upset him."

"Wait," Emery shouted after him. "Can I at least go with the lookout?"

"Why?"

"I can help."

"No, you'd only slow him down."

"I am fast. I run fast."

Lach didn't look convinced. Although Emery was taller and more muscular than the women in his tribe, he still doubted she could run as fast as a man. Emery suspected he didn't want her to go because of Visla.

"I'll be careful."

"Tell her that," he said, shrugged, and left.

"Tell her what?" Visla asked. She appeared out of nowhere with her usual curious expression, now laced with concern.

Emery revealed her plan. She'd already told Visla about her mother's fate a while back. The description of the "bad people" matched those who pushed her mother to her death, Emery explained. Then she fumbled through explaining her mother's story and the travel through the black hole. Visla paid attention to every word, and it seemed she believed her crazy story. After Emery had finished, Visla sat quietly by Emery's side, looking into the distance.

Minutes went by when she finally looked at Emery, found Emery's hand, and took it in hers.

"You should go," she finally said. "I would," she added with conviction. Emery noticed with unease that Visla's eyes lacked the usual luster. They were now haunted by worry and sadness. Visla teared up but smiled through her tears. "It's okay. I know you'll be careful. I would go with you, but my father would worry."

6

SCOUTING

As soon as the sun appeared faintly on the horizon, Lach positioned himself outside of Visla's tent, waiting to see if Emery would go through with it. He said nothing to Emery when she left the tent and was getting ready to leave with Urus, the scout. He stood by but barely looked at her, trying to hide his anger and disappointment. Visla, who left the tent right after Emery, smiled reassuringly.

The heaviness grew in Emery's heart, and finally it felt like a boulder. Emery never had premonitions or visions as her mother did, but in that instant, she experienced a sudden panic that sent her heart into a heavy gallop. For a second, she considered staying, but then realized it could be her only chance to meet the "bad people"—the people who might know where dark matter, the black shards, were and how to unlock them. Hiding her fear under a fake smile, she waved at Visla. "I'll be back soon."

"I know you will."

Emery approached Urus, the scout. He was waiting for Emery with a curious little smile dancing on his lips. He stood relaxed with his hands holding the straps of the leather bag he carried on his back. When the tribe approached the southern lands, they chose Urus, the fastest and most agile young man, for the scouting mission. Urus was the father of the youngest and the most rambunctious child, adored by Visla, a boy named Tam.

Urus walked fast, making deep impressions in the sand that was still wet from the night's dew. Not so fast that Emery couldn't keep up, but fast enough for her to wonder if Lach had directed him to walk fast and tire her out, so she'd be forced to turn back defeated. He could then say, "I told you so."

Emery could easily keep up with Urus, but she doubted his ability to continue much longer at this speed. As the sun warmed up the desert sand, it became harder to walk fast. Eventually, Urus slowed down a little, glancing at her from the corner of his eye, nodding. She showed no fatigue or distress. Emery followed Urus closely, and they walked the entire day through the flat desert devoid of vegetation or even rocks, only stopping to eat a berry cake with dried rabbit meat and to drink some water from their leather pouches.

They alternated between running and walking and talked little. When the sun lowered to the golden-brown horizon, Urus found an area with rocky outcrops and scraggly shrubbery and made a small fire out of the dry branches. After they had settled by the small fire, Urus started the conversation with Emery, eyeing her curiously.

"You learned our language so well."

"Visla is a good teacher."

"You know, she never looked happier. Since you've joined our tribe, she smiles more. She is livelier. You're like a sister to her."

For the first time, someone other than Visla affirmed her presence in the tribe in such a natural and good-natured way. Emery felt a lump in her throat, followed by a warm sensation in her chest.

"Where did you come from?" Urus asked quietly.

This simple question shook her. She looked at him with a piece of berry cake halfway to her open mouth and couldn't say a word in reply. Not even a lie. What could she possibly tell him? She wanted to, but he was expecting a simple answer—the south, the north, the east, or across the mountains. How could she explain the burden of her task, the journey she had made, and the one she would still have to make? Suddenly, the task ahead of her struck her as impossible to accomplish for one person. Despite the bright moon and the stars peppering the sky, heavy darkness enveloped and settled on her chest, as if embodying the wretchedness and hopelessness of her situation. Questions from a man she hardly knew, a stranger, had made her realize how crazy this was.

Emery broke down, crying. Urus averted his eyes and didn't try to console her; he let her cry out her sorrows.

She sat staring at the fire, letting the tears flow freely and land on her tunic. She wondered what Urus thought about her outburst.

Lach was right. I am a wimp.

"I am sorry," she said to Urus.

"Crying is good. Everyone cries."

Emery didn't expect to hear that from a Paleolithic man. There was no masculine judgment, no malice in his eyes when he glanced at her. She saw quiet acceptance and a sympathetic nod instead. She fell asleep next to the fire. Urus observed her for some time, then covered her with a wool blanket.

The next morning, Emery woke up to a gentle tug on her shoulder. Urus stood above her, ready to start the day and get moving. "We walk all day and then go back tomorrow if we don't see anyone."

Physically and mentally exhausted, she had fallen asleep almost immediately after crying last night and slept like a rock. This morning, although slightly embarrassed, she felt refreshed after the deep, dreamless sleep. She nodded and got up.

They moved as fast as they had the previous day, if not faster. Emery loved the fast pace and the wind in her face as she ran by Urus's side. She was thrilled to finally be running toward her goal, getting closer to finding the people who might hold the secrets she was here to uncover.

Urus stopped suddenly and put his finger to his mouth. He crouched, gesturing for Emery to do the same. She squinted, trying to see what he saw, and finally saw a few dark dots contrasted against the golden sand bathed in the bright sun. It appeared they were moving in their direction. Urus crawled toward the figures, and

Emery crawled beside him until they drew near the approaching group. At that point, he stopped moving and hunkered low to the ground, and Emery followed, and then observed as they moved not quite toward them, but slightly west. Emery strained her eyes but couldn't see their hair or eyes—all she could see were their dark silhouettes. She inched forward. Urus, however, tapped her arm and motioned for her to follow him back.

"We must go back now and tell our people what we saw," he whispered.

"Can't we go a little closer to them?"

"No, it'd be too dangerous. They are moving too fast. If we don't warn our people, they might walk right into our camp."

Emery walked back with Urus for a little while, but then stopped and held his arm.

"Are you sure these are the 'bad people?'"

"I'm not. They are too far. But we can't risk it."

"Urus, I must follow them," Emery said, wringing her hands. "You go back and warn our people, and I'll get closer to them."

"Why?" Urus asked with an incredulous look.

"I must know if these are the 'bad people' or not," Emery said, and seeing his worried face, she added, "I have my reasons, Urus. They hurt someone I love."

"Visla will be sad and worried," he said and started walking away, but he turned and added, "Come back safely. Visla won't be the only one."

"I will," Emery said, and returned to the small indentation in the sand behind a series of boulders protruding from the brown ground, where she could watch the approaching people, unseen. Urus was gone; she couldn't see him anymore. It occurred to her that without his guidance, her chances of finding her way back to the tribe were slim. She had paid little attention to the route they had taken. Not only did she risk being on her own with no resources (she still had the knife she'd found, stuffed into the pocket that Visla had sewn to her tunic), but she'd break Visla's heart if she failed to return. She looked back nervously, considering abandoning her post.

It'll be okay. Just concentrate on them now. This is why you came here.
She inched forward.

When she was so close she could almost see their faces, she crawled slower, barely moving, but it still wasn't close enough to make out the features hidden under their dark hoods. She decided to risk it and meet them in person. Rather than coming straight at them, she crawled ahead onto their path and stayed there, pretending to be hurt, but kept her eyes open to observe them (just in case). From what Lach told her, they kidnapped young women instead of killing them. They might take her to where they keep the shards. She'd let them kidnap her and then escape.

They approached her in silence. She kept still until she felt someone kick her, leaving a dull pain in her side. Three men looked at her with surprise in their small black eyes. They were not the same black eyes her mother had—much smaller and shaped differently. Much shorter and stockier, they bore no resemblance to Zoe or her people. They were not the people she needed to find.

She sat up slowly, trying not to make any sudden moves, but they didn't seem alarmed, apparently not considering her a threat. Instead, they plunged into a lively discussion, glancing and pointing at her. One bent down and touched her hair. Emery let him, sensing he was curious. Maybe he had seen no one with blonde hair.

The men, women, and children in the group had thick, straight, black hair and black, almond-shaped eyes and were short, most men not even reaching her height. Intricate geometric designs in black and blue adorned their wool clothes. The men carried bows and arrows with ends made of light stone. She was the subject of their discussion for a while before they asked her questions in an unfamiliar language that sounded hard, staccato. She shrugged and answered in Visla's language, hoping they'd know it, but they shook their heads and chattered some more in their language. Emery stood up slowly and waved, telling them she was leaving. They didn't understand her words, but understood her intentions when she started backing away. Just as she thought she could leave peacefully, several men pulled from the group and surrounded her.

She still didn't think they meant to harm her as they continued talking to her and asking her questions. Instead of answering in Visla's language, she spoke English, asking who they were and what they wanted from her. Hearing her speak English, they froze, staring at her with shock and ... fear.

Emery's eyes widened seeing their reactions. "You know my language? Do you know English? How?"

The men who surrounded her started backing away. One of them, most likely the leader, pointed ahead and clattered an order. The group started moving in the direction the leader pointed.

"Don't go! Please! Tell me, where do you know my language from?"

In response, they walked faster. Emery kept following. The leader shouted something, and the women picked up their small children and walked faster, but the men turned around and faced Emery. They glared at her while fitting their bows with arrows and aiming them at her. She noticed their hands shook as they held their bows.

The leader shouted something.

They're afraid of me.

Stricken with fear, they kept their bows pointed at her.

How could they possibly know English?

Emery put her arms up and backed away, letting them know she was leaving. They started backing away too, vigilant, keeping their eyes glued to her every move, with their bows still pointed at her. The women and children were far away now. Emery turned around and walked back, oblivious to where she was going as the questions and doubts piled up and pressed heavily on her mind. Did they really know English, or were they just frightened by its unfamiliarity? Or how it sounded? She stopped walking and considered following them. Remembering how fearful they were, she changed her mind. They wouldn't willingly go to people they feared.

Now what?

Emery looked around, not sure where to go. She didn't remember where she'd come from. There were no distinguishing features in the surrounding landscape. They had traversed a sandy and rocky plateau with the occasional scraggly shrub or clumps of dry grass. Everything seemed the same, no matter which direction she looked. She hunched, keeping her eyes close to the ground in search of Urus's footprints.

Bending down and inspecting every indentation in the ground, Emery frantically searched and exhaled deeply when she finally found Urus's footprints. They sometimes disappeared in rockier terrain, but she always found them ahead and continued with renewed hope that she'd eventually find the tribe. As she tracked Urus, she imagined Visla's smiling face and Omana's smirks and felt as if she were heading home. Emery deliberated whether to walk through the night or stop and rest. Urus carried with him the blankets, the food, and the flint. With the approaching winter, the temperatures dropped significantly at night. But she risked losing Urus's footprints in the dark. So she curled into a ball and fell asleep quicker than she thought she would.

The morning sun's gentle touch woke her up. But her chilled body refused to move. Grunting, she managed to get up, find the footprints, and continue her journey back. Slowly at first, she increased her pace as the sun rose on the horizon and warmed up her stiff body.

Thrilled, she found a long stretch of ground with more clearly defined footprints; she followed them, running. Suddenly, she stopped and bent to inspect the footprints, and the hair rose on her neck when she saw multiple footprints. Two other sets of footprints overlapped those of Urus's. Someone had been following him. For a moment, she hoped, without optimism, that two other members of the tribe had found him and kept him company on his way back. But the hope vanished as quickly as it appeared. The foreign footprints were much larger. Urus was the tallest member of the tribe and had the largest feet, but these footprints were almost twice the size of his. Her heart pounded in panic, but she still tried to rationalize what she'd seen.

It could be a coincidence. Someone was just walking here. It doesn't mean they were following Urus.

She sped up to full stride to catch up with Urus and his followers. The alien footsteps continued shadowing Urus against Emery's hope that they would eventually veer off. Her throat constricted in dread as she tracked their imprints. With every step, they appeared more ominous, and her heart sank further.

Women's cries and men's shouts stopped her in her tracks. She held her breath and froze as if someone had dumped ice on her. Then she sprinted as fast as her legs would take her. Someone was crying. Someone was hurt. She willed her body to move.

When she reached the camp, she saw two older women lamenting over a body sprawled on the ground and two older men standing nearby with their heads down, mangling their hands in sorrow. A man's back blocked her view of the body. But she didn't need to see it. She knew whose body it was. She felt it. As if in slow motion, as if her body were not hers, she moved toward the figures.

Lach sat on the ground, bent over Visla's bloodied body. With an ashen face and eyes stricken with pain, he held her hands, whispering her name. But Visla didn't respond. Her eyes were closed, and her face was white and glossy like marble. Emery slumped to the ground and gasped, noticing a large gash in Visla's side oozing blood. Her vision dimmed, and her heart pounded in her chest as she checked Visla's pulse, fearing the worst. When she felt her heart's faint beating, she drew several deep breaths, exhaled, and sprang into action.

"She is alive," she said to Lach. "Press your hand on her wound."

After a moment of hesitation, Lach placed his hand on the wound, barely touching it.

"Put more pressure on the wound!" Emery shouted. "We must stop the bleeding."

She waved to the two older women, who were kneeling, crying, and pulling their hair out. One of them was Omana. The other was Urus's mother, Lina.

"Get me something to stitch her wound. I need a needle and some thread," she barked.

The women didn't budge, glancing at Emery, utterly confused.

She repeated her request, but they just glared at her with indignation and disdain. She should mourn with them, not sew, their expressions said, as they scolded her with their brown eyes now brimming crimson.

Emery pointed to the side of her tunic, held together with colorful stitches. "She is alive. She's not dead yet. I need to stitch her wound to stop the blood from leaving her body. Now!" she shouted at them.

They finally understood. Omana, hearing Visla was not dead, stopped crying, stood up, and wobbled to her tent.

"Faster! Run!" Emery yelled. Looking at the amount of blood Visla had lost, Emery feared she had little time left before Visla bled out. Omana returned with a wooden needle and blue wool thread and handed them to Emery, eyeing her curiously, while wiping her tears and her nose.

Emery cut Visla's tunic with her knife and asked Lach to pinch the wound together. He rocked his head in protest, but her forceful look convinced him. Emery threaded the needle, exhaled, and stared at the wound, holding her hand in the air. Having watched movies in which even a novice could quickly do it, she was confident enough. *How hard could it be?*

Damn hard, she quickly discovered. The skin was tougher than she imagined it would be, and the wooden needle was big and dull. Emery felt the cold sweat form on her forehead as she forced her hand to stick the needle in Visla's skin. Lach watched her like a hawk, and after she finally poked a hole in the skin and drew more blood, he grabbed her hand to stop her. Emery elbowed him away.

"If you're not going to help, go away! Or keep it together. I'm trying to close her wound so she'll stop losing blood. I'm trying to save her life."

After three holes, she learned how much pressure to apply to puncture the skin, and the next threads went faster. But not easier—every time she pierced the skin, she felt her hair raise on her arms, and a wave of nausea threatened to overpower her. But she clenched her teeth and pressed on. The threads didn't look good—uneven and covered with blood; they looked like something straight out of a horror movie. But the wound was closing, stopping the blood flow.

Lach wasn't the only one watching her intently. Omana and Lina observed her every move with outrage mixed with awe, whispering to each other.

Emery finished closing the wound, looked up at them, and gave them a new task. "Get something clean to cover the wound. And we need to move her out of the sun," she said, wiping the sweat off her forehead. Lach and two older men carried Visla into her tent. Seeing how much blood was on the ground after they moved her, Emery whimpered.

She lost too much blood. I don't know what to do.

She followed them into the tent and sat by Visla's side.

Lach glanced at Emery with a pleading look.

"I don't know. She lost a lot of blood," she said, taking Visla's hand and shuddering when she realized Visla's hand was white and cold to the touch. Her pulse was barely discernible.

Think, Emery, think. What would Grandma do?

Emery had watched many medical TV shows with Sasha, who, as a nurse, habitually watched them all. Frequently, she'd criticize the doctor's or nurse's actions, shouting with disgust, "That is not how you do it! They have it completely wrong. He'd be dead by now!"

She needs blood. The only way she can survive it is by getting blood. But how? And how would I know whose blood to give her? Lach's blood is probably the most compatible. But there is no way to give it to her. Unless …

An idea popped into her mind. She considered it ridiculous, but couldn't let it go. It was her only chance, and time was running out.

It is worth a try. She needs blood. I heal fast. Maybe my blood has additional immune capabilities that can transfer to her and heal her.

"Lach, we need to give her water and some of that sweet honey," she said to the father, who held his daughter's hand in both of his hands, whispering something inaudible. He didn't hear her. She repeated it louder—she needed him to leave her alone with Visla.

"She needs to drink. I'll stay with her. Please."

"You go get water," he said, half angry and half resigned. They locked eyes, playing a war of wills. The war ended when the tent opened and Meius walked in. He had something on his mind but hesitated, throwing quick, nervous glances their way, sensing a conflict.

"We are ready. What do you want to do?" Meius asked.

Lach looked at him, not understanding at first, but then got up and left with his father without a word. Emery heard them speak outside, but she didn't listen, hurrying to accomplish what she had planned before Lach returned. She took her knife out and sliced her wrist. When the blood started dripping, she held her trembling hand above Visla's mouth. Emery's blood trickled down Visla's throat. Initially, the drops just fell into her mouth as she lay motionless. Emery, afraid she'd choke, was about to stop when Visla swallowed. Emery squeezed her hand, letting more blood drip into the girl's mouth. Visla swallowed hungrily.

"What are you doing? Are you crazy?" Lach shouted at her.

He lurched at her, but Emery, holding one hand above Visla's mouth, thrust the other hand at Lach. She pushed him away, but gently, not using her full force—the silvery ball was barely visible when it left her hand. He landed on his back with a shocked look plastered on his face. The wooden cup he'd brought landed on the ground, spilling its sweet contents.

"I am saving her life. Stay away," she hissed at him.

Emery was past her initial doubts. Seeing how greedily Visla drank the blood, she knew she had done the right thing. It was working. Visla's body gratefully accepted this nourishment.

Lach, stunned, lay motionless on the ground, eyeing Emery with crazed eyes. She tensed, ready to stop him if he tried to impede her again. A few minutes passed, and then Lach started stirring.

"Stay there. I don't want to hurt you. I only want to help Visla," she said to him in the calmest voice she could muster, and added hesitantly. "She's getting stronger."

When Lach heard that, he shifted his gaze to Visla. Seeing her gulp Emery's blood, he didn't know whether to stop this bloody madness or let it continue. Seeing the color returning to his daughter's cheeks, he stayed still, and hope brightened his eyes.

Emery stopped squeezing her hand when she started feeling dizzy. Visla's breathing was even, and her pulse was steady and much stronger. Emery pressed her hand to her wrist to stop the bleeding.

"Visla, you are my little sister now," Emery said in English. "Get better, sweet girl," she said, blinking rapidly, trying to halt the tears of relief.

Lach slowly approached, watching Emery anxiously, and sat by Visla. In a matter of minutes, she looked better and more alive. He stared at his child in disbelief. He tried not to look in her direction, but curiosity won, and he threw cautious glances her way. She sensed his gaze, but ignored him. Then he sat at Visla's side, staring at her as she slept.

"I thought she was dead. I thought I'd lost her," he whispered at one point.

Emery rose and motioned for Lach to follow her. He was reluctant to leave Visla's side, but Emery's relentless stare wore him down, and he finally stood up and followed her outside.

"How did that happen? Who did this?" Emery asked.

Lach hesitated before answering. "They attacked us. They followed Urus and tried to kidnap Visla."

"Who?"

"The 'bad people.'"

"You think they came here to kidnap her?"

"Yes. They came for her. They were watching us and waiting for an opportune moment. I was hunting when it happened. Visla threw her knife at one of them. She must have hit him because he screamed and pointed something at her. He did something to her with that thing, and she fell. I heard the scream and ran back as fast as I could. When I saw her, she was lying on the ground and not moving, and blood was pouring out of her. So much blood ..."

"Why did you say they came for her?"

"I just know," he said, and hung his head, avoiding Emery's stare.

You just know. "Where are the women and children?"

"They are hiding," he said. "We have a plan for when they attack us. As soon as we notice their approach, the younger women take the children and head east to the mountains, where they hide in caves and wait for us to find them. Urus followed them to make sure they were safe."

"And you want to follow them?"

Lach nodded.

"She can't walk now," Emery said, pointing at the tent where Visla slept.

"Meius is building a cot to carry her."

Emery stared at Lach. Something in his eyes and the way he told the story hinted he was withholding something. She knew it wasn't the tribe she and Urus had seen. They were going in a different direction, and their small feet couldn't have left such large imprints in the sand. And they didn't strike her as a hostile group.

No, someone else did that. The "bad people". Why Visla?

"What did they look like?"

"I don't know. They were gone before I returned."

"Who saw them?"

Lach pointed at the old man and cast down his eyes. "My father saw them."

Lach didn't stop her as she walked toward the old man, who was helping another older man, Symon, build a stretcher out of wooden poles and leather they tore off their tents. She tapped his shoulder, and he sighed and stood up. He knew what she wanted from him.

"Tall and dark. Their eyes ..." Meius, Lach's father, said and paused.

"Their eyes what?"

"They are pure hate and menace. Their souls carry all the evil of the world."

"You've seen them before, haven't you?"

Meius nodded, returning to assembling the cot. Emery waited, staring at him, hoping he'd say more. But he didn't volunteer more information. Instead, Lach joined them. Lach probed Meius with his eyes, after which they exchanged a telling glance. Emery sensed they didn't want to discuss it with her, so she let it go, for now. The stretcher was almost ready; they were tightening the leather straps holding it together. Omana and Lina stood nearby, holding blankets to cover Visla with.

After they secured Visla on the stretcher, they walked in silence. Lach, and the two old men, carried the stretcher.

Emery broke the silence by asking how far the mountains were.

"Two days," Meius said, avoiding her stare.

They don't want to talk about it with me. Why?

7

THE MOUNTAINS

Emery walked, glancing at Visla and thinking about the attack. It was obvious they were hiding something from her. Whatever it was, she was determined to find out on her own when she set out to find the "bad people." After Visla recovered, Emery decided she must leave and head south. First, however, she had to take care of her friend. She'd go with the tribe and make sure Visla's wound was clean and remove the stitches in a few days.

Emery knew the road to Visla's recovery could be long and treacherous if an infection developed. The tribe didn't know about germs. Even if she tried to explain, they would not believe her story about the invisible organisms that could kill a human being. But she was hopeful, seeing the cleanliness and softness of the piece of leather Omana used to dress Visla's wound.

Visla slept throughout the rest of the day. In the evening, they made camp and put up a small tent over the sleeping girl. Emery lay next to her, and Lach didn't object, but the color of his eyes seemed to have deepened as he clenched and unclenched his hands on the knife he held, glancing at Emery. She knew he disapproved of the method, but that he was also thankful she had saved his daughter's life, or at least postponed her death and given him hope. She saw it in his eyes when he looked at her. How they changed from being full of ache to sparkling with hope. Before Emery returned to camp, he had been certain his daughter was dead and was already mourning her.

However, when she pushed him without touching him, she realized Lach stopped trusting her. He now viewed her in a different light —powerful and dangerous instead of a harmless stranger. Emery caught his furtive glances and the fear in his eyes. Her time with the tribe was ending.

Emery lay by Visla's side, holding her hand, which had returned to its normal temperature and regained its golden peachy color, just like the rest of her body. Visla was dreaming—her eyes twitched under her eyelids. Fearing she might be reliving the attack, Emery considered waking her up but changed her mind, observing the steady movement of her chest. She needed sleep to heal. That's what Sasha always said. Emery smiled, remembering her grandma. She fell asleep by Visla's side, imagining herself cuddling on Sasha's lap like she did when she was little.

Emery woke up, sensing someone's stare. Visla was awake and gazing at her with an odd expression.

"You are awake. How're you feeling?"

"I feel ... strange. Different."

"You're weak because you lost a lot of blood. But your stomach wasn't affected. We'll put some food in you, and you'll feel much better," Emery said and got up, ready to call for someone to bring Visla some food and water.

"No, it's not that. I don't feel weak. I feel ... strong. Stronger than I've ever felt before. I don't know what is happening to me," Visla said, and extended her hand toward Emery, beckoning her to come closer. "I know what you did," Visla whispered as if confiding a secret.

"What did I do?" Emery asked timidly, afraid the girl remembered she drank her blood and that it upset her.

"You saved my life. You gave me your blood."

"You remember?" Emery felt her face redden. *She resents you now.*

"You gave me part of yourself."

"What do you mean?"

"I can feel your presence inside me. And I know ... things. I dreamed of things."

"What things?"

"I saw you in the arms of a dark-haired woman who was kissing and hugging you. I guessed it was your mother because I could feel your love for her. And then I saw you fight with another dark-haired, and very beautiful woman and float in the darkness among other dark shadows surrounding you. I don't understand any of it, but I sense these were your memories," Visla said, wrinkling her forehead while struggling to recall her dream.

Emery was speechless.

"Your blood. It came with memories," Visla said, and seeing Emery tense, smiled with her usual serenity. "It is okay. I don't mind. Now we are truly sisters."

Visla moved to get up, forgetting about her wound, and winced in pain. She removed the wool blanket covering her, and she gasped at seeing the rough-looking blue stitches on her side.

"What's this? Did you do that?" she asked, looking up at Emery.

Emery nodded. "I know it is not pretty or even good, but it stopped the bleeding. I had nothing else, and it had to be done fast because you'd lost too much blood by the time I got to you ..." She paused and added unsurely, rubbing her forehead nervously, "But it will heal and scar eventually and look better."

"Oh, Emery. I love it! How did you know how to do it? I would never have thought of doing such a thing. Sewing human skin to close the wound. It's brilliant."

"My grandma was a nurse."

"A what?"

"Someone who takes care of sick and injured people."

"Oh, like Omana?" asked Visla.

"Yes, exactly," Emery said, remembering seeing Omana collecting herbs, preparing ointments for the tribe, and curing the upset stomachs of children who'd gorged themselves on berries. "But my grandma also knew how to patch people back together. How to seal their wounds and mend broken bones. Things like that. Speaking of which, I want to ask Omana if she has something for your wound. Stay here and don't move."

Emery stood up and left the tent and was surprised to see everyone up, packing and readying for travel. Emery approached Omana, asking if she had anything to put on Visla's injury to speed its healing. The old woman nodded and rummaged through her leather sack.

"This should ease the pain and keep the hot away," she said, taking out a small leather pouch. Inside was a giant green leaf wrapped around a green paste, smelling strongly of medicine and mint.

"What's this? What's it made of?"

Omana blurted out a few names of plants, and most of them went over Emery's head. She recognized one—the bark of a tree resembling a willow. Remembering the native tribes used willow bark to fend off fever and infection, Emery nodded with approval.

"You know what you are doing," she said, thinking, *I hope you do.*

Omana went inside the tent, and Emery followed. She removed the blanket and the soft leather patch covering the wound and gasped at the sight of the Frankenstein gash, shaking her head with dismay. Visla took it well, hiding her pain. Omana gently spread the green paste, assuring the girl in a soft and melodic voice that she'd be fine.

Visla didn't like to be carried and protested, but Lach and Emery would not listen and moved her onto the cot with the help of the two older men.

The day went uneventfully as they walked into the evening, taking short breaks for water and food. Visla's slender body was not a burden to carry, but Emery asked if she could help. She took over, letting one of the older men rest while she helped carry the cot. It was then she noticed Visla's eyes. She uttered a cry but pretended she had tripped to hide the real reason behind her cry. Visla's eyes had changed color. Her light brown eyes were now grayish blue, but that was not what stopped Emery's heart. With her blood, Visla had gained her golden and black dots, which now sparkled in the sun.

The same dots Emery frequently saw in the mirror. The same dots that sparked many conversations among her friends, envious glances, and exalted veneration from her boyfriends.

Like the night before, she spent the second night by Visla's side. She lay on her side, propped up on her elbow, looking at Visla and gathering the courage to tell her about her eyes. When she finally did, her voice quivered. "Your eyes have changed color."

"Really? What color are they now?"

"They are grayish blue, not brown anymore, and they have the same little gold and black dots as mine."

"Really? That's wonderful. I wish I could see them myself."

"I don't think your father has noticed yet, or anyone else. But he will, and he will ask questions. And I doubt he'll be happy. He didn't like what I did."

"So what? Let him. He knows you saved my life, and he's grateful."

"He may be grateful, but he will never understand what happened and will never forgive me. Even though he knows I saved your life, he doesn't trust me anymore. I don't know how to explain it to him because I don't understand what happened either. Sometimes when people don't understand certain things, they fear them instead. Fear can cause people to behave differently." Emery struggled to explain her budding dread that Visla's transformation might bring unwelcome consequences.

"Nobody will harm you. My father won't let anyone harm you!"

"I know, Visla. I know," she said. She wasn't ready to tell her about her powers, and she worried about hurting anyone in the tribe. If forced to defend herself, she could hurt many with her powers, which she still didn't fully understand or know how to control. After reading the letter, she resented her mother for never telling her about the powers or teaching her how to use them. And now Visla might have inadvertently received them. She must tell her. Show her. Teach her. She dreaded it, despite knowing how open-minded and strong Visla was. She procrastinated, secretly worrying the girl might think of her as a monster.

I will tell her, but not tonight. When she's better.

"We'll worry about it later. Now, let's get some sleep. We must get to the mountains tomorrow. Your father is worried about your safety."

The next afternoon, they reached the mountains.

"How beautiful," Emery exhaled at the first glimpse of the old mountains, partially hidden by feathery, purple-gray clouds. As they got closer, the ephemeral clouds dissipated, revealing emerald forests nestled among golden hills and green valleys.

When they came across the first stream, they refilled their leather pouches with the crystal-clear and ice-cold water. Emery admired the strange, willow-like trees with gnarly trunks hiding among rocks in the foothills. Their marbled, swirly branches moved in welcoming or warning gestures, depending on the time of day and absence of sunshine.

Lach relaxed when they reached the safety of the mountains and turned his attention to his daughter. His eyes grew wide when he looked into his daughter's eyes. Then he slowly shifted his gaze to Emery's eyes. Emery met his gaze—there was no point in hiding it. It would be better if he knew and was prepared before reuniting with the rest of his tribe.

"Why did her eyes change color? They are like yours now," he growled.

"I don't know why or how. It just happened. Something in my blood, I guess. But it's just a color. She is still your daughter. Still your little girl."

"Change them back."

"I don't know how to change them back. I really don't," she said apologetically. "Maybe with time, they will change back?" she added hesitantly.

"What are you?"

"What do you mean? I am Emery. You know me."

"I don't know you. You are a *charnicha*!"

"A what?" Emery didn't know that word.

"You are like them!"

"Like who?"

Emery was getting distraught. Lach feared her, as she expected he would. The inexplicable change in his daughter's appearance and Emery's power must have terrified him. Would the fact that she saved Visla's life be enough to hold his fears and emotions in check before she had the chance to see Visla recover and leave the tribe? He was the leader, and his clan would follow his commands. They will exile me if he just says one word, she thought.

He left, not answering her question—which she quickly forgot about—wondering if she should go now. Sneak out during the night, unseen by anyone.

What about Visla? Are you just going to leave her like that? Unaware of the powers she might have. What if she harms someone she cares about? Or she might have no abilities. Maybe the eye thing is the only thing she got from me? What about her stitches?

Her concern about the girl won, and she postponed leaving until Visla recovered. Then she'd share her secret with her.

By evening, they had reached their camp. Hidden among the trees, set against the rocky hills, the camp was not easy to spot. A small cave, concealed by low-growing brush, was where the parents stuck their children for protection. There in partial darkness, they played with pebbles, and as instructed by the elders, whispered to each other instead of shouting when one won the game.

Everyone except the playing children came out to greet them. The women surrounded the cot, expressing their surprise in high-pitched voices. They all believed she had died. Omana joined them and showed them the stitching with pride, while furtively glancing at Emery. Visla let them stare at Emery's handiwork for a while, then covered it with the leather dressing, signaling she'd had enough gawking. They slowly left her side but stayed together and whispered to each other, glancing at her and Emery. Focused on the wound, they hadn't noticed the eyes yet. Emery exhaled and relaxed her tense and tired body.

Visla was healing unusually fast. Faster than Emery thought possible. And then she remembered how fast she used to heal after an injury. Being physically active and a tomboy, she'd sometimes had injuries that required medical attention. Her school nurses and the doctors had always marveled at the speed at which Emery's bones mended and her wounds healed. Back then, Emery thought little about it, but since she'd read the letter from her mother that she left for her in the secret cabin, she knew her kind repaired their bodies faster. Visla must have received this trait through her blood.

8

YOU LIED TO ME

Six days had passed when Emery attempted to take out the stitches. Dreading it but faking confidence, Emery took her knife and, clamping her teeth, started cutting the blue strands embedded in the girl's skin. Her hands trembled when she cut the first one.

"Can't you just leave them here? That would be a gift from you. A blue strand in my skin from my sister, Emery."

"No, we don't want it to get infected."

"Get what?"

"Get sick inside when dirt gets in."

"Oh," Visla said, but Emery could tell she didn't understand. "You know how big we are compared to smaller animals. Ants, for example. Just imagine that everywhere you look—in the dirt, in the water, and in the air—there are even smaller living things. Ants look like giants to those little things. And those things can crawl inside your wound and sicken it. Like the dead animals we sometimes see on our travels. They smell bad. The little things invade their bodies and make them smell bad as they eat them."

"Oh, that is so interesting. Can you see them? The little things?"

"Yes. With a microscope. An instrument built specially to see them. Now, you must hold still while I do this. It may hurt."

"It's okay. Just do it."

Emery took a few deep breaths and removed the first cut thread. It was easier than she had feared, despite the roughness of the wool. Visla winced but remained silent. Emery continued, and soon all eight stitches lay on the side of Visla's bed. Just a few pink spots appeared in the tiny holes, but no blood oozed out.

"Ugh …" Emery exhaled in relief and wiped her sweaty forehead. "Did that hurt?"

"Not that bad. It mostly tickled."

Lach came into the tent. His eyes widened when he noticed the pieces of blue wool on the bed.

Visla smiled at him when he met her eyes. "I'm all good, Father."

Lach cleared his throat and spoke to Emery without looking in her direction. "I want to speak to my daughter alone."

"Of course," Emery said calmly, and departed. Her heart sank.

Visla looked at her father with surprise. "Why did she have to leave?"

"Because I need to talk to you and not her."

Lach sat on the ground by Visla's mat. He took her hand and looked into her eyes. They were his daughter's eyes, but his heart skipped a beat seeing them up close. Her eyes were the color of a stormy sky, and the golden and black dots shone like lingering light-ning bolts.

"How are you feeling?" he asked; his voice cracked.

"I feel wonderful. I feel strong and happy. I should be dead, but instead, I want to jump out of here and run, but I promised Emery I'd stay in bed a while longer."

"Do you feel different?"

"Different how? Why do you ask that?"

"Your eyes are different."

"Oh, yes. Emery told me. I am more like her now." She giggled.

Lach sat by her bed, mulling something over, and opened his

mouth to say something, then stopped and started again. "She must leave. She doesn't belong here with us," he finally blurted out.

"You want her gone after she saved my life?"

"She's not our kind. She's different and should go away."

"No, Father. I don't want her to go! She is my friend. My only friend, my sister. You can't do that to her! Or me!"

"You'll be okay. You have your own people to keep you company. This girl is dangerous, and I fear what else she might do to you. After talking to the elders, I've decided to take our tribe back north, where our people came from. We'll find a place and stay there instead of moving south for the winter every year. It'll be better that way and safer."

"She can come with us."

"No!" Lach sounded more assertive now. Visla was his daughter and must obey him. "She is not coming with us! And that's the end of it! I'll give her a few days to prepare, and then she must be gone."

Lach stood up quickly and dashed out of the tent, looking pleased he'd said what he intended because up to the last moment, he hadn't appeared so certain he could. He seemed relieved but also heartbroken, because he and everyone else in the tribe knew how much she loved Emery. Lach sighed. It was apparent he was grateful to her for saving Visla's life, but it was also apparent that she scared him. Nobody but him observed what she did to Visla and how she threw him across the tent without touching him. Emery detected fear in his eyes every time she caught his glance.

Now, he had to tell Emery to leave the tribe, and he seemed terrified to approach her with the news. But fearing her influence over Visla more, he went searching for her.

Emery sat on a rock, lost in reminiscing about her mother while watching the angry flames. Seeing the face of approaching Lach, she sensed what he would say and waited with a nauseous foreboding. She felt it in her bones. Lach wanted her gone. Even though she knew she had to leave the tribe and hunt the "bad people," it still hurt to leave Visla knowing she could never return. And she hadn't expected it to happen so soon, before she could tell Visla about the powers she might possess. Emery kicked herself for not telling her sooner.

Lach looked at her sternly. She calmly held his gaze.

"I want to talk to you."

She nodded. "I know."

Lach stood by her side, appearing disconcerted by her self-assurance and calmness. He probably expected her to be angry or to plead her case, but when he looked her in the eyes, a flicker of understanding flashed through them—he realized she wouldn't.

She invited him to sit by her and didn't wait for him to start. "I'll leave. You don't have to worry about me. I want to be sure Visla is okay, and then I'll leave. I need to go my own way."

He said nothing, but she noticed he looked as if a boulder had lifted off his chest. He didn't appear surprised either. Her strange interest in the "bad people" was apparent to him. *He thinks sending me away will save Visla somehow. Well, maybe he's right. Maybe I'm a charnicha.*

"She'll be stronger now," Emery said quietly. "She'll heal faster and be healthier."

Lach nodded, still silent.

"She is still your daughter."

"I know that! You don't have to tell me that. She is my family, not yours, despite what you might think or what Visla might've made you think. She's not your sister, and I don't want you near her," Lach exploded. His eyes, facing the fire, reflected the red flames.

"You would've done the same thing to save her, had you thought about it before I had."

The resentment and fear darkened his brown eyes as he glared her way, moving his lips, trying to answer. His knuckles were completely white when he finally hissed. "I'd never have thought about doing such a sickening thing. Never."

"You would've let her die? You know I've done nothing wrong. I saved her life," Emery said, trying to reason with him. But he didn't want to reason or listen. He had made up his mind, said what he was going to say, and nothing would change it.

Shaking angrily, he got up and said before leaving, pressing heavily and dramatically on each word. "You have three days, and then you must be gone. You can gather supplies before you leave. Take whatever you need. I'll grant you that for saving her life."

She had expected him to say what he did, but his anger surprised her. What she did to save Visla didn't justify his fury and fear. She suspected there was something he was not telling her. She stayed by the fire, thinking about his outburst and Visla for the rest of the evening, not paying attention to anyone else. Only when she started getting cold did she notice the fire was almost out, and everyone had left for their tents. Emery rose and walked toward Visla's tent but stopped short, seeing a dark figure sitting in front. Lach was guarding Visla's tent.

Emery would have to find a different place to sleep tonight. She was at a loss about what to do with herself, having slept by Visla's side every night since she had joined the tribe. She returned to the dying fire and curled close to it. Her eyes held tears, but refused to shed them, depriving her of relief. She was about to lose someone she loved. Again. She had hoped that once she finished her mission, she could go back and live with the tribe and be Visla's sister. Feeling lonelier than she'd ever felt before, her mind wandered off to other people she had lost. She thought of her mother and Sasha. And when she thought of Peter, she quietly moaned. *Peter. Peter. I miss you so ...* and then the tears poured from her eyes. She wept most of the night, and finally her swollen lids refused to stay open and shut when the sun was about to rise.

When Lach saw her swollen red eyes the next morning, for a moment, he seemed to waver as if considering telling her she could stay. But then, as if suddenly remembering the blood and the strange powers, he set his jaw. "No, the charnicha is not staying in my tribe!" he rumbled through his gritted teeth.

For the next three days, she gathered supplies. Women brought her things. A soft and light wool blanket, a new tunic, a leather bag to carry water, dried meat and berries, along with some nuts and seeds. They said nothing to her and quickly disappeared after providing the gifts. Men stayed out of her way and kept their gaze away, except for Urus, who sometimes threw quick, curious glances mixed with embarrassment. But he didn't question Lach's decision. Nobody did.

What surprised Emery was Visla's absence during the next three days. Emery knew she'd started walking around the camp—she'd seen her talking to people. But she never approached Emery and stayed away. She didn't look her way or acknowledge her presence. Emery felt a stab in her chest. Visla was avoiding her.

It must be Lach's doing. He forbade her from talking to me.

Though she understood, Emery was surprised Visla had obeyed her father without putting up a fight, wanting to spend time with Emery before she departed from her life forever. But Visla ignored Emery, mostly talking to the elders in her clan. Lach stayed away and only occasionally glanced at her or Visla.

What did he say to her to scare her like that? How am I going to tell her about the powers she might have? Emery wondered, pondering how to arrange a secret meeting with Visla. *I must warn her.*

But time passed, and the opportunity did not present itself. It was her last night at the camp—she'd be leaving the next morning. Emery considered forcing her way into Visla's tent and telling her in English what to expect. Pacing around the camp, Emery was preparing to barge into the tent when she heard a commotion and Visla's raised voice, interrupted by loud male voices. Lach's voice was among those she heard. Fearing Visla was in trouble, Emery rushed toward her voice.

Visla stood between the two older men and Lach. She was waving her arms and shouting. "You are all liars! All those years, you lied to me! And you, my father, are the biggest liar of them all! How could you? How could you be so cruel?"

"We were trying to protect you ..." Lach pleaded.

"Protect me? From the truth? You've always told me I shouldn't lie.

Lies are for cowards, you said. Truly courageous people never lie. So you are a coward! All of you! Cowards and liars!" Visla shouted, stomping her feet and stirring clouds of dust, but noticing Emery, she grew quiet and still. Then, she said calmly and with conviction, looking into her father's eyes. "I'm leaving. I'm going with Emery and never coming back."

"No, you are not! I will not allow you to leave with her! It's her kind that did this!"

Visla looked at him in shock and then at Emery with hope, as if asking her to deny what her father said. Emery was too shocked and couldn't react, but stood frozen, staring at the group with her mouth open. She didn't understand any of it.

Visla locked eyes with Emery, and neither paid attention to Lach's shouting. "Is it true? Are you one of them?"

"I'm not sure what you're asking of me, Visla. One of whom?" Emery's voice stalled.

Visla's searching gaze stayed focused on Emery's. Having found it, she turned slowly to her father. "You are lying. Again. She's not even from here. She came from a different world through the horrible darkness. I don't know why you are lying to me, but it doesn't matter. I'm leaving, and I'm going to find her, unlike you. You've never even tried. And you can't stop me, you coward!" Visla turned around and left, heading toward her tent.

Emery followed, glancing back at a stunned Lach.

As soon as she reached the tent, Visla started packing. She put another tunic and leather moccasin-type shoes into a big leather pouch, followed by a soft wool blanket, while Emery watched in silence. The girl's determination showed in her stance and her eyes as she coolly inspected the items she planned to take with her. Once she was done, she met Emery's shocked eyes.

"Are you sure about this?" Emery asked. "This is your family. Whatever happened between you and your father, you can repair it. Family is—"

"No, this can't be repaired," she said, clenching her jaw in determination.

"What happened?"

"Later. I can't talk about it now. Are you packed?"

"You want to leave tonight?" Emery's eyes widened in disbelief.

"Yes. I don't want to stay here another night. Let's go!"

Emery went to collect her things, which she had stored in Omana's tent, where she had been staying since Lach started guarding Visla's tent. Omana, seeing them together, sighed and looked pained.

"I knew this day would come. I tried to tell them it was wrong to keep it from you. But they didn't listen. They never listen to Omana."

"Why didn't you tell me?"

"I couldn't go against your father's wishes."

Visla shrugged and spun around to leave.

Omana stopped her and opened her arms. "Come here, my little one."

Hesitantly, Visla let the old woman embrace her.

Before they left the tent, Omana whispered. "Your mother would have done the same. Stay safe." Looking at Emery, she added. "Keep her safe."

When they exited, Lach and all the men stood waiting for them.

Ugh, this is going to get ugly.

Visla marched right at them, seemingly unconcerned. "You can't stop me! Move away."

The men stayed put.

Visla thrust her arms forward, and they tumbled and tumbled to the ground, falling on each other, Lach included. Visla continued walking without looking at them. Emery followed, dumbfounded by how quickly the girl had figured out she had powers. Fortunately, they were not as powerful and deadly as Emery's, and the men were stunned but alive. Lach was the first to get up and followed them on unsteady feet.

"If you follow, I'll push you harder, Father," Visla said without making eye contact with him. "I will hurt you!"

"Visla, please. Don't leave. I did it to protect you. Don't go."

Visla sped up. Emery pitied Lach. The plea in his voice, the sorrow, and the pain were real and stabbed at her heart. It was her fault Visla was leaving her father and the people she knew and had grown up among. Inadvertently, she had caused all this pain: without Emery, Visla wouldn't have left the tribe alone despite what transpired between her father and her, despite the secrets he kept from her. Emery was at the center of this mess and wished she could turn back time and fix it. Maybe she should never have stayed with them and befriended this spirited girl. However, finding a friend like Visla in this strange, ancient world was a miracle and worth fighting for. Lach had let his daughter down. His misery was of his doing, not hers.

9

EXILE

They walked in silence throughout nearly the entire night. The vegetation slowly receded as they walked further from the mountains. The lush trees and shrubs gave way to a sparse scrubland peppered with round boulders. Emery asked for no explanation but wondered what secrets were powerful enough to shatter their strong and loving bond?

Just before the sun painted its first feeble mark on the dark sky, Visla stopped and collapsed to the ground, and quietly sobbed. Her sobs mixed with the sounds of dry grass swaying in the light wind. Emery realized she was solely responsible for the well-being of this young girl, and her knees buckled. She sat beside her young friend and took her into her arms, realizing with a heaviness in her chest that now she was Vista's sister, mother, and friend. How would she care for and protect her when she knew nothing about this world and what lay ahead?

What am I going to do? She thought, stroking Visla's head. The girl sobbed for a while, soaking Emery's tunic with her tears. Eventually, her sobs quieted, and she pulled out of Emery's arms.

"It's going to be okay. We'll be fine. I promise," Emery whispered.

Visla nestled her head on Emery's shoulder, and they sat in

silence for quite some time. A while later, Visla's breathing became even, and her head grew heavy on her shoulder. While Visla slept, Emery didn't dare to move and held her until the sun rose high enough to wake the girl up with its warm touch.

"Oh, I fell asleep. I'm sorry."

"There is nothing to be sorry about. You want something to eat?"

"No, I'm not hungry."

"Drink some water, at least."

Visla absentmindedly drank some water from her leather pouch. "Let's go. I feel better when I walk," Visla said, stretched, and got up, yawning.

"That's okay, but we must talk before we go."

"About what?" Visla asked with a worried look. She probably wasn't ready to talk about what her father had done.

"I need to tell you something. I must go south and search for the ... 'bad people'. I came here to find something important that was meant to save this world and give its people the gift of a long and healthy life. I believe the 'bad people' know where that thing is, and that's why I need to find them."

"What do they have that you want?"

"Black shards. Black, shiny rocks."

"You traveled through the scary, dark world and even scarier black hole to get a black rock?" The incredulous look on Visla's face made her smile. Seeing her smile, Visla's eyes widened in surprise, which made Emery burst out laughing. Condensed into one question, the absurdity of it all seemed hilarious. Emery laughed, and Visla stared at her, speechless. But not for long. Soon, her lips twitched, and she laughed with Emery, batting her thighs with her hands. They laughed until they could laugh no more. Emery rolled on the rocky ground by Visla, holding her stomach.

"I went through all this for a black rock! Black fucking rock!"

Saying the words aloud didn't make it better. Uncertainty crept in again. *I can't take Visla with me. What was I thinking? They'd almost killed her.*

"What is fucking?"

"Oh, you caught that one, did you?" Emery giggled. "It means … It means many things. In the sense I said it, it is a curse. You know, when you do something wrong, when you mess up, you say 'churt.' When I do something stupid, I say, 'fuck me!' Or even when I do something that I'm proud of."

"Oh, fuck me!" Visla said repeatedly, and Emery smiled. A Paleolithic girl swearing in English!

"We can't go south, Visla. I've changed my mind. It's too dangerous. I'll figure something else out."

"I must go south too," Visla said dreamily.

"What? Why?"

"To find my mother."

"I thought you said your mother died in childbirth," Emery said and rose from the ground, staring at Visla.

"She's not dead."

"How do you know?" she asked, and then gasped. "Your father …"

Visla's face confirmed it. "My father came to my tent three evenings ago and told me to stay away from you and that you'd leave us soon. I knew from his expression that talking to him would only make him mad, so I didn't argue. As soon as he left, I went searching for you, hoping to find a way for you to stay with us. I hoped together we could think of something that would make my father change his mind. But I couldn't find you anywhere, so I walked around and heard my father speak my mother's name, and his father repeated it. And what my grandfather said next left me standing there, unable to move, as if I had gotten hit with something heavy."

"What did he say?"

"'Lannea came back for her,' Meius told my father," Visla said, and seeing the confusion on Emery's face, added. "Lannea was my mother's name."

"I don't understand. When? When did she come back for you? Where did she go, and where was she supposed to have come from?"

"Those were my questions. Omana saw me standing frozen. She later told me I looked like I was about to collapse. She helped me to my tent and asked what was wrong. I was still hoping I'd imagined it or misheard. But then, I looked Omana right in the eyes and asked her where my mother was, and her entire face turned red. That poor woman can't lie. She never could. She can keep a secret, but she can't lie. I knew then that my father and my grandfather were keeping secrets from me. Secrets about my mother. I had to find out the truth. Omana left hurriedly, and I didn't push her, knowing my father would be angry at her for telling me the truth. But I promised myself that I would find out what happened to my mother.

"The next day and the day after, I walked around the camp talking to all the elders and asking questions to trick them into telling me about my mother. But nobody would say anything, so I confronted my father and told him I knew my mother was alive and that she had come for me. Then I asked him where she was. He tried to lie, but his eyes betrayed him. He knew I would not stop until I knew the truth."

Visla paused. She wrapped her arms around her knees and rocked back and forth. When she spoke, her eyes shone with wounded indignation at her father's betrayal.

"He told me everything. When I was a six-month-old baby, my mother was taken by the 'bad people.' They raided our camp and killed several of our people who tried to protect her, mostly elders, because the younger men and women had gone hunting and collecting food. My mother had stayed in the camp because she was taking care of me. The reason they didn't take me, my father told me, was because Omana took me to her tent to give my mother some rest right after she had breastfed me. When my father came back, she was gone."

"I am so sorry," Emery said.

"My father decided it would be better to keep this from me and forbade anyone from talking about it. Lannea died in childbirth was the new truth."

"What did your grandfather mean when he said she came back for you?"

"That's what he said. She came back for me. He recognized her. She was searching the camp for me."

"She is alive and well, and she came here to search for you? Why didn't she stay with you and your father?"

Visla didn't answer at first. Her youthful face distorted in a pained grimace, and she waved her hand in front of her face, fighting off tears. "She's alive, but I don't know if she's well because she's one of them now, my father told me. She looks like them and speaks like them," she said, and her voice quivered.

Emery sat staring at her in disbelief. "One of them?"

"One of the 'bad people,'" Visla said, nodding.

"How do you know?"

"My grandfather saw her clearly, and I ... I saw her with my own eyes. Although I've never seen the 'bad people', so can't be sure if she was like them but she looked different from us. She came with another. A man. I didn't recognize her. I didn't know she was my mother when I saw her. I was a baby when she was taken."

"That woman nearly killed you."

"But she wasn't the one who tried to kill me. She just ... stared at me while walking toward me. The other man who was with her hurt me."

"But she didn't stop him either," Emery said and regretted it immediately.

"He was too fast. She didn't have time ..." Visla's voice trailed off.

"Can you describe them? Did they both have black hair and black eyes?"

"And they were very tall," Visla added, nodding.

Emery fell silent and bit her lip. *They changed her with the black shards? But they seemed to be violent. This is different. Are they different shards?*

"What else do you know about them?"

"I only heard stories told by our elders. They take some children and some young women. I don't know how they choose who they take. They take only a few each time, or one. Sometimes they kill the rest, and sometimes they just take whoever they want, ignore the rest, and leave."

Emery eyed Visla, who sat with her eyes downcast, appearing despondent.

It must be so difficult, suspecting her mother may have turned evil.

Emery's stomach churned. "We'll find her, and then you can talk to her and see for yourself. Looks can be deceiving. Just because she looks different doesn't mean she is bad," Emery reassured, but she secretly worried about what the mother-daughter encounter might look like.

Emery suspected they kidnapped young children to change them with the black shards.

Why? She wondered. Are they making soldiers? Is that what they want from Visla?

"We should go. I don't want my father to find us."

"I believe your father wanted to protect you by not telling you about it. You didn't have to spend your childhood wondering where she was. I understand why he did it."

"It was still wrong. She is my mother. I have the right to know she's alive."

"He didn't tell you because he knew how spirited you are. He didn't want you endangering yourself by trying to find her."

"I don't care. He should have gone after her. He is a coward."

"Visla, your father is not a coward. He did the best he could. He cared for you and protected you. If he'd gone after your mother, he'd most likely be dead now, and you wouldn't have a father."

"I hate him."

Emery glanced at the girl and let that one go. They sat in silence. Visla stared at the ground, drawing circles in the sand with a stick. First wide circles, then smaller ones, and then finally she threw the stick away, sighing. Emery drew a breath. *It's time. Tell her.*

"When your father and the others in your tribe surrounded us, you did something—"

"Oh, yeah. I saw you push my father without even touching him. I thought I was dreaming and forgot about it. But the evening I found out my father lied to me, I got so mad after Omana left, I thrust my hands at my tent, and it collapsed. I was scared at first. But then I fixed the tent and tried again and again. I was going to find you and tell you about it, but I had to find out about my mother first. I figured it was something you gave me with your blood. Did you?"

"Yes. I didn't have the chance to share my secret with you. I was afraid."

"Of what?"

"That you might hate me," Emery whispered, avoiding Visla's eyes.

"Hate you? No, I love you, and I love *it*. I am as strong as the men are now. Maybe even stronger. I can fight."

"Oh." Emery smiled. Once again, she had underestimated the girl's tenacity and courage. "I've only recently learned that I inherited my powers from my mother and still am not quite sure how to use or restrain them. I'm surprised you were able to use them so easily and that you weren't scared."

"I was too angry to be scared."

"We should practice together."

"That'd be fun! How?"

"We'll break some rocks, for starters."

Emery and Visla walked for several hours without stopping. They exchanged a few words but mostly stayed quiet. Visla was in a reflective mood, and Emery reminisced about her mother. When the night fell, they made a fire, ate a little food, and then fell asleep after talking about the bright stars winking at them from above. They guessed how far away they were and gave them names. Then they fell asleep, sharing one blanket under a sky infused with familiar stars.

The next day, they started walking early and covered many miles. Emery worried less about Lach finding them, but if he were on their trail, the ground—now more solid and hard—would not leave any footprints. Spreading before them were low mountains or hills that wore different shades of brown, depending on the time of day, and were mostly devoid of vegetation. Having enough food for only a few more days, Emery wondered how they would survive, but Visla didn't seem too worried.

"We'll find food. Food is everywhere; you just need to know where to look. Don't worry."

"You've been here before?"

"Only twice. We keep closer to the mountains when we travel south."

The blue skies suddenly filled with ominous gray clouds, and the air turned hotter. Emery heard Visla gasp and spun to look at her. She saw Visla's face darken as if the clouds were reflected in her eyes. Emery turned around, looked up, and almost lost her footing. An enormous black bird hovered above them, focusing its intense blue eyes on Visla, while its black pupils swung rapidly, scanning the girl's face and body. The bird hovered ominously without moving its wings. Its black feathers glistened as if it had been greased or polished. The bird's eyes, done scanning Visla, moved to Emery's face.

"What the ..." Her words trailed off as the bird, silently and barely moving its wings, slid across the gray sky, disappearing between the clouds and into the distance as quickly as it had appeared.

Visla stared at the clouds where it had disappeared.

"What was that?" Emery asked.

"The bird sometimes appears just before the 'bad people' come."

"Oh," Emery exhaled, remembering. "I thought ... never mind," Emery said, grabbed Visla's hand, and started running east, pulling the girl with her.

"Wait, Emery."

"Let's go. We have to hide from them."

"I thought we wanted to find them," Visla protested.

"We do. But we don't want them to find us. We must understand them better.

"How?"

"I don't know yet. But I know we don't want them finding us like that. They could just kill us on the spot."

"My mother wouldn't kill me."

"Maybe not, but others might. Or they may take you and kill me."

Emery no longer had to pull her along. Visla ran alongside her. After a while, she veered left.

"This way, I know a place we can hide and still see who's coming."

"You do?" Emery asked, glancing at the girl with admiration.

And you were worried that you'd have to look out for her. She'll end up saving your ass!

They ran up a hill, stirring clouds of brown dust behind them. Visla ran up ahead. Emery, who kept glancing back to be sure no one was behind them, suddenly lost track of her.

"Visla?" she whispered.

"Up here," Visla answered from above.

Emery looked up and saw a playful smile brighten Visla's face, looking out from an opening above a rocky overhang.

"Come on, climb up here. We can see them come, but they can't spot us in the cave. The bird doesn't know where we are."

"Clever girl!"

"Clever?" Visla didn't know the word.

"Smart! You are smart. Another word for smart. Clever."

"Fuck me!" Visla exclaimed happily, and Emery chuckled. Emery climbed up onto the ledge and slid inside the small cave. There was just enough room for the two of them to lie down so close their bodies were touching.

"Have you seen this bird before?"

"No. I heard about it only. Omana talked about the bird as if it were an evil spirit that came up from the black world …"

"Black world? What did she mean by that?"

"I don't know. I believed she was just telling me stories. To scare me. Like she usually does with all the kids."

Emery, remembering there were no other young people of Visla's age in the tribe, wondered. *Did the "bad people" take them all?*

An hour passed, and Emery started shifting about in the small space, trying to find a more comfortable position on the hard cave floor, full of sharp protrusions. Perhaps it was time to walk again.

They weren't coming. Then Visla dug her fingers into Emery's shoulder and pointed.

Several black figures circled the area where the black bird spotted Emery and Visla, and then they moved toward them. When they came closer, she realized just how fast they were moving. Too quick for normal people.

My mother ran faster than anyone I know. I run faster, too.

Soon, they were close enough to distinguish their features. Six dark figures were in the area that Emery and Visla had left an hour ago. They were looking for them. Visla was right. The bird must have been their messenger and alerted them. There was something off about the creepy black bird—it didn't seem real. Especially the blue eyes with the moving pupils. Emery considered it might have been changed with the shard, but remembering how it moved, she thought it looked more like a machine. A drone. But that wasn't possible in Paleolithic times, was it?

Thinking about the bird, Emery momentarily lost her focus on the approaching strangers. She wasn't too worried, thinking they couldn't see them in the cave. Visla clutched Emery's hand when the figures started coming toward them.

"They can't possibly see us, can they? The bird had left before we came here. Or did he follow us unseen?" Emery wondered aloud.

Visla's hand tightened on hers as the figures moved faster in their direction. Emery calmly patted Visla's hand, although she was far from calm. There was no doubt in Emery's mind that they were moving toward them purposefully and rapidly.

Emery rose and grabbed Visla's hand. "Let's go," she whispered.

But Visla didn't respond, staring at the people running their way. Frozen, she was mesmerized by the woman. Emery grabbed Visla's arms and shook her.

"Visla! Let's go. Or they will take us or kill us!"

Visla looked at Emery with frantic eyes and slowly nodded lethargically as if she couldn't quite comprehend what Emery was saying. She followed Emery, who climbed down and started running east. Emery turned to make sure Visla was following her, and her heart sank when she saw that instead of running behind her, the girl was plodding toward the woman, who stood waiting for her. Five men clad in tight black bodysuits stood by the woman's side, watching both girls intently, ready to seize them. They towered over the slender girl approaching them—the woman was at least a head taller than Visla, and the men even taller.

Emery hesitated. The tiny, cowardly part of her being screamed to run, but the other, fearless part couldn't leave Visla. She guessed Visla had recognized the woman from the previous abduction attempt, and her curiosity and yearning to meet her mother, with the hope of her love, obliterated her self-preservation instinct. Emery waited for their approach, curious about the woman's intentions. The last thing she wanted was to hurt Visla's mother if she meant well.

When Visla was only a couple of feet away from her, the woman reached out with her arms as if welcoming the girl. Visla hesitated long enough for the woman to come forward, but the woman approached a little too quickly. Visla stepped back, and Emery tensed, ready to protect her. But the woman didn't attack Visla. Noticing that the girl had backed out of her reach, she stepped back and spoke in the girl's native tongue with a deep, slightly vibrating voice, extending her arm to halt the men, who stiffened, getting ready to apprehend Visla.

"Visla, my daughter. You survived. You must be strong. I thought you were dead. I thought I'd lost you."

"Mother?" Visla asked cautiously, although her eyes appraised the tall woman curiously.

"I know you don't remember me. But can't you see I am your mother? Look at me, child. We look alike."

Visla gazed at her for a while; afterward, she turned her head. Emery nodded calmly, encouraging her to keep talking to the woman, hearing no aggression in the stranger's voice or movements. It seemed she wanted to reach out to her daughter, but Emery didn't fully trust her. She resembled Zoe too much. She had the same huge, oval-shaped eyes that seemed deep enough to swallow a whole person. Her long black hair was braided tightly and rested on her chest. The shiny black outfit hugged her slim, athletic body in a tight embrace. Her face was even more arresting and familiar-looking. She wasn't lying; she shared Visla's facial features: high cheekbones, the same straight, beautifully-shaped nose and strong chin, the same full lips, and dimples in her cheeks. The only differences were eye color, hair color, and height. The woman was tall, and her skin was unnaturally gray, emphasizing her black eyes and hair. Visla, with her golden-brown hair and now blue-gray eyes speckled with golden and black twinkles, looked like a smaller and more colorful version of this person who claimed to be her mother.

And yet, Visla hesitated and remained still, observing. "You look different from me," Visla said.

"I am. And you could look like me."

"I don't know. If it's really you, why didn't you just stay with us? Why did you try to take me?"

"Because I want to help you be stronger and smarter and leave this horrid life in this horrible wasteland. You don't belong in the wild. You belong with me. There's so much I want to show you and share with you."

"Come with you? Where?"

"You'll see."

"Tell her, or she won't go anywhere with you." On a hunch, Emery spoke English. And she spoke with enough force and conviction to convey her commitment to protecting her companion.

"And who are you to demand such a thing from me?" she asked in an indifferent tone and perfect English.

"I am her friend."

"She saved my life," Visla quickly interjected in English. "The life you almost took from me."

"She saved you. How?"

"She stitched my wound together."

"Did she teach you this language, too?"

Visla nodded, but the woman didn't see it as she turned toward her companions. They looked at each other for a moment. Emery noticed their eyes move, and something passed between them—a silent communication as if it were telepathic. The men nodded, and the woman turned toward Emery. She lingered on Emery's face, then gazed at Visla. It was then that she noticed Visla's eyes. When she saw the same shiny sparks in her daughter's eyes as in Emery's, her black eyes intensified, and her voice sounded like ice hitting metal.

"Who are you? Where did you come from?" She asked Emery and then Visla, "What did she do to you, daughter? How did she change you?"

"I told you. She saved my life. You tried to take it, but she saved me. I'm with her and not going anywhere without her," she said, striving to sound as firm and calm as she could, but her still-childish voice, stopped by emotions, disobeyed her and cracked.

"That is all right, daughter. She can come too," she said. Her tone was unchanged, indifferent, and so cold. Emery shivered. Her hand instinctively went to her pocket and clenched the stone knife.

Visla turned and looked at Emery searchingly.

"Suppose we go with you. Can we leave anytime?" Emery asked.

"You can, not that you'd want to," she said to Emery, looking at Visla. "A different world awaits you. A world full of wonder."

So you say. We'll see about that. "Visla, do you want to go with her? Is that all right with you?"

"Yes. I think so."

"Let me know if you change your mind."

Emery followed the woman. Visla walked alongside the tall woman, glancing at her curiously but also with a hint of uncertainty. If she didn't know Visla so well, she might have mistaken this uncertainty for shyness. But Visla was not shy. She was wary, and Emery sensed it.

Emery and Visla tried to keep up with the woman and five men. Visla was lagging, so they slowed down and regrouped. Two men now walked behind them, one on each side, and two in front of them.

They are herding us! Emery thought, panicking. Cold sweat crept up her back.

Sensing the woman was the leader of this group, Emery watched her closely, waiting for her to signal the men to apprehend them.

They were agile men who appeared young but also ageless. Their expressionless gray faces, devoid of curiosity and human emotions, worried Emery. Although they were physically similar to Zoe, her people, and Emery's mother, they behaved nothing like them. Their movements were precise and even. They moved forward in unison, like a group of well-trained soldiers or droids.

"How sure are you she is your mother?" Emery whispered to Visla, but the girl couldn't hear her, mesmerized by the tall woman.

Ugh! I don't like this one bit! I don't trust these people.

After two hours of walking, the group halted in front of a rocky hill. Slowly, the woman turned toward them and looked Emery in the eyes intensely, as if her intention was to pierce through her and into her soul, searching for something. Emery assumed an impenetrable expression and held her gaze. While she stared into her eyes, she felt a prick in the back of her neck. Her knees gave out on her, and she collapsed to the ground, hearing Visla screaming. Her mind plummeted into darkness.

"No! What did you do to her?" Visla shouted at the woman.

"She is fine," she said calmly, while signaling to the two men in the back, who picked Emery up, swung her onto his arm, and carried her. "This will relax her."

Visla lurched toward Emery, but one of the men grabbed her arm and stopped her. The girl's head barely reached his chest. She looked like a lost child in that instant, but a child who wasn't afraid to attack someone twice her size. She reached to grab the woman's arm, but missed as the man pulled her closer to him. The woman looked around. Then, she took something from inside her pocket and pointed it at the hill.

The hill transformed and opened up to reveal a gray material, glowing with a portentous shine, from under the brownish rock.

"What's this?" Visla whispered. Her lower lip quivered.

"This is your new home, daughter," her mother answered.

Visla considered trying to flee, but one look at the unconscious Emery changed her mind. No, she couldn't leave her. If this woman is her mother, maybe she won't hurt them. As a mother, she'd do anything for her daughter, wouldn't she?

An oval opening in the gray hill slowly revealed a gaping, dark passage.

The men carrying Emery disappeared into the opening. Visla's mother pointed toward the door, inviting her inside. Though her knees felt like giving in under her, the girl put her chin up and entered, keeping track of her friend. But Emery disappeared into the darkness, carried by the men. Her mother grabbed her hand in a forceful grip and led her inside as the door behind them shut silently. Visla tried to adjust her eyes to the darkness, but the blackness shrouded her so completely that she feared her mother had locked them in a cave where they would die.

But the darkness slowly dissipated, replaced by lights that seemed to emerge from the dark gray walls without an obvious source. The lambent lights lit the dark passage well enough for her to see smooth, seamless walls. Visla has never known light that was not made with fire or walls as smooth as these. Never had she seen anything so bizarre, and she stood with her mouth agape and eyes open so wide they hurt.

The mother stood still, letting the girl take it in and observing her reaction. Visla was alone with the woman in the corridor, now enveloped in a bluish-grayish luminescence. The eerie light brought out the sharp features and dark shadows that seemed to shift under the woman's face, now looking more translucent and grayer. Visla stepped back.

"It's all right, daughter. Everything is all right," she said, and Visla noticed with surprise and horror that her voice had changed too. It reverberated in this strange place, sounding distant and hard.

"Where is Emery?" Visla stomped her feet and tried to shout, but only managed a high-pitched whimper.

Waiting for a response, hearing her heart pounding in her head, Visla didn't even notice when the woman grabbed her hand and pulled her into the corridor—the woman's movements were so quick.

"Let's go."

10

THE GRAY CITY

Absolute and thus terrifying silence woke Emery up. No matter where she was—outside in the forest, on the desert plain, or inside her apartment—there were always sounds. Sounds of life on the streets, of animals, of wind through the trees, or those creaking sounds buildings made for no apparent reason. Sounds she normally didn't notice or pay attention to, unless they were completely missing. A world without sound was wrong. The silence invaded her sleep with its abysmal tentacles, reaching for her heart and brain. She woke up covered in sweat, hearing only her uneven, panic-stricken breathing. Lying on the floor of a small square room with seamless gray walls so smooth and even, she wondered if it was a hallucination or if she was still dreaming. Her heart galloped as she attempted to move her hands and feet to ensure she could. When they moved, she relaxed, raised herself on her elbows, and inspected the room.

She wasn't hallucinating. The walls and the floor were of a seamless and slightly translucent gray material resembling a dense plastic and metal blend, but they felt soft as she pressed her elbows into the floor. Natural light, as if originating from windows, illuminated the tiny space. But there were no windows, and—she realized with horror—no doors. She saw no obvious ventilation system, and yet she had no problems breathing in her small cage.

"Where am I?" Emery spoke loudly. Her voice sounded hollow and different. Hard. No one responded to her question, and the silence became even more oppressive. She got up and walked around the room, examining the walls and the floor for cracks or seams and making as much noise as she could to fill the silence. She found nothing she could pry open. Not even a hairline crack. Her stomach churned in panic. She would die here.

Someone put me here somehow. There must be a door. It's just well-hidden.

She remembered the prick on her neck and Visla's scream, but nothing more. She touched her neck and felt a tiny bump.

They must have carried me here. Visla, where are you?

"Visla?" she shouted.

She didn't get a response. Emery licked her cracked lips and drew a few deep breaths. *Need to find a way out of here and find Visla. I doubt that bitch is her mother.*

Her situation seemed hopeless as she stared at the seamless walls of her prison. Who were these "bad people", and how could they have created something so technologically advanced in Paleolithic times, when people didn't even know metals yet? They must have developed it and kept it a secret. But how and why? Why not share with everyone?

Emery touched the wall and traced it with her hands, searching for imperfections, but again with no results. Her heart beat even faster as she imagined herself as a shriveled gray corpse sprawled smack in the middle of her featureless prison. But the thought of Visla, who probably awoke in a similar gray box and was waiting for her, brought her back to her senses.

Emery sat on the floor, staring at the walls, thinking.

"Focus, Emery. Focus," she muttered. "There must be a way out of this box. Find it."

She closed her eyes and, one by one, she cleared all the thoughts, fears, images, and questions from her mind. She sat unmoving and silent like a statue. Her breathing slowed; her heart barely moved as she concentrated on eliminating everything from her mind. And once she cleared her last thought, she saw a gray expanse of nothingness unfolding like a blank canvas. Her mind drifted through it unhurriedly, searching for an escape route, a door, anything to get her out of this box. She finally saw something that looked like her prison, and she searched the walls for a door. Her golden and black dots floated and settled on one area, outlining a rectangle that looked more translucent than the other walls. Outside it, winding corridors traversed in every direction with no apparent end. A labyrinth. They'd put her into a maze.

Emery opened her eyes, and grinned. "Wow! I didn't know I could do that."

She stood up with a groan, surprised at how stiff her body was. *I must have been sitting for a while.*

She approached the wall from her vision—the one that looked different, weaker, thinner, and faltering. Emery threw her hands forward. The wall moved just enough for her to get through. Her heart was now fluttering like a scared bird, and her hands shook as she squeezed through the opening. It was just as she'd seen it—an endless gray corridor made from the same material as her cell, with the same sourceless, ephemeral lighting.

"Where are you, Visla?" she whispered, then repeated louder, and finally shouted. With no response from Visla or anyone else, she was undecided about which direction to go. On impulse, she turned right. She walked for a while, inspecting the walls, which, just like in her cell, were perfectly smooth and stretched into an endless grayness. Emery stopped when a terrifying thought crossed her mind.

What if there are people stuck in the boxes along the entire length of this corridor? All corridors? What if Visla is in one of them but can't hear me? How would I ever find her in this maze?

The hair stood up on her arms. She leaned with her back against a wall and, looking right and left, bellowed at the top of her lungs. "Visla! Answer me! Where are you? I'm so sorry. I was supposed to protect you, my baby sister, but I fucked up. I should have known. I shouldn't have trusted that dark bitch!"

Crying Visla's name, Emery moved down the corridor for what seemed like forever. With every curvy corner, she tensed, anticipating, hoping, and fearing something would happen—a door would open, a person, or a structure would appear. Anything other than the endless gray corridor. But there was nothing different beyond the bends. She wondered if she was stuck in it, destined to walk it till she died. It even crossed her mind that she might already be dead. Just like the lifeless wraiths stuck in the dark world, she was stuck here in the gray maze.

No, you are not dead. Get ahold of yourself. Find Visla. She might be in danger.

Alternating between despair and bursts of optimism, Emery kept walking and talking to herself to interrupt the oppressive silence. She stopped when she heard a sound up ahead and felt a slight vibration.

Invigorated with hope, Emery increased her pace. As she kept walking, she heard more sounds. They were faint and indistinguishable—whooshing sounds as if something was zipping through space. They reverberated through the corridor, but the sounds only slightly increased in volume as Emery walked toward them. She slowed before every bend in the hallway, and after the last bend, the corridor ended abruptly at a dead end. She looked at the smooth walls before her with her mouth open. When she was about to scream and pound at the strange wall in frustration, she heard the whooshing sounds again.

The sounds originated outside the corridor, so she attempted to open the wall again, just like she had in her cell. This time, the wall at the end of the corridor seemed to open much quicker. *I must be getting better at it.* She gasped as the wall just dissolved before her eyes, as if it were a cartoon or a computer simulation. She stepped back nervously and tensed, preparing to fend off an attack. When nothing happened, curious and eager to escape the maze, she returned to the edge and glanced at what lay beyond the wall. As she approached, she saw lights zip across the dark space that stretched before her.

What unfolded before her made her question her sanity and her understanding of the world as she knew it. Spreading as far as her eyes could see was a ... city! Tall gray windowless buildings and skyscrapers stretched in uneven rows as far as she could see. They shimmered, with lights emanating from their walls, as if they were the source of light themselves. As Emery watched them, the buildings seemed to move ever so slightly. At first, she thought she was imagining it. But the longer she watched them, the more certain she was that the buildings were not static but swayed as if propelled by invisible waves. And as they moved, their walls shimmered more intensely. There were no streets, no foundations supporting the buildings. The buildings floated in the dark space surrounding them. The whooshing sounds Emery had heard from the corridor were generated by the glistening objects emerging from buildings, zipping through space, and disappearing into other buildings like knives into butter. No doors opened for them. No platforms came out.

For a long while, all Emery could do was stand and watch the display of shifting lights and gray shapes, undulating as if they were dancing to the sound of silent music. She couldn't help but admire the spectacle because it was beautiful in all its strangeness, boldness, and sophistication. Even in the twenty-first century, where she came from, no technology existed to build this extraordinary, gravity-defying marvel of architectural violation and oddity.

"Holy fuck! Where am I? Who built this?"

Emery pinched her arm. It hurt.

Now what? She asked herself, looking down and seeing only darkness below and in the immediate vicinity.

How will I get out of here? I'm still stuck here.

Gazing at the swaying buildings, she considered her options. She could retrace her steps and walk back where she came from, or she could search for a way to get inside the strange gray buildings (if they were buildings or something entirely different and unknown to her). She opted not to go back, fearing she might get stuck in a maze and never come out. And she was growing weary, having walked for hours. Her stomach suddenly and painfully reminded her it had missed several meals, and her mouth felt parched.

There must be a way out of here.

Emery sat at the edge and let her feet dangle, observing the bullet-shaped gray objects as they zipped before her. She felt a strange tingling sensation when on her feet. It wasn't strong or unpleasant, and it didn't hurt. The dark air around her swirled, smelling of something slightly pungent and acidic, as if it were electrified. Straining her eyes to see as far as possible into the distance, she didn't immediately notice when something started forming under her feet. When she felt something touch her feet, she pulled them back, giving out a childlike scream. She looked down, and her jaw dropped in amazement. Below, the same gray substance that made the walls of her prison and the corridors and probably the buildings she could see in the distance had created something resembling the bottom of a boat underneath her feet.

"What the heck?"

She dropped her feet down again and waited in amazement as the boat's structure extended up. When it was close enough to her, she touched it. It was solid and soft at the same time—it felt like the walls of the cell and the corridor.

She hesitated at first, but having no alternative and propelled by curiosity, she slid down into the boat. She landed softly, and the boat grew all around her. Soon, she was sitting in an enclosed structure resembling a graceful marriage between a rocket and a boat. The front of the vessel was translucent, allowing her to see the buildings in front of her. There were no buttons, no screens, nothing suggesting this vessel could be controlled manually.

"This is pretty cool, but I seem to be stuck again," she said to herself. "How do I fly you, rocket boat?" she asked, not expecting a response, but to her shock, the boat replied.

"State your destination, my lady," a soft male voice requested.

If she weren't sitting already, she'd certainly be dropping to her knees, hearing the boat that just built itself out of nothing speaking perfect American English.

"Who the fuck are you? And how can you speak English?"

"I am Charon 499. English is my default language. Would you like me to speak another language? I know French, German—"

"What? No! Who programmed you in English?"

"Programmed? I don't know this word. It is not in my dictionary."

"Ugh! Do you have a boss? Somebody who assigns new tasks for you?"

"A boss? No, I don't know this word."

"Do you know anything, fuckhead?"

"I don't know the word fuckhead."

"Yeah, figured as much."

If this thing is mainly designed for transport, its vocabulary is probably limited to directions and maybe names or places.

"Can you go west?" Emery asked.

"Yes, do you want to sail west?"

"Yes, sail away," Emery grumbled. Someone had a strange sense of humor or was a sailing aficionado.

"How far west do you want to sail?"

Emery looked through the see-through front wall and pointed at the first building.

"To the first building."

"The building you are pointing to is not west. It is east. Do you want to sail east instead?"

"Sure, sail east."

"Yes, my lady."

My lady? Emery had thought she had heard wrong the first time, but when Charon 499 repeated the phrase, she marveled at the absurdity of the archaic English phrase used in futuristic or even alien settings. Because as she sailed through this strange world in a boat that made itself out of nothing, she was no longer certain she was still on Earth. The antiquated English added to her confusion and doubt. None of the scenarios she ran in her head made any sense. And then, when she remembered Charon was the entity who transported the dead in Greek mythology, she shifted in her seat, nervously glancing ahead. The surrounding mystery thickened, the puzzles and questions kept mounting, but answers glimpsed for a second, mocking her, then eluded her.

The boat moved forward swiftly but smoothly. She observed other objects disappearing into the buildings, wondering if her boat would do the same. But her boat halted just a few feet away from the gray structure.

"Can't you go inside? Sail inside, I mean?"

"I can, but you do not have permission to enter."

"Permission? From whom?"

"Entry permission."

"Who gives the permission?"

"The building."

"Are you kidding me? The buildings give permissions?" Emery stewed over this revelation while her vessel hovered patiently in front of the building. "So the building is like you? It can talk?"

"Yes."

"Can I talk to it?"

"You must enter to talk."

"How can I enter without permission? Can I ask the building for permission to enter?"

"You can't," Charon 499 said in a monotonous voice. "You'll have to request an invitation from the building occupants before entering."

"Catch 22."

"I don't understand. Is 'Catch 22' an address?" the boat asked.

Emery ignored him, thinking. "Can you ask the building if I can enter so I can get permission from the occupants?"

The boat didn't answer.

"Hello? Did you hear my question?"

"Yes. I can ask."

"Go ahead," Emery said impatiently, after sitting for a while without an answer.

"I did."

"You did what?"

"I asked."

"And? What did it say?"

"You cannot enter."

"Why not?"

"It didn't say."

"Can you ask?" Her voice gained an edge.

"You don't have the correct body to enter without an invitation."

"I don't have the correct body? What the hell does that mean?"

"The building cannot scan you to verify your identity."

"So why did you allow me to enter if you are the same as the buildings?"

"I am not the same. I am a sailboat, not a building. No permission is needed to enter the sailboat."

"Why?"

"No information."

"Never mind."

Emery crouched on the floor, pondering. This boat was not designed to be very smart or helpful. *Maybe for a reason*, she thought. To prevent unwanted visitors from going places they were not supposed to.

"Is there another way to get inside the building? A front door or a window?"

"Information not available."

"Okay, boat. Can you sail all the way down to the bottom of the building?"

"Yes. I can."

"Okay, sail down, then, Charon 499."

"Yes, my lady."

The not-so-smart boat lowered itself until it reached the base of the tall building. Much to Emery's disappointment, there were no doors or other openings she could squeeze through. Worse, since the building was not anchored to the ground but hovered in midair in the surrounding darkness, she could not just leave the boat and try to open the walls.

The boat awaited further commands.

"Boat, can you open your front wall? The front window?"

"No."

Emery shook her head in disgust and took matters into her own hands. Literally. She extended her hands and attempted to remove the front wall. She succeeded and more. The wall moved, but so did the entire boat. It slid from under her body, and she started falling. For a split second, she hoped the boat would build under her as it did before, but she continued dropping and couldn't see the bottom. The gray buildings around her blurred as she fell.

Thinking she was going to die, Emery thought of the people she loved, and her memory flashed their faces before her eyes: her mother, Sasha, Lev, and ... Peter. She had prohibited herself from thinking about him since the time she cried herself to sleep in front of the dying fire. Each time she thought about him since landing in this world, it hurt more, not less. It was as if the pain of losing him was catching up with her. She feared that if it got worse, it might weaken her resolve to continue. Since that night, whenever she caught herself thinking about him, as punishment and a deterrent, she made herself remember the most embarrassing moments in her life.

But now that she saw the buildings flash as she was falling to her death, she could think of Peter all she wanted and remember his blue eyes. One night, his blue eyes had shone strangely as he traced his hands over her naked body.

"You are my Aphrodite," he blurted out.

"I am a what?" Emery laughed.

"You are the embodiment of perfection. Not just your beauty. Your face, eyes, body, and hair couldn't be more perfect. Everything about you is perfection, the embodiment of human beauty. But not in the sense our media portrays it. Your perfection and beauty stem from something deeper inside of you. It is timeless, primal, sexual, and intellectual. Your magnetism and strength have no limits, but encompass everything around you and make it shine with life. You embody life and love. You are my Aphrodite."

"You are silly, Peter. I'm going to forget you said that." But she never did. She remembered everything he'd ever said to her, his every look, and his every touch.

"I've never been more serious than I am now, Emery. Don't forget it. Remember it wherever you go. Take it with you. You are my goddess. Goddess of love. What's more, I believe you will—"

A hard landing interrupted her memories. She grunted as her body slammed down on a semi-solid surface with a thump. It took her a moment to return to her senses and to gather enough courage to check her body for injuries. She moved her fingers and toes first, sighing with relief.

"I am alive," she whispered in astonishment, looking at the foot of the building above. It seemed so high. *Too high for a mere human to withstand the impact without breaking into a million bloody pieces,* she thought. *I should be dead.*

She took her time to relish her seventh life and then sat up and surveyed the area. The material she'd landed on was the same stuff everything else was made of. The gray mix of plastic, metal, and God-knows-what else was probably what had saved her life by lessening the impact of her fall, she guessed after examining its semi-soft surface. When she hit it hard with her foot, it made an imprint lasting almost a second.

Well, I don't know what that stuff is, but I owe my life to it.

"Thanks, stuff!" she said, patting the ground.

11

THE LAB

The surface she'd landed on stretched as far as the eye could see, undulating as if it were built over massive hills and valleys. The amount of effort and resources that were used in the construction of this strange world astounded her. If this was the world the "bad people" had built for themselves, they were far more powerful than she'd imagined. She began doubting these were the people she was seeking and began questioning their humanity and origin.

Realizing the power the "bad people" held, the urgency to find Visla intensified. Emery stood up, feeling every muscle and bone and hearing them complain with strange snapping and popping sounds. She didn't care, feeling no broken bones and knowing she'd recover soon. Bruises, scratches, or sprains would not stop her from looking for her friend. Everywhere she looked stretched the same gray vastness of nothingness—the hills, valleys, and buildings floating above.

Focusing intently, she noticed a giant structure in the distance. It appeared different, almost as if it had a greater depth, and it seemed to be lower than the other buildings. She pushed her aching body to lumber forward. The building was still far away, and she worried she wouldn't make it before her body gave out. But as she doggedly pushed on, dragging her feet, her body surrendered its grumbles, realizing it wouldn't get any rest until it reached the destination set by its stubborn owner. The aches slowly faded, and her steps regained some springiness.

As she approached the giant structure, she noticed that not all the buildings were as high as the one she had fallen from, and renewed hope infused some verve into her gait. Maybe there was a way to reach one of those buildings and find Visla. As she climbed over the hills, she noticed a cone of light shining down on the ground. Surprised, she looked up. The light seemed to originate well above the skyscrapers. She wondered what its purpose was. It certainly didn't provide enough light to illuminate the area below, and it appeared to be missing something. Emery stared at the light, and finally, she understood what was wrong. There were no dust flakes or flying insects near the light. The light was a perfect, bright cone, devoid of even a single fleck of anything. The dread gripped her gut in a tight clasp as she stared at it. *That's not normal. Maybe I am really dead?*

The building sometimes disappeared from her view altogether as she climbed over the hills and the valleys. Walking on the undulating terrain was hard enough. The hills grew slippery as their height increased, becoming nearly impossible to climb. Hungry, thirsty, and banged up from the fall, Emery labored with each step, panting, struggling not to slide down. The last incline was the worst of them all. It seemed to grow in height as Emery climbed it. She slid down after climbing a third of the way up, then again after climbing halfway. After the last failed attempt, she flopped on the ground and held her tears at bay to gather enough strength to climb again. But the tears came pouring out of her eyes. She lay down and sobbed, staring up at the black sky and the floating buildings.

I can't go on. I'm tired. I want to stop.

She closed her eyes, picturing herself falling asleep and never waking up. But instead of sleep, Peter's face appeared, clear and real, as if he were right here with her. "Get up, Emery. You can't give up. The world needs you. I need you."

She gasped and quickly sat up, looking around frantically. Hopefully. "Peter …"

She stood up, amazed at her renewed strength and resolve. She looked up the hill and instead of seeing this ominous, never-ending mountain, she saw a small hill that she could almost jump over. Not once did she slip. She climbed to the top and gasped. Having not seen the building as it was hiding behind the hills, she couldn't believe her eyes when she saw it up close.

"Mother of God!"

Before her spread a colossal building. She slid her hands across its surface and then pushed on it, trying to see if it had the same give as the other walls. It didn't. Its surface was not smooth like everything else around here but appeared to have been constructed with ultra-light concrete widely used in the twenty-first century, just before she began her journey.

The giant had suffered purposeful destruction: broken windows, cracked concrete, and large holes, as if something big had rammed into it. Flames had licked the exterior of the walls, leaving black smudges around the glassless windows. Emery regarded the building, scratching her arms in confusion. Judging from the weathering damage, this building was old. Centuries old. And yet, she had just spent time with a Paleolithic tribe. Where was she? What happened to her? Did the woman transport her into the future? Or was she dead, and this was hell?

No, you're being ridiculous. There's a logical explanation for all this. Concentrate on finding Visla.

Emery saw an open door, or rather, a hole with rubble piled in front of where the door used to be, and scrambled inside, albeit hesitantly, fearing the crumbling structure might collapse on her. As she explored further inside, she exhaled with relief. Inside, the building looked much better. The damage was mostly on the outside, while the interior walls were mostly intact. In its former glory, this place must have been impressive. Concrete, metal, and glass met in arches with extravagant shapes and colors. When the building was lit, it likely dazzled its tenants with its astonishing and unusual architectural style.

Emery wished she had a flashlight to explore all the areas. Broken windows allowed limited illumination from the nearby cone of light, casting ghostly shadows on the walls. As a result, the interior seemed to be bathed in moonlight. In its abandonment and ephemeral beauty, and with hints of former magnificence, this old building felt tragic and magical.

In the center, giant elevators made of glass and metal vanished into the ceiling in a spiraling structure that reminded Emery of a giant seashell.

Intact white leather sofas, chairs, and glass side tables greeted her as she entered an immense room that looked like a lobby. She scoured the area but found no hint of the building's purpose. With no power, the electronic signs and boards stared at her with empty glass fronts. Emery walked around searching for clues but found nothing, as if someone had removed everything that would have revealed its history. Her first impression was of a hotel lobby, but she quickly dismissed it. Although elegant and impressive, the building lacked the elements of comfort inherent in a hotel lobby. It felt more like an office building.

She continued through the lobby, discovering more elevators and stairs. Two of the elevators stood open, revealing their dark interiors. In one, Emery found overturned boxes spilling out into the hallway, once full of papers, now resembling a pile of dried-up mold. She peeked into the stairwell and saw only darkness. She took a few steps, looking up the dark shaft. The steps seemed sturdy enough, and she crawled up on her knees with her hands extended ahead to feel the obstacles. She was anxious but also curious about what she'd find upstairs.

Are you sure about this? What if they collapse on you?

As she scrambled up, fatigue returned with full force. Emery found she needed to give herself an ongoing pep talk to motivate her tired body to keep moving. She needed sleep. But to stop and rest meant delaying finding Visla, who might be in danger. No matter how tired she was, she had to push forward. Crouched, checking the stability of the stairs in front with her hands, she slowly made progress climbing up. Upon reaching the last step, she found herself in a dreary hallway and, seeing a faint light at the end, scuffled toward it, holding on to the walls. The light she saw seeped through the broken windows of an enormous room with walls stacked with equipment and translucent screens. The dead machines and screens looked out of place without power.

Emery gasped. This place looked similar to her mother's lab.

"This thing detects wavelengths. Don't remember its name, but I remember it," Emery exclaimed, walking around the lab. "Oh, my, this looks like an electron microscope! This is a physics lab!"

And as Emery looked around, she recognized more instruments. She didn't know their names or functions, not being old enough when she visited the lab with her mother to have developed an interest in physics. But having an exceptional visual memory, she knew she'd seen this gear or its previous iteration before. She stopped when she saw a stool she recognized and experienced a sudden flashback as clear as day. She saw herself sitting on a high stool with her feet dangling while her mother and Sara looked at something under a microscope and talked in hushed voices. The stool looked just as she remembered. She approached it and touched it slowly with her fingers. It was cool to the touch and triggered no recollections. For a moment, she wasn't certain if it was a memory or a hallucination caused by exhaustion.

There are plenty of stools like that everywhere. Emery told herself, but when she noticed scratches on its surface, she tensed. *No, not like that.*

Emery grabbed the stool and turned it. Her face drained of color as she saw the scratches on its underside. The letter "E" was lopsided, with the lower line sloping down, but this was an unmistakable "E." She stood staring at the stool, remembering the day she had tried to scratch her name with an old, broken pen as she sat, bored, waiting for her mother. She'd never checked if she had succeeded in scratching an "E", forgetting about it as soon as her mother beckoned her to follow her out of the lab after she was done working.

Overcome with sudden anger, she slammed the stool with all her strength. It landed with a loud thump, and she kicked it away.

This is impossible. You are imagining things. People scratch their names on stools all the time. Yours is not the only name that starts with E.

But the strange feeling of déjà vu persisted, and she scrutinized the room again. It was much larger, and the layout differed from her mother's lab. And yet, something about this space made her pulse quicken. As she looked into cupboards and opened drawers in search of clues, she noticed something strange. There was no dust on any of the surfaces. Emery wiped the surface of the desk with her hand. Her hand was clean.

If not for the broken windows, this place would look like its employees had just left. She searched desk after desk. Someone had emptied them all. On her way out, Emery opened one more drawer and froze. There was a photo inside. One lonely photo in a silver frame lay abandoned in the big drawer. It had been a while since she'd seen an actual photo. Most people had floating AI screens or holograms by the time she left college. The only actual photographs Emery remembered seeing were of herself and her mother, proudly displayed throughout her grandmother's house.

Emery picked up the frame with the glass still intact and glanced at the photo. The color and detail were gone. In this dark room, she could only see the outlines of a man, a woman, and a child—judging from the long hair, a girl—standing between them. A family photo. When she looked closer at the woman, her heart fluttered.

"Mom?"

She dropped the photo, which broke on impact with the concrete floor, shattering the frame and the glass into countless sharp bits. Emery backed away, viewing it with dismay. She felt her skin prickle, and she shuddered violently.

This just isn't real. It can't be my mother. This is not her lab. What the hell is this place?

Emery inhaled deeply and, with trembling fingers, removed the broken glass from the photograph and picked it up to look at it again. When she scrutinized the face of the man, she nearly fainted. While the background behind the faces was blurred, his face was much clearer, and his intense eyes were brilliant blue. Wearing a mysterious smile, staring at her from the old photograph was her father, Sergi Orlov. The girl's face was not discernible. It blurred and grew foggier as Emery stared at her.

Emery felt her body enveloped in a dense fog, just like the girl's face. Her mind went blank as if it were detached from her body, no longer hers.

She dropped the faded image and stumbled back. The crunch of broken glass under her feet jolted her from the fog, and she started rationalizing what she'd seen. This was not a photo of her parents. Her father died before she was born; thus, she couldn't have been photographed with him. And his eyes were no longer blue when he first met her mother, but black. This was simply something her tired mind conjured. These people probably looked nothing like her parents in the daylight. It was this place that made her invoke things that weren't there. Emery stared at the image a while longer, then bolted out of the lab without picking it up, even though every part of her body was screaming as if in agonizing pain to take the damn photo and stare at it some more.

Emery walked through all the rooms but couldn't make out much detail in the dark, windowless rooms, and fumbling around crawling on her knees wasn't appealing. Her tired body was giving up and balked at that prospect. At one point, it refused to go any further, demanding rest. She plopped onto the floor, but only for a moment. The guilt clamped her stomach and wouldn't let her rest. With a grunt and a moan, she rose and hauled her heavy body to another area.

A broken window let some light inside a room that was much smaller. It held a refrigerator, sink, and food fabricator/dispenser. Lined against the walls were also chairs and tables, some of which were overturned and broken, as if people had left this place in a hurry. She remembered this type of food dispenser, which the schools started installing when she was in high school. By the time she graduated from college, they were ubiquitous.

A break room. A kitchen. Food!

Trying to be funny to fight the fatigue, but secretly hoping for a miracle, she ordered the dispenser: "Make me a cheeseburger and french fries smothered with cheese and garlic! Oh, and a Coke."

With no power and most likely no ingredients left in the fabricator, nothing happened. Emery took a deep breath, opened the refrigerator, and ... wished she hadn't. There was no smell left, but the sight sufficed in making her cover her mouth with her hand to keep the bile from bursting out. What were once containers filled with food had morphed into oozing goop and gore that crawled out of the containers, overtaking the walls. It was now mostly green and black, but it leaped at Emery with all the ferocity of decay. She shut the door and backed up a few steps, bumping into a cupboard, which opened on impact. The hinges gave out, and the cabinet doors fell to the floor, breaking into slivers.

A bottle came tumbling out of the cupboard. Emery watched it with her mouth agape as the plastic bottle rolled toward her and stopped just inches from her feet.

"No way!"

She picked up the bottle and held it as gently as she could. The liquid inside looked clear.

Water?

When she tried to unscrew the cap, the bottle disintegrated in her hands, and the water spilled over her tunic and onto the ground, sinking into the gray-blue carpet.

"No!" Emery exclaimed and kneeled on the floor, trying to salvage the water. But the old carpet soaked it up like a thirsty sponge. She ransacked the cupboards but found no more water or food.

Crap!

She shuffled back into the main lab and flopped on the concrete tiles. Keeping her heavy eyelids open felt like a chore she couldn't do anymore. Her body seemed too heavy and disconnected from her mind, as if she were in a dream. *If I'm asleep already, closing my eyes won't matter. Only for a little while,* she told herself. *Just a few minutes. I won't sleep, just rest ...*

Her eyes closed, and she immediately plunged into a deep sleep.

~

"Stella! Stella! Where are you, girl? Stella. Come here, girl!" A man's voice cut through Emery's sleep.

She didn't open her eyes, thinking she was still dreaming.

But then she heard the man's voice again. "Stella, come here, my girl. Stella! I've been looking all over for you."

The voice sounded quite real. Emery jumped, listening to determine the sound's origin.

"Stella! Stella!"

She decided it was coming from below. Emery ran toward the stairs and trod down as fast as she could in the dark. She hesitated before stepping onto the last rung.

You don't know who that is. I don't care. It is someone who can talk and tell me where I am.

Emery peeked from the bottom of the stairs. She saw the back of a tall, slender man standing in the lobby, shouting the name "Stella" again. His voice sounded full of angst and sorrow.

"Stella, my girl! Stella! Come back, please. You might get hurt if you go too far."

"Who is Stella?" Emery asked, emerging from the staircase.

The man turned, and when he glanced at her, a glimpse of hope landed on his gray, sorrowful face. He looked almost identical to the people who had accompanied Visla's mother, except his face looked grayer. He didn't look old, appearing to be in his twenties, but his face looked worn out, as if its owner was in constant anguish. His vacant expression, however, was in stark contrast to his fatigued face, emphasized by the dark gray bodysuit he wore.

"Have you seen her? Have you seen my dog?" he asked Emery.

"Your dog?" Emery repeated stupidly. The notion of a dog in this strange realm seemed absurd. She must have misheard.

"Yes, my dog, Stella. She jumped the fence again. Have you seen her? Have you seen my Stella?"

"What does she look like?" she asked hesitantly. There was no dog here. There couldn't be a dog here.

"Big, white, and fluffy. She looks like a white wolf—a white husky, except her eyes are golden brown."

Emery shook her head. "I'm sorry. I haven't seen your dog," she said quietly.

The sad man looked around hopelessly, hung his head, and then lumbered for the exit. He seemed to be heartbroken over his missing dog, which made her think of her Regis. She understood his anguish; she would have been equally heartbroken had he gone missing.

Emery didn't follow him, believing he wasn't real. She deemed the entire experience a dream or a figment of her imagination. But once she heard his steps outside, she jumped up and ran after him. If he were real, he could help her. He seemed harmless.

"Wait," she yelled after him.

He stopped and turned around. "Do you know where my dog is?"

"No, I don't, but I'll look for her. I promise."

Apparently, he didn't believe in her ability to find his dog because, nodding absentmindedly, he turned to leave.

"Wait! How do you get to the top?"

"Just sail up," he said, shrugging his shoulders and pointing up.

"But I don't have a boat anymore. It broke."

"They don't break. They can't break," he said, glancing at her sideways. "Who are you? You look different."

"I am Emery. I am also looking for someone. My sister. Can you help me?"

"How can I help you? Who is your sister?"

"I want to go up. Can you tell me how to go up to all those tall buildings?"

"You can come with me if you want." The tone of his voice conveyed nothing. No annoyance, no curiosity, no anger.

"Really?" she asked incredulously. Seeing him nod apathetically, she added, "Sure. Thank you! I'll come with you. What's your name?"

"Thomas," he answered after a long pause.

Thomas summoned his boat: "Titanic 101, pick me up."

Titanic? He has a wicked sense of humor.

As soon as the words left his mouth, the boat started taking shape under his feet.

"Make it big enough for two people," he added.

Emery inched closer to Thomas, and the boat built its bottom under her feet.

When it was ready, Thomas gave it a command. "Take me home."

"Yes, my lord."

12

MEETING ELENA

"W here do you want to go?" he asked Emery after the boat was ready to sail.

"I ... I don't know," she said.

"You don't know where your sister is?"

"No. I don't. I am lost."

Thomas eyed her, and although he feigned disinterest, she noticed a hint of curiosity in his black eyes. "You can come with me."

"Where are you going?"

"Home."

"Thank you. I will come with you if it's not too much bother," she said as politely as she could. "Who names the boats?"

"We do," he said, looking at her askance. "We all do. It's our right to name them whatever we want."

"Why did you name your boat Titanic? Isn't it a bad omen to name your boat for something that sank like a rock on its first journey?"

"Titanic didn't sink. It was the first ship that carried people past the solar system and returned safely."

"Oh," Emery said, and instead of trying to convince him he was wrong, she observed him quietly. Either he didn't know or was utterly confused. Traveling outside the solar system was not possible in her time. And this was the past ... Or maybe she was dreaming, dead, or on some other planet.

The boat sailed upward, and in just a few moments, it headed straight for a sizable gray building without slowing down. Emery braced herself for impact, but the boat went through the wall smoothly as if it were fusing with it and then disintegrated on the other side of the wall. The interior was a spacious apartment, austere in its simplicity. Although windowless, the lightly colored walls illuminated by the familiar sourceless light made it feel surprisingly pleasant. She felt ... welcomed, as if the walls radiated something friendly and satisfying. Or perhaps she was just tired, and the bright space felt comforting.

While Emery looked around what appeared to be a living room, Thomas disappeared from her view. She heard him talking to someone somewhere deeper within the dwelling.

A woman followed Thomas as he returned. As tall and gray as he was, the black-haired and black-eyed woman was dressed in a light blue suit that fit her body as if it were made specifically for her. She carried a see-through tablet that folded into her hand to match its shape. When she saw Emery, she seemed genuinely surprised for a split second, and Emery felt relieved observing an emotion, even if it was just surprise. But as she reverted so quickly to her vacant expression, Emery thought she had only imagined it and felt a pang of disappointment.

"You were right. She is real. Is she a wildling? What is she doing here?" She asked Thomas, not taking her eyes off Emery. Hesitantly, she advanced a little and looked Emery up and down.

"I am Emery. I'm searching for my sister," Emery said, and started to sweat under the woman's unblinking stare. She rubbed her hands and smiled nervously. *Maybe I shouldn't be here.*

"Your sister?" the woman asked and seemed eager to ask more questions, but was at a loss for words. The tablet she held tumbled to the floor, but it didn't break. Her gray face turned darker. She ignored the tablet and touched Emery's face with her gray hand, which felt cold and metallic. Emery pulled back.

"I am sorry. I didn't mean to scare you. It has been a while since I saw a wildling. I'm Elena."

A wildling? Doubt crept into Emery's mind. The hand that had touched her didn't feel human, and yet they both looked and behaved like humans and spoke perfect American English, just like the boats.

The woman stepped back and pointed at Thomas. "My brother and I have lived here for a very long time. We seldom leave our quarters. I'm sorry we can't help you find your sister. We wouldn't know where to look."

Just like Thomas, except for the initial surprise at seeing her, she displayed no emotions. She showed no displeasure at the unexpected visitor, nor fear nor curiosity.

Maybe they are not people? Or they are just good at hiding their emotions.

The emotionless siblings stood facing her, appearing entirely uninterested in their visitor. At the same time, they didn't seem to mind her being in their apartment. Emery tried to think of something to say to fill the silence, but her mind was blank. Her stomach's loud rumblings released her from the awkward moment, reminding her it was time to tend to her mistreated body.

"Do you have any water? Food?" Emery asked. Seeing their blank stares, she continued. "I haven't had anything to eat in a while. If you don't have any food, that's okay, but I'm desperate for water. If I could just have a glass of water ..."

They gawked at her for a while and then exchanged glances.

Thomas shrugged. "We don't have food. Or water."

Emery didn't ask, suppressing the urge to scream into their unmoved faces. *How can you have no water or food? You are lying, or ... you are not human.*

"You don't ... have ... water?"

"She doesn't know," Thomas said.

"She is a wildling and too young to know and remember."

"But she speaks our language."

"Yeah. You are right. That's strange. Maybe she learned from the Minders. No, it can't be. She wouldn't look like she does."

Noticing Emery's confusion, Thomas turned to his sister. "We could try the *Origin*?" he asked her, whispering the last word as if it were a secret.

"I don't know," she intoned.

"We should help her, Elena."

"You are right. We don't want her to die here," Elena said, mulling over something. Then she asked. "What do you usually eat? Or drink?"

The first thing that popped into Emery's mind was cheeseburgers and fries—she was starving. She quickly reconsidered. She had to think of something simpler that they might have or know where to find it.

"Bread, vegetables, fruit? Water?"

"Bread?"

"Yeah, you know, ground-up grains made into bread," Emery tried to explain.

"What kind of bread?"

"Regular loaf. Wheat, rye, or whatever you have in your kitchen would be great. I'm not picky." Emery said. *I'm guessing they don't eat bread.*

Elena picked up the tablet and asked it to translate bread into a chemical formula.

"Wheat. It may work," she said and beckoned at Emery to follow her.

Through a gray hallway, they entered a room that held only a glossy white counter and a glass box suspended above it. Elena placed the tablet under the box, which immediately lit. Blue and pale-yellow lights flickered, and then a clear piano version of the Magic Flute played from the box, followed by a man's voice announcing that the pill was finished. A round silver pill, the size of her thumb, popped out from under the box and landed on a small white plate shaped like a flower petal that materialized underneath.

Thomas peeked over Elena's shoulder. "Are you sure it's safe for her to eat?"

"I don't see why not," Elena said, handing the plate to Emery. Seeing her hesitation, she added. "It won't hurt you. Wolfgang never makes mistakes. He's been making our Elements for centuries with no mistakes."

Centuries? What does she mean by that? Maybe she's crazy. Wolfgang. How weird. I am about to eat a bread pill made by Mozart.

Emery took the pill and carefully inserted it into her mouth, readying herself to spit it out if it tasted foul. Her eyes opened wide in astonishment as the pill quickly dissolved in her mouth and burst with a flavor and richness she didn't expect from the tiny capsule. Emery moaned with utter pleasure, closing her eyes as the taste of perfectly baked bread spread in her mouth. It felt warm, as if it had just left the oven. Emery relished the experience a while longer—it had been so long since she had tasted bread. It tasted heavenly and was very satisfying, as if she'd eaten half a loaf.

When she finally opened her eyes, the siblings gazed at her with a strange expression that bore a tiny hint of desire and envy.

I managed to make them feel something.

"Thank you. That was fantastic," Emery said, and burped loudly. She laughed uneasily, covering her mouth.

"I'm sorry," she said, and asked unsurely. "How about water? Can Wolfgang make me some water?"

They cast a quick glance at one another. Although they said nothing to each other, a mutual understanding, possible only for people who spend their entire lives together, passed between them. Elena put her tablet under the box with instructions for making water. Wolfgang lit up with its blue and light-yellow lights, but instead of the Magic Flute, the pill machine sounded three high-pitched tunes and flashed red lights.

"I'm sorry, my lady, your request could not be achieved."

"Why not?" Emery asked.

"No perfect ingredients, my lady."

"You said something about the *Origin*?" Emery asked Thomas. She smiled, hoping not to sound pushy or rude.

"I'm not entirely sure if you could use the *Origin*, but I can take you there."

A human being can't survive without water. If their machine can't make water, how can they be alive, just swallowing pills? Tired of guessing, she abandoned caution and simply asked.

"You don't drink water?"

Thomas's eyes showed a hint of surprise as he looked at his sister and opened his mouth to say something, but Elena stopped him quickly. "Why don't I take her, Thomas?"

"Are you sure? I'm the one who found her. I should be responsible for her."

"Yes, I'm sure. Why don't you get into your Atlantis for a while?"

"I guess so. Are you sure you don't want me to come along?"

"Yes, I won't be long," Elena said and added, glancing at the ceiling. "Atlantis, launch. Enjoy your ride, Thomas."

"Yes, my lady," a pleasant woman's voice answered from somewhere above their heads. The room darkened, and classical music came on. Emery didn't know what it was; she didn't know classical music well, but it sounded great played through their top-notch sound system. A white, bullet-like space rocket materialized out of nowhere and surrounded Thomas. He had only enough time to wave at them before he was enfolded by the little rocket. Then the room darkened even more, and stars and planets appeared before them, and soon the room wasn't a room anymore, but a vast expanse of space that stretched in all directions as far as the eye could see. Emery, not expecting it to look so natural and multidimensional, almost lost her footing, feeling momentary vertigo as if she were falling through outer space.

The rocket quivered and moved. Emery had just recovered her balance but stumbled again, trying to move out of the rocket's way, which seemed to head straight at her. But the rocket didn't move—it was an optical illusion, just like the rest of the room. The surrounding space smelled and felt different, as if electrified, charged with something smelling slightly acidic and sweet.

Elena grabbed her just in time. "Come. Let's go. He'll be at it for weeks. Who knows where he'll go this time."

"What do you mean, go? Like, actually go somewhere, or virtually?"

"What's the difference? Come on."

Elena approached a wall, and it opened without her doing or saying anything. She stepped out, and a boat materialized under both of them.

They flew through the emptiness in silence for a time. Emery could tell Elena wanted to tell her something. She hesitated, opened her mouth, hesitated again, but then finally spoke in a tone that sounded apologetic and even a little worried. "The dog ... he doesn't do that often. Only once in a while. It's not worth mentioning to anyone."

"The dog?" Emery looked surprised. She had already forgotten about the dog. "Oh, the dog. I won't tell anyone," Emery said decisively, although her first impulse was to ask whom she shouldn't tell about the dog and why. But she didn't, hoping Elena would continue.

After a long pause, Elena regarded Emery and spoke in a measured voice. "I know he was not supposed to remember it. But it's the only emotion he remembers. He is not harming anyone. He wanders around looking for it. Sometimes he disappears for ages, but always comes back, and then he forgets again. It's not that important. It's just a dog."

Emery bit her tongue, suppressing questions that kept popping up. She remained silent but relaxed her body and took on an amiable expression to show Elena she was not a threat, with nothing at stake, and that she deserved Elena's trust.

"It's just a glitch. An insignificant glitch. They don't need to know. You won't tell them, will you?"

"I promise," Emery said, trying to sound as sincere as she could, given she wasn't certain what she was promising.

Elena must have believed her because Emery's promise calmed

her. Only after Elena had relaxed, did Emery notice she had been tense before. As the word "promise" left Emery's mouth, Elena's facial features smoothed out, and her body eased into her seat. It was a subtle change, barely visible, but Emery noticed it.

Emery looked out the front window and gasped at how fast they were flying or sailing (according to the boat's point of view). The surrounding buildings blurred, and the infrequent cones of light shining from above looked like an abstract painting. Although strange and desolate, the view of the strange city that spread before her eyes arrested her breath, as she sat spellbound by its extraordinary beauty and resplendence.

She was startled when Elena broke the silence. "I will help you find your sister if I can," Elena said.

"You will? Thank you, Elena. You've been so kind to me."

Elena looked at her as if she'd seen her for the first time. "Kind?" She asked, silently repeating the word as if hearing it, not knowing its meaning, and trying to understand it. They remained silent until the end of their trip. Emery, engrossed in her thoughts, didn't notice when the boat stopped.

"We are here. Come, let me take you to the *Origin*."

The boat had taken them to ground level and stopped by an actual rocky outcrop, not the gray malleable material everything here seemed to be made from. They stood facing the stone for a few long seconds.

Elena walked toward it, glancing back at Emery. "Don't be scared. It is just a cave. An ancient cave," she said.

"I'm not scared."

Elena approached the rock and placed her hand on its surface. It opened silently to reveal the entrance to a dark cave, its interior smelling of moist dirt. As they entered, the darkness gave way to dim emerald light originating from the focal point of the large circular area.

"Wow!" Emery exhaled, stunned at the wondrous spectacle unfolding before her—a small spring shot out of the ground. Chest-high spurts of water as clear as a pristine mountain stream glistened in an emerald light that emanated from below. Emery stood gazing at the spring, amazed at its brilliance and tranquility. In that magical moment, she forgot where she was. This place made her think of a story about a sacred spring her mother had read to her when she was a child. Stalactites hung from above in delicate, thread-like long fingers, casting webby shadows and emerald drops to the ground, from which stalagmites reached out with their slender stalks as if accepting the drops as precious gifts with their crystal fingers. As they collected the drops of water, the light scattered them into rainbows onto the walls, which glistened with ever-changing colors.

While Emery admired the cave, Elena stood quietly, observing her. Her gaze was focused on Emery's face with an intensity that would have shocked Emery had she been watching Elena. But she was lost in her reverie, awestruck by the sight in front of her, trying to comprehend what she was seeing. When she finally glanced at Elena, her companion had her expression under control and reverted to indifference.

"What's this place?"

"It is the *Origin*."

"The origin of what?" Emery asked carefully.

"Of everything," Elena answered slowly and added unsurely. "Of us. Of you and me, I suppose."

She doesn't know?

Emery asked no more questions about the spring, realizing Elena either didn't know or didn't want to tell her. *You rarely use such profound names for objects without a reason*, Emery thought.

"Do you come here often?"

"Not at all. I've been here only twice since I can remember. With Thomas."

Elena didn't elaborate, and Emery didn't press. She walked along the walls of the cave, exploring it, stopping at the far side, which appeared different from the other walls. It was completely black and didn't glisten. The moisture didn't adhere to it.

"What's behind this wall?"

"Nothing. Why don't you try the water?"

"It doesn't look the same as the other walls. Are you sure?"

Elena nodded.

Emery walked toward the spring, speeding up in the last few steps, drawn to its coldness and freshness that settled as fine mist on her face, chest, and arms. It reminded her of the springs she used to stop by with her mother to refill their bottles during their hiking trips. They never bothered to filter the water from the mountain streams and never got sick from drinking it. Emery had later wondered why her scientist mother didn't worry about germs hurting her little girl. Only after she read her letter did she understand their immune systems were more efficient and much faster at responding to foreign "invaders". She wished she knew more about it and how her powers worked, and found herself in one of her occasional bitter moods toward her mother for failing to explain them in her letter, and she had a sudden urge to curl into an angry ball and feel sorry for herself. But then, remembering the torn pages, she rebuked herself for doubting her mother and quickly snapped out of it.

As she stood by the spring, mist settled on her tunic. She shivered —not from the cold, but from how refreshing it felt on her tired body. Emery folded her hands into a cup and filled them with water. Before she started drinking, she smelled it with suspicion. But it smelled just as it appeared—clean and fresh.

The taste of the water surpassed its appearance and smell. Emery drank until her stomach felt heavy and started gurgling. She drank until she could not drink anymore, long after her thirst had waned, while Elena watched her. Emery noticed her expression this time. The same one she had when Emery ate the bread pill. In it, Emery saw a trace of desire and bitterness as Elena swallowed as if she had drunk the water herself.

Emery wiped her chin and smiled. "Don't you want to try it? It's the best water I've had in my life."

Elena walked hesitantly to the spring. She didn't drink but ran her fingers through it timidly, as if the water frightened her. She must have liked the sensation of the cold water on her fingers because she did it repeatedly and with less caution each time. Emery wondered how old she was. She appeared to be in her twenties, yet ageless. If she were like Zoe, she might be hundreds of years old or even more. *Wait. Didn't she say something about Wolfgang making her pills for centuries? Nah. I must have misheard her.*

When Elena played with the spring, she appeared much younger. She watched the droplets dance in the air with the amusement of a child witnessing something extraordinary for the first time. As Emery watched Elena, for some strange reason, she pitied her. This woman had never played with water before or ... if she had, it was such a long time ago that she'd forgotten.

Elena moved her hand away from the spring, inspecting the droplets on her skin. Then, her attention turned to her jacket, which was also covered with tiny droplets. She was mesmerized by them, but sensing Emery's curious gaze, quickly composed herself and smothered the light in her eyes, replacing it with indifference.

As if she'd never experienced water. *Doesn't she shower? Swim?*

The suspicion that Elena was not entirely human returned. Although Emery's mother and Sara were changed with the black shard, they ate, drank, and showered. Her mother loved to swim. Any chance she got, she'd jump into even the coldest mountain lake and swim like a fish. These people, or whatever they were, were entirely different. Emery had changed her opinion of whether they were human beings several times already. They looked human, but their gray skin lacked the brightness of human skin. But so far, she hadn't experienced the uncanny valley effect, the profound revulsion she felt when she had first encountered the humanoid robots at the Museum of Artificial Intelligence (the failed experiment in creating mechanical intelligence that killed thousands of people in the 2030s). Also, the names they used for their appliances and boats suggested they were at least familiar with human history. The "my lady" phrase, although it irritated her, also hinted at human origin. Who else would use such a strange, archaic expression with implied superiority, if not a narcissistic human?

Emery was tempted to ask, but she bit her tongue. Elena might get angry and abandon her, or she might be upset. Emery did not want to offend her, beginning to like this strange woman. Seeing glimpses of emotions escaping Elena's control, Emery suspected she was hiding and suppressing them.

"How can I assist you in finding your sister?"

Daydreaming, Emery jerked at hearing her voice. "I don't know."

"When did you last see her, and where?"

"Oh, I'm not sure. I think I've lost track of time. Maybe a few days ago? As for where, I don't know."

"You don't know where you last saw your sister?"

"That's just it. I came here from somewhere else. That's why I don't know where I was when they took my sister. I don't know the name of the land I came from or how I got here, either ..." Emery's voice trailed off as she realized how dumb she sounded.

Elena showed no reaction. "Who took your sister?"

"Her mother and—"

"Your mother took your sister?"

"No, she's not my mother. She is her mother. I am not even sure of that. She said she was, but I'm uncertain Visla believed her," she said and paused, looking into Elena's eyes, trying to draw out an emotional response, a glimmer of understanding from her. She found it difficult to explain how much finding Visla meant to her to someone staring at her with eyes lacking emotion.

She continued, pleading with her eyes. "I know how it sounds. Visla is like my sister, but she's not my biological sister. She is my friend. My best friend. I think, no, I'm sure that she saved my life when I first came here. We've become friends. More than friends. We were more like sisters. She is the most wonderful human being in this world. I must find her and make sure she is okay."

"You came from up there. Didn't you?"

"Up there?" Emery asked, not understanding.

"From the wasteland. Where the wildlings live."

"The wasteland. You mean the desert?" The wildlings. *Does she mean Emery's clan or the other clan I saw while scouting?*

"Where did you come from?"

Emery hesitated. Should she tell her the truth? Tell this strange, emotionless woman that she came from the future through the black hole? Trusting her intuition, Emery told her the story. Not the complete story. Enough to test her reaction at first.

"I am from Seattle. From the United States. I came here through a time machine my mother built and then traveled through a black hole and ended up in the desert," Emery said quickly and exhaled, thinking Elena wouldn't believe her wild story and would laugh in her face (if she could laugh). To her surprise, Elena listened without even the slightest blink. She watched, nodding pensively and calmly, as if Emery were telling her she was visiting from a neighboring town.

"Ah," she said, appraising Emery as if she had seen her in a new light. "What year did you arrive from?"

"It was 2047 when I left. I don't know how long I was in the black hole. Sometimes it seems like it was eons ago and sometimes like it was just yesterday."

"Why did you come here, Emery? Why did you go through such an ordeal to come to this forsaken wasteland?"

Her calm and even tone stood in stark contrast to the surprise, outrage, and even anger implied by the question.

"What you call a wasteland is not so bad. People survive up there just fine." Emery believed she ought to protest Elena's attempts to disparage her actions. "I'm here to save the world," Emery said with a voice that sounded weak and unconvincing. She had realized the absurdity of her quest and grown accustomed to it, but when someone else, a stranger, noticed and commented on it, it stung like hell. Emery averted her eyes to hide her ache and shame.

"To save the world? To save it from what?"

"Self-destruction. I'm to release dark matter, locked by the—"

"Self-destruction? That's nonsense. What're you talking about?"

"The world was unbalanced and is about to collapse."

"And that was in 2047?"

"Yup."

For what seemed like an eternity, she stared at Emery, thinking. Emery deemed it was important to convince her she wasn't crazy and continued talking. "The universe was unbalanced and on the verge of self-destruction because there wasn't enough dark matter to keep it stable and replenish it. You see, dark matter is what the universe is made of. It changes from its invisible, weightless state to normal matter. Normal meaning visible, you know ..." Emery said and glanced at Elena to check if she was following. Satisfied, she continued, "... but dark matter was locked by the ion implosions thousands of years ago. It was my destiny to go back in time and restore the balance by releasing the black shards, which in fact are condensed dark matter—"

"Emery, the world didn't self-destruct. Someone lied to you."

"Huh? How could you possibly know that?"

"Because I was there after 2047, and the universe was still there."

Emery backed away and searched Elena's face for signs of deceit. But she looked sincere in her emotionless expression and didn't appear to be the type to fib. "When in the future? What year?"

"I was born in ... 2358."

"What year is it now?"

"3090."

"It can't be." Emery's face became ashen, which in the emerald light seemed even whiter. If Elena wasn't lying, it meant Emery had traveled into the future instead of into the past and had sacrificed her life and the love of her life for nothing. The world didn't end. Her mother had sacrificed her life for nothing. All this was just a lie, concocted by Zoe. In the end, Zoe won—she got rid of her, even though she ended up in the dark dimension all by herself. The realization hit her hard. As the anger and regret weighed heavily on her and then suddenly dissipated, she felt empty and depleted. Elena's words repeated in her mind like an echo: "Someone lied to you."

Elena observed her silently and with indifference, but when she saw the tears beading Emery's long eyelashes, her face changed. Her lips and eyes and eyebrows twitched in tiny movements, and her lips curled up and down. Emery's tears triggered a sensation that Elena wasn't able to process.

The two women stood silently, outwardly observing each other, but consumed by their thoughts.

"Who told you the world would end?" Elena asked finally. Her tone of voice had lost its flatness, as if it had gained a few layers in the last few minutes. But it wasn't just her voice that changed. Emery could see Elena was struggling to revert to her emotionless expression. She eventually relapsed into her cool persona, although clearly not as quickly as she believed she ought to have. A faint echo of what she had experienced remained, softening her expression. At that moment, Emery considered her pretty in a quiet, but interesting way. She reminded Emery of old oil paintings of nobility. Her high cheeks, large eyes set perfectly on her face and framed by long, curvy lashes, topped by full lips, which even though they were gray, had the softness and curvature of human lips. The stately nose accentuated her royal looks.

"I should report you," Elena whispered more to herself than to Emery. "It's my duty to report strangers; it's the protocol."

The hair rose on Emery's neck. "Will you report Thomas as well?"

Elena looked at Emery with cool eyes. Her mouth was moving in tiny movements, but no sound was coming out.

Emery interrupted Elena's conflict, answering her question. "Zoe Brie told me the world would end. My mother's enemy. I don't even fully understand the feud between them. I think Zoe was jealous of my mother's power and wanted to get rid of her. She concocted a story so outrageous that it rang true. Powerful and resourceful, she corroborated it with actual events and facts that she made happen. She even destroyed England trying to convince my mother, but—"

"She did what?"

"She vanished England with the black shards she sequestered from the Russians."

"Who are you?" Elena asked, taking a step back.

"I am Emery, I told you ..." Emery didn't finish, noticing Elena had started trembling, then shivering violently after taking a few more steps back.

Thinking she was having a seizure, Emery rushed to her side to steady and comfort her. "How can I help?" she asked.

Elena didn't respond, staring at Emery. Her eyes moved in their sockets back and forth as her body convulsed.

"What's wrong?" Emery wailed. She wanted to console her, but was afraid to touch her. The need to help overcame her hesitance, and she embraced Elena in an awkward hug—she was much shorter, and her head rested on Elena's chest. She half-expected to be pushed away, but Elena didn't object, staying in the embrace, still shaking.

"I have no idea how to help you."

Emery's attempt to sound calm didn't quite work, so she just gently stroked Elena's shoulder. A few minutes passed; the spasms slowly lessened, but Emery didn't ease her embrace until Elena completely calmed down. Only then would Emery release her.

"Are you okay? Can I do anything?"

Elena shook her head. A look of determination settled on her face as she quickly composed herself. She looked into Emery's eyes. "I'm not used to interactions with wildlings. There is so much peculiar ... energy around you. I think my body reacted strangely. We need to leave this place. Let's talk on our way back," Elena said, heading toward the cave's exit.

Inside the boat, Elena wasn't talkative, grappling with the decision she had made and dreading the conversation she was about to have with her brother, cognizant that there were many unspoken questions between them already. Questions she was unwilling to ask before, anticipating what the answers would be and fearing the consequences. Questions she now had to ask.

Emery's anger and humiliation had evaporated in an instant after experiencing Elena's strange panic attack. Alarmed, Emery oscillated between two equally disturbing notions—believing Elena had a neurological disorder or that she was a robot, and she malfunctioned. Either might impede her help in searching for Visla, which now became her priority, considering her mission might have been a lie according to Elena's version of the past events. If she were to believe

Elena that her quest was just a hoax, finding the shards slid down on her urgent list. She had to find Visla and get out of this place.

Her intuition whispered Elena was telling the truth. If she had bad intentions, she wouldn't have helped her to get food and water; instead, she'd have notified someone, and they would have snatched her already and thrown her back in her silent prison. No, Emery decided. Although Elena was different and aloof, she was not like the others who captured and imprisoned her.

"Are you okay?" Emery asked.

Elena glanced at her, acknowledging her question, but took a moment to reply. "I think so."

"What happened to you?"

"I don't want to talk about it," Elena said, waving her hand. "Tell me more about the person who vanished England and sent you here."

"Why?"

"I have my reasons. I'll explain, but I must be certain you are telling me the truth."

"I have no stake in it and no cause to lie to you," Emery said and told Elena the story about Zoe and her brother, Sebastian Brie, and her mother. It took her longer than she'd expected, as emotions kept interrupting her story as she relived her mother's disappearance and losing Peter. Engrossed in her story, she didn't notice the boat coming to a standstill in front of Elena's building. Elena listened to her every word, watching Emery's face.

"So now that you know everything, tell me why you wanted to know this crazy story that had had no connection to you."

"Let's go inside," Elena said, folding her hands strangely, appearing uncomfortable. "Here, take this," Elena added, taking a tiny silver object from her pocket. "It's Thomas's. If you insert it in your ear, the building will scan you as him."

Emery didn't hide her surprise. "But the building let me in when I came with Thomas."

"As a guest, but ... it's better not to repeat it too many times. It's better that way ..."

The concern in Elena's voice dampened Emery's desire to argue or protest. She nodded and took the earbud, but secretly wondered why Elena carried her brother's scanning device.

Elena told the boat to enter the house, and it responded politely, "Yes, my lady," and did what she'd asked.

Thomas was still inside the rocket exploring distant worlds, and the living room still resembled outer space. Elena led Emery past the rocket, deeper inside the apartment, and into a smaller room, furnished with floating sofas and chairs. *Well, if buildings float, why not chairs?* Emery chuckled, admiring the view that started to materialize after Elena snapped her fingers and the ceiling.

Mountain ranges with snow-covered peaks emerged from the walls and surrounded them. They looked so real, Emery had the sensation of being immersed in the middle of an alpine valley. Even the moving clouds and the bright sun peeking from behind the mountaintops seemed real. A fresh breeze swept across Emery's face and toyed with the lock of her hair that escaped from her braid as she marveled at the view. To add to the reality, the breeze carried with it the smell of pines. Emery didn't know or care if this was only a holographic image or something even more sophisticated, because the moment she walked into this room, she felt its tranquility and comfort. It was as if she had stumbled into an oasis after being on a long and exhausting journey through the desert.

"This is incredible. So beautiful," she whispered, squinting at the fake sun.

"I am glad you like it. This is one of the places I travel to ski. Over there, past that peak," she said, pointing at a distant range.

"Ski as in actual mountains?"

"Don't be ridiculous. Snow doesn't exist anymore." Elena said with a scornful hand gesture. "We can talk here without being heard," she said and pointed at the ceiling with her index finger. Soon after, classical music reverberated through the room. Elena slid her finger through the air, adjusting the volume to be loud enough to muffle the sound of their conversation if anyone happened to be monitoring it, but quiet enough to hear each other.

Being heard by whom? Emery wondered but didn't ask, sensing she might find out soon. Emery had felt the slight change in Elena and her growing trust, but perceived that Elena took longer than most people to fully confide in someone. Perhaps she had her reasons.

Elena summoned the white, cloudy sofa with her eyes, and it glided toward her. She sat in it and eyed Emery. Emery followed her cue and sent a stern look at the comfy-looking chair floating above her. But the chair ignored her and stayed put. She looked at it more sternly, but the chair didn't budge.

"Okay, what's the trick?"

Emery looked at Elena, and she could have sworn she saw amusement in her eyes. It was fleeting and elusive, but it appeared as if Elena was teasing her.

"Chair, come here," Emery said, but the chair didn't obey her. Emery looked at Elena. The amusement was gone from Elena's eyes. *I must have imagined it.*

"It doesn't recognize you. They are programmed to specific people, so they can do a better job of comforting," Elena explained and sent the unruly chair Emery's way with her eyes.

Cautiously, Emery sat in the chair, which immediately wrapped around her in the softest and warmest hug she had ever received from a ... chair. It felt almost as if a pack of cuddly dogs were embracing her. She immediately felt a pang in her chest when she remembered the furry friend she had left behind. *Regis, my boy. I miss you so much.*

"Are you all right?" Elena asked, noticing Emery's pained expression.

"Yeah. I miss my dog. And my mother ... not necessarily in that order ..." Emery blinked to fend off tears. *Not now. Not here. Calm down.*

"Ah, a dog. It's so strange that such a creature can cause a human to ... hurt," Elena said pensively. "Stella wasn't my dog. I don't remember when the dog disappeared and don't really remember her. I suspected it had died or gotten lost. He never forgot her. Any mention of dogs brought memories back and spells of grief. My brother loved that dog more than he loved anyone or anything else."

"Why wasn't he supposed to remember the dog?"

"He wasn't supposed to remember he loved the dog," Elena said; her face warped in a peculiar expression.

Emery didn't understand, and her expression showed it.

"Why not?"

"It is not who we are now. The change … the change eliminated the nonessential aspects of human nature."

Nonessential aspects. Love? Does she mean love in general or love of the dogs? Emery caught herself grimacing. "The change?"

Elena shifted in her seat. "I'll share with you what I remember about the change, and before the change. I promise," Elena said, seeing Emery's expression. "First, let me tell you what happened after you left," Elena said and paused.

After a moment, she drew a deep breath—the first and only deep breath Emery saw her take—and continued in a flat voice. "The world didn't end. Not in the sense you thought it would. But it transformed. Worldwide heatwaves, followed by thirstwaves, wreaked havoc on crops. In 2360, food and water shortages affected everyone, even the richest. Millions of people died of hunger and thirst. Chaos ensued, but the worst part was that nobody did anything about it. No one thought of a solution before reality hit the world. It came quicker than anyone expected. As you can imagine, certain parts of the world were impacted more than others, and people died quickly. There was no time to mourn them. It was then that the disappearance of England resurfaced."

"Really?" Emery grimaced. "Why? Nobody except for the conspiracy maniacs discussed it anymore by the time I left. What happened?"

"Italy happened," Elena said and peered at Emery with an odd expression, as if waiting for her to finish the sentence.

"You mean … Italy disappeared too?" Emery asked, and seeing Elena nod, added, whispering. "Who did it, and why?"

"Nobody knew who was responsible and the reason at the time, but that is not what was important."

"The disappearance of Italy was not important?" Emery snorted.

"The entire human race was dying. Italy didn't matter that much at that point. What mattered is where it led from there," Elena said and paused, gazing at Emery.

"I'm listening."

"By that time, the ion explosion had been thoroughly studied and used in various ways. When Italy disappeared, the ion monitoring equipment went berserk, and everyone knew that an ion explosion was one of the factors involved. The other was unknown until a certain ... figure ... came into play. A man named ... Sebastian Brie—"

"No way! That Sebastian?"

"Based on what you have told me, I have few doubts. When I heard your story, and you mentioned Zoe and Sebastian Brie, everything fell into place and started making sense to me. Sebastian Brie played a major role in human history. And now I think I understand why. He was still furious about his sister and returned to avenge her while trying to wreak havoc and destroy humankind."

"Avenge her, how? Italy had nothing to do with Zoe's disappearance. I did." Emery's voice sounded weak. She felt queasy.

13

THE CHANGE

Visla woke up to voices she didn't recognize. When she opened her heavy eyelids, everything seemed enveloped in fog, as if she were dreaming.

A woman's voice sounded loud and clear: "Ah, you are awake. Good. We can start then."

Visla blinked to clear the blurriness out of her eyes. She saw a faint outline of a person above her. She recognized the voice, but she couldn't remember whose it was.

"Visla, my daughter. Can you hear me?" she asked in English.

Her memories charged back before her eyes, and her heart started galloping. The blurriness dissipated, and she saw with anguish the woman claiming to be her mother glaring at her from above.

"Where is Emery? What have you done with her?" Visla rasped.

"Why do you think I've done anything to her? She is fine. She is relaxing and waiting for you."

"I don't believe you. I want to see her."

"Calm down. We've got something important to discuss now. Before the change."

"What change? What're you talking about?" Visla tried to sit up, only to discover with horror that she was tied inside some strange container connected to even stranger-looking white boxes with blinking lights and dark webs of shiny, narrow twines that connected them to her body. She panicked and started wiggling to loosen her restraints.

"What are you doing to me? What do you want? I want to leave. I want to go back home. Let me go," Visla cried in anger and fear, looking at the woman claiming to be her mother. "Please let me go. I don't want to change. Please, Mother ..."

"I will. Once the change is done. That's what I wanted to talk to you about. I want you to understand what will happen to you and what to expect when you wake up after this is all done."

"What change? I don't want any change. Please let me go. If you are truly my mother, let me go, please," Visla pleaded, sobbing; her tears formed a salty pool by her side.

"You'll be fine. Better than fine. Your life will change for the better. You will not know or remember certain things. But don't worry. These things are unnecessary and only make human lives miserable. You'll be free and will live your life to the fullest. There's no reason to be scared. It'll take less than a day, and you'll wake up a different person and will thank me then."

"I don't want to be a different person. Please let me go. Mother! Please!"

"Shush," she said and gestured to the women standing behind her to approach the table. "I'll be with you when you wake up."

"Is that what happened to you?" Visla screamed. "You were changed into the monster you are? I don't want to be like you! I hate you! Let me go ..."

Visla wanted to scream, experiencing fear she had never felt before. It pressed against her eyes, blinding her and paralyzing her body in an agonizing grip, obstructing her breathing. One dark-eyed woman shoved something in Visla's mouth as she gasped for air. Another woman attached more shiny lines to her head, chest, arms, and legs. Visla saw her mother calmly observe her as she bit hard into the object the woman put in her mouth. When she bit into it, it slowly dissolved and flowed deeper into her throat, filling it. Her heart pounded so hard it hurt. As she struggled to breathe, her body spasmed. Before she finally lost consciousness, she was certain she was dying.

I am dying. How could you, Mother? That was her last thought just before her mother slammed an opaque lid on top of her.

14

RUN, EMERY, RUN

W hat happened? What did he do?" Emery asked, shifting to the edge of her cloudy seat.

"He admitted to vanishing Italy and threatened to annihilate the entire world if his demands weren't met."

"What were his demands?" Emery's heart beat faster in anticipation. The chair responded to her increased heart rate by holding her tighter. She struggled to free herself from its embrace. "How do I tell the fucking chair not to squeeze me so tightly?"

"Just relax. The chair aims to comfort you when you get upset. It can sense it."

"I don't want it to do it. How do I stop it?"

"You can't."

"Why not? I don't like it. It feels like a straitjacket." Emery shifted violently and fell off.

"Why are you so upset? The chair won't hurt you."

"I don't like having no control over furniture. I don't need hugs from a fucking chair." *Why are you freaking out? It's not like the chair is going to bite you. And how would you know what a straitjacket feels like, anyway?*

"Calm down. It's just a chair. Don't you want to learn the rest of the story?"

"Yes, of course I do. Sorry. Go ahead. What did he want?"

"To have ultimate power over the Department of Energy and to replace its head, who was—"

Elena was interrupted by a loud click and a change in the appearance of the walls. The mountains disappeared, and the walls turned dark gray. The drab colors slowly brightened in the center of one wall, and Emery could see two people standing and looking straight at them. Surrounded by a brighter blue-gray, dark silhouettes hid their features. She guessed from their outlines that one was a woman and the other a man.

"Elena," the woman said. "I see you have a visitor. Would you mind telling me how she got into your quarters?"

Elena responded calmly to the woman's inquisitive tone. "She was lost and asked for help."

"You didn't answer my question. How did she get into your quarters? She's not one of us. You should've reported her immediately. The moment you noticed her, you should've notified us. We have protocols for this, and for good reason. You know that, Elena. Don't you?"

"Of course I do. I don't need a lecture, Lady J. I knew what to do, but she didn't seem dangerous. I saw her lying on the ground and took her with me. She was lost and needed to rest for a while. No harm done. Now you know she's here. What do you expect me to do now?" Elena asked.

Elena did not lose control of her voice throughout the conversation, keeping her black eyes on the man. The tone of her voice was neither subservient nor arrogant toward these people, who appeared to be her superiors. She sounded just as Emery remembered her speaking when she first had met her—like a machine. Elena reverted to her dispassionate voice when speaking to these people. This made Emery realize that her presence altered Elena's behavior. The change was nearly indistinguishable; nevertheless, Elena acted differently toward them.

"Why did you help her, Elena?" the woman asked; her tone was spine-chillingly calm.

"Because she needed it. That's all."

The man did not speak, only observed them quietly, without moving at all. While Elena responded to their interrogation, Emery, still on the floor, shifted her gaze between the woman and the man, bewildered. Who were these people, and why did Elena have to report her presence to them? They must have been part of the group that had kidnapped her and taken Visla. But this woman's voice was not that of Visla's mother. These were different individuals, but they were still interested in her. They must have realized she'd escaped and were now looking for her. But how did they find her here? Elena had no time to send them a message—she'd been with Emery this entire time. Thomas, busy traveling in his rocket, couldn't have reported her. If neither sibling had informed on her, who did? These gray beings must have other means with which they spied on others. It was probably the holograms. It must involve some sort of transmission—a two-way communication system and a method to monitor the occupants at their will, Emery guessed. They must have seen her sitting here and talking to Elena.

Emery felt no fear, only astonishment mixed with curiosity. It occurred to her that if she went along with them, if that was their plan, they might lead her to Visla.

She was about to say something to them, but Elena, as if sensing her intentions, ended the conversation quickly. "Come and get her, then." Then she jumped down from her cloudy chair while gesturing at the walls.

The transmission stopped.

Elena grabbed Emery's hand and tugged her along with her, deeper into the apartment. "You must run, Emery. You have little time before they come to get you."

"But they might lead me to my sister. They may lead me to Visla. I should wait and go with them."

"No!" Elena shouted, her angry outburst surprising Emery. "If they get you, they will change you. You might never remember your sister or your mother," she said, adding quietly, "You certainly won't remember how you ... felt about them."

"Change me? What does that mean?" Emery asked, and her mind immediately went to the black shards and what they did to people. If this were the case, she had nothing to worry about. She had already been changed by the black shards. At birth.

As if guessing what she was thinking, Elena blurted. "No, it is not your black shards. It is something else entirely. You must run, trust me. If they change you, you will not remember that you needed to find your sister. You must try a different way to search for her. But you must hurry because they're coming. You can use the boat, but not for very long. They will track you with it," Elena said, and opened a side wall, which opened to the familiar vastness of dark space and floating buildings they had traveled through before.

"Go." Elena pushed her out of the apartment.

"Why are you helping me?"

Elena hesitated briefly. "I have a brother. I'd do anything to find him."

The boat formed around Emery as she fell. "I will try to find you," she heard Elena say, just before the boat enfolded her in its belly.

I feel like Jonah, Emery thought, and almost giggled. "Boat, do you know how to get to the *Origin*?"

"Yes, my lady."

"Take me there, please."

"Yes, my lady." The boat lurched forward and carried her toward her destination. Emery suddenly realized how tired she was and lay on the floor to rest her eyes during the boat ride. She awoke when the boat suddenly spat her onto the ground and then rudely dispersed before her eyes without so much as an apology. Rolling on the ground, Emery cursed the boat for the unexpectedly harsh landing. "That's not how you treat a lady, shithead!"

Banged up again, Emery rose from the ground, straightened, and looked around. She was not anywhere near the cave. Instead, she was on the same strange elastic bottom as before, but this time, she could see no buildings. Only the oppressive grayness. Not having paid attention to where the boat went when she traveled to the *Origin* with Elena, she did not know what direction to take and wasn't even certain why she'd wanted to go there. For lack of other ideas, and only knowing the name of that one destination she could convey to the boat, she'd decided to go here first. Counting *eeny, meeny, miny, moe,* she picked *moe,* and started walking, hoping to find her way back to the cave.

The dark, smooth wall in the cave had intrigued her. She didn't believe Elena when she'd said there was nothing behind it. She felt a pulse and a slight vibration when she rested her hand on the wall. If nothing else, there was water in the cave and a place to rest without being seen from above. Her eyes felt like they were on fire: swollen and rough, and didn't want to stay open, but after what Elena had shared with her, Emery didn't want them to find her. Elena acted scared that Thomas would be found out for remembering the love for his dog. Did they do something to him to make him forget? Why? Was Elena changed in this way, too? Emery had perceived a slight alteration in her behavior since they had met her, as if their encounter had triggered suppressed emotions to resurface. More and more, Emery was becoming certain Elena was a human being, not a robot.

Elena was about to tell her about Sebastian and his impact on the world. Emery sighed, wishing she knew what it was. It could have explained what was happening now, all this weirdness.

Her head pounded from lack of sleep, and her other body parts screamed, wanting to coil up and rest, but she pushed it to move forward, not having anywhere to hide. Hence, she shuffled her aching feet forward, scanning the surroundings for pursuers. The consolation that she wasn't being followed wasn't enough to make up for the darkness and silence. At that moment, her frayed nerves could hardly endure the oppressive silence and stillness around her. Seeing a faint light in the distance, she tried to shuffle faster, but her mistreated legs had developed a mind of their own and refused, folding under her. The light proved to be one of those holes up high on top of this strange place.

Walking toward one of those cones, she noticed that the light emanating from them appeared natural, and she speculated whether this was a way out of this place. As she got near enough to stand directly underneath it, she saw the sun blinking at her through the hole. *This might be an escape route. If I could get a boat, I could fly up there and leave this fucking place. What about Visla? Are you going to leave her here? What if they "change" her, whatever that means?*

Emery sighed. She wasn't fooling anyone. She could never leave Visla. She'd find her, and they'd escape together. With or without Elena's help.

15

COME WITH US, ELENA

The wall opened, and four people stepped out of the boat. Three men and one woman entered Elena's apartment with an air of superiority, as if they owned the place and merely allowed her to stay there. The boat they stepped out of was superior, too. It was a much larger and more luxurious vessel, designed to carry more passengers, and it included additional protective measures—it waited for commands from the right people before disintegrating. This remarkable vessel was specially designed for elite members— the Minders, the special guards of the Masters. People like Elena couldn't contract boats like this one.

While the three men tramped around the apartment, searching for Emery, the woman stayed behind, observing Elena. They didn't bother to ask Elena if her guest was still there or to ask for an explanation. Boorishly, they invaded her space, disrespected her, and scoured her apartment, looking for Emery, assuming Elena was hiding a fugitive.

The woman watched Elena for a moment, piercing her with her cold eyes. "You let her go?"

"Was I supposed to keep her by force? I'm not equipped for that."

"Why didn't you report her in time?"

"I didn't think it was necessary."

"You broke the protocol, and now you'll have to face the conse-quences."

"What consequences? What're you saying?"

The three men came back, shaking their heads.

"All right. You come with us," the woman said and nodded at the men, who immediately grabbed Elena's arm and pushed her toward the boat. She didn't protest, knowing it would be pointless to object or try to fight the guards, who were trained as the ultimate protectors, the ultimate killing machines. Elena avoided glancing back at Thomas, who was still in his rocket, unaware of what had happened. He would be dumbfounded not to find Elena on his return. Not wanting their attention on Thomas, she let him be. He might be confused and worried, but he'd be safe.

And he was. Dumbfounded. But not immediately. He returned from his trip moments after Elena had left, escorted by her silent guards. He hadn't planned to return so quickly, but zipping through the Canis Major constellation, he had thought of Stella, and thinking of her, he remembered Emery and had a sudden desire to see her again and talk to her. Ask her questions about the place she traveled from, but hopefully without his sister knowing.

After searching all the rooms and finding them empty, he surmised Elena and Emery were still at the *Origin*. It surprised him; he thought Elena would be back by now. She disliked leaving him alone for long. He knew it was because of the dog. The dog he wasn't supposed to remember. But he did. And when he did, his chest felt heavy, as if a monster had woken up from under his bed and come out to torment him, crushing his chest and tugging on his soul, digging out deep, suffocating sorrow.

After it first started happening, Thomas couldn't stay in one place. He wandered all over the city looking for the dog, knowing he would not find it. But he kept looking, just to keep the monster off his chest. Elena noticed something was wrong when he stopped traveling in his rocket as much as he used to. She asked, but he refused to speak about it. After she followed him once and heard him cry out for Stella, she confronted him and suggested they should let the Masters know so they could fix the issue with another change, but the look on her brother's face made her not ask again. Ever. Those memories hurt him; she knew him well enough to see his torment, but it seemed he would rather suffer through them than forget. He didn't want the change. Thomas knew his sister wouldn't understand it. And she didn't. Until today.

He plodded all around the living area several times, listened to music, and paced again, but Elena was still not back. He was at a loss. Usually, it was Elena who made all the decisions, took care of everything, and was there for him. She was just so much better at it. Always focused. Always calm and dependable. Always there for him.

I should check on Elena, he finally decided. It's not like her to disappear for this long.

He opened the wall with an impatient hand gesture and stepped out and into a boat. "To the *Origin*," he ordered sternly.

"Yes, my lord," the boat answered and drifted away, carrying its worried passenger into the darkness.

When the boat sailed closer to its destination and lower to the ground, Thomas peered out the front window, searching for any sign of his sister. Not seeing any movement outside the cave when he disembarked the boat, he guessed Elena and the young visitor were still inside. But to his astonishment, the cave was empty.

"Elena? Where are you?" Thomas yelled, even though he knew she wasn't there.

He left and yelled again. He got no answer. His voice produced no echo. Deep silence surrounded him. For the first time since he could remember, the silence overwhelmed and terrified him. He left the cave and walked around, yelling and searching for his Elena. He couldn't think of other places Elena could have taken Emery. *Did the wildling take my sister? No, why would she? Keep looking.*

It was then that he almost stepped on a dark figure lying on the ground. He gasped and bent down.

"Elena?" he whispered, but soon discovered his mistake when he saw her face. Emery lay on the ground, appearing unconscious.

"Emery? What happened? Where is Elena? Wake up." Thomas shook her, trying to wake her up. First gently, but when she didn't respond, more violently until he finally succeeded.

Emery's eyes opened to slits. Seeing Thomas, Emery attempted to open her eyes wider and croaked, "Where am I?"

"Where is Elena? Where is my sister? What did you do to her?"

"I did nothing to her, Thomas. She stayed home," Emery said, her eyes opened wide now. The sleepiness was gone, replaced by an alarm, which spread down her spine in a slow, chilling crawl. "We came back from the *Origin*, and I left."

"She is home," Emery said quickly, seeing how upset he was. "Why don't you go back to your place and check?" Seeing he was getting even more upset, she continued. "Why would I do anything to her? She most likely saved my life. Twice now. I wouldn't have survived without water or food, and then she kicked me out to protect me from the people who wanted to take me and do something to me, which I still don't understand. You both have been very kind to me."

"She's not home."

"Are you sure?"

"Yes, I'm sure. I just came from there." He surprised Emery by raising his voice.

Emery recoiled. She didn't think he was capable of shouting.

"I am reporting you," he said, looking at her somberly.

"No, wait, Thomas. Elena told me to run because they found out I was in your apartment. She pushed me out, saying they were going to change me. Please don't. They must have taken Elena. I'm so sorry, Thomas. Don't let them know where we are. If they get us, we might not be able to find your sister or my sister. I can help you find her and get her back. Please ..."

Tears rolled down her cheeks. Heavy, long-overdue tears, hot with sorrow, guilt, and exhaustion, burned her cheeks as she wept while she gazed at Thomas with pleading eyes.

Thomas stood above her. At first, still upset, he tried to ignore her pleas, but then, perplexed by her tears and her words, he listened. As he saw the misery and sorrow pouring out of her, Thomas shifted the weight of his body, moving his feet as if walking, but he stayed above Emery, watching her. The uncertainty and turmoil darkened his gray face as he stood over her, pondering. Deciding. He then crouched beside her and hesitantly put his hand on her head.

"I won't report you. Don't do that thing with your eyes, please. It makes me ... it makes my chest do what it does when I miss my dog. Tell me again what happened. Why are they after you?"

"I don't know why they are after me. Honestly."

Slowly, Emery calmed down, and her sobs waned. Surprisingly, Thomas's stiff hand on her head felt comforting. With a voice raspy from crying, she told him her story. He listened without interrupting, emotionless, as if she were reciting a mere shopping list. When she was done, he said nothing for a while. Then he breathed. "I see," he uttered and lapsed into silence.

"Do you know where they've taken her?" Emery asked.

"I'm not sure. Maybe. I think so."

"Has it happened before? What will they do to her? She's done nothing wrong."

"They might want to fix her."

"Fix her? What do you mean? There is nothing wrong with her."

"We were supposed to report you. We are expected to report any strangers—any wildlings, or anyone that looks different—if they ever show up here. Not that it had ever happened before. Possibly to someone else, but not to us. You are the first stranger we've ever seen. The protocol clearly states we are required to report strangers. We didn't. They might think we are both broken."

"Thomas, what do you mean, 'fix' you? What does it mean? What do they do?"

"I wouldn't remember my Stella anymore."

"You mean they would erase your memories?" Emery asked,

panicking. *They'll lobotomize me. And Elena and Thomas. And Visla? Is that it?* "Do they erase your memories during the change?"

"Not exactly. Not remembering certain things is part of the process, but it's more than that. I think it's very complicated, but I'm not privy to the details."

"Whatever they do, we can't let that happen," Emery said and peered at Thomas. "You want to remember Stella, don't you?"

"Yes. I do. I don't want to forget her."

"Do you think Elena would want the change?"

Thomas waited before responding, mulling over the question. "No, I think not. Maybe before. Maybe many years ago, but not now."

"Then we must find your sister and stop this nonsense."

Thomas became lost in thought again.

Emery, suddenly energized, rose to her feet and looked around. She jerked when she noticed a boat zip above her and grabbed his hand, pointing up.

"It's just a maintenance boat," he said calmly. "They are just delivery and maintenance boats. They bring us clothes and furniture."

"Oh," she said.

She looked around her and swallowed when she noticed the cave ahead. She had almost made it back to the cave but collapsed from exhaustion just before getting there.

While she gazed at the cave, Thomas slowly got up, stood behind her, and gently tapped her shoulder. "I know how to get to where they took her," he said calmly.

"How?"

Thomas pointed at the cave. "In there. We can get through the wall. I think."

"You think, or are you sure?"

"I am almost sure, but it's been a while. Let's try," he said and headed inside.

Emery followed. After Thomas opened the entrance, Emery drank water and splashed some on her face and neck. Thomas observed her. "What does it taste like?"

"Sweet, cold, like a mountain spring with a hint of pine and honey," Emery said, and seeing his reaction, the longing in his eyes added softly. "Why don't you try?"

"I can't," he said with resignation in his eyes.

"Why can't you?"

"We were not made that way. We don't drink or eat anymore."

"How can you survive without water? It's impossible."

Emery couldn't wait any longer. She had to know, even if the consequences of her curiosity might prove dangerous, or that Thomas would not speak to her anymore. "Are you ... still human?"

Thomas nodded. "We are, still are," he whispered. "Even though we tried not to be. I don't recall the details of the change. I don't even remember it clearly. It happened a long, long time ago. And I was still young ... and ... dumb. All I remember was that humanity had to go through a change to save itself."

"From what?"

"I think the starvation. Elena was older. She might remember better. I ... remember very little," Thomas said, and then hunched, resembling an abandoned rag doll with his forlorn gray face.

"You know what? Forget about it for now. It'll come to you. Just like Stella's memory did. You'll remember. I am sure of it," Emery said, half-believing what she said. "Let's find Elena now."

Thomas didn't hear her, or if he did, it didn't change his stance. He stood lifeless, with his head low, eyes closed, and his arms hanging down by his sides. Emery touched his shoulder, and, on an impulse, embraced him. At first, his limp body remained still, but after a moment, when Emery gently patted his back, he shuddered. She felt him jerk and then shiver in her embrace, but she continued to hold him, sensing he not only didn't mind it, but somehow needed it.

"It's okay. It's all right," she repeated tenderly.

After a long moment, he pulled out of the embrace and looked up at Emery shyly, acting embarrassed, as if the hug was a great sin or a transgression.

Emery smiled. "You never had a girl give you a hug?" she asked.

She meant her question to be humorous and ease the awkward tension. But it had the opposite effect. His mouth curved downward, and his black eyes showed hurt. When he shook his head in slow motion, Emery felt grief oozing from his soul—she could almost see it spreading around him. She took his hand. "I'm sorry, Thomas. Let's find your sister," she said and led him to the black wall.

Seemingly calm, Emery fumed inside, thinking about the injustice done to this man. He'd never hugged a girl. Never kissed a girl. Never slept with one. *Whoever did this to him is a fucking monster! Now, they are trying to do this to my Visla.* Emery cried tearlessly. *No fucking way, you bastards. I'm not gonna let you hurt her.*

They stopped at the wall. Thomas glanced at it and then at Emery. There was doubt in his eyes.

"Can you open it?" Emery asked.

"I don't know. I remember going through here, but I don't remember opening it. But I'll try."

Thomas toyed with his tablet and then stared at the wall. Nothing happened. He tried again. There was a slight vibration, but the wall didn't budge. Thomas wasn't giving up. He tried again and again and again. But failed each time.

Emery tapped his shoulder. "Let me try."

He moved aside, shaking his head, skeptical of Emery's abilities, but also slightly intrigued. "I don't think you'll be able to ..." His words trailed off, blending into the surrounding silence. He stood frozen in astonishment as Emery tossed her hands at the wall, and the black barrier receded silently after it was struck by the silvery blue waves, revealing a dark corridor behind it.

"How? How did you do it? What are you?"

"I don't know for sure, but if you remember my story, I have an ability, a special ... talent I use occasionally. It's kinetic energy. I don't understand it, as I only recently learned I'm able to harness and use it. But I use it only when I have to. When I need to protect myself or someone I care about. It's a burst of energy that feels like it's growing in intensity, pressing on my body, and then bursting out. I can actually see it. It's like a heat wave, but it's silver or bluish silver, sparkling with golden dots. It's quite pretty ...

"... when I use it, I feel this intense relief, this blissful calmness. The angrier I am, and the longer I wait to release it, the bigger and stronger the wave is."

"Oh." That's all Thomas said, but she noticed his curious expression, which he quickly smothered with indifference.

Emery poked her head inside the dark corridor. "Do you know where it leads?"

"To the Genesia Center. It's where ..."

"Oh. Where they change people?" Emery guessed, seeing the look on his face.

"I believe so. Yes."

"Are you ready?" Emery asked and extended her hand toward Thomas. "We should stay together in the dark."

"Okay," he said and took her hand.

16

REMEMBER ME

They moved through the ominous darkness of the winding corridor for quite some time. Emery was leading, feeling the space in front of her with one hand while holding Thomas's hand with the other. To break the oppressive silence, Emery asked questions.

"How many of you live in this underground city?"

"Underground? Hmm. I guess we are underground. I've never thought about it like that. Forty, fifty thousand, I think."

"Does your city have a name?"

"Diamond Eldorado."

Emery didn't comment on the strange name, which neither fit the look and feel of the gray city nor made any sense. "Have you ever been up? On the surface?"

"No, why would I? It's uninhabitable now. Isn't it?"

"Who told you that?"

"It's a known fact. Everyone knows that. It's a wasteland."

"Thomas, people live up there. I lived up there for months and am alive and fine. Who told you it was uninhabitable?"

"Hm ... I never actually thought about it. It's just something I've known, but I don't know how I know it."

"Weren't you ever curious?"

"Curious? No. Not really. I'm not sure." Thomas peeked at her from under his brow and paused. The long pause transformed into a deep silence as Thomas reflected on her question.

How can they not want to see what's out there? That is not normal behavior for human beings. They erased their curiosity along with their feelings. Like empty gray vessels, they hide in their gray cells and don't even dream of escaping. Emery shivered at the thought. And yet, Thomas remembers the dog he loved a long time ago. Maybe all is not lost.

"How is it up there?" Thomas asked. "Can you show me sometime?"

"Of course. I will take you and Elena on a trip to the desert and to the real mountains. Then we'll have a fire at night, and you can gaze at real stars."

"You can see stars from up there?"

"Yes," Emery said, choking with emotion.

Thomas did something strange. He squeezed her hand. Such a human gesture. She squeezed it back and was glad the darkness hid her tears from him. Her heart throbbed for him and the life he never led.

They walked for a long time, holding hands.

Emery stopped when she felt a wall in front of her. Cold, flat stone wall. She told him they had reached a dead end and let go of his hand, then explored the wall with both hands, searching for a way through. She felt no door handles, cracks, or anything else that might open a door if there was one.

"I will have to use my powers again, Thomas," Emery whispered. "Do you remember what is behind here? I don't want to emerge into a room full of people."

"I remember an enormous building, full of lights and glass, and colorful screens, and an elevator that went up and down. I remember riding it a few times before the ..."

"Before the change? You remember events before your change?"

"I just did." Thomas gasped in surprise. "I remember some of them. A few things. They are more like flashes of people; maybe a sky, or a big body of water, but nothing that I can make sense out of."

"That's better than nothing. More will come. You'll see," Emery said, this time believing it. "Are you ready?"

Thomas nodded.

Emery thrust her hands at the wall, which opened silently to a room lit with the same sourceless lights, but dimmer. They entered cautiously, looking around the room. Stacked against the wall were several containers that looked like a cross between a see-through casket and a space rocket, similar to the one Thomas used for his space explorations. Emery cautiously opened all the containers, and to her relief, they were all empty. Thomas looked like a ghost, staring at the containers. His mouth and eyes were wide open.

"What is it? Is it where they changed you?"

Thomas nodded. "I remember these ..."

"How old were you?"

"I don't know. Young. In my late teens, I think."

They jumped at a noise. Voices accompanied by the sound of something rolling on the floor were approaching.

"We've got to hide," Emery said, pointing at the containers. "We don't know how many are coming," she explained, seeing his shock. "Quickly, we must hide."

Thomas didn't look too enthused at the prospect of hiding in the containers that brought back painful memories.

"Come on. Let's go. We'll follow them after they leave."

Reluctantly, he followed Emery and headed toward the container. Emery was surprised at his extraordinary cat-like agility when he effortlessly jumped inside the tube, barely touching it. She jumped into the second tube, trying to repeat his graceful jump and hitting her knee on the edge of the container. Compared with Thomas, she was a clumsy child.

As soon as she settled on the bottom of the container, the voices got even closer—they were already in the room. Emery could hear three distinct male voices, but couldn't understand what they were saying through the container. Straining to hear, Emery jolted when she felt a bump and then movement. They were moving her container. Emery tensed and readied to jump and fight if they opened the lid. But they didn't. They made some noise and bumped her container again, moving it closer to the wall.

"That will do it," one voice said so loudly she could hear it clearly. They were so close to her now that she could see their shadows moving through the slightly opaque walls.

"This is an older model. I wonder why they wanted to use this one on her. They should have been destroyed," the second voice said.

"Not my business. I do what I'm told. I don't wonder about matters I'm not supposed to. You should do the same," the third voice said dryly. Emery had a strange sensation; this man's voice sounded familiar, but she couldn't pinpoint it. Strangely, her heart beat faster.

"Yes, of course. I just thought it was strange. These models are no longer used on the wildlings."

"We've got to go back. Let's go," the third voice said.

After the voices receded, Emery emerged from the container. Her face was pale, and her hands were rolled into painful fists. And that is how Thomas found her when he gracefully jumped out of his hiding spot.

"What's wrong? What happened, Emery? Are you hurt?"

"Did you hear that? They used this one on a wildling! We are too late. They used it on Visla. They changed my sister. Motherfuckers. They'll pay for this." She hissed the last words.

"You don't know if it was your sister. It could be someone entirely different. Come on, let's follow them."

It didn't help. Emery's stomach was tied in a tight knot as a wave of fear, disappointment, and anger swept over her. She opened the container they'd brought in and jumped inside, inspecting it while squatting on its smooth bottom. She cried out when she found a hair.

Her forehead wrinkled, and her lips twisted into an angry scowl as she picked it up and held it between her fingers, showing it to Thomas. "This is Visla's hair. This beautiful golden-brown hair is from her head. They changed my Visla." She straightened her back.

The look of determination and anger on her face made Thomas take a step back.

"Before you go with me, I must tell you I'll make them pay for what they've done. I know these are your people, but I have to make them pay for this. You must know that in case you want to try and stop me from hurting them. You can't. But I don't want to hurt you, so if you've changed your mind, you must go back—"

"No, I'm not going back. They took my sister to change her against her will. They are no longer my people. I am going with you to find her," he spoke with a quiet confidence and without hesitation. And Emery felt warmth in her heart. She was grateful to have someone with her, even if that someone may not be ... entirely human.

Emery darted out of the room first. Thomas followed closely. The men were no longer visible, but Emery could still hear them in the distance. The familiarity of that man's voice still haunted her. They followed the voices through a hallway made of the same material she'd seen everywhere else. This stuff was pervasive throughout this dreary city.

The voices disappeared. Emery glanced at Thomas, and he nodded to keep going. They stopped at one point, surprised to see an actual door in the hallway. It didn't have a handle or a knob of any sort—only a small oval indentation in the middle. Perplexed, Emery touched the oval, but the door didn't magically open. Then Thomas tried, but it didn't open for him either.

"What now?" Emery whispered. "Should I try to force it open?"

Thomas shrugged. "I don't know."

Emery put her head against the door, trying to listen. She shook her head. "Let's keep going. We can come back if we find nothing else."

They continued through the hallway and finally reached a large, open area with high ceilings and ample light. Two men stood in a corner, talking. Emery was leading, and upon seeing them, backed up a step. With an extended arm, she stopped Thomas from entering the area. She turned toward him and put a finger to her lips. She pressed herself against the wall, pondering her options. Remembering how she had killed two powerful men, almost killing Peter simultaneously with just one thrust of her hands, she was almost certain she could do it again. But should she? Could she attack unprovoked? They needed information on how to locate Visla and Elena, and the dead don't talk. Emery glanced at Thomas, doubting he could fight; she couldn't and wouldn't put him in that position—it was her fight. Thomas and Elena were in this situation because of her. She needed to talk to one of the men separately.

"What are you doing here? This is a restricted area."

Preoccupied with planning her next move, Emery jumped at the sound of a man's voice. He must have hidden behind the door they just saw and come up behind them quietly.

There it was again—the familiar voice that made her heart skip a beat. However, she still couldn't quite place it. She couldn't see him clearly in the dim light of the hallway, but something in his posture, in the way he cocked his head asking a question, sent a shiver down her spine. She desperately needed to know who he was, even though she didn't understand the sudden desperation. It was so profound; she felt her entire body become frigid in anticipation. No sound came from her dry throat as she tried to say something.

"I asked you a question. Who are you?"

"We are lost. I'm looking for my sister," Thomas said calmly, and stepped forward so the man could see him first instead of Emery.

The stranger with the familiar voice pointed at the ceiling and activated the lights to illuminate the hallway. When she saw him in full light, her jaw dropped, and she let out a tiny whimper. He looked like a younger version of Peter, barring the color of his eyes, skin, and hair. Her Peter stood before her.

You are crazy and imagining things. It can't be Peter. But his voice?

"Peter?" she managed to whisper. Her heart thrashed in her chest, sounding louder than her whisper, squirming in her chest as if it wanted to break out.

Distress and surprise showed on Thomas's face when he glanced at her. He tensed. "You know him?"

"My name is Konrad, not Peter," the man said in a firm voice. "You must come with me. You shouldn't be here," he said, staring at Emery's blonde hair and blue eyes with suspicion.

Emery was becoming increasingly uneasy under his stare. She couldn't hear or feel her chest beating anymore. Instead, her body seemed alien, not belonging to her, and not responding, as if her mind was separated from her body by a million miles. She stood inert; her arms flopped to her sides as conflicting emotions and yearnings raced through her body. One moment, she imagined falling into his arms, certain he was her Peter; another, she wanted to run from him as doubts crept in. This man looked like him, sounded like him, and had the same mannerisms, the same unassuming confidence. And the same slim but strong body that she had caressed before. But this man's eyes were not blue. They were black, like Thomas's eyes. His skin was gray, not sun-kissed like Peter's, and he was younger. Ageless, really, like the rest of them. No, this man was not her Peter. Why, then, did she feel like he was? Why did her heart beat faster for him? He certainly didn't behave as if he knew her. It couldn't have been Peter. It was impossible. Weren't they separated by centuries?

This is crazy, Emery. This man is not Peter. He can't be him. It's hope playing mean tricks on you. If you're in the future, Peter will have been long dead by now. He is not Peter. Run.

"Come on," the man said, pointing the way.

Emery, spellbound, followed obediently.

Thomas glanced at her and got between her and Konrad. "Wait. We'll go back the way we came. There's no reason for you to go out of your way and bother anyone. We'll just go back, and nobody needs to know we were ever here."

"It doesn't work that way, I'm afraid. What's your name?" the man asked him.

"I'm Thomas. Thomas Graves. I was just searching for my sister and got lost. Please let us go."

"I can't. Come with me, please. I don't want to use force. You'll answer some questions, and I'm sure they'll let you go."

"Who? Who will let us go?" Emery finally regained her voice, but wasn't pleased with how puny it sounded.

He didn't answer, assessing her. And she felt it again. Despite realizing the absurdity and impossibility, despite the difference in his appearance, her heart was certain this man was her Peter. He didn't remember her, but the way he searched her eyes made her heart toss in her chest, rendered her breathless, and gave her hope. Was it possible he felt something, too? Remembered her?

"Okay, let's talk to whomever we need to talk to," Emery said.

Thomas didn't budge. Emery waved at him. "It's okay, Thomas. It'll be okay. I am sure they'll let us go, right, Konrad?"

Konrad nodded and pointed the way. As they proceeded through the large open area, the other two guards followed them silently, indifferently. Emery guessed they'd overheard their conversation already and were following Konrad's lead, who, she thought, was the authority figure, the one in charge. The big room opened up to another one, which was even larger and different from anything she'd seen in this unicolored world. She couldn't help herself and uttered a surprised laugh. Konrad glanced at her, but she didn't see it.

"Holy shit!"

They were in a cathedral. The walls, ceiling, and floors were intertwined and blended in countless shades of gold and silver. High above, arches reached incredible heights in glittery, undulating webs and vanished into the distance. The marble walls were studded with diamonds and silver. As Emery scrutinized them more carefully, she saw the faces of men and women—but mostly men—portrayed on the walls with mosaics in various shades of diamonds, emeralds, rubies, and other gems. The imposing portraits of men and women gazed at them from various heights, nooks, and crannies. She thought she recognized one face, although she couldn't think of a name to go with it. There were no portraits of saints or crosses, but the breathtaking monumentality of this place evoked spirituality while diminishing one's self-worth and confidence. She felt insignificant in this place, and she guessed it was the architect and builder's intention.

"What is this place?" she asked Konrad.

"The Silver House," he answered matter-of-factly. "Let's go," he urged her. He pointed to a crystal staircase that spiraled almost to the ceiling.

"You've got to be kidding me. You expect me to climb all the way up there?"

"Climb?" he asked, surprised.

Thomas went up the stairs first. As soon as everyone was on the stairs, they started moving up. First slowly, then much faster, but not alarmingly fast. As they glided up, the room came to life. Through the crystal walls of the staircase, they watched diamond mountains, clouds, and trees replace the diamond faces as the stairs went up. The optical illusion created by the movement gave the impression that the images came to life as they ascended. Floating and shifting shapes. Tree branches and mountains elongated, curved, grew, or disappeared as the stairs moved up, revolving around their axis.

For the second time since she'd found herself in this world, she was awed. First time by the spring, and this time by this magnificent creation, unparalleled by anything she'd ever seen. Thomas, just like Emery, admired the splendor with his eyes and mouth wide open.

"You haven't been here before?" Emery whispered.

"Long time ago," he whispered back. "I remember the staircase."

When they reached the top, Thomas grabbed and held on to the silver banister, looking down with amazement. Emery joined him and admired the view for a moment before the guard pushed them to move. The view from above was equally spectacular. The floor looked like a diamond sea—waves moved in and out in natural motions, mimicking the ocean so accurately that Emery was fooled for a second, thinking she was looking at the Pacific. A sudden sadness crept in as she wished she were back home, walking the beach with Regis running ahead and sniffing everything.

She felt Konrad's eyes on her; she looked at him and pointed down. "You don't recognize me, but maybe you'll recognize this? It's the Pacific Ocean. You used to live near it. It's where you're from."

He looked down, but when he looked at her again, his eyes betrayed no recognition or emotion.

Emery teared up in grief and anger. "What? Nothing? What did they do to you, Peter? Why don't you remember me?"

"Come on. Let's go." The Minders were getting impatient, but Konrad ignored them and kept his gaze on Emery and her eyes, now full of tears, now shining, enhanced by all the shimmering gems. They looked like blue diamonds, blending with the surroundings. The golden and black dots gleamed through her tears as she stared at him with anguish.

His emotionless stare unsettled her even more. She stomped her feet in anger.

"Remember me, Peter," she said.

Konrad, as if suddenly waking up from a trance, averted his gaze and pointed ahead. "Continue," he said calmly. "This way."

Thomas didn't notice Emery's tears, or that they had started moving, still watching the sparkling ocean below. One of the Minders pushed him forward. "Move," he barked.

Emery straightened her back and followed Thomas, wiping her tears with quick, angry movements. The three men led them to a room that almost matched the splendor of the rest of the building.

Diamonds were definitely easy to come by in this world, Emery thought. This room was studded with them from floor to ceiling, and they seemed to move in energetic ripples, resembling a fast-flowing river. The men pointed to chairs and then stood behind with their arms folded. She'd seen this gesture before, many times—men in the Secret Service, the army, and the police had the same stance, the same look on their faces, and folded their arms the same way. Trained soldiers. Trained assassins?

"Sit here and wait," Konrad said.

"Wait for what?" Emery asked.

"Wait for the Masters to come and ask you questions."

"Masters?" Emery scowled. "You had no Masters in my time, Peter. You'd never say anything so dumb when I knew you in your time ... our time." She sat and turned away from him. But not for long. She turned and glanced back and saw him immersed in thought. Emery noticed a slight change in his posture. He'd neglected to fold his arms. Instead, his hands rested on the back of Emery's chair. His mouth tightened into a narrow line as he stared at the wall ahead.

Is something happening under his mask? Emery thought, lingering on his face.

The room brightened, and a screen lit up. The same two people who'd talked to Elena in her flat sat across from them. Emery remembered Elena addressing her as Lady J. They looked so real that she thought the screen was perhaps a camouflage to make her think they were somewhere else. The Masters sat, observing them in silence. A third person joined them, and Emery jumped in her seat as she recognized Visla's mother. She sat near the female Master and said something to her. The female Master nodded, but seemed uninterested.

Then she heard the other woman speak. Her monotonous tone and robot-like mannerisms were so unnerving, Emery couldn't understand what she was saying. She caught disjointed words (wildling ... different ... eyes) while she stared at Visla's mother, hoping she'd say something about Visla. That she was safe and unchanged. But Visla's mother ignored Emery, gazing into the distance above her head, dispassionately and silently. Emery wouldn't have it.

"Where is Visla? What did you do to her?" Emery shouted, rising from her chair. Immediately, a hand pushed her down.

Konrad, gently but firmly, held his hand on her shoulder while whispering. "Just listen and say nothing until asked."

"I will not! Get your hands off me!" she said without looking at him and glared at Visla's mother. "Where is she? Answer me!"

Lady J said something to Visla's mother. The mother shrugged. The man remained silent, just observing.

"Why?" Lady J asked. "Why do you want to see her so urgently? What do you want with her?"

"Visla is my friend. She helped me and saved my life. I—"

"Visla is my daughter, and she is not your concern anymore. You must forget her," Visla's mother interrupted.

"Not in your dreams," Emery hissed and got up. "Thomas, lie down! Now!" she shouted, pushing Konrad away with one quick thrust of her hand. He didn't expect it and staggered back. She thrust her hands at the three men, including Konrad. "I am sorry, Peter, for hurting you again."

The men fell.

"Come on, Thomas, let's go," Emery said, offering her hand to him to get him on his feet, but there was no need. He jumped up gracefully. Emery glanced at the screen and saw all three of them watching her with an intensity she didn't expect from them.

"I'm coming for you!" Emery shouted at Visla's mother.

Thomas, speechless, followed her. She stopped by Konrad's body to check if he was still alive. She shook him, but he didn't respond. "I killed you this time," she whimpered. A sudden darkness enveloped her and permeated her mind and soul as if she were transported back into the void. And at that moment, she was okay with that.

Thomas kneeled by Konrad and listened to his chest. "He's alive," he said, glancing at Emery. She didn't respond. He tapped her on her shoulder. "We should get out of here. They'll come for us."

"He's alive?" Emery exhaled deeply with interrupted breaths. The darkness started dissipating, and she saw Konrad's face again. He looked peaceful.

"Yes, he is breathing. Let's go, or they will kill you."

"Okay," Emery said, relieved, wiping tears that suddenly welled in her eyes.

They exited and headed for the staircase. The moment they stepped onto it, it started spiraling down. The danger didn't detract from the breathtaking beauty of the room as it spun around them in a rainbow of diamonds.

No one was waiting to apprehend them at the bottom of the staircase. They ran back the way they'd come, looking back nervously, but saw no pursuers. Emery slowed, stopped running, and turned toward Thomas.

"I don't want to run, Thomas. Since I don't know where to go to find my sister, I'm going to wait for them so I can find Visla and Elena. You should go back, though, and wait for your sister."

"No, Emery. I told you this is also my fight now, and who's to say they won't come for me, too? I am not leaving you. If you think we should wait for them to get us, we'll wait, but I think it's too danger-ous. We should search for your sister and Elena. I doubt they'd tell us where they are. Even if we asked politely. And not after what you'd done."

Emery, impressed with his resolve and surprised by the slightly sarcastic tone in his voice, smiled. "You are right. But how? Do you know how to find them?"

Thomas nodded. "We must leave this place."

"You think the Masters are not here?"

"No. I think not. I think they all meet somewhere else. This place is just a front. A place of worship—to awe you with its importance and to discourage dissent through a demonstration of power."

"Okay. Let's not waste time then and go," Emery said and followed him back the way they came. He hardly made a sound as he ran. She could barely hear his feet on the gray floor as he gracefully glided on his long legs. She couldn't even hear his breathing. Perfectly balanced with an effortless stride, like a natural runner, he ran ahead of her, making her feel like a clumsy rhinoceros. Emery was surprised no one followed them. Maybe Thomas was right. This entire area was only for show and housed a few guards while they conducted their business elsewhere.

As soon as they left, Thomas called for a boat, and the obedient vessel materialized around them. Emery was not in the mood to ask questions. She sat thinking about Konrad, whom she had nearly killed, as she had nearly killed Peter. When not directly looking at him and seeing him move and talk, she started having doubts that this Minder was her Peter. She admonished herself for losing focus, imagining it was him, and almost jeopardizing their mission. She tried to convince herself that she was just tired. But she knew she was deceiving herself. She had been more emotional since she had come to this dark place, as if making up for other people's lack of emotions.

Thomas let her be and contemplated the view out the window, looking forlorn. Emery guessed he was worried about Elena. The boat stopped. Thomas walked first. Emery absentmindedly followed him, only to be astonished when she realized he had brought them back to the old lab. He, walking fast, led her through the door and into the basement—somewhere she hadn't explored yet.

It was dark in the basement, but Thomas fished a little silver gadget out of a hidden pocket and shone a light down the corridor ahead of them. The bright beam proved indispensable as it illuminated the treacherous decay ahead. The floor had caved in places, leaving gaping holes to the sour-smelling abyss below. They hopped over the voids and climbed over the jagged mounds, which rose in sharp concrete chunks and mangled metal, until they reached a door. A huge metal double door. To Emery's surprise, the door was secured with an enormous, old-fashioned padlock. She hadn't tried her powers on metal, but before she had a chance to try, Thomas reached for the lock, fiddled with it, and the monstrous metal clasp slipped out of the lock. He then removed the padlock.

"How did you do that?" Emery asked.

Thomas avoided looking directly at her. "I opened it years ago when I was looking for Stella."

"Oh," Emery said, and again saw him in a new light. He hadn't stopped surprising her. She was wrong about him. He was bold and curious, exploring places that were most likely off-limits to him, or at least not encouraged to enter. She wondered who'd locked this giant door, why, and when. This padlock looked ancient and out of place, not befitting the modern structure above the basement.

The door opened with a long, creaking groan, followed by a metallic clang as if it were lamenting and livid, disturbed from a long sleep.

They entered a large area that appeared to have served as storage a very a while ago. Dilapidated cabinets, shelves hanging haphazardly from the walls, broken lights hanging loosely from the ceiling, and rusty metal and crumpled plastic containers littered the floor.

They navigated through the obstacles and reached a long, empty hallway, then arrived at a laboratory, which Emery recognized as a twenty-first-century genetics lab. She could even identify a few instruments, such as centrifuges, microscopes, autoclaves, and incubators. Other contraptions, too damaged to be recognizable, cluttered the floor, accompanied by broken glass bottles, tubes, and flasks. The debris crunched under their feet as they crossed the demolished workshop.

Yet another hallway led them to another research room that was in complete disarray. Emery stopped, seeing the front of a heavily armored military tank embedded in the wall.

"What happened here? What is this place, Thomas?"

"I don't know. Ancient ruins."

"Ancient ... ruins." Emery paused. Thomas seemed impatient, but she ignored him, staring at the tank. "This is from my time. A tank ... in the lab ... military tank in the lab. Was there a war, Thomas? This is so confusing. Where are we? When are we?"

"Elena remembers more from the old times. She knows more than I do about the change and what happened before the change. You should ask her."

"You don't know the history of your own country?"

"We don't. We don't learn history. Learning history is not authorized."

"What?" Emery's knees buckled under her. She had to sit down. Behind her tired, swollen eyes, her brain buzzed with a thousand thoughts.

"What's wrong?" Thomas asked.

"Who forbids you to learn history, and why?" Emery asked. Her voice reduced to a hushed whisper as she spoke, barely moving her pale, dry lips.

"The Masters ... well, they don't forbid us, it just ..." Thomas said, and his voice trailed off. He contemplated the question and his response before continuing. "It's just not something we can get from the Essential Library."

"Essential Library?"

"The library is accessible from our quarters. We can get music and art; we can travel anywhere we want to. Ski, climb mountains, sail ..."

"But you can't learn anything about the history of your country or any other country?"

Thomas shrugged. "Nobody wants to learn about the past anyway."

"How about books? Can you read books?"

"Books?"

"Forget it," Emery said, seeing his face. Something was very, very wrong with this place. Even more than she'd suspected. She realized once again Thomas could not answer her questions, as he was condemned to ignorance by his Masters, whoever the sick fuckers were. She had to get answers from the source—from the Masters themselves.

"Okay, let's continue," Emery said, getting up. "No books," she said bitterly. Her hands curled into fists. The anger restored some of her energy and resolve. "Let's find these motherfuckers who prohibit books and learning about history."

Thomas led her through another hallway to a small door. He opened it, revealing a staircase. The concrete steps were in terrible shape. So bad, Emery doubted they'd be able to ascend them. But Thomas surpassed her expectations again and showed her the way. He knew where to step and which steps to avoid and gracefully climbed up, maneuvering through the treacherous concrete jumble. Now and then, he felt his way in the dark, touched Emery's shoulder to make sure she was behind him, and encouraged her with a gentle pat, which melted her heart.

The stairs ended at a small landing that was in better shape than the lower sections but stuck out in midair, defying gravity. Another huge padlock secured a metal door at the platform's end. Emery doubted he'd come all the way up here looking for his dog. Even the smartest dog on the planet, Regis, couldn't have climbed up here and opened the padlocks and doors. There must have been another reason. She didn't ask. Maybe someday he would no longer be afraid and would tell her.

Thomas lifted the padlock off, cracked the door open, and carefully peeked through the opening. Assured there was nobody near the door, he opened it wider, and they entered a shadowy, narrow corridor with surprisingly low ceilings. The corridor ended at another door with yet another padlock. Emery chuckled at the sight of such an ancient locking mechanism. With a cocky smile, she reached for the padlock to lift it off its mechanism, but to her surprise, this one was still very much locked.

She glanced at Thomas with surprise. "You didn't open this one?"

He shook his head.

"Why not?"

"I heard voices behind this door, and I left."

"So you don't know what's behind there?"

"Not really, but I suspect that is where all the Masters meet."

"How do you know?"

"I've seen them go in there," he said and then added, giving her a sideways glance. "On a couple of occasions."

"You've seen the Masters go in there? Did they see you?"

"No, of course not. I've seen the Masters, accompanied by the Minders, go in there. I followed for a while. A short while."

"How do we open this monster, then?"

Like a wizard, from his pocket, Thomas produced what looked like a tiny knife or a pen. He messed with it and then cut the bulky metal with it as if cutting through a cake.

"Perhaps you could wait here," he suggested.

"No. Why? We'll go together."

"You'll attract attention with your hair and your eyes. Everyone would see right away that you don't belong here."

"I see what you're saying, but I must go with you. I can't just stay behind and do nothing."

"No, it's not like that. I'll return for you once I see it's safe, and we'll go together."

"I don't think it's a good idea. They might just take you, too. They know you are with me and may snatch you immediately before asking questions," Emery said, then fell silent. Then her eyes brightened with an idea. "How about you pretend to be my captor?"

"Huh?"

"My captor. Pretend you just caught me and are bringing me to be interrogated. I think you could pass for a guard."

Thomas didn't look convinced but nodded. "I don't think I can pass for a Minder," he said, paused, and added hesitantly. "We can try."

"Do you have other ideas? And not the one about you going by yourself. I didn't like that one."

He shook his head. "No."

"Here's what we'll do. You walk behind me with a stern look, and I will hold my hands behind me as if they are tied. It will work. I've seen it in movies."

"In movies?"

"You don't know what a movie is?" Emery asked, seeing a blank expression on his face.

Thomas shook his head.

"One of the greatest inventions of humankind. I'll explain later," Emery said, sighing and shaking her head. "But now let's go. We need to find them before it's too late."

Thomas opened the door and strode in a deliberate march, pretending to be a guard escorting his captive. She shuffled in front with her eyes downcast and her hands behind her, feigning fright and humiliation. Thomas was behind her with the sternest expression he could muster, but he wasn't a great actor, and he looked more scared than scary.

They walked down a hallway and entered a brightly lit room that reminded Emery of a doctor's waiting area. Several Minders passed without paying attention to them, and Emery exhaled with relief.

So far, so good, she thought, feeling immensely proud of her brilliant idea. Then everything changed instantly. They reached a dead end, and as they approached it, it darkened, revealing ten dark, expressionless Minders waiting for them in a frighteningly intimidating row.

"Shit," Emery said. When she looked back, Thomas was no longer behind her. Two men had grabbed him by his arms and moved him away from Emery. She assessed the group of Minders staring at her silently, motionlessly, as if waiting for instructions. Thomas resembled a scared child, standing so hopelessly between them. The look on his face was enough to awaken her power, which immediately surged through her. She concentrated and raised her hands, about to thrust them at them, hoping to overpower them all in one swoop. But instead of a thrusting motion, her hands flopped down to her sides, as a sudden sharp nick on her neck knocked her off her feet. She landed hard on the floor but didn't feel the impact and didn't lose consciousness. To her horror, she couldn't move; her body didn't respond to her brain. She felt the saliva drop from her open mouth, which she couldn't close.

Two men picked her up and carried her, holding her on their broad shoulders.

"What did you do to her?" Thomas asked. "I was supposed to take her to the Masters," he protested. Emery was impressed by his commanding tone but doubted they believed him. She wouldn't have.

"We'll deal with you later," one Minder, who was obviously in charge, said, looking at Thomas. Then he turned away and motioned at the other Minders. "Take him away. They are not interested in seeing him yet. They only want her."

Emery wanted to scream in protest, but her mouth was numb. They carried her to a well-lit hall and placed her on a raised table. Even though she couldn't move, they tied her ankles and hands to the table anyway. One of them opened her eyelids and inspected her eyes with his cold black eyes, and then they deserted her, tied down like a rabid animal. Trapped and paralyzed, she lay on the table in the middle of the room in total silence and stillness, while her mind screamed behind her ears in alarm.

Emery didn't hear the two women enter. Visla's mother planted her heavy gaze on Emery's face. Then she inspected her entire body like a machine, scanning it for imperfections. The other woman, who came in seconds later, scanned her unhurriedly with an even heavier stare, as if a venomous snake slithered all over her body.

"Where did she come from?" the second woman asked Visla's mother.

Hearing her voice, Emery recognized her as Lady J. Evidently, she held a grudge against Emery, immediately appearing at her side to intervene and probably hurt her.

"Visla said she came through the darkness."

"What darkness?"

"I don't know. That's all she said."

"She speaks our language, but she's not one of us. She has powers no one else has. How did she learn our language?"

"I don't know. Does it matter? We are just going to change her, aren't we?"

"Perhaps." The woman was noncommittal, scrutinizing Emery's body. When she reached her eyes, Emery noticed a flicker of interest pass over her face. There was a barely discernible alteration in her demeanor, betraying her curiosity. Whether it was the color of her eyes or the golden spots or both, she didn't know, but she sensed she had made an impact. Then, to Emery's horror and humiliation, she cut the upper part of her jacket down to her chest and inspected her breasts. Emery couldn't feel her touch, but she could see her hands go over them a few times. *What the fuck?* Emery screamed silently. *And why did you have to cut Elena's jacket? Why are you worried about the jacket? They are about to butcher you!*

Visla's mother waited impatiently for the woman to finish her examination. Emery guessed she had her own plans for her, suspecting she wanted to wipe her memories of Visla so she'd stay away from her.

Lady J, however, must have reached a different conclusion about Emery's fate.

"You may go now, Marianne. Your role here is done. I'll call for you if I need you," the woman said and waved her hand dismissively. As she said that, the wall facing the table lit up with a hologram showing two men and a woman sitting and observing them.

Marianne, obviously ranking lower on the status ladder, obeyed and turned toward the exit. While slowly walking away, she kept turning and glancing pleadingly toward the woman and the hologram, hoping someone would ask her to stay. Nobody paid attention to her or stopped her. She turned to leave again, not getting the results that she wanted. She stopped and tried persuasion once more before leaving.

"She is no wildling, and she possesses powers beyond our understanding," she said, glaring back at Emery. "I think you should let me change her." They didn't even bother responding to her, and she finally left.

"What do you suggest we do with her?" The male Master spoke for the first time. He spoke very slowly with a strange inflection, dragging his words and ending each one with a question. It wasn't quite an accent or a speech impediment, but more of a mannerism that, if received in high doses, would be unnerving or even frightening. When he turned his head, Emery noticed his hair was strangely styled, or perhaps it just grew that way. The front was raised while a half-curl, half-wave stood up at the back of his head. Emery found this hilarious, despite being tied up and examined like a lab rat. *Nice hairdo, dude.*

"What do you think of her? Who is she?" The Master asked.

"I'm not sure ... but she's definitely not one of us. She might be a different type of wildling. She has nipples," she said, and paused, and added with certainty. "I think it's imperative to understand her powers in their entirety. We should not change her. We must process her brain in the idiomefuge."

"That will kill her," the Master said dispassionately.

"We don't need her alive. You've seen her. She won't cooperate willingly. We only need her brain. Unchanged."

"Are you sure?"

"I am. The idiomefuge will give us a comprehensive understanding of her brain and her powers. We can use that to our advantage."

"Proceed then. You are sanctioned."

Emery desperately wanted to shake her head or scream that she would cooperate, but her helpless body was not responding, paralyzed with whatever they had injected her with. She was ready to sell her soul to the devil for a chance to escape.

"How long will it take to know what she is?"

"A few days. Week at the most."

The screen went blank, and the Masters were gone. Lady J found Emery's eyes and stared into them searchingly.

She wants to see me scared, Emery thought. *No way, bitch. I'm not afraid of you, and you are not getting my brain.*

Not getting the results she expected, the woman had grown weary of standing and gestured at the Minders. "Take her to level 'S.'" She ordered them.

"Yes, Lady J," the Minder answered curtly and obediently, pushing the table, which moved forward quickly and with ease, much to Emery's dismay.

17

UNEXPECTED HELP

All Emery could see was a gray, seamless ceiling as the Minders moved her down several hallways and through rooms until they reached a round and well-lit room and left her in the middle. Her heart started beating faster, and she thought and hoped it was a sign the drugs were wearing off. She shut her eyes and lay trying to devise an escape plan, but her brain kept spinning and buzzing and seemed locked in a loop, refusing to function. Then, her heart started beating even faster. It beat at such a rapid pace that Emery panicked, fearing it would explode.

"You're going to be okay, baby," a voice whispered in her ear. She opened her eyes, but there was nobody in the room with her. She closed them again and saw an image of her mother smiling at her. "Concentrate, Emery, concentrate, baby. You can do it."

Mom, I need help. Help me, Emery silently called to her mother. Then she remembered the technique she'd used to escape her cell and focused on clearing her mind. This time, it took much longer because her heart refused to calm down. Every time she thought she had it under control, it started its frantic pounding again. She recalled her mother's face, and eventually she calmed down enough to clear her mind and concentrate on trying to break the restraints on her wrists and ankles, praying her powers worked telepathically. She visualized her cuffs breaking. First, a thin line appeared—a tiny crack that deepened and spread through the thick bars on her wrists. And she felt it that time—her powers rising within her. The golden dots swirled and morphed into a thin, shining blade, which, like a lightning bolt, sank into and then sliced through the manacles.

Before she knew whether she had broken her chains, the table started moving. Panicking, Emery struggled to rise, but her body was too heavy and foreign. To her relief, her foot moved, reluctantly and with a delay. Then her fingers moved. She tried to move her head to see who was taking her, but her head felt like a giant boulder.

While being transported to an unknown destination, Emery focused on regaining the feeling in her body. Stealthily, not to alert whoever was moving her, she made tiny movements with her hands and feet and was slowly regaining feeling in her arms and legs as she felt blood gradually returning to her numb body. She opted to wait for the right moment when she was fully recovered to strike when they least expected it. Reassured by the sound of only one set of footsteps, Emery was preparing to attack. The table stopped suddenly, and she felt the restraints being lifted off her wrists and ankles. She gasped, seeing the face she had least expected gazing at her from above. Konrad, looking unharmed and well, pressed his finger to his lips and looked around. Assured they were alone; he picked her up and carried her.

Is he helping me, or is he taking me to my brain surgery room? Emery's instincts, usually accurate, couldn't decide whether to trust him. Her thoughts, still full of cobwebs, alternated between believing Peter had finally remembered her or that he was so angry she had killed his people and nearly killed him that he had taken it upon himself to transport her to her death.

He carried her through a gray wall that opened into a small room that may have been used as a storage room with boxes stacked against two walls. He then gently positioned her on the floor with her back against the wall. Then he sealed the wall behind them.

"We'll sit here and wait. They can't find us here—it's an old, unused storage place that doesn't have surveillance installed. Only a few know about it, and the ones that do are no longer in this building," he whispered and added, seeing her curious expression. "I have an elevated security clearance."

"Are you helping me?" she whispered back with lips that were still half-numb.

He hesitated and gave her a sideways glance and a noncommittal nod.

"Why are you helping me? Do you finally remember me?"

Konrad shrugged and didn't answer, staring at the wall, thinking, deciding, wavering. Emery watched him, unafraid and getting increasingly calmer the longer she was in his presence. With every passing second, her body grew stronger, losing its drug-induced shakiness, and her confidence returned more robust than ever, infusing her veins with fire. Feeling bolder than she ever had in this strange, dark city, she was ready to take on the entire building if she had to.

Konrad finally looked at her. When his black eyes met hers, she nearly passed out. She'd only experienced that kind of openness in someone's eyes once in her life—when Peter looked at her. Konrad looked at her with the same expression as Peter had.

"I'm not sure if it's a memory. I don't know what it is. Having experienced nothing like this before, I can't put a name to it. But something happened to me when I looked into your eyes when we got to the top of the stairs ... when you made your eyes drop diamonds. Something powerful has gotten hold of me, and I can't go on not knowing what it is. I had to speak with you, and I ... had to see you. As soon as you left, I followed you. Listening in on their conversation and hearing their plans, I knew I had to help you and get you out of there. I couldn't let them kill you. And I don't know why. I've never been so confused. But I'm certain that I can't go back to my life without saving yours ..." His voice trailed off, and he lowered his gaze to the ground.

Emery wanted to touch him. She stopped herself, terrified he might find her touch unbearable. She watched this powerful man, the trained killing machine, looking lost and sad, and tried to soothe him with words.

"You were a police officer when I knew you. A detective. You never hurt people, but helped them instead. You were the most honest and brave man I've ever known. People loved and respected you. Even after you retired and stopped working, they still wanted to be around you."

Konrad looked up and seemed intrigued. "A police officer? Like a Minder, a guard? Like I am now?"

"No. Not like you are now. Much more. Much, much more. You didn't just blindly follow orders, but only if they made sense. You were a damn good detective with a sixth sense for locating missing people. I couldn't imagine you not doing the right thing—protecting people who couldn't protect themselves from harm, and finding and bringing to justice the scumbags who hurt them."

He said nothing, staring at the ground again. Although she couldn't read him, she sensed his confusion and melancholy, and the need to touch him only increased. She longed to touch his skin, his hair, and his lips that had kissed her with passion and tenderness in her previous life. She clasped her hands tightly and fought the urge to stroke his cheeks and then just watched him, surprised but also moved at her sudden limerence. After a while, he sensed her gaze and looked at her. Silently, he watched her eyes, her lips, her hair with his black eyes, which, although intense, held the same gentleness as Peter's eyes. They sat silently, gazing at each other, with their backs against opposite walls. Emery was oblivious to the passing of time, studying him and wondering what he was thinking. Was he remembering her? Was he even thinking about her?

They both jumped, hearing a noise behind the wall. Someone was shouting and running in the hallway, separated from them by only the thin wall that could easily be opened with their tablets.

After the initial startle, Konrad sat still and calm, indicating he had it under control. Once the shouting and footsteps faded in the distance, he stood up and listened. Then he took a small tablet, put it against the wall, and scanned it with his eyes.

"Once they leave the building, we can leave," he whispered.

"I can't leave without my sister, Elena, and Thomas. I must find them and take them with me. That's why I'm here."

Konrad gazed at her. Thinking. Wavering.

Certain he would refuse, Emery opened her mouth to try to convince him, but he said calmly, "I know where the man you came here with is, but I don't know where Elena or Visla are."

"Do you know where Visla's mother is? The woman who was at my side first and wanted to change me?"

"Oh, Marianne. I can find her. Why do you want to find her?"

"Visla is her daughter. She might be with her. That's my best guess. If she is not, I'll make her tell me where Visla is. But I don't know how to find Elena. She's Thomas's sister."

"You'll make her tell you. How?"

"I have no intention of hurting her, if that's why you are asking. But I think I can convince her to let me take Visla back with me. She is her mother, after all." From the blank look on his face, Emery gathered he didn't know why it mattered. "Just trust me ..."

"Trust you?"

"Yeah, believe in me. Believe that I have the best intentions for Visla and, therefore, her mother. Because no matter what kind of mother she is, Visla wouldn't want her hurt—she loves her."

"Loves her?"

Emery glanced at him with surprise. "You don't know what love means?"

He exhaled a deep sigh. "I trust you," he said. "We can get Thomas now. I'll search for Elena and Marianne," he said, pulling out his tablet. He worked his gadget for a while, then looked up at Emery. "I have their locations."

That was fast, Emery thought, but said nothing.

"Stay with me. Follow me closely. If I spot anyone on my tablet, we'll have to hide, if there is a place to hide."

"If there isn't?" She asked, dreading the answer. He'd have to use force on his people to protect her. Would he be able to?

He moved his shoulders in an attempted shrug, as if saying he didn't know, but looking at his face, his set jaw, and slits where his eyes used to be, Emery sensed he had made his decision. She would find out soon what it was. Would she be able to kill him if he turned on her? Unlike Konrad, Emery had not decided yet.

Konrad left the room first, looked around, and then motioned for Emery to follow. He looked at his tablet again and moved fast along the corridor, Emery on his heels.

At one point, he stopped, grabbed Emery's arm, motioned for her to stop, and then touched his tablet. Emery staggered as the floor below them moved silently, fast but smoothly, designed to carry its passengers in comfort, just like the boats. They moved down a few levels that looked similar to each other—dim and empty corridors stretching both directions as far as the eye could see. Stopping at the umptieth level, Konrad again stepped first, glancing at his gadget. Then, the floor resumed moving, carrying them forward again like baggage on a conveyor belt.

They were carted along like that for some time. Emery couldn't resist the urge to glance at Konrad, trying to guess his thoughts. But his face was impenetrable now. She didn't mind. Just looking at him made her feel alive and happy. Whether he was her Peter, it didn't matter now. She felt peaceful in his presence. When they finally stopped, the wall ahead of them opened, and they saw Thomas curled up on the floor of a small, dark room. Worried he was drugged or worse, Emery darted to him and shook his arm. He wasn't drugged or hurt. He jumped when she touched him and stared at her for a while before he realized who she was.

"Emery ... how did you find me?"

"Konrad did," Emery said, stepping aside so he could see her companion behind her. Thomas shuddered at seeing him.

Emery noticed. "Don't worry. He is helping us. Are you okay? Can you move? Because we must go now."

Thomas got up gracefully, as usual. "I'm okay," he said and whispered as quietly as he could. "Do you really know him?"

Emery shrugged.

They left her cell and returned to the conveyor belt, but to

Emery's surprise, they didn't go back the same way. The belt took them in the opposite direction.

"Elena is close," Konrad said.

Thomas touched Emery's elbow and whispered. "Are you sure we can trust him?"

"I think so. No, I'm sure."

"I don't want him to hurt my sister."

"He won't. He saved me from death. They were going to take my brain out and throw the rest of my body away. He found me and rescued me, even though I nearly killed him," Emery whispered so fast, she ran out of breath with the last word.

Konrad pretended not to listen to their whispers, but Emery noticed his stillness and alertness. He was eavesdropping. She grinned to herself.

Thomas glanced at Konrad and then Emery, then focused on his tablet as they drifted down the corridor.

They moved for only a few minutes before they stopped again. Konrad opened the wall, and at first, Emery thought the cell was empty. Only after her eyes had adjusted to the darkness could she see Elena's slim body huddled against the far side of the cell. She didn't move or say anything when the wall opened.

"Elena," Thomas exclaimed. "Are you hurt? What did they do to you?"

"Thomas? Is it really you? How did you find me? Are you okay?" Elena exclaimed, peeling herself off the wall.

"It's really me. Emery and ... Konrad are here ... to help."

"Emery?"

"Yes, it's me. You didn't think I was going to leave you here? Have you been held here all this time?"

Elena nodded. "Who is Konrad?"

"A friend who is helping us," Emery said and glanced in Konrad's direction. She didn't notice a reaction to the word "friend," as he was paying attention to his gadget.

"We need to go. We have a long way to go before we reach the Gardens," Konrad said.

"The Gardens?"

"That's where Marianne lives."

"No! Why do you want to see her? You can't trust her," Elena shouted and moved as if to run.

"I need to know where Visla is, and I think she knows."

"She won't tell you. You must find your sister another way."

"I don't have time to find another way. She must tell me, and she will. Visla may be with her."

Elena stopped protesting, but was not convinced. She kept watching Konrad with interest but refrained from asking questions. Thomas grasped her hand and ushered her out of her cell. She squeezed his hand, and his eyes shone. Emery noticed, and her heart fluttered with delight.

As they rode the moving corridor for a short distance, Konrad called up an elevator on his tablet, and they went upward. High up. Thomas and Elena stood close to each other in the elevator. Emery was worried at first that they'd changed Elena already, but seeing her face and the way she held on to her brother, she knew that not only had they not done it yet, but that Elena's capacity for emotions had increased. As if the angst of the solitude and the separation from her brother had breached her dispassionate carapace, allowing emotions to seep out.

With her concentration centered on Elena, Emery didn't notice Konrad's covert sidelong glances at her. He'd secretly watch her every move, but only when her attention was directed elsewhere.

The elevator opened onto a garden. Emery's jaw dropped when she saw it. It was full of flowers, shrubs, weeping willows, fast-flowing rocky brooks, and birds chirping happily while flying from flower to flower. Inconspicuous classical music was playing in the background. The garden felt so real that, for a moment, Emery thought they might have gone to the surface. But she soon discovered with disappointment that this, too, was an illusion. Beautiful, but an illusion nonetheless. A few gray people, who Emery guessed were Masters, sat on benches or walked the pathways, but they disregarded the visitors.

Glancing at his tablet, Konrad guided them through the narrow pathways. When Emery saw a rosebush that took her breath away, she bent down to smell it. There was no smell, and there was no rose. Her nose went through the beautiful hologram, and she felt silly afterward. She knew it was fake, and yet she had tried to smell it. *Fake rose. Fake birds. The garden is all fake.*

Konrad watched her reaction as she grieved the rose's nonexistence.

"Why go to all the trouble? Why not just go up and plant a garden? A real one?" she rumbled, staring at them and expecting an answer. "It doesn't make sense."

"Go up?" Konrad asked. "You can't make gardens up there," he said, with a certainty that quickly waned into doubt when he saw Emery's face. "Can you?"

Emery shrugged. "Why couldn't you make gardens there? Who told you this? Up there above us are sun, dirt, and water. All the ingredients to grow real gardens. All a rose needs to flourish is up there on the surface. You were lied to."

"Sun, dirt, water," Thomas and Konrad said in unison. Thomas, in a dreamy voice, whereas Konrad sounded skeptical. Thomas nodded. He believed her.

Konrad pointed the way and walked ahead of the group until he reached a glass wall. He turned to face them. "This area contains private residences. I can't view all the rooms, only the hallways, storage rooms, kitchens, and common living rooms. We may run into armed guards if anyone expects us here, so be prepared," he said, trying to glance at everyone, but his eyes gravitated toward Emery.

Then he pressed on the glass, and an oval opening appeared, exposing a large gray hall. From there, they went up in an elevator, unnoticed and uninterrupted by anyone. When they halted before an arched glass door, Konrad's brow furrowed as he tapped his tablet with confusion.

"What's wrong?" Emery asked.

"I don't understand. I was certain she lived here, but now nothing shows up. As if someone blocked me and I can't open this door."

"Do you think they realized that you're helping us?" Elena asked.

"I doubt it. Nobody saw me helping you."

"Are you the only one around here with the high-security privilege?" Emery asked.

"Oh, no. There are several others with similar or even higher rank."

"Are you a Sage?" Elena asked.

Konrad nodded.

"What's a Sage?" Emery asked.

"A Minder with an elevated rank. He leads other Minders, and has special privileges and access to more areas," Elena explained.

"There are not that many Sages around. It would have taken them some time to figure out what you were doing. Something else must be going on," Elena said.

"She doesn't have the clearance or the capability to scramble my tablet. Unless ..."

"Unless she is a Sage herself," Thomas finished Konrad's sentence.

"She would have to be at least a Golden Sage to scramble my tablet. I'm a Silver Sage, a step below."

"Can you open the wall?" Emery asked, getting impatient.

"No."

"Okay, let me. Step out of the way," she said, and not wanting to waste more time, she thrust her hands forward, but the wall didn't give way. She tried again and failed again. She wrinkled her forehead and stomped her feet. "Shit."

She inspected the door and noticed a thin film covering it. "This must have a protective layer that absorbs and dissipates kinetic energy. Is there another way?" Emery asked, looking at Konrad impatiently.

He didn't reply initially. Then he said warily, "There is an emergency exit we could use."

"Okay, let's go then," Emery pushed, seeing his reluctance to move from his spot by the glass door.

"If we enter through the emergency exit, the security system will be alerted, and we could be spotted. It's more dangerous."

"Is there another way?"

"No."

"We don't have a choice then. Let's not waste any more time." Emery gestured forward. "Lead us to it."

Konrad led them through a path to a lower area and stopped by a wide door with lights surrounding its frame. He opened it with his tablet, slipped inside, and led the way down the corridor. At the hallway's end, Konrad stopped and motioned for them to wait. Then he disappeared into a room and was gone for a few seconds that felt like long minutes to Emery. As she waited, fearing he would not return, her heart beat faster and faster. But he returned and led them through two empty rooms.

The third room appeared empty when they entered it, but then they saw Marianne standing in the corner with her hands behind her, staring at them in disbelief. "How did you get in here?"

"Where is Visla? What did you do to her?" Emery demanded and moved toward her in hurried strides.

"Don't come any closer," Marianne said, pointing something akin to a small gun at her while eyeing Konrad. "I'll kill you if you come any closer."

"I mean no harm. I just want to take Visla back with me. Back where she belongs. She can't stay here."

"Here you go again. Visla is nothing to you. She is my daughter, and she'll stay here with me because she belongs with me, her mother, not some stranger."

"She belongs with you? You may have given birth to her, but you have not been a mother to her. You could have returned to her and taught her about the real world and how to grow a real garden, but you chose to stay in this artificial, hollow world. And you want her to stay here with you and never know the scent of real flowers? Never touch their delicate petals, never see the sky, never play in the water? Bring her here and let her tell me that she wants to stay. If she does, I will leave and never return. But I want to hear it from her lips. So, my lady, the sooner you get her, the sooner we'll leave."

"She's not here," Marianne said, but without conviction.

Emery noticed that her speech evoked a reaction in Marianne. She seemed to withdraw. Emery waited. But as moments passed with no response from her, Emery became impatient, seeing Konrad's growing restlessness.

"Where is she then?"

Marianne shrugged and shook her head.

"Fine. I'll find her myself."

Emery stomped past Marianne, ignoring the little gun pointed at her, and stopped by a wall. She thrust her hands forward, and it collapsed and dissipated before her. Marianne aimed at Emery, but seeing Konrad step forward, aimed at him instead. Then Thomas stepped forward, and she aimed at him. Elena was the last one to step forward. Marianne spun from side to side in chaotic movements between the people advancing at her.

In the meantime, Emery went through the opening she'd made to another area and continued breaking down walls while shouting Visla's name louder and louder as she searched Marianne's quarters, demolishing them. Her frustration grew, and her confidence faded as her search turned up no trace of her sister. Was she wrong in thinking Marianne had Visla with her? Emery crossed the room in one gigantic, angry leap and faced Marianne.

"What have you done to her? Where is she?"

Marianne didn't wilt under Emery's furious stare, but her hand holding the gun lowered down to her hip. She breathed in deeply. "She is my daughter ..." she started saying, but then paused; her expression took on a curious look. "What is she to you that you are looking for her with such determination, risking your own life? You could have escaped by now and returned to that wasteland that you think was so special. What do you want with her?"

"I'm her friend. I only want to protect her and bring her back to her world."

"Friend," Marianne intoned the word gravely, but without grasping its meaning. "What can you offer her that is greater than what I can give her?"

"What can you give her?" Emery hissed. "A life in this forsaken dark prison?"

"I can give her immortality."

"Wonderful. A never-ending life in this forsaken place where people make fake gardens, fly to fake stars, and spend time on fake mountains. And you want that for your own daughter? How noble of you. You must feel very powerful and virtuous, offering such a gift to your baby girl. Did it ever occur to you to ask her what she wants?"

Marianne didn't answer for a while, observing Emery's face. Then she sighed. "It's too late. She's been changed already."

"No," Emery shouted. "I'm gonna kill you—"

Konrad stepped between them, seeing Emery's hands raise at Marianne. "She's lying," he whispered into Emery's ear. "Visla has not been changed yet."

"How do you know?" Emery asked, not bothering to whisper.

"I get notified every time we get a new member."

"A new member?"

"A new resident of the city. They get assigned their Brilliant Numbers, apartments, and permissions."

"Assigned Brilliant Numbers ..." Emery said senselessly. "That's what the Masters do. Isn't it? This is what this is all about—kidnapping real people and changing them into machines."

"Into machines?" Marianne and Elena asked in chorus.

"Yes, into machines, devoid of basic human emotions. You don't feel, you've lost your curiosity, you don't eat or drink, and you deprive yourselves of the most fundamental elements of what makes us human. Don't you get that? Any of you?" Emery snorted and scowled at everyone.

Thomas was the only one whose face wasn't blank. He understood. Elena stared at her with her mouth open as though she wanted to protest. Marianne seemed confused, and Konrad stared at her expressionlessly.

Emery's frustration and anger culminated in tears as she stood surrounded by beings who couldn't cry and didn't understand the reason behind crying. And yet they were captivated by it and guessed she cried because of them, but couldn't quite grasp why. Each dropping tear grew heavier, laden with everyone's silence. As she wept, Konrad watched every tear as if it were priceless diamonds, and her lips as they trembled and bowed in sorrow. As he watched her, his face changed. His black eyes shone and deepened, as if they'd gained an extra dimension.

He looked at Marianne and clenched his teeth. "Where is she, Marianne?" Konrad asked with a tone that conveyed absolute authority, but Marianne ignored him. "Why the deception? I know she hasn't been changed."

"Why are you here, Konrad? Why are you with her?" Her tone, seemingly emotionless, took on a hint of recklessness.

"I'm helping her."

"Why?"

Konrad had no answer. His eyes widened, and he opened his mouth, only to close it again. Emery watched him, holding her breath, waiting for his answer, and was crushed when he fell silent.

"We don't have time for this. We must go," Elena interrupted. "Otherwise, they'll find us and change or kill us. Tell us where Visla is. If she says she wants to stay with you, we'll leave. I promise."

Emery wiped her tears. "I only want to know that she is where she wants to be. If she wants to be with you, I'll leave. You have my word."

Marianne wavered momentarily, then looked up, and the ceiling opened. A tiny rocket similar to the one Thomas used for his starry expedition slowly lowered to the floor. When it reached the ground, it dissipated. Visla sat up straight, appearing to have just awoken from a deep sleep but otherwise unharmed. Her eyes and hair were still brown, and her face was pale, but not gray. She rubbed her eyes clumsily.

"Visla!" Emery exclaimed and kneeled by her friend. She gently embraced her and stroked her hair and cheeks, scrutinizing her face. "Are you okay?" she asked in the girl's native language. "Did she hurt you?"

"Emery?" Visla asked in a raspy voice.

"Yes, it's me. I've finally found you."

Visla folded into Emery's arms. Emery stroked and kissed her head.

"Am I still me, Emery? Or did she change me?"

"Yes, my beautiful girl, you are still you. You recognized me and remembered my love."

"The last thing I remember is being in some strange gray tube, and she said I was going to be changed," Visla said, pointing at Marianne. "Another woman put something in my mouth, and I couldn't breathe and passed out. I thought I was dying. But I feel fine and the same and remember everything."

"She didn't change you." Emery glanced at Marianne and added as softly and unassumingly as she could, "Do you want to stay with your mother, or do you want to go back?"

"Stay here? No! I want to go back." Visla didn't hesitate with an answer but asked timidly while glancing searchingly into Emery's eyes. "How about you? Do you want to stay here?"

"Absolutely not. Let's get out of this hellhole. Can you walk?"

"I think so," Visla replied and stood up. She took a few unsteady steps, guided by Emery. She stopped and regarded her mother with her kind brown eyes. "Thank you for not changing me."

Marianne seemed uncertain about what to do or what to say. Her arms moved as if to touch Visla or embrace her, but stopped in midair as if she wasn't sure how. Visla sensed it and quickly wrapped her arms around her. At first, unsurely and clumsily and with a slight resistance, Marianne put her arms around Visla, and her uncertainty and her struggle melted. Her eyes widened, then softened as Visla nestled herself deeper into her arms.

"I couldn't follow through with it. After seeing you, I wasn't certain anymore and needed more time to think. I wanted to talk to you first. I ordered the old machine to be delivered to me because I knew how to change its programming, and went through the normal steps of the procedure as planned. Nobody suspected anything, having had no reason to doubt my intentions. After we started the machine, everyone left. I got you out of there and hid you up here before anyone could see you after the change. I intended to create a new identity for you, but never had the opportunity before all of your ... friends showed up ..."

"Will you come with us?" Visla asked.

"What ... what would I do up there?"

"What you did before. Be my mother."

"And live instead of pretending. But we must hurry. If you want to go with us, we must go now," Emery said.

Marianne hesitated briefly, but then nodded. Visla grinned and seized her hand.

Konrad scanned the area before they left Marianne's quarters. He nodded, confirming it was safe. They walked into the Gardens, which were now empty. The few Masters who had been enjoying the holographic image had left the area as if on cue. That is when Konrad noticed something wasn't right. He stopped and extended his arms to stop everyone in their tracks. Emery glanced at him, and her eyes opened wide when she saw his transformation. His body tensed, and yet it became cat-like, graceful, and stealthy while his muscles became more defined, his knees bent slightly, and his arms slowly moved to his pocket, where he held his gun. He pulled the gun with lightning speed. "Watch out!" he shouted at Emery, pointing his gun ahead.

Emery gasped, seeing the Minders, who had materialized out of nowhere and assembled before them in a row, blocking their exit through the garden path.

"Don't come any closer," Konrad said calmly. "I have this situation under control. I am escorting them where they need to be, obeying Master E's orders."

"We are aware that you're helping the wildlings. Lower your gun and give them up," one guard, who seemed to be in charge, said. "Stand down, or you'll be executed."

"I can't do that. Let us through. I don't want to hurt you, Sylvester. We've worked together for a long time. You know me."

Sylvester ignored him and gave a sign to one of his companions, who stepped toward Emery and aimed his gun at her. Konrad shot him, knocking him down with his face twisted in a grimace of surprise. They didn't expect it. Before the Minders were able to respond, Konrad fired more shots in succession with a speed that defied logic, and three more fell. Marianne moved in front of Visla and fired at the Minder, who had aimed his weapon at her daughter. But Visla went around her, and twisting her mouth in a sneer that was half-grin, half-fear, thrust her hands at the guards. Two fell immediately, and the third staggered and then pointed his gun at Visla. Marianne turned around to look at her daughter and saw her lips tremble in an irresolute grimace. She quickly turned and fired her gun at the Minder, who had just gotten up, shaking his head rapidly after being struck by Visla, and quickly directed his gun at her. He and Marianne fired simultaneously.

Elena and Thomas, not having weapons, ducked for cover, unsure of what they should do instead. Emery, seeing the guards pointing their guns at them, thrust her hands at the Minders, killing seven in one swoop. But the two others, who were standing further away, staggered, quickly recovered, and aimed at Emery. Konrad fired his gun and killed them, but not before one fired a shot at Emery. As if in slow motion, Konrad twisted halfway toward Emery, opening his mouth and his eyes wide in horror, expecting her to be hurt, and saw her standing in one place and then suddenly appear a few feet to the left, with no perceptible movement, dodging the shot. The only sign that something had just happened was Emery's white face and her hair that loosened from her braid and swayed around her face as if a gust of wind had struck it. He thought he saw a blur, but then maybe he just imagined it. He kept his eyes on her for a second more, then shifted his gaze back to the Minders.

And Emery was just as perplexed at what had just befallen her as Konrad was. She felt an energy jolt when she saw the gun barrel staring at her, and something happened right behind her eyes. A pop, a shift that spread throughout her body, and as it did, she felt her body lose its mass and transform into pure energy that lifted her and pushed her to the side. Her heart was racing, and she felt coldness spreading through her arms and hands, which soon felt like icicles.

Did I ... did I ... just dodge a bullet?

She caught Konrad's glance as he was turning toward the Minders. He noticed she thought. There was no time to think and try to understand this unexpected corporal experience because there might still be enemies she'd have to fight. She poised and prepared to strike any remaining guards who might have survived her first attack. But they didn't. They lay lifeless on the ground. Seeing their vacant eyes, Emery knew she had killed several of them. Konrad had killed the rest without hesitation. As she gazed at him, a warm and tingling wave of affection and pride filled her body from her head to her toes. He had protected her. Surrounded by dead bodies, all she could think of was to kiss him and look into his eyes. His face showed no emotion, although it seemed darker than before. Emery whirled around, rousing from her daze, hearing Visla's frantic scream.

"Mother ... what's wrong?"

Emery saw Marianne on the ground with Visla by her side. Elena jumped toward Visla and kneeled on the other side of Marianne, who appeared conscious but hurt. A big gouge on her side was oozing a gray substance, which pooled by her side in a viscous puddle.

"Can you help her, like you helped me?" Visla asked, looking at Emery with pleading eyes. "Please?"

"I would if I could. But I don't think I can. It doesn't appear as if your mother has ... blood running through her veins like you and I have. I don't know how to help her."

"I think I can. But it'd require some time. We should get out of here," Thomas said, taking off his coat and kneeling by Marianne. "Sit her up," he directed Elena and Visla. He wrapped his coat tightly around Marianne, while Visla and Elena supported her. Then he picked her up.

Emery, noticing Visla's ashen face and quivering lips, touched her shoulder, encouraging her to go. "Come on, let's get going," she said. She wanted to assure Visla that Marianne would be fine, but she couldn't lie to her. Marianne didn't look well.

"Where to?" Thomas asked Konrad.

Thomas's voice seemed to have released Konrad from the spell he'd been under since killing several of his men.

He probably worked with them frequently, Emery thought, seeing his torment. He killed his colleagues to protect me.

"This way," Konrad answered sharply, tilting his head and then walking in that direction. His expression was still unreadable, like before, but his jaw moved as he worked his hands into tight fists, and his eyes seemed even darker, shadowed by some internal struggle.

They hurried through the Gardens to the elevator and to an area where Konrad summoned a boat with the tablet he'd taken from one of his fallen colleagues. The boat appeared: a special, larger boat, so they'd all fit in.

"To the Moonlight," he told the boat.

"Yes, my lord," the boat replied and moved forward. Marianne's gray face became lighter, looking almost white. She closed her eyes and rested her head on Visla's shoulder. Visla held her mother's hands and cried.

"Are you sure about the Moonlight elevator?" Marianne asked. "They may wait for us there."

"Where else could we go?"

"How about the old Dark Lab?" Marianne suggested.

"Has it not been completely destroyed?"

"No, part of it remains open. Not in very good shape, but better than the alternative."

"Do you know how to get through the Dark Lab?"

"I do," Thomas raised his hand.

Konrad apprised him with his impenetrable gaze. Then he shrugged in agreement.

"Dark Lab, please," Thomas said.

"Your destination may not exist anymore, sir. Are you sure?"

"Yes, I am sure."

The boat said nothing more and continued sailing through the gray landscape. Elena eyed Thomas with suspicious and worried eyes, but reserved her questions for later. She knew of his frequent trips in search of Stella, but she didn't expect he had gone exploring so far away from the apartment. Now she started doubting he was only looking for his dog.

"Are we going to the place where I found you?" Emery asked Thomas.

"Not the same," he replied hesitantly, glancing at Elena, who was now glaring at him.

Emery didn't push, sensing he didn't want to upset his sister more than he already had.

She tried not to look at Konrad, to let him grieve his friends in peace—if that was what he was doing—but her rebellious eyes kept finding his face. He sat straight, looking ahead through the front window, lost in his thoughts. Emery noticed his hands were clasped together tightly and wished she knew what he was thinking. Was he mourning his fallen comrades and furious at himself for killing them? Was he angry with her? He avoided her eyes. His eyes hid amid the shadows of the darkness, which shrouded him like a heavy cloud.

They reached a building, which, like the other lab, bore signs of time, fire, and explosive damage. Konrad dismissed the boat, which promptly disappeared, and Thomas steered them through an opening that appeared too treacherous even to approach. Chunks of wall hung loosely from the metal threads, threatening to fall at any time. Although carrying Marianne, he glided as gracefully as ever, stepping over the jagged edges with a step as light as a dancer. The ragged opening, Emery guessed, might have been a window at one time. She estimated the building's age to be approximately the same era as the other lab. She wondered why it was named the Dark Lab and why it was never destroyed or covered with that gray stuff. What was its purpose?

Thomas navigated through rubble scattered across a large area that might have served as a lobby in its previous life.

As they went deeper into the building and away from the windows, the damage was not as prevalent. Broken furniture, computer screens, and other unidentifiable electronic equipment were scattered everywhere, cluttering the floors. The surface seemed to be still in good enough shape to walk on. *Good old-fashioned stiff and stable concrete*, Emery sighed. *Never thought I'd miss concrete.*

Thomas led them through many rooms that had once been functioning laboratories. Emery identified some as chemistry, others as genetic, recognizing overturned and broken equipment as centrifuges, incubators, DNA cyclers, and PCR machines. When they arrived at the last lab, Emery stopped abruptly, seeing something on the floor.

"What the ..."

In what she felt was slow motion, she moved toward the object. Her face grew paler with each step. She wanted to go faster, but her body completely disobeyed her and dragged, as if suddenly gaining a few hundred pounds. Her heart thumped as she labored to get to the thing lying on the floor, screaming for her to hurry. But once she was close, she didn't reach for it but stood white like a zombie, looking at it with distrust as if she feared it wasn't real and would dissolve before she could get to it. She finally bent down and picked up a broken name plaque that had fallen off the door, most likely when someone had slammed an ax through it. The fire ax was still embedded in the door, still fiery red, as if still holding on to the anger that flung it there.

Emery held the plaque in her trembling hands, thinking she was hallucinating. The unbroken first half of the plaque said: "Dr. Olesya S. The rest of the plaque lay scattered on the floor in broken pieces. She saw the broken "k" and an "n" and an "s" move before her eyes like in a magic trick, forming a familiar name: Dr. Olesya Solensky.

"What is it?" Elena asked. "What's wrong?"

Thomas, still carrying Marianne, had already left the room, but seeing nobody behind him, returned. "We must go," he urged. "We need to take care of her."

Emery put the broken plaque in her pocket. "What was this place?" she asked him.

Thomas heard the quiver in her voice and glanced at her with surprise. "Not sure. I stumbled upon it."

"I don't understand any of it and don't know what it means," Emery said and asked Konrad the same question.

He had also noticed her distress, and his eyes softened. "What I know is that the change was perfected in the Dark Lab, and that's why it wasn't embedded underneath but left as a memento."

Emery shrugged in frustration. "Embedded underneath? What does that mean?" she asked, with lips as white as her face. "Covered with this gray substance, as everything else is in this place?"

"Yes, everything old was covered."

"Come on, let's go." Thomas's anxious eyes pierced Emery's. She was surprised at the intensity of his angst. She nodded and followed him as her mind whirled with unanswered questions.

Everything old was covered. That would confirm Elena's story and that I didn't travel back in time. Why was my mother's name on the door of this lab? It could be a different Olesya Solensky, or maybe I am mad, and all this is just in my imagination. Or maybe I really died in the black hole.

"I'll tell you everything I know," Elena said. "But let's get out of here first."

Emery nodded distractedly. It couldn't possibly be her mother's lab. How could it be?

Thomas once again navigated through yet another dark hallway and to another door, which was secured with another giant padlock. Thomas, with his hands full, carrying Marianne, pointed at the padlock with his head and glanced at Emery. She guessed it was already open, and she was right. She removed the padlock, opened the door, and uttered a tiny shout, seeing the tallest skyscraper yet. It seemed to have no end, narrowing into a point as it disappeared into the darkness above them.

This windowless skyscraper was unlike the other gray buildings, and it was from a different era. Much older. The material looked unfamiliar to Emery. A cross between glass and concrete, the monstrosity was deeply embedded in the gray floor and not hovering like the others. What Emery found odd was that there were no other buildings around. Just this lone, tall strangeness.

"Why couldn't we get here on the boat?" Emery asked.

"This building is in a separate area, sealed off from others. And there are no boats here. You can't call one in. I tried," Thomas said.

"How do we get inside?" Emery asked, not seeing any doors or windows.

"Follow me," Thomas said and proceeded to walk around the building. A little further away, he pointed down with his eyes. "Open it."

"Open what?" Emery asked, not seeing anything where he pointed.

"There is a small indentation in the hatch below. Press on it."

Emery kneeled and moved her hands over the ground. Konrad moved to her side and felt for the handle, helping her. At one point, their hands touched. Konrad moved his hands away, avoiding her eyes. Emery, disenchanted, searched more fervently and found the indentation. She pressed it, and a hatch opened, revealing a dark passage beneath. Konrad stepped down first, using his tablet as a flashlight, followed by Thomas, carrying Marianne, and Elena. Emery stayed and looked back at the building they had just left, memorizing it. *Don't go anywhere. I'll be back.*

The stairs led them down a dark corridor and then up another set of steep stairs. No padlock this time, but a keypad greeted them at the top.

"The door is unlocked," Thomas said.

Emery swung the door open and entered a circular room. The interior looked like any other gray building, except for a crystal tube embedded in its center. The tube sparkled with a million lights from within.

"What's this thing?" She whispered in awe.

"This is the shaft that goes up to the place you wish to go—the wasteland. It is much older, but it probably works the same way the Moonlight does," Konrad said. He approached the tube and inspected it. Finding a small depression, he pressed it, and the tube opened. Just as he guessed, it was a lift that ascended softly once they were all inside. It was a small space with not much room to spare. They all barely fit in it. Emery used the opportunity and stood as close as she could to Konrad, letting her body touch his. He flinched but didn't move away. Nor did he look at her.

"Does this Old Lab have a power source?" Emery asked.

"Power source?" Konrad asked.

"Yeah. The elevator is working. It must be connected to something powering it."

Konrad shrugged. "I don't know."

They emerged into a round rotunda. Konrad waited for everyone to leave the elevator and then faced them, still avoiding Emery's eyes. "I'll open the door, and you can leave safely. You must hurry and hide before they organize another search mission."

"You are not coming with us?" Emery asked, feeling the blood draining from her face.

"No. I must face the consequences of what I've done..."

"That's suicide and total nonsense. You were protecting us. I'd be dead if it weren't for you..."

"But I killed others. I must succumb to justice, as I swore to the Masters I would—"

"Fuck the fucking Masters! We didn't want to kill them. They ambushed, abducted, and tried to change us against our will. How is that for justice? We were just fighting back for our freedom, and you helped us. It was noble and the right thing to do."

"I understand, Emery," he said quietly after a moment of deliberation. "I know and don't hold it against you, and I would do it again and again but must do what I swore to do."

"Don't. You can't! I can't survive losing you for the second time. I can't lose you again. Please, come with me."

"I can't ..."

"They'll execute you," Thomas said. "They'll kill you on the spot without a trial and without asking questions. I know. I've seen it happen before."

"You have?" Elena asked, widening her eyes and leaving her mouth open.

"Yes, two people tried to escape through this very place. But they didn't get very far. The Minders killed them. They disintegrated their bodies; they fired so many times. There was nothing left."

"What were you doing here, Thomas?" Elena asked in a low voice.

"I was looking for Stella."

"Who's Stella?" Konrad asked.

"His dog," Emery said quickly. "Come with us, and I'll tell you all about me and where I came from and about Peter ..."

"I can't ..."

"We must go, Emery," Thomas said. "Marianne will not last much longer if she doesn't get help."

"Please, Konrad, come with me ... Peter, please. I can't bear losing you again." Her voice broke with emotion. She grabbed his hand with both of hers.

Konrad slowly pulled his hand back and looked into her teary eyes. The emotion and tears intensified the golden spots.

"I need you," she whispered, but did not take his hand again.

He clenched his teeth, looked away, and opened the wall, then dashed back into the capsule. His full lips were pressed together tightly, and his eyes narrowed as he fought the temptation to look back.

"Fool," Elena hissed. "Stupid, righteous idiot. It won't be justice that he'll get."

Emery wept, looking at the tube. "That's the way he's always been. Righteous. Always righteous and always doing the right thing according to his moral code. Only now his code is all screwed up, but once a cop, always a cop."

The wall closed after they left the circular room. Elena faced Emery. "It's not your fault. It was his choice. He did what he wanted to do. What he needed to do. It's not easy to change someone who was designed and trained for centuries to serve their Masters. He did what he thought he had to do."

Emery didn't respond. She couldn't talk, afraid that if she had uttered another word, she'd never stop crying. Her eyes felt as if they were drowning in the dark depths of her skull. The first time she lost Peter was hard, but this time it was even harder. If Visla hadn't been here, she would have turned around and followed him. She would have stayed with him and died with him in that fake world. But she had to be certain Visla was safe. Afterward, she'd search for him. They might keep him alive to get information, she hoped.

Marianne knew the outside world already, but Thomas and Elena absorbed every detail when they emerged outside for the very first time after their change. Every rock, every shrub and tree—no matter how scrawny it was—every blade of grass, every crevice, cloud, and every bird that flew by, they studied with fascination. Thomas, sturdier than he appeared, was still carrying Marianne with the same ease as in the beginning.

The daylight brought the grayness of their faces out. While it blended well in the darkness below, now it looked uncanny and less human. Visla led the group toward the mountains, to her hiding places.

18

THE VALLEY

D o you want us to take over and carry her for a while?"
Emery asked Thomas.

"No, I am all right. Let's keep going. Is it much further?" he asked Visla.

"No, the first hiding place is not very far. We can stop there, rest, and take care of my mother."

"Is it safe?" Emery asked.

"Yes, it's well hidden."

"They won't stop. They will find us, Visla," Marianne said. Her voice sounded weaker.

"I know, but they won't find us there. I promise."

"They will not stop. I know. I am one of them," Marianne said, and Emery detected a hint of bitterness in her otherwise monotonous tone.

They continued their journey through the desert until they reached the first rocky hills overgrown with spindly shrubs and yellow flowers with bright orange centers and spiny green leaves that grew in the crevices. The flowers, although a different color and larger, reminded Emery of thistles. Elena reached hesitantly to touch a flower, and when her fingers touched the petals, her face lit with awe. "They are real," she whispered. "Real flowers. So delicate... so beautiful."

"Let's go," Thomas urged Elena, seeing her falling behind, mesmerized by the flowers. She followed the group, but turned to admire the yellow treasures as if they were precious, prize-winning heirlooms, and she wanted them etched in her memory.

"There will be more flowers on the way," Visla said.

Everyone stopped when they reached a stream. The stream, although confined to the middle of the channel and not as wide or impressive as during spring snowmelt, had ample flowing water, which splattered on the rocks and made the comforting whooshing noise streams usually do. Visla stepped into the flowing water, careening through it to cross it, followed by Emery. Elena and Thomas stopped at its edge, observing the swift current with apprehension.

"What's the matter? You haven't seen a stream before?" Visla shouted at them from across the stream.

"It's okay, Thomas. Step onto the rocks. You just have to be careful not to slip," Marianne whispered into his ear.

Emery waddled through the heart of the stream in her handmade sandals, water splashing up to her thighs. It felt good to be out under a blue sky again, standing in a real creek and experiencing a real wind moving through her hair. Her soul ached from losing Konrad, but her body was coming back to life, refreshed by the cold water, the sun warming her after the prolonged stay in the darkness, like apricity warms the air during winter. The bright sky returned the shine to her eyes.

Noticing their hesitation crossing the stream, Emery returned to the bank and reached her hand out to Elena. "It's okay. The water won't harm you. Come on. I'll help you. The water is cold, but it's not harmful. Trust me. Just like the water in the *Origin*. Remember? I've seen you touching it. I've seen you liking it. This is the same; it's just bigger."

Elena took her hand but still hesitated. "Are you sure it won't hurt me?"

"Yes, I'm sure. Why would it? Water doesn't hurt. Water is life."

Elena put her foot into the stream and quickly pulled it back, uttering a tiny shriek. Emery gripped her hand, not letting her go. "It's just cold water. You'll get used to it."

Elena examined her wet foot, but seeing no signs of damage, delicately, like a ballerina, slid her foot back into the stream.

"See, it's not so bad," Emery said, coaxing her to put the other foot into the water. "I've got you. Hold on to me." Emery guided Elena through the stream, showing her where to step to avoid slippery rocks. Elena concentrated on crossing, but at one point she stopped, looking at her feet with a worried expression. "My feet. They feel strange. What's happening?"

"They are just cold because the water is cold. Once you're out of the stream, your feet will get warm again."

Elena continued, although her steps were more laborious and careful. Once Emery helped her get on the bank on the other side, she rushed back to help Thomas. "Come on, Thomas. I know you can do it by yourself, but you can hang on to me if you want," Emery said, reaching out to him with her hand. He readjusted his arm and held Marianne in one arm, then grasped Emery's hand and walked into the stream. He yelped when his feet touched the cold water, but soon after, the anxiety left his face, replaced by awe and then joy, and he let go of her hand. Emery glanced at his face, and her face lit up in a smile. He liked the feel of the water. Emery had the impression he'd be playing and splashing in it if he hadn't been carrying Marianne.

After they crossed the stream, they followed the face of a steep hill that paralleled the channel. This must have been the northern side of the hill because it was covered with lush green vines adorned with delicate white flowers.

Then suddenly, Visla stopped and moved the green vines apart, revealing an opening between the rocks. "Be careful now. This passage is narrow and dark, but not very long. Hold on to me and each other, and I will guide you through it."

They followed Visla through the passage and emerged into a small green valley, enclosed by hills on all sides, with a tiny brook running through the middle. Visla sprinted across the green sanctuary while everyone enjoyed the view, Elena and Thomas, with their eyes wide-open and gaping mouths. She came running back with a smile on her face. "Everything is still in there. We'll be safe here. Come on, this way."

On the far side, there was a cave. Situated a little way above the ground, the interior was dry and clean. A broom made of stiff grass and a polished piece of wood leaned against the wall by the entrance, and judging by its frayed ends, it was used frequently. Neatly stacked branches by a circle of stones greeted them near the opening to the cave, and a stash of carefully folded colorful blankets further inside.

"We leave some supplies here in case we need to come here and hide in a hurry. There should be some red berries and grain stashed here, too." Visla continued to talk nervously while spreading the blankets on the ground. When she was finished, Thomas gently lowered Marianne onto the soft mound. "You're going to be fine. Thomas will fix you," Visla said softly in her native tongue.

Emery wondered how much Marianne remembered of her old language. She'd greeted Visla in her native language when they first met, but it sounded rehearsed, as if she had hurriedly relearned just enough to communicate with Visla to gain her trust. But then again, she had sounded strange to begin with. Thomas removed his jacket, which was still wrapped tightly around her midsection, opened her thin black jacket, and inspected her wound. It was still oozing the gray viscous substance. He took out his knife, unfolded it, and manipulated it, changing its appearance to resemble a silvery wand.

A magician.

"Hold still and don't move now," he said to her. She didn't react or answer, too weak and close to losing consciousness. "I am going to close the rupture now. Emery, can you help?"

"Sure. What do you want me to do?"

"Keep her skin together while I glue it," he said, and showed her how to do it.

Emery did what he asked with only a slight hesitation before pinching Elena's skin, while he glued it together with the wand. She noticed that Marianne's skin was nothing like hers. It was not connected to the underlying gray substance but enveloped it tightly because of its extreme elasticity. Emery found it to be slightly porous inside, firm yet soft and cold, but surprisingly pleasant to the touch, and not metallic or cold as she had previously imagined.

"What is this thing?" Emery asked, pointing at the gadget.

"I don't know its name. I found it," Thomas said, glancing at Elena. But his sister wasn't paying attention to him, as she sat at the mouth of the cave looking at the valley, hypnotized by its beauty. When a bird flew by the first time, she recoiled in panic, but then, seeing what it was, followed it with her eyes until it disappeared into the sky.

Visla nervously wrung her hands as she watched Thomas perform the surgery on her mother. "It's like what you did to me, isn't it? To halt the blood from flowing out of me?" Visla asked Emery. "Will she be okay?" she asked Thomas.

"I don't know. I've done what I can."

Visla kneeled by Marianne and swept a lock of her black hair off her mother's cheek.

"Let her rest now," Thomas said.

Visla nodded and ran outside. "I'll get some berries," she shouted, not looking back. Once her back was turned, her lips twitched and tears ran down her cheeks. She went in search of berries, but mainly to cry unseen by anyone. The cruel world had returned her mother to her for just a brief moment, and now was threatening to take her back once again. Take her back after she'd just risked her life to save her daughter and committed to being her mother again.

Visla sat by a bush with her back to everyone, picking berries and weeping silently. One wouldn't know she was weeping except for the occasional sob spasming through her slender chest.

Emery sensed Visla needed to be alone at the moment. Besides, she realized, she wasn't the best person to console her friend now. Her own grief was being suppressed, pushed down deep into her chest, just waiting for a trigger to rip through her and escape. Instead, she occupied herself with mundane chores and went in search of more firewood. Thomas joined Elena at the entrance of the cave. Elena glanced at him and then laid her head on his shoulder. He took her hand.

"What do you think?" he asked.

"It's incredible. I expected nothing so beautiful up here. I never even wanted to go up and see for myself. And I don't even know why. It was so easy to do all along. Why didn't I want to explore, Thomas? What's wrong with me? What's wrong with us?" she asked and glanced at him. Seeing his expression, she sighed. "You did, didn't you? You wanted to go up to the surface and see it for yourself. Didn't you?"

"I did. I wanted to see what it was really like up here, but I lacked the courage. Once ... I almost did, but then I saw the murder of the two people attempting to escape, and I never went back."

It was dusk before Emery made it back to the cave, carrying a handful of small branches to start the fire with. Elena and Thomas observed her as she arranged the small pieces of wood in the fire pit and then added larger branches on top.

"What are you doing?"

"I'm going to make a fire. It'll be cold here during the night," Emery announced, and noting their faces, guessed they probably didn't feel the cold. She smiled. "Let me guess, you've never seen an actual fire? You are in for a treat."

Visla returned carrying a wooden bowl full of red berries. "Do you need help?" she asked Emery.

"It'll take me a long time to start a fire rubbing sticks together unless you've stashed a flint somewhere here."

"I am not sure. I'll look," Visla said and disappeared into the cave. She returned with a triumphant look on her face that still bore signs of crying. "I found it. I bet my father ..." her voice faded away. She threw the flint to Emery and rushed off to check on her mother. Emery started striking the flint, creating sparks. The siblings watched her with fascination, following the glints with their eyes. Thomas's eyes resembled those glints, sparkling with excitement.

When the fire started crackling, Elena uttered a tiny cry, sounding like a child, full of wonder at experiencing something new. Emery tossed more wood onto the fire. It roared to life as it hungrily swallowed the dry branches. Emery sat by Elena as the darkness enveloped the little valley. She put her hands toward the fire to warm them. Elena watched her and did the same. She quickly pulled her hands out as the fire suddenly crackled. "Don't put your hands too close to the fire, or you'll burn them. Don't forget, it's not a hologram," Emery chuckled.

Visla cuddled with her mother. She covered herself and Marianne with a blanket and closed her eyes, hoping her closeness and her warmth would help her heal. Emery walked over to check on Visla, and seeing her asleep by her mother's side, smiled a tiny, sad smile and left, grabbing a bowl of berries before she settled by the fire.

Emery took a few berries from the bowl and munched on them while sitting by Elena. Thomas and Elena, enthralled, sat speechless, gazing at the dancing flames. Not long after Emery started the fire, the first stars appeared. Thomas shifted his gaze from the crackling blaze to the stars, not sure which fascinated him more.

Elena withered into herself, woefully watching the fire and had not said a word for a long time, and Emery was fine with it, preoccupied with thoughts about Konrad and the strange lab her mother was in some way connected to. Neither Thomas nor Elena seemed to know much about it. But there must be someone who knows exactly what that building was and what had happened there. Once she had them all safe and away from danger, she'd get back to the lab and find Konrad. She sighed deeply, thinking about him but dismissing the thought that he was dead. Having not experienced a sudden bolt of sorrow, or a thunder of grief, she was convinced she would have if Konrad had been killed; she held on to the idea of him surviving until she rescued him.

"Thank you," Emery jerked out of her reverie, hearing Elena's voice. She'd forgotten they were sitting by the fire with her.

"Thank you for today. This is the best day of my life. Thank you for giving it to me. If I were to die tomorrow, I'd die having touched a real flower and walked through a real stream, sitting by a real fire, and gazing at the real stars with my brother by my side and with you. Thank you for this gift."

Emery nodded absentmindedly. Although glad Elena and Thomas had escaped the gray land, she had just now realized how great of an impact this new reality must be for them. In their dull, monochromatic city, they were protected from everything. From the elements, from danger. This environment she'd brought them into might prove too dangerous for them. She knew practically nothing about them. What they were made of, what they needed to survive. Maybe she'd made a huge mistake taking them with her. How would she protect them? Perhaps it was best that Konrad didn't come. She couldn't bear his dying here before her.

"You mustn't worry about us, Emery. We'll be okay. Help your sister. I'm not sure whether Marianne will survive. She'd lost a lot of essence," Thomas said, as if reading her mind.

"Is there nothing you can do for her?"

"I don't know. I've never done it before. I've only seen this tool being used to heal someone once. That happened the second time I went to the Dark Lab. I was looking for Stella when I heard a noise. I hid behind a fallen container when the three Minders came into the lab, looking for someone. No, they were not looking for me, Elena," Thomas added quickly, seeing her face. "They didn't know I was there. They were looking for a woman, from what I overheard. A chunk of metal fell from the ceiling and pierced the guard's chest. The other two used the tool to heal him and then tossed it to the side. This thing rolled down into a crevice, but they didn't bother searching for it. I retrieved it after they had left. The guard was okay right after they glued his rupture, but he didn't lose much essence. Marianne had lost a lot."

"This might sound like a strange question, but what do you mean by essence? Is that your blood?"

"Blood?" Thomas asked.

"Yes, blood. It's what keeps your body working. The heart pumps it through your body, distributing oxygen and nutrition. Is that what the essence is?"

"I don't think so," Elena said. "When they changed us, they eliminated the need for blood and nutrition. As you've probably inferred, we don't eat. We don't drink…"

"How do you survive, then?"

"We have self-sufficient bodies. The medical and physical inventions of the twenty-third century led to a fundamental change and revolutionary improvement of humanity. The Brilliant Genesia—"

"Improvement?" Emery breathed out. "Brilliant Genesia? Brilliant? You don't feel, you don't love, and you don't eat. How is that an improvement to humanity? It sounds like dehumanization to me, not an improvement."

"When it happened, the Earth had been suffering devastating climate change and immense food shortages. Billions of people starved. This change was inevitable, and the Brilliant Genesia saved humanity by offering survival. It was that or death. Death to everyone and humanity."

"It seems to me the change didn't save humanity but morphed it into something else. Something entirely new," Emery offered, and then grew silent, thinking about the world before she had left it. Full of armed conflicts, starving children, social injustice, prejudice, and worst of all—greed. Super Greed was the new name coined for the ultra-rich, who, in a race with each other, had amassed as much money as they could at the expense of the poor. It was a new extreme appetite to gather as much wealth as possible, no matter the cost, unmatched by anything else in the world's history. Maybe she should know more about the changed people before judging them. Perhaps they were an improvement?

"So everyone on Earth transformed into self-sufficient bodies filled with the gray stuff you call essence?" Emery asked.

Elena hesitated before answering; Thomas averted his eyes.

"I don't think everybody was as lucky as we were. The process … the change was … expensive …"

"Are you saying that people had to pay for it?"

"Yes. To change and survive, people had to pay for it."

"That's fucked up. You are telling me the rich people paid and were saved, and all the poor people died of starvation?" Emery said and shivered as an ice-cold wave swept over her.

"I suspect that's what happened. It was—"

"We've not been told the entire truth, Emery," Thomas interrupted, seeing his sister struggling to explain it. "But this is what we've been told all our lives. The Brilliant Genesia saved our lives, but not our parents."

"What do you mean? Why not your parents?"

"Our parents lied to us when they took us to be changed. They told us that everyone would be changed, including them, but there was not enough money for everyone. They sold everything they could, but it wasn't enough, so they paid for us only. We didn't know that then. They left us a note explaining, apologizing, and wishing us luck."

"How long ago was that?"

"Seven hundred years ago," she whispered.

"Seven hundred years ago," Emery repeated and clammed up. Her forehead wrinkled, forming a web of angry lines while her lips pursed in a grimace. "Not true. I went back in time through the singularity. The dark shapes told me I would travel back in time. Isn't this the Paleolithic era? People still make their tools out of stone and don't even know how to extract and process metals yet. Why would you lie to me ..." she said, trying to evade the truth with anger and sounding like a cantankerous child. Emery leaped up to leave.

Elena touched her arm to stop her, but Emery pushed her hand away.

"I'm not lying, Emery. We were interrupted before when I tried to tell you what I know and remember. Please sit down."

"Elena doesn't lie," Thomas said. "And she doesn't have any reason to mislead you. You saved us."

Hearing this, Emery looked into his black eyes and burst out crying. "I didn't save you. I barged into your life and disrupted it. You'd be safe in your apartment if I hadn't pushed myself on you ..."

"No, Emery. You saved us. We know that now. You showed us the truth and offered a choice."

"Emery, you did not go back in time. You traveled into the future. Whoever or whatever the dark shapes were, they lied to you or just simply didn't know."

"Why do you keep saying that?" Emery sobbed. "My mother showed me the way. She guided me to this world ... Maybe I chose the wrong one? I didn't pay enough attention to what she tried to show me and messed up. Messed everything up ..."

"No, you didn't. Nobody can travel back in time. Time travel was possible in my time, but only into the future. No one ever succeeded in traveling back in time."

"But I came through the black hole ... the dark shadows told me time looped there, and I was the only one who could do it. I was the special one. The chosen one ..."

"I know nothing about that, Emery. You must be devastated by this. The lies you and your mother were told."

"If this is the future, who are the people on the surface? You said people who didn't change died. If they are the survivors, why are they not technologically advanced? Why are they using stone tools?"

"I have no answers for that, Emery," Elena sighed. "I wish I did, and I wish I knew as well. They deceived us, too. We've been told that the Earth has not been livable all this time and was only getting worse. That this was a horrible wasteland where nothing grew, and that the only living things were the Mutant wildlings who cannibalized each other. The Minders kept hunting them on the Masters' orders and tried to help them by changing them."

"Mutants ... who told you those lies?"

Thomas and Elena answered in unison, sounding like robots. "The Masters did." When they realized their mechanical answers were as if someone had programmed them to answer in such a way, they exchanged uncertain glances.

"The Masters told you? Master E told you and that woman Master? Master J or was it Lady J?"

"Well, yes. Maybe. I'm not sure who told us. There are more

Masters than the three you saw. They never told us that in person," Thomas said, wrinkling his brow, trying to remember.

"How so?"

"This information was always with us. Since the change. We knew life on Earth was no longer possible, and the only way to survive was to stay in our city."

"I see," Emery said. *They implanted their memories with lies.* "Who are they? The Masters? Do they have real names?"

"Don't know," Thomas said, looking down at his feet. "I'm sorry we don't have the answers you are seeking. We've never asked them ourselves, lacking curiosity and courage. We've been ... kept in the dark for most of our lives."

"Are you all immortal? The stuff you are made of makes you immortal, doesn't it? You didn't finish telling me about Sebastian."

"I really don't know for sure if we are immortal or can just live long. They promised us immortality. But is it true? They lied about everything else," Thomas said, and paused. "I wondered what it would be like to die after I saw the Minders murder the people trying to escape."

"There is not much left to tell about Sebastian. It was such a long time ago, and I barely remember it," Elena said. "He got what he requested. He was put in charge of the Department of Energy. Once he obtained and solidified his power, he then usurped the Department of Defense and Treasury and merged them into the Department of Genesis and Change. He became the most powerful man in the world. In the chaos, no one tried to object or gave a damn about him and his affairs. Everyone scrambled to survive," Elena said, and delayed her story for a moment, eyeing Emery. "But that is not what he is remembered for," she added slowly.

"What is he remembered for?"

"He invented the change."

"He invented it? How? No, this can't be right. Sebastian Brie was not an inventor or a scientist. He was ..." Emery hesitated, not finding the right words to describe Sebastian, whom she only knew from meeting him once and from her mother's letter. "He was a charming globetrotter, devoted to his sister. But I don't think he had any special talents, and he was not a scientist. Must be a different Sebastian Brie."

"It might be, but I doubt it. He cried Zoe's name just before he died. He yelled he had finally avenged his sister."

"Avenged his sister? How? I pushed her into the dark dimension. It makes no sense," Emery said, rising from her seat. She lumbered back to the cave, sat by Visla, and looked at the sleeping girl. The anger and disappointment she felt dissipated almost immediately when she saw her little sister sleeping, curled up by her mother. The innocence and peacefulness of her face melted Emery's rage. She sat a while longer with her elbows on her knees, supporting her chin with her hands, and watched Visla, feeling calmness transcend into her. She kissed Visla on the cheek and then rolled off the mat and sauntered to her place by the fire, next to Elena.

"How did he die?"

"Murdered. Sebastian was killed by the resistance. The bullet ripped his chest open."

"The resistance?"

"Many people opposed the change, demanding the government save the planet rather than just a chosen few. They ultimately formed the resistance movement. The resistance was strong in the States, having been backed by more progressive and powerful young politicians with huge public support. They mobilized the masses in a last attempt to save the planet and stop the change. With their members in the White House, Pentagon, and Secret Service, they could get to Sebastian. But it mattered little. Everything was already in motion. The richest had already bought into the idea behind the change and would not stop. All the best secret agents, police officers, and special forces were bought with the promise of immortality to serve the wealthiest. There was nothing the resistance could do. It was over. They tried and fought, hijacked army equipment, trying to destroy the research centers. Perhaps that's why there were two labs. The second one was built secretly and hidden from view, so the change could progress as planned."

"Immortality," Emery guessed. "He offered them immortality. They couldn't refuse it. How could they? They had all the power and money, and yet were still going to die one day. But how did the change work? The change you went through was so completely different from what Sebastian could have done with the black shards. And he didn't have enough, did he? He must have had help developing the change you experienced." Emery fell silent. The lingering suspicion that her mother might have been involved in the change's development returned and settled in the pit of her stomach. The anguish reflected on her face. Sensing her unrest, Elena and Thomas gazed at her, deliberating on how to comfort her if she needed it.

Once the powerful wave of angst passed, a sudden and overwhelming need to sleep descended upon her. She closed her heavy eyelids, curled up on the ground by the fire, and fell asleep instantaneously. Elena glanced at Emery's bare arms, got up, found a blanket in the cave, and covered her. Then she gently touched her cheek. As Thomas watched his sister, his eyes opened wide in surprise.

Emery slept for twelve hours and would have slept longer if it weren't for Visla, who persistently hovered around her and kept touching her, checking if she was awake. When Emery woke up, Visla immediately materialized by her side. "You are awake. Good. Come and look at my mother. She keeps sleeping and doesn't want to wake up. I don't know what to do. Can you help?"

"Okay," Emery said, yawning. "How long have I been asleep?"

"Long time," Visla said and tugged on Emery's sleeve, pulling her toward Marianne.

Marianne didn't look any better. She was either asleep or unconscious. Emery couldn't tell.

Thomas had just returned from gathering firewood and joined Emery at Marianne's side.

Funny how quickly he adjusted. Already doing chores. Emery smiled, watching him carefully arranging the twigs and branches in the pit.

"How is she?" Emery asked him.

"No change. The same as yesterday."

"Hmm." Emery put her head on Marianne's chest and heard a faint thumping sound. She sat and glanced at Thomas, gathering her thoughts before asking him an awkward question.

"Thomas, I need to ask you something. It may sound strange, but I need to know to help Marianne."

"Ask. You can ask me anything."

"Do you have a heart?"

"A what?"

"An organ that pumps nutrients to all your body parts so they work."

"I don't know," he answered unsurely.

"We have a Central Drive," Elena, who'd just returned from outside, chimed in. "It maintains a constant pressure in our systems."

"Okay," Emery said pensively. "So you have an organ and an essence. What about other body organs? Kidneys? Liver? Lungs? You must have lungs because I can see you breathe."

"We have lungs, but I am not sure whether we have the other things you mentioned."

"Yeah, it makes sense. You don't eat or drink. Therefore, you don't need a liver or kidneys. You probably don't have a stomach either."

"Why are you asking?"

"She isn't recovering. I was wondering if any major organs were damaged when she was shot, which could explain her lack of improvement."

"Oh," Thomas said, seeming unsure.

"We can't give her our blood?" Visla asked.

"I don't think so. It might hurt her even more. I doubt her essence is organic."

"Is what?"

"Living. Like our blood. Your knife is not organic. It's not living."

"Is there anything we can do? I can't lose her now." Visla didn't cry, but the golden spots in her eyes intensified.

"I know," Emery said and embraced the girl while glancing at Elena. "What's the stuff you had in your kitchen? The pills you take? What are they for? Why do you take them?"

"They are Elements. We take them to keep our essence stable."

"And how often do you have to take them?"

"Every three to six months. Why are you asking?" Thomas asked, looking at Emery with an odd expression.

"It could help her recover quicker. What do you think?" she asked, glancing hopefully at Elena and Thomas.

Visla's eyes widened, beaming with hope. "Where can we find these Elements?"

Elena was slow to respond. So was Thomas. "We can only get them from our Element processor in our kitchen," she finally said.

"Oh." Visla's face dropped.

"What's in it?"

Thomas shrugged. "I don't know."

"I don't know either," Elena said, seeing Emery waiting for an answer.

"You don't know what you put in your bodies? Let me guess, the Masters told you to take them?"

"Well, yes, but everybody must take them. The Masters take them too. Otherwise, our bodies would disintegrate."

"Hmm." Emery mulled something over in her head. "You are telling me that without the Elements your body will break down in a few months?"

Elena and Thomas looked at each other and nodded. Although Thomas's nod was tiny and unconvincing—almost nonexistent.

"Yes," they answered together. "We believe they would."

"You knew you might die within a few months without your pills, and yet you still left. Why?" Emery asked, raising her arms in frustration and shock.

"They would have killed or changed us. We didn't want to change this time. A few months out here is worth dying for," Thomas said.

"We've lived a long time," Elena added.

"We have ourselves a conundrum then," Emery said.

"A what?" Visla asked.

"A problem we need a solution to," Emery said and added, looking at Visla. "Come on, let's go outside. I need some air."

Emery led Visla to the other end of the valley. She held her hand and was quiet during their slow walk.

"You are too quiet. I don't like it," Visla said. "You are thinking of doing something foolish. Aren't you?"

"Come on, let's sit," Emery said, directing Visla to a large flat rock. They sat, but Emery was still silent, not ready to say what she needed to say, anticipating Visla's reaction.

"Just tell me."

"I want to help your mother, Visla. She needs help. And the only way to—"

"Fuck me! No! You're not going back there! I forbid you! I don't want to lose you, too."

"You will not lose me. Your mother might not survive without those pills. And neither will Elena and Thomas. They are in this mess because of me. It's the only way to save them. You mustn't worry about me. I'm very powerful, and my strength is only growing and evolving as I learn how to use it. Nothing will happen to me. And they won't expect me. Who'd be foolish enough to go back?"

"You, obviously, but so would I. I'm coming with you."

"No, you can't. You must take care of your mother, Elena, and Thomas. They are like children here. They don't have a clue what to do or where to go. You must guide and help them while I'm gone. Without you looking after them, they might get killed. You are strong and smart, and I know you'll keep them safe until I return. I will return. I promise."

"You can't go by yourself. They'll kill you. Elena or Thomas should go with you."

"It's better that I go by myself. One person will be less likely to be detected. I can sneak in without anyone knowing. I'll be okay. I suspect the Masters have a way of tracking them. It's a hunch I have."

"I don't understand, but I trust you. I still don't think you should go alone," Visla said, frowning, but when she noticed Emery's expression, she stared at her expectantly. "What? Tell me."

"The Elements are not the only thing I need to go back for—"

"It's about Konrad, isn't it? That you thought he was your Peter. Is that why you want to go back?"

Emery looked at Visla and noticed how she had grown up in just a few days. Her eyes reflected a level of seriousness and a new depth that hadn't been there before. Emery moved a strand of Visla's soft brown hair from her face and kissed her cheek. Visla sighed and leaned her head on Emery's shoulder.

"Yes, that's one reason," Emery said.

"Why is he so important? He's not your mother, your father, or even your brother. Why do you care about him?"

"That's another hard question, Visla. It's like your father and your mother. They were in love and had you—"

"In love?"

"Yes, in love. When two people want to be with each other more than anything at all in the entire world."

"Like I want to be with you?"

"Not exactly like that, but similar," Emery said, laughing. "People love their children differently from how they love their parents or siblings. And different yet, how they love that special person in their lives."

"Special person," Visla said, furrowing her forehead.

Emery remembered that there were no boys or girls of Visla's age in her tribe. The girl has never had a crush on a boy. She had never felt her heart beat faster for anyone. "Are there other tribes like yours out there?"

"Yeah. Up north, where we came from."

"How often do you see them?"

"We only go back there when it's too hot down south. So, not very often."

"Hmm," Emery said and shrank into herself until Visla tugged her on the sleeve.

"What is the other reason?"

"What?"

"You said that he was one reason you wanted to get back there. What's the other reason?"

"You perceptive, clever girl. Yes. There is." Emery fished the name plaque out of her pocket and held it in her hand before showing it to Visla.

"What's this?" Visla asked and took the plaque from Emery's hands.

"This is my mother's name—Doctor Olesya Solensky."

"Your mother's? I don't understand. I thought your mother went to a different world to be reborn."

"That's what I believed as well. You know, I also thought I had gone somewhere other than where I had planned to go. I must understand this, Visla. I must know if this was really my mother's name plaque or just some strange coincidence."

Emery stopped, noticing that Visla had fallen silent and was staring at the ground, moving a small rock around with her foot. Moments later, Visla looked up at Emery. Her expression was that of a sad child; her eyes glistened with tears, and her chin trembled. But she held her tears back.

"Now I understand why you must go back. You need to know what happened to your mother."

Emery nodded. A tear made its way down Emery's cheek and fell on Visla's hand.

"I wish I could go with you, but you are right. I can't leave my mother alone."

"Do not go back to your people until I come back. I think you must be careful when we bring your mother back to your tribe."

"Take her back to my tribe? Why would I do that?"

"Don't you think your father would want to see her?"

Visla wavered with an answer. "I'm not sure, Emery. I don't know. Do you think my parents were ever in love?"

"Usually, that's what happens when people have children. Children are born when their parents are in love. Well, not always, but usually."

"I'll think about it," Visla said. "I'll ask my mother if she wants to go back."

Emery shook her head, admiring the wisdom of the young

woman. "Will you stay in this valley or go somewhere else while I'm gone?"

"I wanted to go further east into the mountains, but my mother can't walk. Thomas can't carry my mother all the way. It's too steep. I'll wait for you."

"I'll be back soon."

"I know."

∼

It was dawn as Emery sat outside the cave with Elena and Thomas, talking in low voices. They were against her going alone, but didn't attempt to persuade her otherwise.

"Here, take this," Elena said, taking her tablet out of her pocket. "It may help you. And this," she added, handing her a small oval object.

"What's this?"

"With this, you can easily get into our place. With it in your ear, you'll be able to detect people approaching from far away. I'm not sure if the tablet will be helpful to you, but take it just in case," Elena said and touched the screen of the small tablet. "If you press here, you can see the walls that you can open with it."

Elena looked Emery up and down, assessing her size. "You are smaller, but I think it might work. You should take my clothes so you can blend in."

Emery agreed eagerly and switched clothes with Elena. Elena simply removed her clothes without even the slightest sign of embarrassment at showing her body. Emery couldn't resist glancing at her breasts, which, although shaped perfectly, lacked nipples. That's why Lady J inspected my breasts. She wanted to know if I had been changed like she was, Emery thought as she undressed. Her cotton tank top, now thin and frayed, covered her breasts, but Elena didn't look.

Emery had to roll up the sleeves and the bottoms, and the pants were loose, but she loved all the pockets. Elena couldn't fit into

Emery's tunic, which had been made for Visla and was even too small for Emery.

"Don't worry. I'll think of something later. I'm going to wrap myself in the blanket for now."

"Visla might have other clothes here. Ask her when she wakes up."

Next, she tiptoed to where Marianne slept and grasped her hand. Cool to the touch, her hand was dry and heavy. Emery held her breath, dreading she was dead, but seeing her chest rising and falling in slow, labored movements, she exhaled, relieved. Visla was still asleep beside her. Emery gently searched Marianne's pockets, looking for the gun. Marianne opened her eyes and regarded her with surprise. Emery pressed a finger to her lips, pointing at Visla. "I need your gun. I am going back to get the Elements, so you'll heal faster," Emery whispered.

Marianne's eyes widened. "No," she whispered back. "They'll kill you. I'll recover without it. Don't go."

"They won't kill me. I'll be careful. You need the Elements to survive. And I have unfinished business down there. Tell me where your gun is."

With her eyes, Marianne pointed to the pile of blankets. "Visla hid it there."

Emery sneaked past the sleeping girl to search the pile. She found the tiny gray gun, stowed it, and returned to Marianne's side. "Do you also have a tablet like Konrad had?"

"Yes, do you need it?" she asked and took the small tablet from her pocket. Her gray hands trembled.

"I don't know, but I'll take it with me. Thanks for the gun."

"It's not only a gun. It's also a flashlight. There are buttons on the left side …"

Emery reached into her pocket, pulled out the tiny weapon, and inspected the blue buttons on its side.

"How do I open the entrance to the elevator?" she asked Marianne.

"With the tablet. You press the button on the left side and slide sideways, facing the rock wall. The door to the elevator chamber will open." She found a small silver pin in her side pocket and handed it to Emery. "Insert this in your ear. Any main door and elevator should open for you with this in your ear."

"Is it programmed for you? Will they know when I open doors with this?"

"No, I stole this one from the storage cabinet for Visla. It's new and not assigned to anyone. By the time someone realizes a door opened with it, you'll be far away."

Emery was about to leave, but Marianne seized her arm. "Thank you."

"No problem. You rest and get better. Is there anything else you need from down there?"

"No, stay safe. If anything happens to you, Visla would be ..."

"I know. I love her too."

On her way from the cave, she grabbed a handful of berries and a little grain cake Visla had made the night before. She glanced at her one more time and left. Elena and Thomas were waiting for her outside the cave. They had told her they only needed two or three hours of sleep a night, spending most of it staring at the stars or the fire.

The siblings accompanied Emery to the hidden passage.

"Are you absolutely sure you don't want company?" Thomas asked. Elena glanced at him, displeased.

"No, thank you for the offer, but it's better if I go alone. It'll attract less attention that way. This is my fight, not yours."

Elena was relieved.

Thomas pleaded with his eyes. "Come back," he whispered.

"Look after Visla for me. If anything happens to Marianne..."

"We will. I promise," Elena said. Thomas nodded.

"Thanks," Emery said and started to go, but before leaving, she asked them if they knew and had access to the internet.

"The what?"

"The internet is where you can find all the information in the world. You simply type or ask about anything you want, and it usually provides the information you need. Can your tablet do that?"

"We use our tablets to request places we want to travel to from the Essential Library."

"We ask the Masters when we want..." Thomas started, but his voice trailed as he understood the implications of what he had just said, and he grimaced with revulsion. "Every year, we give our list of questions to the Masters, and they send the answers to the Essential Library." As he continued explaining their knowledge base to Emery, he grew visibly agitated. "Now that I think about it, we never had any important questions to ask anyway. Everything we know, we know from them. And I never questioned it. It never occurred to me that there was anything wrong with it."

"I didn't either, Thomas," Elena said quietly, touching his shoulder. "But we know now."

19

GOING BACK DOWN

Emery lied to everyone. She didn't want to go back by herself. But she wanted to uncover the truth about her mother alone. During the entire journey back to the portal leading down to the dark city, she felt uneasy. The dread growing in her gut was already weighing heavily on her as she neared the shaft that would take her back down. Was her mother involved in the change, and if so, how? She could not eliminate the possibility that she had somehow ended up here while passing through the light. The shapes did not give her enough information, or maybe they had simply lied to her. Maybe everyone had deceived and manipulated her. What she feared the most was discovering her mother had lied to her. If she was immortal, as Emery suspected, she might still be here, working in some dark lab. Or maybe she was no longer immortal and long gone—her powers and her immortality stripped from her when she traveled through the light.

Mother, what happened to you? Where are you?

Emery inhaled deeply, held Marianne's tablet in her shaking hand, and approached the rocky hill hiding the elevator entrance. The rock opened silently, and she entered. Although she expected it, she still jumped, startled, when the door closed behind her, taking the daylight and fresh air with it and leaving her in total darkness.

I'm back in the hellhole.

The darkness didn't last long. Soon, the crystal tube lit up, and the elevator opened. She stalled momentarily, glanced back, then entered with a woeful smile dancing on her lips. As the dazzling-with-lights elevator took her down to the bottom level, she played with the pin in her ear, adjusting it to ensure she had inserted it correctly. She didn't know if she had or not—she couldn't hear anything, but the lights came on, the elevator opened, and she had to keep moving to avoid being spotted. Remembering the gun, she took it out and inspected it. She pressed a blue, slightly translucent button, and something shifted inside the tiny barrel, pushing out a glass tip, which then emitted a bright light. Emery left the elevator and found the steps leading to the outside.

Emery shivered at the sight of the familiar grayness as she emerged. When she looked at the Dark Lab, she whimpered. Two dark, glassless windows and a front hollowed by bullets in an upward arch made it look like the building was sneering at her with an unwelcoming and sinister grin. She shrugged, shoving away the uneasy feeling, and climbed through the jagged opening.

Once inside, she turned the flashlight on and headed for the lab, but delayed entering the room, taking a long look at the red ax glistening threateningly in the bright beam. Emery inhaled, held her breath, and went inside, pushing the door open with her sweaty, trembling fingers.

It was an office, and it was apparent from its imposing size, the high ceilings, the quality of the furniture, and the overall feel of the room that it was the office of someone of high rank and importance. Enormous windows spanned the entire length of two walls, and abstract artwork hung between colorful glass bookcases and cabinets on the remaining walls. Several chairs surrounded a huge amber desk. The bookcases held no books but glass tablets and round glass balls of different sizes and colors.

The surfaces were free of dust, just like in the other lab. Nothing in this room told of passing time except for an overturned chair at the desk and the ax's shiny tip protruding into the room. The enormous windows looked out into the darkness.

Emery roamed the room, examining the glass tablets and the balls, but put them back on the shelves one by one, disappointed. They bore no markings, nothing distinguishing one from the other aside from the color. The cabinets had no handles or indentations. She tried to push them and then kicked them, but they did not budge.

She tried the desk drawers. The first two were locked, but the largest one on the bottom opened, revealing more glass tablets of various sizes and colors. She rummaged through them, took some out, and inspected them again. Not finding anything of interest, she looked around the room, and her gaze rested on an amber box on a corner table. The box had slits matching the sizes of the glass tablets, and Emery guessed they must fit into the openings. Hoping for a hologram that would explain the lab's purpose, she inserted one of the glass tablets into a matching slit, but nothing happened. How could it? The building had no power. The machine sat on the table, mocking her.

"Crap!"

Emery eyed the ax in the door. Her imagination took her on a short but horrifying trip. She saw her mother's terrified face while attempting to escape a manic man holding the red fire ax. As she tried to run past him, he raised his weapon high above his head and then brought it down with all his strength; a crooked grin spreading over his shadowy face. Emery shuddered just before the hard metal hit her mother, breaking free of her hallucination. She gritted her teeth and grabbed the ax. It did not budge. Thrown at and lodged in the door years ago, it had bonded with it and its poignant history, refusing to relinquish its role as a reminder of the room's past.

Emery braced herself and tried again, but there was no movement. She pulled her gun out and pressed another blue button. The glass tip retreated, and the barrel of the gun slid forward and opened. She delayed only a second before aiming at the cabinet and firing.

Surprised by the impact of the tiny weapon, Emery peeked through the large hole it made. To her disappointment, she saw more glass tablets stacked inside. "More useless glass!"

She then fired the gun at the locked drawer, which opened with a loud clank. When she saw what was inside, she gasped and backed away. From a few steps away, she stared at a gold-engraved crystal plate honoring Doctor Olesya Solensky with the 2224 Nobel Prize for her achievements in the development of preontechnology. Emery shuffled forward, took the plate, and inspected it with shaking hands.

Preontechnology? What's that?

Along with the plaque lay a glass tablet. Emery put the tablet in her pocket. She went back to the lab and combed for clues there, but all she found was lifeless lab equipment scattered on the counters and the floor. From the lab, she continued through a door into a narrow hallway blocked by aluminum carts filled with equipment and glass tablets. She noticed a door at the hallway's end and moved the heavy carts out of her way.

To her astonishment, the door was locked. *Something important must be there,* she thought, and shot the lock. The impact sprang the door wide open. A pang of disappointment shot through her as the room proved to be a small storage room full of equipment and cases of glass tablets and balls. Emery scanned the room and left. She walked a few feet and jumped over the carts, but stopped in her tracks, having a strange tingling sensation in her stomach that she had missed something. Something in that room was not quite right. She went back.

This time, she examined the room inch by inch but still couldn't pinpoint what her brain had registered as out of place only a few minutes ago. Narrowing her eyes, scrutinizing all the walls, she leaned on a half-empty shelf by the far wall and scrambled to keep her balance when it moved away from her. What she thought was a solid surface, a solid wall, was an illusion. Once she regained her balance, she pushed the shelf further. The shelf disappeared into the wall, and Emery followed it, finding herself in a circular room that resembled the chamber where she had started her journey. Only gravity still controlled her movement, rather than weightlessness, and the console was missing. This crystal capsule looked identical. She touched it, wondering if it would activate. It remained dark and locked. With no power and no black shards, the crystal tube stayed lifeless and useless.

What would be the point anyway? She'd have to go back into the terrifying dark dimension, find her way to the black hole, only to travel into the future. She might even discover nothing ahead—no future for anyone. But part of her still held a shred of hope that traveling back in time was possible; she just needed to confront the highest-ranking Master and get the truth out. The truth about time travel, the change, this place, and the reason behind all the subterfuge.

The need to find Konrad, which she'd put aside for the time being, kept stubbornly resurfacing, gripping her stomach in a tight hold, demanding her attention. She gritted her teeth. *I'll find him. Later.*

She realized she wouldn't find answers here. The glass tablets probably held the information she was seeking, but she couldn't play them. Emery left the chamber, found her path back to the lab, and retraced her steps through the labs, heading toward the entrance.

She stopped by the army tank with its long barrel jammed through the outside wall. The rational Emery just shook her head, dreading she'd find things she might regret seeing, but the snoopy Emery shrugged and climbed on top of the steel turret and grabbed the hatch cover. It took all the strength she had, but she finally opened it and peeked inside. As she feared, there were dead bodies inside—or rather, desiccated skeletons—with their mouths open, baring their teeth in mirthless grins. She climbed inside in a fit of momentary insanity, satisfying her curiosity about the resistance.

All the bodies were mostly bones, with some hair still stuck to their charred skulls. Emery performed gymnastic moves she didn't know she had to maneuver over the skeletons to reach the second compartment. A woman's body lay sprawled on the cold steel floor, making Emery flinch. Her long dark hair draped across the metal decking in dark curls. Emery sensed the girl was young and immediately thought of Visla. She died fighting for what she believed in: to save her planet and her people.

Emery kneeled by the girl, noticing something shiny in her curled hands. "I'm so sorry," she said to the girl, gently loosening the grip of the bony fingers and taking the shiny object.

It was a round, silver coin. Larger than the one-dollar coin she'd seen in her grandpa's collection. Engraved on one side of the coin was the elongated image of Earth, displaying all seven continents. The other side showed an engraved profile of a young woman. Encircling her head, the words spelled out, "She who protects our Mother Earth lives forever."

She held her breath, looking closely at the profile, which resembled her mother's, tracing her face with her finger and whispering. "Mother? How?"

Emery put the coin in her pocket. She wasn't convinced the profile was her mother's and blamed her overactive imagination, but couldn't leave the coin behind. *You see her everywhere because you miss her.*

Emery left the tank and crawled out of the building. She shook like a dog would after getting out of a lake and let out a deep breath, glad to be out of there, and examined Elena's tablet. The instant she touched it, the boat started to build around her.

"Where to, my lady?" the boat asked, once it had finished constructing itself around Emery.

"Home," Emery said, touching her earpiece.

"Yes, my lady."

The boat took Emery to Elena's apartment without incident. Emery asked the boat if it was connected to the internet, but the boat didn't understand.

"Still not smart," she muttered.

"What's that, my lady?"

"Never mind. I said, you are smart. Smart boat."

The boat didn't know how to process this sarcastic statement. It remained silent until the journey's end.

Emery ran to the kitchen and asked Wolfgang to make the Elements. Wolfgang spat out a silver pill onto a small plate.

"This is going to take a long time," she muttered. "Wolfgang, can you make me twenty of these? Twenty Elements, please?"

"This quantity exceeds your allowance, my lady. I can only make one more for the second occupant. Would you like me to make it now?"

"Shit!"

"Could you give me the chemical composition of shit, my lady? I don't know what that is."

"Never fucking mind, mindless machine. Just make me one more Element."

"Yes, my lady." Wolfgang's monotonous voice suggested he didn't hold a grudge.

"You'd think they'd be more creative with the voice of one of the most talented musicians of all time," Emery grumbled. "Where am I going to get more Elements?"

"You can get more if the ones dispensed to you were lost or damaged, my lady."

"Oh? Awesome. So ... Wolfgang, if I were to tell you the two Elements you just made for me got lost, you'd make more?"

"Yes, my lady."

"Okay, then. Make more?"

"Have you lost your Elements?"

"Yes, I have lost my Elements. Make two more. Please."

"Yes, my lady."

Wolfgang spat out two more pills, and Emery repeated her lie, thinking that fooling the machine more than once would not work. To her surprise, Wolfgang continued to believe her fibs even though she was standing right in front of it with her hand full of silver pills. Once she had thirty, she stopped. "That will last for a while."

She left the kitchen, but she thought of something and ran back.

"Wolfgang, can you tell me the chemical formula of the Elements?"

"Yes, my lady," Wolfgang said, and recited a mouthful of chemical formulas.

Emery's interest in chemistry was spotty. She had paid attention to the parts that interested her but ignored the ones that bored her, and still ended up with straight As, acing all the tests. She didn't know what the compound or compounds the machine listed were, but she memorized them anyway.

"Thank you," Emery said, and left the kitchen and the apartment.

She summoned the boat, which promptly materialized for her.

"To the old lab," she ordered the boat. It was time to find and confront the bosses.

"I'm sorry, my lady. I don't know that destination."

Shit! Why didn't I pay attention when Thomas ordered the boat to fly there?

"An old building ... made out of concrete," Emery muttered. "It's from the old world."

"The old world? Do you mean Africa, my lady?"

"Africa? You can fly to Africa, boat?"

"Yes, my lady."

"Is there an old building there?"

"There is a building there."

"Okay," Emery sighed. "Take me there. Sail to Africa, boat."

While the boat sailed through the dark city, Emery looked out the window, searching for familiar landmarks. The boat stopped in front of the old lab.

I'll be damned. Africa, the old world, where humans originated. These people are ... masters of dry humor. *Masters*, she laughed silently and without humor. All the strange names of things, the archaic "my lady"s, "my lord"s. Twisted. *Who came up with all this weird shit?* Emery wondered.

Emery entered the old building, but instead of finding the stairs leading to the Masters's quarters, she headed for the physics lab. She now had a light and could go into the dark rooms she couldn't explore before. Before she did that, she picked up the photo from the ground and slid it into her pocket without looking at it.

The dark rooms held no secrets. More equipment—whole or in pieces—more broken glass, and lights cluttering the floors. Each step she took made a crunchy echo, which, although annoying, was preferable to the eerie silence in this creepy lab.

The last room was a windowless office. Monitors with their lifeless faces lined all the walls in an unbroken, lustrous line. Emery saw her reflection in the screens and jumped—her face looked different, alien-like.

A monstrous glass table occupying the central part of the room held a model. When Emery came near enough to see it, the skin on her arms formed goosebumps that felt as if someone had thrown barbed wire on her. Facing her was spread a model of the chamber. The upright crystal capsule was displayed prominently inside the circular room, with the console next to it. The outside walls were lined with a complex system of machines and instruments connected by a web of tubes and wires.

Emery stood with her mouth and eyes wide open, staring at it. She felt the blood drain from her face as she imagined that her mother had designed the chambers. *And then what? She was tricked into disappearing into her own creation? No, it makes no sense. Oh, Mom. I hope you had nothing to do with all of this.*

With a heart that felt like a huge, heavy stone that took up too much space in her chest, making drawing breath an almost impossible task, Emery left the lab and headed for the passage leading to the Masters' Quarters—the people who had orchestrated all this mess. It couldn't have been her mother. Her mother had no evil in her.

She navigated through a maze of obstacles, finally reaching the lab with another military tank sticking out from the wall. Propelled by morbid curiosity, she sighed and climbed down the tank after wrestling with the mangled, charred hatch.

There were four skeletons inside—two still in their chairs and two on the floor in the second compartment. Emery searched the interior and found another coin on the chest of one body. Its owner, an older woman, judging by the long gray hair, had drilled a hole through it, threaded a silver chain through, and hung it around her neck. With an apologetic smile, Emery gently took the chain off the skeleton's neck and inspected the coin. It was the same as the one she'd found in the other tank. She hung it on her neck after a moment of hesitation, realizing she was robbing a grave. "I am sorry."

Emery scrambled back up the broken staircase and through the padlocked doors, finally reaching the familiar, narrow, claustrophobic corridor. Creepy shadows flitted across the low ceiling that felt as if it was going to fall on her at any moment. She opened the last door and found herself in the area resembling a doctor's waiting room again. It was empty. Emery wiggled the earpiece, but she still heard no voices or footsteps. She took out Elena's pad and touched it.

Elena's tablet was blank, providing no help with directions. She checked Marianne's tablet, which wasn't working here either, it seemed. Emery would have to find her own way through this building. Emery tiptoed along the empty hallways, sticking close to the walls with her gun ready until she reached a door.

To her surprise, the door was not locked. She leaned against it while holding a gun, and it opened wide with just a slight push of her foot. The lights came on, and she entered a room filled with black spy birds. She backed out of the room, expecting an attack, but the black monsters remained still and silent, sitting on gray shelves. She went inside and looked at them closely. The size of a bald eagle, the impressive birds looked at her with blank stares, the whites of their eyes reflecting in the bright lights. Most birds were damaged: broken wings, chipped beaks, and cracked bodies revealing a gray underlayment. Emery guessed this was their graveyard after they were no longer useful. She picked one, surprised by how light it was, peered inside its body through a hole where its wing used to be, and saw an array of pegs, wheels, and electronic chips hanging in disarray.

Emery left the bird room and walked further through empty rooms and hallways, but found no sign of anyone living or working there. The lights were all dimmed, and the air was cold. Thomas had explained to her that this building was hidden from everybody but the Masters and privileged Minders. He saw them go in and out, but that was the extent of his knowledge of this place and whether it was where the Masters conducted their business or lived. Now that she had explored it, she doubted it was and doubted the Masters got in and out of their building this way, guessing they must have another hidden, but more convenient, way to get in and out.

Emery stopped at another door. She put her ear to the wall and listened before trying to open it with Marianne's tablet. Hearing nothing, she turned the tablet on, and the door started opening slowly, as if hesitant to let her in. It opened into darkness. She flipped a switch on her gun and directed the flashlight at the ghostly murkiness ahead.

The passage was a narrow suspension bridge strung between two buildings. Stinking of old rubber and diesel, the bridge felt soft and unstable underneath her feet. She shone the light on the bridge and discovered that it really was made of a black rubbery substance. She touched the rubbery handrail, but not trusting its strange stickiness, she didn't grab it but crept over the wobbly bridge with her arms outstretched for balance, glancing at the black void underneath. Looking down, she tripped over a tear in the rubber and, screaming at the top of her lungs, grabbed the railing with just one hand. Her knuckles were completely white as she held on to the railing, expecting it to break at any moment. With her heart pounding, she dragged herself to her leaden feet and reached the other side in sluggish, shaky moves. The door at the end of the bridge was a welcome sight.

It opened with the tablet Marianne had given her. Alarmed by the squeaky noise it made, she closed it quickly behind her and held her gun, ready to fire. The earpiece was silent while she navigated through narrow corridors, which, to her anguish, all came to a dead end. She checked each end with Marianne's tablet, and finally, the last one showed a darker rectangular area. Emery thrust her hands at the wall, which dissolved slowly. The moment she crossed the opening, the wall rebuilt itself behind her.

She was in a large room; its intense brightness was amplified by diamonds and silvery threads entrenched in the walls. It was as if shimmering rivers were running the length of each wall up to the high ceiling, where they met in the middle, tied together in a diamond-studded lily, its petals and veins outlined in silver.

Rows of cloudy chairs floated in rows above, seducing with their cozy seats, waiting to accommodate their Masters in a soft cuddle. They encircled a diamond fountain, spewing diamonds of various sizes. Corridors emerged from all around the circular room through intricate arches. Emery guessed the room looked like a shining star from above.

I bet the Masters meet here and think up all the lies to tell their minions.

Each arch leading to a corridor had a two-letter diamond sign on top. Emery paced around the room. She chose one with two letters: "E.K." The corridor led to double crystal doors, whose center parts were carved into stylized "X" signs, their edges delineated with gold borders.

As expected, the doors lacked handles, doorbells, or any other latching mechanisms or clues about how to open them or alert the occupants that their guests had arrived. Emery preferred not to announce her presence. She'd already made enough noise.

As she stood facing the door, she remembered Thomas's words as he slipped his little shiny gadget into her hand before she left. "This thing will cut through anything. I mean anything. Take it." She took it hesitantly, believing she would not need a knife, and now she was glad she had.

First carefully, then with more force, Emery cut an opening in the door—just large enough for her to slip through. Like in the Silver House, opulence screamed at her from the diamond-studded crystal walls. Picasso and Van Gogh were locked in a staring match with each other across the hall. The Degas dancers seemed to be moving as the crystal chandeliers studded with gems cast their light on them.

She heard music and loud voices up ahead, past the long hallway. Marble floors covered with Persian carpets muffled her steps as she walked down the hallway toward the sounds of music.

Before she placed her foot into the massive living room, she could make out dark silhouettes moving on the crystal and marble walls. The room was shrouded in shadowy darkness, interrupted by occasional explosive flashes emitted from a gigantic screen displaying a movie. Judging from the music and the clothes, it looked like an oldie —filmed in the nineteen-eighties or nineties.

A man and a blonde woman sat watching the show from their cloudy chairs. Emery wasn't sure which shocked her more: the blonde hair or the movie playing. Neither Elena nor Thomas remembered what a movie was. Apparently, they were reserved for the elite. Master E and his blonde companion were utterly involved in the film, watching intently. It was too dark to see their faces, but Emery recognized the man's strange lock of hair on the back of his head. It was the same Master E she'd seen on the screen during her inquisition. She watched them for a moment, deciding how to proceed. With her gun pointed at them, she tiptoed around to the front so that they could see her.

"Enjoying your movie, Master E?" Emery asked, with a healthy dose of sarcasm in her voice.

They both jumped and observed her for a while before the man finally responded. Emery expected his voice to falter, seeing her pointing the gun at him, but he calmly pointed at the ceiling. The movie stopped playing, and the room brightened with lights. The chairs lowered down, and the Master got up and gazed at her. As he recognized her, his full red lips curved into a malicious smile. The malevolent grin churned her stomach in an instant. His beady black eyes sparkled with a mix of interest, malice, and spite, while his blonde companion gazed at Emery blankly with no interest, no irritation at the interruption, nor even the slightest surprise showing on her face. Almost as if she didn't understand that an armed visitor was pointing a gun at her companion. Beautiful beyond belief, the blonde goddess simply set her unblinking, beautiful blue eyes on Emery and smiled with the innocent smile of a child.

"Should I leave now?" she asked with a melodious and slightly husky voice.

"No, you can enjoy yourself watching me having fun with this thing," he said in the sticky voice of a lizard. "You are brave. I give you that much," he said to Emery, still smiling. "But you are also incredibly stupid."

"How so?"

"You thought you could just waltz in here and kill me with this little gun of yours?"

"I don't see why not, but not before I ask you a few questions, which I expect you to answer without delay, because I'm short on time."

"You are short on time, and you don't even know it."

His self-assurance troubled Emery. She'd witnessed Elena killing a guard with this gun and remembered the hole it made in the cabinet; she was certain it could do severe damage to this man, who did not appear strong or fast. Staring at him, she discovered that his face and body were not of the sculpted, smooth consistency of the rest of his people. Instead, disturbing bumps lurked underneath his skin, resembling a worn-out pillow that shifted as he spoke. Emery shrugged, shaking off the sensation that something was crawling under her own skin as she stared at his gray, slightly moist skin. There was something surreal about him, something completely unreal. With red lips, squinty eyes, and eyebrows shaped in a raised arch as if he were in a state of constant surprise, Master E had the face of a reanimated clown. And a familiar clown. She thought she ought to have recognized him; she just couldn't put a name to his face.

"What would you like to know?"

"Who are you? Who invented this sick change, and why are you lying to all of your people? Why eliminate their emotions? Why don't you let them watch movies or learn about history? What do you hope to gain from this?"

"Your little mind would not understand this concept, no matter how much I try to explain."

"Why don't you enlighten me, then?"

"No point in trying. I've tried in the past, but there was not one human being who could understand the brilliance of my plan and its absolute necessity, elegance, and beauty. Only a limited few in the history of humankind have ever reached the unrivaled pinnacle of human intelligence and forethought as I have. And honestly, girl, I don't see that special sparkle of intellect in you."

"You think you are one of the greatest minds? You are comparing yourself to Albert Einstein, Marie Curie, or Stephen Hawking?"

"No, I'm not one of them. I surpassed them centuries ago. I am the ultimate ideal being. Master of the human race. Master of all races, as a matter of fact. I've mastered perfection," he crowed, extending his arms in a swooping gesture.

"Mastered it? You are a complete lunatic. You dehumanized people, depriving them of the very thing that made them human— curiosity and love, you deranged imbecile. How many people have you perfected or murdered? How many died because of you? And how were you able to convince them to go through something so radical, so atrociously inhumane? So alien?" Emery asked.

Watching his face light up with delight in anticipation of her solving the puzzle, she knew the answer. "They didn't know? You tricked them. You never told them the entire truth. Keeping people ignorant, illiterate, and fearful is a way of controlling them. That's it. Isn't it?"

He chuckled with the glee of a child committing mischief without consequences. "Brilliant, right?" he asked.

"Sick. It's sick ..."

Master E paused and grimaced. "I knew it. They told me you were special, but you're not. You are just a puny, mediocre human, lacking imagination and the brainpower to comprehend what I've accomplished. Your little pea brain can't handle the significance and elegance of—"

"Who invented all of this? It obviously wasn't you. You lack the brains and look like a guy who'd steal someone else's work, twist it around, and take credit for it. Who invented it? Was it Sebastian Brie? Or someone else? Who was it?"

When he started laughing, his lumpy face twisted in knobby twirls as if there was something alive and crawling underneath his skin. Emery, appalled and fascinated with his bizarre appearance, stood silent, observing him, calm on the outside but screaming inside. She needed him alive, but the hand holding her gun seemed to have developed a brain and despaired in the tight hold, wanting to plunge a hole in his lumpy chest. "Tell me! You motherfucker!" She yelled, and her voice cracked. "Who invented the change?"

"Why the hell do you need to know that? How would that change your tiny world? You know what? I am already tired of you. You are not as interesting as I thought you might be. You ask the same pedestrian questions and sound as dumb as everyone else. I was hoping you were less mediocre. We could have had fun together. I'll let Elijah play with you and find out where you came from. He'd have so much fun with such a pretty thing. I'll give you one thing. You are good-looking. You have superior genes. Too bad they'll go to waste," he said and waved his hand. The smile left his face abruptly as his lips curled into a cruel pout.

A wall opened to two Minders, aiming their guns at the stunned Emery. She pressed the trigger, but the gun didn't fire. She pressed it again, but the gun remained silent. Her heart sank.

"Your gun doesn't work here, stupid girl. You don't think I'd allow just any gun to work in my home?" Master E chuckled. "I've protected my area from the likes of you. Take her away," he directed the Minders.

Emery dropped the gun and thrust her hands at the approaching guards. But they didn't fall as she had expected. She repeated it, but the guards didn't even stagger. Emery looked at her hands with surprise. Master E laughed. His blond beauty giggled mindlessly and stared into the distance without comprehension.

The Minders closed in on Emery. She was no match for the tall, muscular men without her power. But she would not go out without a fight. Once they were close enough, Emery kicked one in the groin, but he didn't even flinch. One of them grabbed her arm in a painful clutch, and the other tried to grab the other arm. She elbowed him in the stomach, to no avail. With expressionless faces, they dragged her away. Shocked, she wondered why her powers didn't work on these

Minders. But as they dragged her away, she noticed their black uniforms were outfitted with a semi-translucent outer layer. Gritting her teeth, she realized it was a crumple layer designed to absorb kinetic energy. She sighed, wondering who Elijah was.

"Don't hurt her," Master E shouted. "Elijah will take care of her."

"You fucking coward. Make others do your bidding for you," Emery shouted as the Minders dragged her away. "You can't even stand having the company of a real person, a real woman, with you because you fear she'd laugh right in your idiotic clown face. That's why you're hanging around with a mannequin. You pathetic piece of —" Emery slumped to the side, as one guard slapped her face with his large, gray hand. She felt the sting on her face and another on her neck. She lost consciousness.

20

DIVIDED

Konrad reached the base of the elevator shaft and headed toward the old lab. His pace, fast in the beginning, slowed, and he eventually stopped before he reached it. He looked back and took the few remaining steps toward the building and crawled through the opening. Then he sat on the jagged edge, glancing back. He spent his entire life obeying orders, making sure others obeyed them, and, if not, finding the noncompliant and bringing them to justice without hesitation. But that was before he ran into Emery. Now he sat on the rubble, remembering her blue eyes that had carved themselves into his soul and fighting the urge to run back to be near her, look at her, and listen to her voice when she spoke. The old Konrad urged him to turn himself in and answer for his actions. The new Konrad hesitated, realizing he was afraid of dying. If he died, he would not see Emery again.

The old Konrad won. The new Konrad still doubted himself. Inexperienced child.

This was the first time, instead of walking with his usual confident stride, he dragged his feet, trudging through the countless labs and back to the other side. He hesitated again before summoning a boat and ordering it to sail to the Minders' headquarters. Once he arrived at the drab building where there were no diamonds, no silver, only depressing gray walls, he just walked in, announcing himself loudly. The head of the Minders, Philip, threw him a stern look. "Where are they?"

"Outside. On top."

"You helped them."

"Yes."

"We'll find them. And you'll be dealt with by Master E himself. He has asked to see you if you were found," he said, then turned to several Minders standing behind, ready. "Take him to level 'S'," he ordered. Konrad didn't protest or resist them. He let them herd him to his prison cell, from which he most likely would be escorted to his death after being questioned by Master E. He wondered why. Master E never questioned mere Minders who broke the rules.

The guards left him standing in the middle of his tiny cell. He lay down and stayed like that for the rest of the day and night. He didn't sleep but stared at the ceiling, thinking about Emery. Her eyes and lips were forever imprinted in his memory. He felt a sudden urge to sink his hand into her hair. Konrad didn't know what was happening to him. Emery had asked if he remembered her. He didn't. But when her eyes had shed the tiny diamond-like tears, a vivid memory raced through his mind. In his memory, she was touching his lips with hers and looking at him in a way that constricted his chest strangely. He couldn't breathe, and yet he wanted more of her touch and more of her eyes looking into his. Had he known and forgotten her, or had she somehow hypnotized him with her extraordinary powers?

Remembering what he felt when their hands met and when she pressed her body into his in the elevator, Konrad jumped up so quickly that he almost fell over backward. He fought with all his willpower to stop his knees from buckling under him, overwhelmed by the memories.

Suddenly and without warning, all traces of loyalty and guilt he carried evaporated as the urge to see her overtook his entire mind and body. He had to break out of his prison. He struggled to draw breath as a heavy weight pressed against his chest, urging him to hurry.

With no weapons and no tablet to open doors for him, he had little chance of escaping. He paced the little cell back and forth so many times and so fast that the soft floor beneath him retained his footprints.

The door swung open, and two guards gestured for him to come with them. He didn't protest, relieved they'd only sent two people to get him. Konrad was one of the best Minders if not the best. Everyone knew that. They must have assumed that he had resigned himself to his fate and would not try to escape. After all, he'd come back and turned himself in.

Konrad waited until they were inside the elevator, knowing it was where the surveillance equipment frequently malfunctioned. He took both of them down at once. He rendered them unconscious with fast, efficient movements, so quick, they didn't have a chance to react. Besides, they did not expect an attack. Insubordination among the Minders was not something they ever encountered. Before he left the elevator, Konrad collected their guns and tablets. He then ran to the back exit. He knew this place inside and out and knew which way to go to avoid being spotted. Soon he was sailing back to the old lab. Tapping his fingers on the boat wall, Konrad impatiently waited for the ride to be over.

Without hesitation, he ran through the labs and then to the elevator. Inside, he banged his hands on the crystal tube in frustration, fearing he had waited too long and wouldn't find her.

She's probably dead already in the wasteland. No, she said there are real flowers up there. If flowers can survive, so can she.

Once he was outside, the bright sunlight hit his eyes, and, not having experienced the sun before, he covered his eyes with his hands in panic. When the sun didn't hurt his hands, he slowly removed them from his eyes and looked around, squinting. He was not panicking anymore. What he saw stole his breath. The color of the sky reminded him of Emery's eyes, and the golden sand under his feet of her hair. White clouds drifted through the sky unhurriedly;

the sparse grass swayed in the wind; and the gentle breeze brushed against his face. These new sensations filled him with a wonder he had never experienced or had long forgotten. When he saw the yellow flowers, he knew Emery was telling the truth, and the Master had lied to him and everyone else. There was life up above. Flowers grew here. The sun filled the air with warmth, and the zephyr caressed his face with its soft fingers.

After his initial earthquake of emotions, of wonder and awe, he felt mad at himself. He remembered what Emery had once said to him. "... you had no Masters ..."

Konrad had never taken part in the excursions in search of wildlings because they didn't align with his job duties. His responsibility was to ensure all rules were followed and to discipline anyone who broke them. The wildings didn't break city rules and therefore didn't concern him. He thought little about them, and he knew only what he'd been told, indoctrinated into the deception since the change. The wildlings couldn't survive up in the wasteland and cannibalized each other. The good Samaritans, the Masters, helped them by offering them the change. Konrad never questioned it, seeing nothing wrong in rescuing people from death, but now he knew it wasn't an offer but a forceful act. Now he knew the wildlings didn't eat each other or need help to survive. Now he knew the wasteland wasn't a wasteland.

For all those years, he was a part of the mechanism, normalizing and enforcing the atrocious actions of the Masters. How could he have been so blind? Konrad hung his head and walked, looking at the ground. That was when he noticed the footprints in the sand. He counted them. Four sets of footprints. Thomas, carrying Marianne, Elena, Visla, and Emery. Emery!

With his eyes glued to the ground, he followed the tracks. Hopeful that these were their tracks, he increased his pace, and his anxiety lessened as he believed he was getting closer to seeing Emery. He paused, seeing water rippling and splattering over rocks in the stream. Konrad knew it was a stream because he frequently ran holograms of streams and rivers in his apartment; the sound of the flowing water calmed him. Although he'd been to the *Origin* several times, he had never touched the water. No one ever told him it would hurt him, but it was a common assumption everyone shared. Water was to be avoided. And yet, the footprints ended at the water's edge. They'd crossed the stream and must have survived because their bodies were nowhere in sight. He paced up and down the bank, then bent down to touch the water with the tips of his fingers.

Just like Elena before him, he yanked his hand from the water, not expecting the coldness and the strange wetness. After inspecting his fingers and seeing they were intact, he put his hand back in the stream and held it longer this time, and moved it back and forth, amazed at the water swirling around it. Then he stepped into the current and started crossing it, slipping on rocks and getting splattered with water. To his surprise, he liked the chill on his skin.

Instantly, he felt younger and recalled an image of splashing in the river with other boys. Boys. Young people. He was young once; he realized. And as the thought crossed his mind, he stopped amidst the swift water of the stream. He just now fathomed there were no children in the city. He somehow sensed it was wrong, but he didn't know why.

Konrad found the footprints right after he made his way across the stream and followed them until they disappeared again. He walked further, expecting they'd reappear, but not seeing them, returned to the spot by the hill where they vanished. He grabbed the vines in both hands and put his foot on the wall, expecting to find a solid foothold, but when his foot disappeared into the wall, he quickly pulled it out. With both hands, he moved the vines apart and gasped, seeing a hidden passage. Without hesitation, but holding his breath, he entered the narrow, dark corridor. When he emerged on the other side, he gasped again at the beauty of the valley, welcoming him with its serenity. Visla saw him and dropped a bowl of berries. She searched her pockets and found a knife, which she pointed at him.

"What're you doing here? Did you bring the others with you?" she shouted.

"No. I am alone. I came back after realizing I must ... I must see her. I must see Emery."

Visla moved a few steps forward. He didn't hold a gun, and he looked like a different person from the one she'd first met down in the city. Even though he had helped them escape, he was still one of the Minders. They stared at each other for a while. Visla did more glaring than staring, gripping her knife tightly and still pointing it his way. But her stern face slowly lost its edge as she observed him shifting his weight from one foot to another and blinking.

"Where is she?" he asked.

Visla put her stone knife back into her pocket. "She's not here."

"Where is she?" Konrad asked with such distress, and she immediately felt sorry for him.

"Come in," she said, pointing toward the cave.

Konrad followed her silently, his anxiety building.

Elena and Thomas greeted him with their mouths wide open. Elena was wearing a leather tunic adorned with yellow flowers instead of her blue city jacket and pants.

"What are you doing here? Did you find her?" Thomas asked.

"Find who?"

"Emery. She went back—"

"She went back down?" Konrad asked, and his face tensed. "Alone?"

"She didn't want anyone with her. I would've followed her anyway, and then she'd have to deal with me, but I had to stay with my mother," Visla said.

Konrad apprised Visla, who stood with her hands folded defiantly, looking him straight in the face.

"You're not afraid of anything. No wonder Emery risked her life for you."

"Yeah," Visla said and hung her head for a moment. "She risked her life for me, and now she went back to get the Elements, convinced they might help Marianne recover faster."

"How is she?"

Elena shook her head and pointed to the heap of blankets further back in the cave. Marianne was asleep; her breathing was heavy. Konrad crossed the cave in a few steps, kneeled by her side, and listened to her breathing.

"Why do you think the Elements would help?"

"I don't know. They are supposed to stabilize us, so we thought it might be good for her," Thomas said unsurely.

"Maybe," Konrad shrugged. "When did she leave?"

"This morning. Early this morning."

"I just missed her," he said, and gritted his teeth. "Where did she go?"

"She wanted to go back to the old lab. She saw something there that she wanted to examine. And then she was going to Elena's flat to get the Elements ..." Visla said, and paused, staring at Konrad with a guilty expression.

"Then?"

"She said she needed answers."

"She went to find the Masters," Konrad guessed, and turned on his heels.

"Wait, I'm coming with you," Thomas shouted.

"No, you are not," Elena interjected.

"Yes, I am," Thomas said. "She risked her life to help us. I'm going to do the same."

"Suit yourself," Konrad said. "Just stay close and don't slow me down."

"I won't. Do you have an extra gun?"

Konrad glanced at him. "Do you know how to use it?"

"I'll figure it out."

Konrad nodded and handed him a gun. Larger than Marianne's, but still small enough to fit in a pocket.

"Be careful," Elena said. She didn't try to convince him again. He had made up his mind, and even though she didn't want him to go, she knew it was the right thing to do and was proud of him. Her younger brother had so much more courage than she had.

21

ELIJAH

Emery regained consciousness as the Minders were strapping her into a metal contraption on a wall, which reminded her of a medieval torture device. They abandoned her in the dreary room. She and the contraption she was tied to were the only two features here. She was alone for a long time, during which she concentrated on loosening her restraints, but before she could get her hand free, the door sprang open and a man walked in. The shackles they had put on her were much stronger than those they had used on her before. She couldn't break them in time.

He was the spitting image of Master E, but younger, and his body or face didn't remind her of an old pillow. His face wasn't expressionless, nor as smooth as Thomas's or Elena's. It seemed to have a life of its own, as if it were a musical instrument, and emotions played a silent symphony underneath his gray skin. His black hair was also different. Not the thick black waves, but delicate and soft like you'd expect on a baby's head. The hair stood up as if styled by someone who might have read too many fantasy books. Like the head of Medusa, the locks and half-locks and spindly projections pointed in all directions and moved ever so slightly. What shocked Emery were his lips. Full, sensuous lips —with beautiful curves that would send any girl into a jealous fit— were twisted in the most malicious grin she'd ever seen. Lips made to kiss and love breathed out hate in an evil smile.

"Who are you?"

"Guess?" he asked, and his grin widened.

"You are his son ... Master E's son. You are Elijah."

"Well, you are not as dumb as he said you were. There is a certain family resemblance ..."

"Yeah, the same evil face."

His boisterous laugh filled the room and bounced off the walls in a sinister echo. "Not dumb, but not smart, either. There's quite a fight for you at the headquarters. I think they want your brains." He snickered. "Maybe I'll save some for them. I don't know. What am I going to do with you? They say your name is Emery. Emery, what? Do you have a last name, pretty Emery?"

"Not for your ears. I won't soil my name in your presence."

His laugh seemed strained this time. "You'll tell me your name soon enough. You'll tell me everything, pretty Emery," he said, strolling to the opposite wall. It opened to a monstrous cabinet that held bizarre, sharp instruments artfully displayed, as if it were an exhibition in a museum of horrors and torture. All shapes and sizes —curved, spindly, serrated, shiny, black—all would make but the strongest of hearts wilt. He stood by the open cabinet, grinning and waiting for Emery's reaction. Waiting to see fear.

"Evil and a coward, just like your daddy. You can't face a woman smaller than you and fight her on even ground? Instead, you resort to tying her up and torturing her. You are as pathetic as your clown daddy. Clown and a joker, what a pair." Emery laughed in his face.

The ghastly smile was still plastered on his face, but Emery could see she had hit a nerve. "What's the matter? Are you afraid of me, boy? Do you think you can scare me with your little boy toys? Have you ever looked at yourself in the mirror? Wipe that jester smile off your face if you want to be taken seriously. You are just a little boy playing with toys. You are not a man and never will be," Emery said, laughing.

"Shut up. You cunt! You'll stop laughing soon," Elijah said and turned toward the cabinet, trying to select the perfect implement and hiding his expression from Emery. The smile was gone. Instead, his lovely red lips curved down into a revolting sneer, exposing his super-white teeth. He chose a long, curved knife with a serrated edge. When he turned around to face Emery, his reptilian smile returned to his red lips. He showcased the knife, turning it around, tracing its edges with his fingers, while avoiding her stare. But eventually, he couldn't help himself and glanced at Emery, who not only did not look afraid or worried but grinned at him mockingly.

"Don't hurt yourself with that thing. It's not made for little boys. It was meant for real men."

Elijah threw a fit. He screamed in an immature, screechy voice, stomping his feet and throwing his arms around in a tantrum, like a child in a toy store demanding his parents buy him whatever he wants. As he waved his arms, the long, sharp blade nicked his thigh. When he realized it, the strange half-curls on his head animated as if propelled by strong winds, and his mouth and eyes opened in a big "O."

"I will show you who's the man here, bitch," he drawled.

He stomped toward Emery, wielding the knife in front of him. She realized she might die at the hands of this crazy boy-man, but she would never give him the satisfaction of showing her fear. She looked him right in the eyes, defiantly, proudly; her eyes threw blue lightning daggers at him. As he approached, she could smell his breath, foul and acidic, and see the infinite hate in his black, bottomless eyes. His stare settled on Emery's bracelet. He stared at it for a moment, frowning, then cut it with a quick move of his long blade. Emery blinked to stop the tears from escaping. *Not Visla's bracelet, you bastard!*

She mustered all her energy to hold off her anger and stay calm. "You don't have to do it, Elijah. You don't have to listen to your father. What happened to you? Where is your mother?" Emery changed her approach, softening it, hoping to hit a different nerve.

"Do not mention my mother," he screeched.

He plunged the knife into her stomach slowly while looking into her eyes, expecting fear to emerge at any moment. Not seeing any, he pushed the knife further and then slowly turned it. Emery's eyes darkened. The golden dots in her eyes glowed like fire, but she showed no fear or hurt and did not cry out in pain. But the concentration it took to hide her pain was too much to bear. Her head slumped to the side as she lost consciousness.

"How do you like that, bitch? Am I man enough for you now? Huh? Wake up, fucking bitch. Wake up. I'm not done with you," Elijah screamed.

He poked her arm with the knife, and when she didn't respond, he inserted the knife into her arm. She didn't react. Blood poured out of her, staining the gray floor.

Emery regained consciousness when he stabbed her arm, but she didn't show it, feigning a blackout. She focused on unlocking her restraints, realizing that it was her only option. The pain in her abdomen felt like someone was twisting a fiery hot iron. She focused all her inner strength, and she felt the cuffs on her right wrist loosen while her left arm was being ripped open by Elijah's knife.

With a quick move, she freed her right hand and opened her eyes. Seeing the knife move toward her throat, she grabbed his wrist and twisted it. The knife fell to the floor with a loud clank, but she didn't release his hand and twisted it harder, pressing on it with all her strength. She felt her fingers go through his skin and felt something break and give way while his deafening screams for help, first muffled by the concentration and effort to penetrate his skin, became louder, unbearable, and pierced her ears. She let go, seeing his face lose awareness. He flopped to the ground like a rag doll.

With her hand tarnished with his viscous gray essence, she tried to reach the restraints on her left wrist but couldn't reach them, as her neck, also tied to the wall, inhibited her movements. She concentrated again on untying the restraint, but Elijah was already getting off the floor. He found the knife he had dropped and held it with his undamaged left hand.

"Die!" he screamed, flailing his massacred hand.

Emery instinctively protected her throat with her arm, but realized she was done for. He was about to kill her soon. She couldn't remove the restraints quickly enough, so she shut her eyes tightly and thought about Peter as the murderous boy/man lunged at her.

She held her forearm in front of her throat to protect it, waiting for the blade to slice it, but the pain that came was not what she had expected. Instead of plunging deep into her skin, the knife only nicked it. Surprised, she quickly opened her eyes and thought she was dreaming, meeting Konrad's eyes.

"Emery," he whispered, his voice breaking. "What has he done to you?"

Thomas came out from behind him. "Quick. We need to stop her essence from escaping her body. She is draining badly," Thomas said after inspecting her wounds. "Give me the thing," he added impatiently, seeing Konrad immobilized, distraught by the sight of Emery's injuries. "Konrad, give me that thing!" he shouted, hitting his arm. "The thing that heals wounds. I left mine with Visla. Quickly."

Konrad handed him the healing wand, similar to the one Thomas had used to glue together Marianne's wound. Then he dragged Elijah's body away from Emery. He had killed him with just one powerful hand thrust to his temple.

"Will it work on her?" Konrad asked as Thomas readied the silvery wand to close Emery's wounds.

"I don't know, but I don't see why it wouldn't. We don't have any other options," Thomas said, and seeing the dread in Konrad's eyes, he added. "I know how to do it. I will not hurt her."

Thomas parted Emery's coat and, with Konrad's help, closed Emery's stomach wound, while her head swayed from side to side as she slipped in and out of consciousness. It worked as well as it had on Marianne's skin. The bleeding stopped immediately, but Emery's pain increased. She clenched her teeth, holding back tears. Konrad gently untied her restraints while Thomas tended to her arms, gluing the bleeding wounds.

"What are you doing here? How did you find me, and why are you together?" Emery whispered.

"He came back looking for you," Thomas said, glancing at Konrad, who kneeled by Emery's feet, removing the last restraint from her ankle.

"He did?" Emery said and smiled. She felt no pain at that moment. "He remembers me ..." She held her head up, searching for something with her eyes. She couldn't see it.

Konrad noticed her anguish. "What is it? What are you looking for?"

"My bracelet. Visla made it for me. This scumbag cut it off my hand. I need it."

Konrad searched the floor, found the bracelet, and gently inserted it in her hand. She smiled, and then her head tilted to the side as she lost consciousness again.

"Emery," Konrad whispered, taking her hands in his. "Emery ..."

"We need to go, Konrad. We must get her out of here," Thomas said with urgency. Seeing Konrad staring at Emery with such immense grief, Thomas added gently. "She'll be okay. She's strong. We must go. I'll carry her while you protect us. I believe you are much better at it."

Konrad nodded and clutched his gun. "I'll go first," he said, regaining his resolve upon hearing the word "protect." He *was* good at that.

He left the room first. There was nobody around to stop them. The Minders had orders to stay away when the young Master E was "working." The corridor was empty. Thomas carried Emery with ease —she was even lighter than Marianne. Konrad held both guns while glancing at Emery's chest, making sure she was breathing.

"Wait." Emery woke up and tried to free herself from Thomas's arms. "We can't leave yet. I need to know who started this whole thing."

"Not now. We must get you out of here. You've lost a lot of your essence."

"I'll be fine. I heal fast. We must find out who's behind all this and stop them before they hurt more people."

"I closed your wound, but I don't know what damage he's done to you. I know nothing about the internal organs you mentioned before. We can't risk it."

"We must, Thomas. We must," she cried out weakly.

"Emery, listen to me. I promise I will come back with you and help you find the answers you seek. But now, we must go. I will not risk your life for answers. We must go before they find his body," Konrad said.

Emery tried to protest, but Konrad gestured with his finger to his lips, hearing something in his ear gadget. He motioned for Thomas to stay put while he sprinted forward. Three Minders came marching toward them. They stopped when they noticed them and didn't immediately reach for their guns, not understanding what they were seeing.

Konrad fired three times, and all three fell without so much as a cry of surprise. He didn't feel bad this time and didn't ask for forgiveness. After all, they let Elijah torture her and try to kill her.

He'd heard rumors about Elijah's secret room and wildlings disappearing instead of being changed, but he never paid much attention to gossip. Today, the memory of the rumors had ambushed him as soon as he set foot in the elevator, unifying with the need to find Emery. The pressure to hurry had intensified and grown into panic as Konrad and Thomas headed toward the Master's headquarters. His inner voice told him to find Elijah's torture chamber, pressing him to rush. He followed this secret voice without hesitation and found Emery with not a moment to spare.

For years, he had shunned and hid from others this extraordinary perception, this sixth sense, believing it to be against the policies of the Minders and something he'd be killed for if it became known. His intuition warned him to keep his gift a secret, sensing no other Minders had it. Having witnessed executions of Minders who hesitated killing uncooperative wildlings, he knew that being different was punishable by death.

As he ran to find Emery, he questioned his past deeds. Why did he never challenge the murder of the wildlings? And why didn't they stir his emotions then, as they do now? Why didn't he protest when they brought the wildlings and dragged them to their cells and the interrogation rooms to be changed or to be killed? Emery was right. They needed to know the truth. He had just realized he needed to know it as much as Emery did. Would that be enough to vindicate his past actions in his own eyes? In Emery's?

"I promise you. We will find out," Konrad said with conviction as he gazed into her eyes. She believed his eyes.

He said we will find out, not you will find out. He said we ...

"Okay, let's get out of here." She sighed.

Konrad picked up the guns of the three Minders he'd killed. He stuffed two in his pockets and the third one into Thomas's back pocket. Then he continued down the corridor, heading toward an elevator shaft, stopping occasionally to listen. More Minders were in the elevator, advancing their way. More than he could fight by himself without putting Emery at risk. She noticed his troubled expression when he glanced back at them, trying to decide what to do.

"Put me down," she whispered to Thomas. "Take your gun and be ready."

The pain shot through her when Thomas put her down as gently as he could. She swooped her hair off her forehead and set her jaw, wrestling with agonizing pain while she set her feet firmly on the ground, ready to fight.

The elevator opened, and eight Minders poured out with their guns pointed at the fugitives. Emery didn't wait for all of them to be out. She thrust her hands, hoping to have enough strength left to eliminate at least a couple. But she did better than a couple. With the fear and the fight for survival came extraordinary strength. She saw the blue waves encircle the Minders. Five fell immediately without a sound, the sixth staggered and fell, and the remaining two were not fast enough to react before Konrad and Thomas shot them both at once.

Using her powers exhausted her. She staggered, but Thomas

caught her before she hit the ground. He carried her to the elevator while Konrad dragged the bodies out to make room for them.

"How did they know we were here?" Thomas asked.

"It's probably this," Konrad said, removing the earpiece and stomping on it. "I should've known."

Emery was conscious, but her face had turned white.

"We are getting out of here alive. Hold on, Emery," Konrad said. "Can you run carrying her?"

"Yes, she is light."

"We're going to have to run to an exit that isn't known to many. That is the only way to avoid them now that they know we are here. Turn right and run. Don't look back. I'll catch up. At the very end of that corridor, turn left and keep running."

Thomas did as Konrad instructed. He ran and didn't look back, even when he heard shots. He ran, ignoring Emery's pleading whispers to wait for Konrad. Instead, he clasped her tighter and ran with all his strength. At the corridor's dark end, he turned left and kept running, even though he was becoming worried, not hearing shots or shouts anymore. Without Konrad, he was unsure how to leave this place. But he kept running. And hoping Konrad would make it.

"Ugh, you run fast," Konrad huffed behind them.

Thomas turned around and ... smiled. Konrad stared at him with bewilderment.

"What did you just do with your face? How did you do it?" Konrad asked.

"I don't know. It happened on its own. I was glad you made it with hardly a scratch, and my face just reacted," Thomas said, looking at Konrad's torn jacket and his arm oozing essence. "Let me tend to your arm—"

"Later," Konrad said, waving his arm and pointing the way. "We are near the exit."

"Are they—"

"No one is behind us anymore. We are safe for now."

Konrad ran ahead and then stopped. He scrutinized the ceiling, the floor, and then glanced back at his tablet. He moved a few feet forward, bent down, and touched the floor. It opened onto a dark shaft into which he jumped without hesitation. After a second, his face appeared in the shaft. He looked at Emery with sudden despair, and with a voice that didn't obey him, and kept cracking, he asked Thomas to lower her into his arms. When Konrad felt her body in his arms, he nearly lost his balance—not because of her weight, but because a profound and strangely familiar feeling overwhelmed his entire body. Paralyzed by this sensation, he stood still and silent like a pillar. Her body felt so right in his arms, as if she'd belonged there all along, and he never wanted to let go. Emery sank deeper into his arms and nestled her head on his shoulder. She heard his chest move faster.

Peter, my Peter. You remember us.

"What's wrong?" Thomas asked, glancing at Konrad's inert body and ashen face.

"Nothing," he said in a shaky voice. "This way," he added, taking a small step down a dark corridor, then another, and finally regaining his composure, he began moving fast, almost running. Thomas volunteered to carry Emery but received no response from Konrad or Emery. When they finally reached the end of the long, dark hallway, the wall opened. Thomas was about to step out, expecting a boat to build around him, but Konrad stopped him.

"No, no boats. They can find us."

"What then? Jump?"

"No need," he said, and moved his foot forward and tapped the floor at the base of the wall. A flat, dark shape emerged from the floor and slowly turned on its side, providing a slightly concave raft. Konrad pointed at it. "Go on. It's safe."

Thomas stepped onto the raft cautiously, but as it remained steady, he moved forward, making room for Konrad and Emery.

"What is it?" Thomas asked as the raft moved forward. It wasn't as fast and smooth as the boats, but it moved efficiently through space. Without the sides, the air felt cool as the raft sailed through the air. Emery shivered. Konrad instinctively put his arm around her, but she didn't feel it, plunged into her feverish sleep again.

"It's an old boat. They don't use it anymore, and nobody remembers them."

"Nobody except you?"

Konrad waited before answering. He'd told no one about his explorations, deceiving himself that he was merely doing his job by inspecting every nook and cranny in his city because, as its protector, he needed to know everything about it. He had always suspected, but never admitted to himself, that this need was something more than performing his duties. Something deep inside him that he didn't have a name for. Something he told no soul.

"You were curious," Thomas said.

Konrad looked up at Thomas. "Curious?"

"That's what Emery said about me. I went places I wasn't supposed to because I was curious. I wasn't supposed to be curious."

"I don't know. I had spent a lot of time with the construction crew when they were erecting all the buildings. That's how I know about places that were used for staging in construction. When no longer necessary, they were all forgotten."

They drifted in silence. Konrad gazed at Emery, who rested in his arms, asleep like a baby would in a parent's arms, knowing she was safe.

"How does this thing know where to go?" Thomas asked.

"It only goes to one place—the older lab building, Africa."

"Oh."

The raft lowered to the ground once it arrived at the ancient lab. Konrad and Thomas moved quickly and silently through the labs and to the elevator.

22

I REMEMBER

Visla squealed in happiness and excitement, seeing Konrad emerge from the secret entrance to the valley. Her face dropped when she saw Emery's pale face and blood on her clothes.

"Emery!" she shouted, running toward them. "What happened? Is she alive?"

"She was attacked. She's alive but weak."

"She shed a great deal of blood and could use some nourishment. Give her your berries and the other things you make. And water," Thomas said, coming out of the passage.

Elena emerged from the cave running, hearing their voices. "Thomas. Are you all right?" She asked, seeing the red substance on his clothes.

"I'm okay. Emery is hurt."

"Bring her inside. I know what to do," Visla said in a commanding tone. She ran ahead and prepared a bed for Emery. Konrad gently lowered her onto it. Visla opened the part of Emery's blue jacket that wasn't cut and examined the wound. The glue held well; no blood oozed out of it.

"I know little about the organs inside your bodies, and don't know if anything was damaged inside her. I only know she lost a lot of her essence ... blood before I could close her wound."

"Thank you for saving her life," Visla said, getting up in search of something. She returned with her stone knife, which she stuck into her wrist without delay, and held the bleeding wrist above Emery's mouth. The blood dripped slowly onto Emery's parted lips. Some spilled, reddening her lips, which stood in sharp contrast to her pale face.

"What are you doing?" Konrad asked.

"What she did for me when I was hurt. She needs blood, and that's the best way. That's what she said, and she was right. She kept me alive this way."

As the blood dripped into her mouth, Emery swallowed it in tiny gulps. After a few moments, Emery's eyes opened. When she understood what was happening, she grabbed Visla's hand.

"That's enough. You can't give me more. You are so pale."

"Emery," Visla said and smiled. "You're back."

"Glue her hand, Thomas," Emery said, stroking her friend's cheek. "You shouldn't have done it. You gave me too much."

"Shush, Emery. I've done what you've done for me. I am healthy, and you need to recover quickly."

"How is your mother?"

"The same."

"But not worse?"

"I don't think so."

"I have the Elements. They are in my pocket." She took the pills out of her breast pocket and gave them to Visla. The girl took them and inspected them with interest.

"Wait," Konrad said, covering Visla's hand with his. "Why do you need them?"

"They are for all of you. Elena said that you must take them every six months to keep your essence strong. I want to give it to my mother, so she'd recover faster."

"You must ask her when she had one last. The same goes for you," he said, looking at Elena and Thomas. "When did you last take one?"

"I don't remember. Four months ago? Wolfgang reminds us to take them," Elena said.

Konrad stared at Thomas, who was fidgeting and procrastinating with an answer.

"Thomas?" Konrad pressed.

"Eight months ... maybe nine."

"How? Why? What were you thinking?" Elena gasped.

"I tricked Wolfgang into believing I had swallowed the pill, but I hid it in my sleeve. I just wanted to see ..."

"See what? How quickly you could die?" Elena asked.

"No. I wanted to know how long I could ..."

"You wanted to remember Stella? To feel?" Emery asked.

Thomas nodded, avoiding Elena's eyes. "Every time I took a pill, I forgot her right away. I only remembered her later. And I didn't want to forget about her or other things ..."

"That's exactly what I thought," Konrad said. "You are still alive and well—"

"Are you well?" Elena interrupted, gazing at Thomas intensely.

"I'm very well. Actually, I've never felt better. I remember my Stella, and I remember ... our parents. Glimpses only of our mother's golden-brown hair. When I first saw Visla, I remembered our mother. She had the same eyes and hair."

Elena gasped. "But your essence? You could have died. You could die at any moment."

"At least I remembered, and I felt things. I don't want to forget anymore," Thomas said somberly and looked Elena in the eyes. "I don't want to live like that anymore ... Like I wasn't alive, visiting fake stars when I can love the real ones."

"I suspect the pills are not given to us to preserve our essence," Konrad said. "I believe they are given to us to keep our memories from returning. For a while now, I've suspected the pills were not what they told us."

"You've suspected it? Was it your intuition? Your inner voice? A hunch, maybe?" Emery smiled when she said the last word. "Your hunches were always spot on."

"You know about my hunches?"

"Of course I do. That's one of the endearing little quirks of yours that made me fall in love with you."

"You fell ..." Konrad's voice broke. He couldn't speak.

"It's okay," Emery said, taking his hand and squeezing it gently. "You'll remember one day. And you'll feel it too."

Konrad sat on the bed of blankets Visla had prepared for Emery and enveloped her, surprised at how naturally he had done it. As if his body remembered it, but not his mind.

Thomas took Visla aside and tended to her wrist, while Elena stood at the cave's entrance, shaken, as her world flipped upside down. She worried that if this was true—the pills to repress their memories and to stifle their emotions—what lay ahead of her? What would she remember? Were there memories she shouldn't remember? Thomas remembered their parents. Was she ready to remember them? Elena sighed and returned to the cave. She stopped by Marianne and sat beside her. Marianne was asleep; her chest was rising in small but steady breaths.

"Could we give her some of our essence?" Elena spoke, breaking the silence.

"What? Why?"

"Seems like it worked for Emery when Visla gave her essence to Emery. Maybe it would work for Marianne. We ought to at least try?"

"How would we do it?" Thomas asked.

"The same way Visla did it." Elena and Konrad said at once.

"It may work," Emery said. "You take your pills orally. We could give her a small amount at first ..."

"I'll do it," Elena said and, with no reluctance or uncertainty, pulled her hand out for someone to cut it.

"Thank you," Visla said, approaching Elena with her stone knife.

Elena nodded, and Visla made a small incision on her wrist quickly and expertly. The essence was thicker than blood and dripped slowly into Marianne's mouth, which Visla parted and held open. After a while, Konrad approached and volunteered to give some of his essence.

"You can't give her too much, otherwise you'll be too weak," he said, taking the knife from Visla.

Elena didn't want to stop, but Thomas chimed in. "He is right. You can't give too much. I'll give her some too. That way, we won't make ourselves vulnerable."

Elena nodded and moved aside reluctantly. She wanted to be the one to save Marianne, although she wasn't certain why it felt so important. Konrad quickly cut his wrist and let his essence dribble into Marianne's mouth.

Thomas approached Elena and glued the nick on her wrist, glancing at her face and searching her eyes, which she kept averting from him. "What's wrong?" he asked.

"I don't know. I feel strange ... not myself. It hurts right here," Elena whispered, touching her chest. "But I'm not hurt. I don't understand what's wrong with me."

"Nothing is wrong with you. You are beginning to feel things."

"Feel things ..." Elena whispered. "It hurts."

"It does. Sometimes," he said quietly, and added after a pause. "Without that pain, I hurt even more. I yearned for it, and that's why I didn't want to take the pills so often. I wanted to wait until I felt worse. But I never did. I was going to tell you about it. Later. Much later. After I was sure."

Elena finally looked him in the eye. "You are so much wiser than your older sister."

Thomas patted her hand and went to check on Emery's wounds.

"You are getting quite good at this," Emery chuckled. "You are going to become our doctor soon."

"Doctor?"

"Yeah, someone who fixes people when they are sick. Like you fixed me."

"And how is my fix doing? How are you?" Thomas asked as he moved her coat aside to look at the wound on her stomach.

"I'm better. I told you I heal fast. Faster than other people. It's a gift I have."

Thomas shook his head, not sure what to think of Emery's

wound, which looked redder than before. So much different from Marianne's wound, which, after he had sealed it, left no mark. He got up and approached Marianne's bed, then gestured for Konrad to stop. He took the knife and moved his wrist above Marianne's mouth, about to cut it, but she intercepted his hand.

"What are you doing?" she asked.

"Mother, you are awake," Visla squealed.

"We are giving you some of our essences so you can recover," Elena said.

"Why? Emery is back. Did she not get the Elements?" she asked. Watching everyone's faces, she continued with dismay. "What's the matter? Someone better tell me why we can't just use the Elements?"

"We think the Elements make us forget," Elena said.

"Forget what?"

"Everything. The change takes away our memories, our curiosity, our will."

"No. It can't be. I've been taking the Elements all my life and remember everything."

"What do you remember about your life before the change? Do you remember your daughter?" Thomas asked. "How do you even know she is your daughter?"

Marianne opened her mouth to speak but paused, glancing at Visla, then back at Thomas. "They told me to get my daughter because she needed to be changed."

"Who told you?"

"Lady J."

"Did she tell you why? Why her? Why Visla, specifically?" Konrad asked.

"She is a Mutant who will pass her mutation to future offspring if not changed."

"A what? A Mutant?" Visla asked. "What's a Mutant? Pass what?"

"I don't know ..." Marianne's voice trailed off. After a pause, she spoke in a monotone, devoid of emotion, staring blankly at the cave's ceiling. "I was prepared to change my daughter without knowing why. I blindly followed orders I didn't understand. Now, I can't remember why I never questioned the change and why I never, not once, thought there was something wrong with it."

Marianne shifted her gaze to Visla. "You knew I was your mother. How did you know?"

"The elders recognized you when you came."

"Do you know what a Mutant is?" Emery asked Konrad.

"Not exactly. Someone who behaves differently from others. Specially trained Minders went up to search for and bring the Mutants in."

"How did they know they behaved differently?" Emery asked.

"The birds?" Visla said, studying her mother's face.

"Yes," Konrad answered for Marianne. "They used the birds to observe the wildlings and report any Mutant behavior."

"And you don't know what that Mutant behavior is?" Emery asked.

"No. It was not my sector," Konrad said. "I didn't think about it or question it," he admitted.

"Hmm," Emery said and became quiet, remembering how different Visla was from her tribe members. She was the only one who hugged and kissed the children and her father. Visla was more emotional than others in her clan, or couldn't hide them well enough, which could have been why she was chosen. The Masters wanted to eliminate emotions from the wildlings' gene pool. They eradicated emotions from their people and suppressed their memories. *But why?*

"You know, don't you?" Elena asked.

"I suspect, but I'm not sure."

"What is it?" Visla asked. "Why am I this Mutant thing?"

"They are misusing the word, which can have a negative meaning if not used correctly. But it could also be a positive thing."

Emery noticed the golden dots in Visla's eyes intensified and started glowing as the girl's angst mixed with curiosity increased. "How?" Visla almost yelled.

"Mutant means that someone differs from others, either in their abilities or looks. Those differences can influence how people survive and live in positive or negative ways," Emery said, grimacing, not pleased with how she had explained genetic mutations. "It sometimes gives people an advantage. Like animals that live in hot climates have larger ears with lots of little blood vessels that help them cool themselves."

"Oh. Am I a bad Mutant or a good Mutant?" Visla asked, cocking her head. Her hand inadvertently went to her ear.

"You, Visla, are the best Mutant there ever was," Emery said, smiling.

"Really?"

"Yeah, really. You have more emotions than anyone in your tribe. I've noticed you kissing and hugging children and your father. I suspect your mother was the same way. That's why they kidnapped her, and then you, because you were related to her."

"Oh," Visla said, and Marianne echoed. They locked eyes. Visla smiled.

Marianne tried, but all she managed was a grimace. "I don't remember," Marianne whispered.

"You might be right," Konrad said.

Emery noticed he was preoccupied and sent him a curious look.

He saw the look and continued, albeit hesitantly. "Once, I stumbled on an interrogation of a woman wildling. She had hair and eyes like Visla. The Minders were asking her questions, playing a hologram recorded by the bird in the background. I saw her embrace other people and touch them with her lips and do what you do, Emery and Visla—smile. Back then, when I saw her doing it, I didn't understand what or why she'd do something so strange. I know now she was kissing them," he said, and looked Emery in the eyes. And it was as if Peter were looking at her. The same penetrating stare that dove right into her heart.

Peter, my Peter. You are coming back to me.

"What're we going to do now? We can't stay here," Thomas said. "They'll search for us and will find us eventually."

"They will." Konrad nodded. "They'll send all the Minders from the city to find us. We need to leave as soon as Marianne can walk."

"I can walk," she said. "I feel much better."

Marianne wasn't lying. She looked much better. Her eyes had regained their shine and intensity, and her skin was not as pale. The treatment had worked. All she had needed was to recover some of her essence.

"You said your father was planning to go back north to reunite with the rest of your kin. Maybe we should join them?" Emery asked Visla.

"I don't know if we should. They'll be afraid of her," Visla said, pointing at her mother with her eyes. "Who knows what Father told them? They might fear everyone. Maybe even me. They were already wary of you because of what he had told them," she added, looking at Emery. "They might attack us when they see us. My father is—how do you say that? Hot head?"

"Hot-headed? Yeah. He is. But once you tell him everything, and once he sees your mother—"

"But he never went after her. Why didn't he? I would have. Maybe he didn't love her."

"We should at least try, Visla. You'd be safer with your people."

"I would be safer with my tribe? What about you?"

"I meant we'll be safer in a bigger group. All of us."

"We can try. I can go first and talk to them."

"Where are they now?" Marianne asked.

"Probably still in the mountains, gathering supplies for the journey north."

"Let's go," Marianne said. "We don't have much time before they find us."

"You're right. Konrad found us. He crossed the water."

"Yes, the trained trappers wear special shoes and pants to cross water if they have to."

"Trained trappers," Emery scoffed.

Marianne shrunk into herself hearing Emery's scowl.

Visla wrapped supplies in blankets and tied them into knots, fashioning them into makeshift bags to be carried suspended on wooden poles or on their backs. Thomas, Elena, and Visla each hauled one as they left the valley. Even though her wound still hurt, Emery kept it to herself. She insisted she felt better and wanted to walk, but Konrad shook his head with such force she just laughed and let him carry her.

Marianne walked more slowly than usual, but looked much better. Visla smiled every time she looked at her. Thomas and Elena walked side by side, looking forward to exploring outside the valley. Emery guessed they had explored it many times already and were ready to experience new scenery. Elena had inspected every scraggly bush and flower in the valley, touching and smelling them in awe and wonder. Thomas, fascinated with the night sky, spent the nights gazing at the stars and slept a few hours during the day. He was looking forward to seeing more stars. Both siblings were eager to leave and see what else was out there. Before leaving, Elena picked up a yellow flower and brought it to Marianne.

"I know it's not a rose, but I thought you might still enjoy it," she said, placing the flower into Marianne's hand.

Marianne took the flower between her fingers and brought it to her nose. The flower didn't have a strong or super sweet smell, but she must have liked it, because her eyes shone while she was admiring its delicate petals and its rich color.

Visla walked by her mother, and at one point, took her hand in hers. Marianne did not take her hand away, although in the beginning, her stiff hand looked awkward in Visla's smaller and softer hand. But just a while later, the warmth of Visla's hand pervaded her gray body, thawing her from inside, and causing a sensation she didn't want to end. She relaxed her hand, which fit more naturally in her daughter's clasp. As she strode holding hands with her child, her stride gained a bit more lift.

They walked east for several hours and into the night until Visla stopped by a small hill covered with a few shrubs and trees. They camped without making a fire to avoid attracting attention. Konrad had laid Emery on the blankets, Visla spread out for her under a small tree, and then lay by her side. She took his hand and held it tight and soon fell asleep, despite the throbbing pain in her belly.

Visla stopped by and touched Emery's forehead, noticing droplets of sweat.

"What?" Konrad whispered.

"She might have a fever. I must collect some herbs tomorrow to put on her wound."

"Fever?"

"Yes. She is hot. Feel her forehead."

Konrad touched Emery's head. "Is that bad? Why?"

"The wound may be infected. That's what Emery told me when I got hurt. She made Omana spread an herbal paste on my wound. It helped. I'll do it tomorrow."

"How did you learn my language?" Konrad asked. "No other wildlings know it."

"Emery taught me. I taught her ours."

"I see."

The next morning, Visla came to Emery's side and opened her jacket. Emery was still sleeping when Visla inspected her injury, alarmed to see yellow pus oozing out of the red and swollen wound. Emery was hot to the touch. Gently, Visla spread the paste on the affected area. Emery moaned, winced, and woke up.

"I'm done," Visla said. "Rest a while longer. I'll be right back with a berry cake for you."

"I'm not hungry. I'm okay. We can go now."

Visla ignored her, shook her head, and left.

Emery moaned again.

"You are in pain," Konrad guessed.

"A little," she said and grabbed his hand. "Better now."

He held her hand and then did something that surprised him more than anything else he had done so far. He kissed her hand. When he looked up at her, her blue eyes glistened with tears. She touched his cheek and felt him shiver.

They walked the entire next day, stopping for brief water and snack breaks. Konrad carried Emery, who demanded to be put down whenever she woke up from her feverish dreams.

"I can walk. Put me down."

"No."

In the early afternoon, they could already see the mountains in the distance. In his excitement, Thomas paid no attention to his step and kept tripping over rocks. Elena couldn't keep her mouth closed, awed by the beauty of the mountains. "What's that white substance on top?"

"It's snow," Visla said.

"Snow. Snow is ... real?"

"Of course it's real. You'll soon get to see it up close. Touch it, even," Visla said.

Marianne walked by Visla, and after a while, she took her daughter's hand and was rewarded by her radiant smile.

By evening, they reached the foothills of the mountains and set up their camp. Again, with no fire. Visla put more paste on Emery's wound and sat by her side. Konrad guessed from the way she glanced at him that she wanted to speak with Emery alone. He rose quietly and left.

"How are you? And don't lie to me. I can tell you are in pain. Your wound is infected, and you have a fever. I don't know what else I can do."

"It hurts. I won't lie to you, but I'll get better. My body heals faster. You know that ..."

"I know. You've told me. But you also told me about the ... inter thing ..."

"Internal injuries? I think I'm okay. It doesn't feel like anything important was punctured. It's just the blade was long ..." Seeing Visla's expression, Emery regretted saying the last part.

"You don't know that. We must go even faster tomorrow so we can catch up with my people and Omana. She knows herbs and roots you can grind and drink and get better. And some of the spiny bushes for her potions only grow in the mountains."

They withdrew for a moment, comfortable in their silence.

"Is he really your Peter?"

Emery nodded and teared up. The fever made her more emotional. "I think he's starting to remember me. Remember us."

"Is that even possible? How?"

"I don't know. Just a year ago, I wouldn't have believed a fraction of the things that have happened to me. I was just a regular American girl who didn't believe in fairy tales. Sometimes I think I am dreaming. I can't explain it, but I know it's him. I feel it's him."

"Hmm. I think I know. When I first saw Marianne, I felt a connection to her," Visla said and sighed. "I hope she remembers me and my father soon. I hope she remembers her real name."

"She will with your help. I can see the difference in her already— she is not as cold. I see the way she looks at you and how she is drawn to you. I think she remembers being your mother," Emery said, and her mind immediately slumped into a resentment mode, thinking about her mother. *Would she have gone through with it if Zoe hadn't pushed her into the capsule, or would she have returned to me? Mothers are not supposed to abandon their children, no matter how noble the cause may be.*

"You think so?" Visla smiled. "You must sleep now. We'll have a long day ahead of us tomorrow. Rest. I'll call your Peter back," she added, winking.

Konrad came back and lay beside Emery. She pressed her face against his chest, which, although not as warm as a normal human body, felt comforting in its familiarity. She wanted to ask him so many questions, but lacked the right words. For her, it had been just a few months since he'd held her in his arms. For him, it was centuries.

I'll ask tomorrow, she decided, closing her heavy eyelids.

23

TROUBLED REUNION

B ut the next day, she didn't get the chance to ask. Visla's pace kept everyone focused on not tripping on sharp rocks and falling off the ravines while navigating the winding switchbacks and climbing the steep inclines. Elena kept glancing at the peak of the mountain, hoping to see the snow, but it was hidden behind hazy clouds. The crisp morning air turned laden with moisture and heavy as they climbed higher into the clouds. Thomas noticed Konrad had slowed his pace and volunteered to carry Emery for a while.

He refused, but Thomas insisted. "It's better I carry her for a bit than carry you. If you completely exhaust yourself, you'll be of no use to her. Let me."

Konrad reluctantly relinquished Emery into Thomas's arms. He trusted him. He'd seen him carry her effortlessly and with gentleness. And yet he stayed close behind him, watching his every step.

The group of fugitives increased the pace even more, following Visla's lead, who seemed to fly up the mountain as if she had suddenly gained wings. The sun hid behind the sharp peaks, and the air became sharp with coldness and stung everyone's lungs. It was getting difficult to walk with the darkness setting around them, but

Visla pressed on. She knew the way and shouted warnings back at them when she noticed a sharp bend, a rock on the path, or a treacherous hole in the ground.

Just before a turn that would have put them past the ridge, Visla stopped suddenly, putting a finger on her lips.

"Wait here," she whispered. "We are close to my father's camp. I'll talk to my people and be right back."

Thomas carefully positioned Emery on the blanket Konrad had spread for her and then peeked around the bend. He saw a fire in the distance.

Emery woke up and looked at Konrad in confusion. "Where are we?"

"We are close to Visla's people. She went to talk to them."

"Someone should have gone with her. I don't quite trust her father. He might not let her go."

Marianne, hearing that, started following Visla, but Elena stopped her.

"Wait. That girl knows how to handle herself. She is quite resourceful and resolute. You should wait and let her talk to her people."

An hour passed, and then another. Marianne paced back and forth between Elena and Thomas—who sat by Emery—and Konrad, who alternated between keeping watch and checking on Emery.

"We should see what—" Elena started saying, but a man's voice from behind the bend interrupted her.

Konrad had just returned to Emery's side and had not seen them coming, and his jaws clenched as he admonished himself for carelessness.

Visla emerged, accompanied by her father carrying a torch, and Omana, carrying her medicine bag. Omana hurried to Emery's side, glanced at her pale face, touched her feverish forehead, and shook her head. She opened Emery's jacket and tried to see her wound, but it was too dark. Thomas approached and directed a beam of light on her injury. At first, Omana was taken aback, recognizing the gun in his hand as a weapon that had killed many of her tribe members in the past. But as she gazed into his eyes, she relented and inspected the wound with his help.

When Visla's father saw Marianne, he stopped and stared at her with his mouth agape. He started to say something, then stopped. Marianne stood still, letting him observe her.

"It can't be. Nobody comes back from there," he whispered in his language. "And if you do, it's only to kidnap one of us." He approached Marianne and brought his torch close to her face. She winced but remained still and calm. Expressionless. Emery watched their interaction, holding her breath. Visla stood behind them, watching, but Emery couldn't see her face. Was she worried about what her father would do or what her mother, now Marianne, would do?

"Lannea?" Lach asked, uncertainty in his voice. "Is it you?"

Hearing her previous name, Marianne staggered a little, stepping back. She touched her twitching cheek as if checking if she was awake or real.

"She's not my Lannea," he delivered his assessment in a somber tone. Only Emery and Visla understood him. Lannea folded her hands and was still staring at him with an unreadable expression. The siblings and Konrad waited for a translation. Konrad, tense and focused, watched Lach like a lion ready to pounce on its prey.

"She is different. Changed. I don't know this woman and don't want her in my camp. I don't want any of them in my camp. Tell them. They can take the *charnicha*—the white devil—with them," he growled, staring at Emery.

Konrad sensed his unfriendly tone and slowly moved his hand closer to the pocket that held his gun.

"No, Konrad. You don't need to do that," Emery whispered. "Everything is going to be okay."

"Let's go, Visla. You are coming back with me. Omana, come," Lach shouted in a raspy voice. "We are not helping the 'bad people' or the white devil."

"Father, I am not coming with you," Visla said calmly. "If you don't want to help, go back. I won't stop you," she added, holding her head high and piercing his gaze with her blue-gray eyes that shone like two steel knives on which the orange torch flames moved as if in a warning dance.

"You are coming with me," Lach said. His tone increased in intensity. Konrad's eyes narrowed.

"Oh, shush, Lach," Omana said, standing up. "You are acting like a stupid child. Your girl did something no one else has done before. She's done the impossible by bringing one of us back. She brought your woman back from the dead—the mother of your child. Now, be grateful and welcome her and the people who helped her, regardless of their looks, and stop behaving like a child. These people do not look like they want to hurt us."

Lach had never been told off before. He now stood with his mouth open, startled and insecure. The medicine woman stood up to him. Lach seemed unsure of himself, gripping his torch tightly. Omana ignored him and addressed Visla as if the girl had suddenly grown up and become a leader.

"Let's get her back to camp," she said and gestured for Thomas to pick up and carry Emery. Thomas obliged the formidable old woman without understanding what she and everyone else had been saying, and was ready to follow her. Konrad didn't move, watching Lach, whose wide eyes kept moving from Omana to Visla. Lach gripped his torch in both hands and, with his feet planted firm, plopped himself smack in the middle of the trail, preventing Thomas and Elena from getting past him. Omana pushed her way past Thomas and nudged Lach out of the way. "Move, fool. She needs my help, and quickly."

"I can't let you do that," Lach said, recovering his voice. "They're not going to my camp."

"It's not your camp," Omana and Visla said at once. "It is our camp."

"You are forgetting something, Lach," Omana said. "A long time ago, our tribe agreed that the tribal medicine elders overruled the current leader if the leader endangered the life of one of our people. This is a rule that we've always obeyed, and you can't break it, otherwise—"

"Otherwise, the tribe might take your leadership away and elect a new leader," Visla finished Omana's sentence. "Move, Father. A tribe member needs help, and you are endangering her."

"She's not a tribe member," Lach shouted.

"She became part of our clan when she saved your daughter's life. Everyone agreed and accepted her, except for you. You need to work out what is clouding the good judgment that you've always had. Visla told us they saved her. They endangered their own lives to save your daughter and your woman. They were victims too, escaping the real 'bad people'."

Omana pushed her way past him and turned around, making sure Thomas went through. "Let's go," she said. Thomas didn't understand her language but understood what she expected of him and followed. So did Elena. Visla took Marianne's hand and followed. Omana waited for Konrad, who was still standing, watching Lach.

"Let's go. He won't attack you. He is not that stupid."

Visla translated what Omana said. "She's right. She's right about everything. Come on, Konrad."

He slowly moved forward, still vigilant, still observing Lach from the corner of his eye.

Lach threw up his hands in resignation. "You'll regret it. We will all regret bringing them into our camp. They will only bring us bad luck."

The group moved up the trail and toward the distant campfire. As they got closer, they could see people wandering around the camp. Some were standing and waiting for them. The women stood back, holding their curious children behind them, gawking at the outsiders. The men were watchful, their bodies unnaturally still and tense, scrutinizing the strangers as they walked past. When they saw Konrad, they tensed even more, and their hands slid down to their pockets, where their knives rested. One man narrowed his eyes and clenched his knife. Urus, who stood by him, touched him on the shoulder and whispered something in his ear. The man relaxed a little and glanced at Marianne. Konrad took no notice of them, following Thomas, who, unsure where to go, stopped. Omana directed Lina to help her care for Emery and then pointed to a tent. Thomas carried Emery inside.

Omana was right. Although people stared at Thomas curiously, no one protested when he carried Emery inside the tent—Emery was one of their tribe members. Whatever Lach had told them about Emery didn't stick.

Lach's father, Meius, approached Marianne and looked at her with astonishment.

"Lannea. It's really you. I'm glad you are back," he said, extending his hand toward her.

"I am sorry, I don't remember you … yet," she answered him in his language and offered her hand, matching his gesture. The old man enveloped her hand in both of his. "It doesn't matter. I remember you," he said and added, looking around the camp as if soliciting a response. "Everyone remembers you. You were a good wife to my son and a good mother to my granddaughter."

Some nodded hesitantly, some didn't react at all, and some whispered to each other, eyeing Marianne. Children poked their heads from behind their mother, peeking at the strangers.

Lach stood farther away, hiding in the shadows of the night. He didn't object or approve. Soon, a small crowd gathered around Lannea, staring at her with curiosity but without prejudice. A woman, Lannea's age stepped forward and touched her hand. "Do you remember me? I'm your friend, Mora. You must tell me if you need anything. It's good you're back with us. This is where you belong, Lannea."

Lannea listened to the woman, looking her in the eyes. "I remember your eyes."

Mora smiled, showing her white teeth. "You remembered me."

"You remember Mora, but not me, your man?" Lach came out of hiding, pointing a finger at Lannea. "Maybe it was a good thing they took you away," he hissed; his eyes shone with fury. Then he turned around and left.

Visla rushed to her mother's side. "I don't know what's with him, but you mustn't worry. I'll talk to him. He'll come around."

"Maybe," Lannea said, not too convinced. She stared as he walked away into the night that swallowed him like a dark cloud.

Moments later, Thomas and Elena found a spot by the fire. Not friendly, but not outwardly hostile, the tribe watched them. Visla sat by her mother. Lach was nowhere to be seen, but nobody searched for him.

Konrad stood by the fire, glancing at the tent where Emery was tended by the two women. Visla noticed his stare, got up, and gestured for him to follow. "You want to see her, don't you?"

He nodded and followed her. "Why do they keep calling her Lannea?"

"That was her name before they kidnapped her."

"I see. It fits her."

Emery rested on a bed of wool blankets. Omana was smearing a paste on Emery's inflamed wound. Lina sat by Emery's side, holding a wooden cup full of steaming liquid. Emery smiled at seeing Konrad and Visla.

"They are taking good care of me. Except this thing tastes like shit," Emery said with an exaggerated grimace. "I'll be better by tomorrow. You'll see."

The two women finished tending to Emery, covered her with blankets, and left, glancing curiously at Konrad. Omana's lips curved into a good-natured smile. She muttered something as she was leaving the tent, glancing at him and Emery. Visla heard her and grinned. She kneeled by Emery's side and gently patted her arm. "I know you'll be as good as new tomorrow. Omana is a magician, and you heal like a cat, you said. I'll leave you two alone now. Goodnight."

Visla kissed Emery on her forehead and stood up. "Make sure she's nice and cozy tonight," she said to Konrad and winked at Emery.

Konrad lay by Emery, folded his arms around her, and buried his face in her hair.

"Your hair. It has a smell. Fragrant, like ... like the flowers we saw on the way here."

"You smelled the flowers?" Emery chuckled.

"I remembered something."

"What?"

"I remembered another woman. Glimpses of her. I thought it was you at first, but her hair was black, and so were her eyes."

"It was my mother. Olesya. You remembered her."

"Your mother?"

"You loved her, too. For years, I believed she was dead. I'd been told she had died in an accident. Years later, I found you, and you helped me find out what truly happened to her. And that is when we fell in love. Do you remember that?"

"No. But when I look into your eyes, my chest is not big enough to draw breath. In those moments, I feel we are connected through space and time. When I am with you, the boundaries of time fade when I grasp or maybe only glimpse the tie that binds us together. It could've been yesterday, hundreds of years ago, or thousands of years in the future. You are my time. You are my universe. I spent hundreds of years alone and was fine, and now I can't stay away from you, even for a moment. You have power over me; you pull me in. Is that what love is?"

"I think so. Before I met you, I felt nothing like it. The moment I saw you when I was spying on you through the windows, I knew you were in this universe for me, and I knew I was in trouble."

"Why?"

"Because you loved my mother. And I thought she loved you. That's why I convinced myself that I was doing something very wrong, inappropriate, and wicked by falling in love with you. I felt guilty, as if I was betraying my mother, even though you two were never together, but despite the guilt, I couldn't stay away from you."

"Can't you love two people at once?"

Emery's smile broke through her tears that flashed in her eyes. "I don't know. Maybe. Yes, but differently. You can love many people. You can love them like a brother, sister, mother, lover, or friend. But for many people, the special love is only shared with the special one. If you are lucky enough to find them."

"You are my special one, then," he said and touched her cheek.

24

TROUBLE ON THE HORIZON

Emery was true to her word and felt better the next morning. And it showed. The color returned to her cheeks, and her appetite matched that of a lioness. Omana checked her wound and smiled, nodding and mumbling something unintelligible. The wound was still pink, but the swelling and the pus were almost gone. Visla ran into the tent carrying sheep's milk and berry cakes. Emery inhaled her food, while Konrad watched her in fascination. His throat moved as if he were swallowing the food with her.

"How is your father?" Emery asked with her mouth full of cake.

"I don't know. He is not at the camp. He left last night. Nobody knows where he is."

"Sometimes we want to be alone when going through something traumatic."

"Traumatic? I don't know this word yet."

"When something upsets people. When people die or disappear or stop loving one another," Emery said, throwing a shy glance at Konrad. "Or sometimes, even when people are very happy, they get overwhelmed with emotions and can't be around other people who are not experiencing the same."

"So you think he is happy that my mother is back?"

"I don't know. Maybe part of him is and part isn't. Or perhaps he mourned for her and thought of her as being dead. And now she is back, but different. Give him time."

Visla left, thinking about what Emery had said. She was about to look for her father, but now she was uncertain what to do.

That day and the next were spent around the camp. Thomas, seeing the men gather wood for the fire, joined them. They mostly ignored him, however, and watched him when he wasn't looking. The women gathered in a tight circle, whispering and glancing at Elena and Lannea. Finally, Omana stepped out and motioned for Lannea and Elena to come. The women watched curiously as the changed walked toward them. Without hesitation, Mora took Lannea's hand and asked her to join them. Visla smiled lightly, knowing it was Omana's idea to involve them in food collection and preparation, even though she was perfectly aware they didn't eat.

Elena examined everything, smelled everything, and even tried to taste a red berry, but quickly dropped it, and wiped her hand on her tunic. The women sang the names of the foods in their melodic language, and Elena repeated them joyfully, like a child learning a new skill. Visla's lyrical language sounded natural when spoken by her.

Lach was not back. But the tribe seemed not to miss him or feel the need to look for him. Life in the camp proceeded as usual, except for the men's furtive glances at Konrad and, less so, at Thomas.

On the third morning, Emery awoke to loud shouting and screaming. Konrad got up and peeked outside. "They are shouting at something or someone. I'll check. I'll be right back."

Emery didn't wait. She was tired of staying in bed. Both the redness and the fever were gone, and the wound was healing. True to her nature, she was recovering quickly. She felt strong enough to walk around without hobbling or holding her stomach.

As Emery left the tent, she saw two dark shadows moving on the ground. Emery squinted at the sky. Two black birds circled above them. Women and children screamed in panic, men shouted, and gathered spears and knives.

"They found us," Emery whispered. "How? You turned off your tablets, right?"

"Yes, we all did," Konrad said with certainty.

"Do you carry any other tracking devices?"

"Huh?"

"Something in your bodies, perhaps? Like an electronic chip?"

"Oh, I see what you mean. No, the earpieces are trackable, but we destroyed them all."

"We must leave immediately," Visla shouted, running toward Emery. "They found us. Gather whatever you can, and let's go," she added, looking at Konrad.

He nodded. "Show me what I need to pack," he said to Emery, heading back to the tent.

Emery was lost in her thoughts; her forehead furrowed with a disturbing suspicion. "Is your father back yet?" she shouted at Visla, who was already running back to her tent to pack. She shook her head in reply and kept running.

Emery pointed, and Konrad packed blankets, knives, and food into leather bags. Then they joined the rest of the group, already packed and heading out. They all had somber expressions and avoided looking at the newcomers.

They think we brought the birds. That we betrayed them.

Thomas and Elena joined Konrad and Emery at the end of the procession. Visla and Lannea joined them later. They appeared distraught.

"What's the matter?" Emery asked.

"Her tablet is missing," Visla said, pointing at her mother.

Emery's face turned white. "When did you notice it missing?"

"Not until today, after we started packing."

"Was it turned off?"

"Yes. Of course." Lannea seemed hurt by her question.

"Pushing the button turns it on, doesn't it? Anyone can do it?" Emery asked merely to hear it from Lannea. She knew how easy it was to operate.

"Yeah, it's very easy."

Emery said nothing and slowed down, letting Visla and her mother move further ahead of them. Then she whispered to Konrad. "Are you good at tracking people?"

"Tracking?"

"Finding people who might hide behind the group, following from a distance."

Konrad glanced at her, surprised. His surprise quickly gave way to understanding, as if he had read her mind.

"You think that ..."

"Yes. I do."

Konrad searched Emery's eyes, hesitating.

"Go. I'll be okay. I feel fine. The pain is gone. I'm almost completely healed."

Elena turned around as Konrad was leaving and gave Emery a questioning look.

"Later. I'll tell you later. Let's walk and not attract attention," Emery whispered.

At one point, Visla turned around and, not seeing Konrad by Emery, fell back, waiting for Emery to catch up to her.

"Where is Konrad?"

"He went back to get me another blanket. I'll need as many as possible going north."

Visla regarded her somberly, then muttered. "You are not a good liar, Emery. Tell me the truth."

Emery sighed and couldn't find the words to tell her what she suspected.

"Tell me," Visla insisted. Emery pursed her lips.

Visla studied Emery's pained face and paled. "You think that my father ..."

Emery nodded and averted her eyes.

"And Konrad went to find him?"

"Yes. But don't worry. He won't harm him."

As they walked for two hours, heading northeast, the terrain became tougher to traverse. Fallen trees and thick brush slowed their pace but covered their footprints, and the trees, taller and thicker now, hid them from the birds. There were other, easier routes, but they chose this one, knowing they'd be harder to spot. They climbed higher and higher, and at one point, they reached an area where fresh snow covered the ground. Elena and Thomas couldn't help themselves and touched it. The coldness, the softness, and the flakiness surprised them. Thomas took some in his hands and watched it melt. "What's this?"

"It's snow. I remember it," Elena said.

"Remember what? Snow?" Thomas asked.

"I remember seeing it. I remember snow and a green tree full of lights and bright round balls."

"You remember the Christmas tree," Emery said.

"Christmas tree?"

"Yeah, during the winter—"

Shouts interrupted Emery's description of Christmas. Lach was shouting. "Leave me alone. No one will believe you anyway. Get your dark hands off me, you devil!"

Everyone turned and saw Konrad pushing Lach in front of him. Lach's hands were tied behind his back with a thin gray bracelet. Konrad ignored his shouts and held him in an iron grip, pushing him into the middle of the group. Surrounded by his clan, Lach stopped yelling and looked defiantly around. "Tell them what you did," Konrad ordered.

Lach didn't understand English, but he understood what he was asked. "You tell them," he said, sneering. "They won't believe a word coming out of your dark mouth."

Visla stared at his father as he strained, trying to free himself from Konrad's grip, and, noticing something, lurched at him, reached into his pocket, and pulled out a small tablet. Her mother's tablet. "Tell them what you did," she said to him in her native language, narrowing her eyes. "Tell your people what you did out of hate and stupidity." The longer she glared at him, the more disdain and disappointment showed in her eyes.

He stood facing his daughter, searching for forgiveness in her stormy eyes. Seeing only scorn, he shut his eyes, emitted a hollow moan, and fell to his knees.

"They wouldn't harm you," he cried, looking around his tribe. "They'll just take them back and leave us alone. We could go back to the way we were before the white devil came. As long as they are with us, the 'bad people' will follow until they get them back. I did it to protect us all. They don't belong with us. I don't want them here. Nobody wants them here." Lach's shouts turned into sobs.

"They wouldn't do anything to me? Have you forgotten that I almost died?" Visla hissed. Her lips trembled as she gazed at her father, whose slender body spasmed in sobs. "They are enraged by our escape. They'll kill us all without hesitation or remorse."

Lach kept sobbing; his stare was fastened to the ground.

"He stole it from her," Visla said, showing everyone the tablet and pointing at her mother. "He took it from her and made it so it would tell the birds where we were. He wanted to make it look like they had betrayed us. But it was my father, your leader, who betrayed us all."

Visla turned to her father. "You are no longer our leader. The tribe will decide whether they want you to stay or ban you forever. I, for one, do not want to look at you. You disgust me."

A circle of angry stares surrounded Lach, who was kneeling and quietly sobbing. He avoided people's stares, especially his daughter's.

Visla gave the tablet back to her mother. "Make sure it's off," she said in English.

"I'd already turned it off when I found him," Konrad said.

"Let's not waste more time," Meius said, glancing at his son with distress. "We must go now. Get up, son. We'll cast our judgment on you later."

The stars were already up in the sky when they finally made camp. Emery refused to be carried, even though she longed to be in Konrad's arms. Fueled by anger at Lach for betraying everyone, but mostly for hurting Visla, Emery walked fast. Visla walked by her side with her head hung low. Even in the night's darkness, Emery saw that her face was sunken in sorrow. Not anger, but sorrow. Regret. She had just gotten her mother back, but instead of celebrating, she was mourning the loss of her father.

Nobody set up their tents that night but covered the children and themselves with blankets and slept in brief intervals, interrupted by the sounds of the forest.

"Why did he do it?" Konrad whispered as they lay under a tree, bundled in blankets. "Why would he risk the lives of his people?"

Emery didn't respond right away. "I think he's hurting and has been since they took Lannea away from him and Visla, and it finally broke him. The pain transformed into misdirected anger. This is the downside of human emotions. When we are hurting, we do things that might be construed as hateful and selfish, while in reality, they may be just cries for help or simply self-defense. You'll understand when you remember more."

"When or if?"

"When. You already remember more. Every day, you remember more."

Emery paused and looked away. Her eyes glazed over as she slowly turned toward Konrad. "What I don't understand and what bothers me is the abysmal hate that Mister E and his son carry. If the change involved the obliteration of emotions, why can they still hate?" She asked and then added in a barely audible voice. "Can you ... hate?"

Konrad said nothing for a long time, staring into the distance. "I'm not sure," he said finally. "I know what the word means, but I don't think I've ever ... experienced it. If I have, I don't remember it."

The entire next day, the tribe and the newcomers walked. Nobody talked, nobody laughed, and people avoided looking at each other. They had to make a tough decision. Punish Lach and cast him away, or forgive and let him stay. The tribe was already small, and losing another member meant more work for the others. Besides, Lach had been a good leader for a long time. Fair and level-headed.

Visla kept close to her mother and Emery. She was quiet and kept her gaze on the trail ahead. Her red-rimmed eyes and dark rings spoke of a sleepless and haunted night.

Emery's hands twisted into fists. You stupid, stupid fool! Look what you've done to her.

They stopped in a valley surrounded by trees. Snow patches covered the higher areas, and the air held a crisp promise of more of it coming. Emery inhaled deeply, recognizing the familiar scent of pines. It filled her lungs with the woody, resinous and slightly sweet perfume of the forest. It calmed her frayed nerves. She wasn't looking forward to the task ahead. Despite what Lach did, she hadn't stopped liking him or even admiring him for his desire to protect his clan.

The atmosphere within the tribe was grave as they readied to pass judgment on Lach. Visla was silent, going about the chores of making camp and preparing food. Emery noticed her lips were pursed, and her hands trembled as she mixed the grains with water and milk to make her cakes. But she didn't console her, knowing the girl well enough that she needed to be alone before making the toughest decision of her life.

After everyone gobbled their food, they called Lach, who sat alone at the camp's edge, staring at the mountains. He had lost his confidence—the expression on his ashen face was grave and even sad. He kept his eyes on the ground as he walked to his trial. Not once did he glance at his daughter or anyone else.

Meius stood up, and silence descended on the camp as everyone looked up at him.

"We are gathered here to vote on whether to keep Lach in the camp or banish him. Everyone knows what he's done, but I will repeat it, so everyone is clear. Lach stole the thing from Lannea that calls the birds and tells the 'bad people' where we are," he said, and then turned to Lach. "Are you admitting your guilt, Lach?"

Lach slowly nodded, but didn't look up or say anything.

"Speak up, son."

"Yes. I do."

"I will not ask why you did that. That is between you and your conscience. I will ask only if you regret it. Before we vote, anyone can ask you questions or speak on your behalf."

Lach said nothing, and his father didn't press him. Complete silence enveloped the camp, broken only by the crackling fire. He finally looked up and focused his gaze on Visla.

"Forgive me, my daughter. I was only trying to protect you from these monsters."

Visla replied quickly. "The people you call monsters have repeatedly saved my life. They are my friends and my family. If you wish for me to keep calling you my father, you must accept them into the tribe," she said slowly and then cleared her throat, trying to keep her voice from breaking. "And into your heart. Because I love them all."

"Cast me away then, because I can't let them into my heart. Ever," he roared, staring at her, wide-eyed.

Visla's face tightened as she turned away from her father and sat on the ground, facing away.

"Does anyone have questions for Lach?" Meius asked.

Nobody said anything. Lach's father was about to start the voting, but Emery put her hand up.

"I have a question," she said, looking at Lach. "Well, more of a statement than a question," she mumbled.

He didn't look at her. The silence deepened as everyone stopped breathing.

"Lach. You accepted me into your camp and into your heart when I most needed it. If it weren't for your daughter, you, and your tribe, I wouldn't have survived." Emery started in a shaky voice. "You behaved like a true and noble leader, accepting a stranger who looked and behaved so differently from everyone you knew. Only the best of us can shed their prejudice to save lives. You've done it at least once; you can do it again. Because it's in you. The mercy, the forgiveness, and the compassion are all in you. You have it. You just have to reach deep down into your soul and find it again. For Visla. For your daughter, whom you love more than the prejudice you hold against people you don't even know. You are asking her to choose between you, her father, and her mother, whom she mourned and longed for all her life. She can't. Don't make her, because if you do, her life will no longer be the same. You'll take something away from her that can't be replaced and give her a burden she'll have to carry on her shoulders all her life."

As she spoke, his head raised slowly, and he glanced at Visla, who, hearing Emery speak, turned to face her father. She met his gaze, and something happened to him when he looked into his daughter's teary eyes. He started sobbing. The deep, tearless sobs writhed through his chest, shaking his entire body. But this time, the sobs were not those born of anger and hate, but of love and guilt.

"I am sorry, my daughter. I am so sorry. Somehow, somewhere, I lost my way. Still lost, but not lost enough to want to lose you or hurt you. No longer will I push you to choose, but I will leave the tribe instead and not stand between you and your mother. Forgive me, child. If you can. For everything. For lying to you ..."

Visla did not answer. She sat unmoving, seemingly untouched, as if she'd not heard him. Every single eye was on her. She still didn't move, staring into the fire. Even the newcomers, who couldn't understand the words being spoken, felt the gravity of the situation. They felt the heartwarming urge in Emery's voice. They heard the sorrow in Lach's voice. But they were waiting for Visla's answer.

Lach's father broke the silence once it became unbearable.

"Does anyone else want to speak on Lach's behalf?"

Nobody spoke. "It's time to vote. Anyone who wants Lach gone from the tribe, raise your hand."

Three people raised their hands. Two younger men and one woman. Everyone still had their eyes on Visla. She moved her hand, and the air became laden with heavy silence as everyone held their breath in anticipation, expecting her to cast her father away. But she stood up and spoke. Her voice was steady now. She looked him in the eye.

"I forgive you, Father. For everything. I know you wanted to protect me, and I know you are hurting. I'd do anything for you to stop hurting except renounce my mother and my friends. If you can accept that, I don't want you going anywhere. I want my father with me. Forever. Will you accept them?"

The father and daughter locked eyes, and the silence held everyone captive in its crippling grip. Lach nodded, and a stream of tears escaped his eyes and soaked into his tunic. "I will," he said in a voice hoarse from crying.

The fire flickered as the breath was exhaled out of the lungs of the spectators. And with that, the tension dissipated. The children went back to their chatter and protests as their mothers tried to tuck them in for the night. Lach remained on his knees. Visla walked to him and extended her hand. He wiped his tears, took her hand gently, carefully, and got up. Still trembling, he opened his arms coyly, tenderly. She fell into his arms, stayed there long enough to allay his sobs, and then led him away. He looked more like a child now, being led by his mother after being scolded and forgiven. Omana searched and found Emery's eyes and grinned at her with her wise, brown eyes sparkling like amber in the sun.

"What happened?" Konrad asked Emery.

"She forgave him."

Konrad looked worried. "They're not casting him out?"

"No."

"What if he tries something again?"

"I think he learned his lesson."

"Maybe we should destroy all our tablets?"

"No," Emery protested with so much force that Konrad looked at her with surprise.

"Why not?"

"We might still need them."

"For what?" Konrad turned his entire body to look at her, and a shadow passed over his face and eyes when he saw her expression.

Emery fidgeted.

"Tell me."

She took a deep breath. "Do you remember when we passed the lab, and I stopped to look at something?"

Konrad's forehead wrinkled as he tried to remember. "Yes, I remember."

"When I went back, I stopped there and picked up a sign."

"A sign?"

"A door sign. It used to hang on the door of the office. It had the name of the person whose office it was."

Konrad looked confused. Emery pulled the sign from her pocket. The flames immediately caught the shiny piece, reflecting their red tongues on its surface, as if wanting to destroy it. Konrad took it and looked at it blankly. "Olesya? Your mother?"

"My mother's last name was Solensky."

"Do you think this was your mother's office?"

Emery nodded.

"It could be a coincidence. People share names, don't they?"

Emery didn't answer, but pulled the photograph from her pocket and handed it to him.

Konrad looked at the photo for a long time. Emery could see a flash of recognition on his face.

"It's Olesya. I remember her sitting across from me at a table. She was crying and saying something, and then she jumped up and ran away. That's the only memory I have of her."

"I must go back, Konrad."

"Why?"

Emery struggled to explain it to someone who didn't remember his parents and the love he felt for them.

"Because I want to know if she was ... involved in inventing and implementing the change. I must know that because I can't go on living without knowing. It may be hard for you to understand. Believe me, I don't want to go back there. Part of me doesn't want to find out."

"What if she played a part in it? What would you do? How would that change things?"

"I don't know. But I must know."

Konrad was silent for a moment, observing her with his piercing eyes. "When do you want to go back?" he asked quietly after a heavy pause.

"As soon as Visla and everyone else have safely traveled north. After I'm sure they'll all get along."

"I promised you I would help you find the truth. But I didn't think you wanted to go back so soon. I thought we had months or even years to think about it and plan it. It's dangerous. They are on high alert, searching for us everywhere."

"And in the meantime, they'll kidnap more people and change them or kill them. They must be stopped."

"And you intend to stop them how?"

"I don't know. I must find out how and why it all happened. Then, I'll know ..."

"Two people can't fight hundreds of highly trained, professional soldiers who'll kill you without hesitation. And I wouldn't be able to help you because I'd be dead long before you."

"I realize it's dangerous. But would they expect us back there? Or would they send everybody they could out on the surface to find us? We went back to get Visla and her mother. Now, there is nobody left there for us to go back for."

"I don't know how to find what you want to know. We'd have to get to one of the Masters alone. But they are heavily guarded. And since your last visit, there'll be more guards around them. We'd need to think this through. We might need some sort of distraction," Konrad said, and immediately started thinking of a plan. He might not have liked the idea of endangering her, but she noticed the challenge excited him. What the Masters had done to him and others incited his need for justice. He craved the challenge of outsmarting the villains and then bringing them to trial if there ever was one.

"Do you know what these things are?" she asked, taking out one of the transparent tablets she'd taken from the lab.

Konrad took it from her and nodded. "Yeah. I know what they are. They are recordings. Where did you get it?"

"The lab. And my mother's office."

"We don't know if it is your mother's office. Not for certain."

"I have a hunch," Emery muttered.

"We are not going back until you've fully recovered."

"Won't be long," she said and looked away.

Konrad could tell something was on her mind. "What is it?"

"When I went to the old lab, I saw something that only my mother could have created. A model of a chamber with a capsule for time travel—"

"For what?"

"Time travel. I came here through a capsule like that."

Seeing the incredulous look on his face, Emery laughed. "You look so handsome when confused. Goofy, but handsome. I realize it's hard to believe, but it is the truth. I'd never lie to you."

"I believe you. I've seen the capsule myself."

"You've seen the time capsule?" This time, Emery's expression was incredulous. "Where? In the old lab?"

"No. In the basement. Underneath the Silver House. It has not been used, and it has been locked for hundreds of years. For a while, it was heavily guarded, but I haven't spent much time in the Silver House for a while, so I don't know if it still is under watch."

"Are you serious? If it's under the Silver House, it has power and—"

"No." Konrad's voice suddenly gained a sharp edge. "It's dangerous. Time travel was forbidden because it could distort the universe."

"Distort the universe, how?"

"I don't know, Emery. I'm not a scientist," he said and paused, then continued with a softer voice. "It has to do with energy transfer through time that stresses the foundation of the universe and its charge, and distorts it in the process. Some argued that if stressed enough, the universe could break or implode on itself."

"I will not do anything stupid and definitely not anything that could cause the world to collapse. You know, I came here to save the world ..." Emery said and regretted it immediately. She wasn't ready to tell him yet. And yet, here she was blabbering about it because her feelings were hurt.

"What do you mean?"

"It's a long story. I'm too tired to tell you tonight. I will. Some other time."

"I doubt the capsule is operational. It's been a while since I was assigned to the Silver House. They might have destroyed the capsule to avoid temptation."

"Ah," Emery said, suddenly feeling tired and deflated. She closed her eyes, and soon her head rolled back on the blanket.

"You're tired. You should sleep," Konrad said and bundled blankets on top and around her, and she fell asleep soon after. He watched her for a while, amazed at how her blonde hair became golden in the fire's light. Then he got up and went for a walk. The conversation with Emery stirred something in him. Whether it was a memory, a longing, or something entirely different, he didn't know. But it was something that would not let him sleep tonight or the next night. He needed very little sleep, but he stayed by Emery's side every night because his mind and his body silently screamed when he was more than a few feet away from her. And he felt an almost primal need to protect her.

He walked around quietly, not to wake anybody. One of the tribe members who kept watch calmly observed him but didn't seem bothered by his moving about the camp. And so he spent the night walking and gazing at stars, thinking about Emery, trying to remember the past, and gluing memories together. The sun was rising when he was about to return to Emery, but halted, seeing something in the distance that hadn't been there a moment ago. He strained his eyes.

And then he bolted back to Emery. "Wake up, Emery. They are coming."

"Who?" Emery asked, her blue eyes still dreamy and her hair tousled from sleep; she looked more beautiful than ever, and for a moment, Konrad forgot about the danger and stared at her, speechless.

"What is it, Konrad?" she asked again, more alert this time.

"They have found us and are coming. We must get up and let everyone know."

"Okay." Emery regained her wits and got up quickly. She ran to the nearest sleeping person and woke them up. "Get up. We need to get ready and leave. The 'bad people' found us. Let everybody know."

She went to several other sleeping tribe members and shook their arms. The rest woke up at the noise of people getting up. Soon, the entire tribe was awake and getting ready to leave.

Lach looked like he'd been hit when he heard the news. "It's all my fault," he said. "It's because of me they found us."

"Let's go, Father." Visla seized Lach's arm and tried to pull him with her to follow the group. But he gently freed himself from her grip. "I must stay behind and protect my tribe. It's all my doing—my anger, my stupidity—I must fix it and fight them."

"No, Father. We must all go. We can escape. There's still time."

"No, there isn't. Tell your mother I'm sorry for the way I behaved."

"Tell me yourself, Lach," Lannea said, taking her gun out of her pocket. "I'm staying with you."

"No, you're not. Both of you are coming with me," Visla cried.

"There's no time, Visla." Emery joined them. "You must take your people—women and children—and go deeper into the mountains. We'll catch up to you after we deal with them."

Visla stared at Emery, blinking rapidly, trying not to cry. But suddenly she felt like a child again, small and vulnerable. "But I can fight. I can help you—"

"I know you can fight. That's why you must go with them and protect them. You have the most important job. Protect the ones who can't protect themselves. Go, Visla, now. Trust me. I'll bring your parents back to you," Emery said, pointing at the women and children staring at them and waiting for directions. "They need you. Go," Emery said, pushing her gently toward the women and children, then turned to Konrad. "How many were there?"

"Around twenty."

Elena watched Visla as she walked toward the group of women and children. Her gait was unsteady and faltering, and she appeared uncertain and scared. Elena ran after her and proclaimed, "You can do it, Visla. You are brave and strong. We'll be back."

Visla was greeted by Omana as she made her way to the group. Seeing the eyes of women and children on her, waiting for directions, Visla straightened her back and addressed the group in a steady voice: "Keep the children close to you. Carry them if you must. Tell me immediately if you need help. Let's go."

25

THE FIGHT

The younger men joined Emery and Konrad, getting their knives and spears ready. Konrad gave Thomas and Elena his extra guns, and they silently took them. Their expressions hardened as they walked toward their enemies like warriors getting ready for a battle.

Konrad was accurate in his estimation. Twenty-one dark figures were approaching fast. Seeing them approach, Emery knew they had made the right decision in sending the women and children ahead. The tribe could not have escaped the long-limbed predators moving effortlessly through the rocky terrain. Like a pack of dark demons, the expressionless figures moved with one purpose—to kill. To murder without hesitation. Without thought or remorse.

Konrad stopped everyone behind a switchback, planning a surprise attack. He directed everyone to hide behind the trees and boulders and not to come out until he gave them a signal, then climbed up the steep rock face. Emery watched him with amazement and affection as he moved up the rock as if he were a mountain goat.

Silence, uninterrupted even by the sounds of birds or wind, befell the forest like a heavy cloak, as if it sensed that the impending battle required a moment of silence before it broke. The tribe and the changed waited, unified by the suspense of the approaching enemy and the fight looming ahead. Elena stood by Thomas, trying not to move. She held her breath, and suddenly, her body started shaking violently. Thomas looked at her and panicked. "What's wrong?" he whispered. "Are you hurt?"

She shook her head and held on to her brother's arm. He gently embraced her, remembering how Emery calmed him with a hug. It took a moment for her to stop shaking in his arms. Then she pulled out. "I'm all right now," she whispered. "Really," she added, seeing Thomas's worried expression. Thomas jerked and looked away, hearing a whistle. They glanced at each other and readied their guns.

From his perch high above ground, Konrad, seeing the enemy approach close enough for an attack, whistled, mimicking an eagle call. Emery, hiding behind a tree, secretly wondered how he had learned to do it in such a short time. Once they were below him, he fired several quick shots at the dark shapes below him. They looked up and returned fire, breaking the rock face and covering themselves in sharp rock flakes and dust that penetrated their eyes.

At that moment, Emery stepped out and thrust her hands forward, sending several of them to the ground. She quickly hid behind the rock, while Lannea, Thomas, and Elena stepped out from the other side and shot at them. Then Lach and five of his men emerged from behind the trees and threw spears at the attackers.

Konrad continued shooting from above, constantly changing positions, jumping from rock to rock like a gazelle. Emery was ready to thrust her hands at the two remaining Minders, but she tripped on a root, cursed, and fell. One o,f the attackers shot Malek, knocking him down. The other one aimed at Emery, trying to shoot her, but Lach threw himself between her and her attacker and fell to the ground, hit in the chest.

Thomas with his gun, and Urus, with his spear, killed the last attacker at the same time. Thomas stared at the gun in his hand as if it were a poisonous snake. Urus approached the Minder he had slain and removed the spear from his body, grimacing in disgust at the gray substance that covered his spear. He wiped his spear in the snow and looked around, ready to plunge his deadly weapon into another Minder, but there was no one else attacking them. He kneeled by his friend's side. "Malek," he said with his voice breaking. Malek moaned, holding his side. Urus paled, seeing the blood pouring out of his body, and then searched for Emery with his eyes.

The gray substance oozing from the dead Minders, when it met the snow, sizzled, evaporating in a misty cloud. Emery stared at it and shuddered, realizing that they were right—moisture could destroy their essence. Then she glanced at Konrad. *I could lose him just like that if moisture ever gets inside him.*

Elena shifted her gaze between the bodies, her gun, and her brother. She shot at them, but she wasn't certain if she had hit anyone. She felt a heavy weight lift off her chest, and she wondered whether it was relief, but didn't know the reason.

Emery ran to Lach, who lay on the ground, motionless, blood spilling out of the hole in his chest. "Why did you do that, Lach? I promised Visla I'd bring you back. You foolish man."

She checked his pulse and exhaled in relief. "He's still alive. We must patch his wound and carry him back. Quickly," she said, and waved at Thomas.

Thomas put his gun away with a sigh of relief and sprinted to Emery. He quickly glued Lach's wound with his gadget. Emery noticed Urus's desperate glance and rushed toward him. She inspected Malek's wound and put her hand on Urus's shoulder. "He'll be all right. We'll fix him," she said and signaled Thomas to come.

Once Thomas was done gluing Malek's wound, two younger tribe members picked Lach up and carried him. Urus wrapped his arm around his friend and helped him walk back.

Konrad climbed down and looked up and down at Emery. "Are you okay?"

"Yes, I am fine. It's Lach who got hurt protecting me. Come on, we need to hurry to catch up with the tribe and have Omana fix his wound."

"Go on," Konrad said. "I must collect all their guns and tablets. I'll catch up."

Emery nodded and ran after the men carrying Lach and joined them in their climb up to reunite with the women and children of the tribe. Men took turns carrying Lach. Even though they walked fast, they didn't catch up to the tribe until early morning. Visla must have been keeping up the pace. The five men who accompanied them, including Malek, kept glancing at Konrad, Elena, and Thomas with reverence, seeing them in a new light. Fighting alongside them, they had not only proven themselves worthy of being part of the tribe but also had formed unbreakable bonds.

When they caught up with the group and Visla saw her father covered in blood, carried by his tribe members, her hand flew to her mouth, and she ran to his side. "What happened?"

"He put himself in front of me. He saved my life."

"Father, don't die. Please, don't die," Visla pleaded, holding his hands.

Emery realized he'd lost too much blood to survive without a blood transfusion. "You know what we must do now?" she whispered to Visla.

"I do," Visla said, and took out a knife from her pocket. "I'll do it first."

"Wait. If we do that, we might change him, just like I changed you with my blood. I'm not sure he'd like that," Emery said, grabbing Visla's hand to stop her. "Maybe we should ask the men to give him their blood?"

"No, he is my father, and I will give him my blood," she said, and, glancing at Emery, added, "Don't worry, I'll take the blame. I think our blood will make him heal faster."

Emery nodded and let Visla cut her wrist and dribble her blood into her father's listless lips.

After Visla had fed enough of her blood into her father to make her lose the color on her face, Emery stopped her. "It's my turn," she said.

"He is my father. You shouldn't have to do this."

"He saved my life. And you've already given him too much. Go find Thomas and ask him to take care of your wrist."

Lach remained lifeless. Emery kept checking his pulse and the wound on his chest. The shot to the right side of his chest must have caused a lot of damage to his lungs. Emery feared he'd suffocate, breathing blood from the punctured lungs, and turned him on his side. *I wish Grandma were here to tell me what to do.*

Visla returned and sat by his side, holding his hand. Emery got up to make room for Lannea, who immediately took her place by Lach's side.

Meius stopped by his son's side. "How is he?"

Emery shrugged. "I don't know." She couldn't lie to him. Lach's chances seemed slim. Meius noticed her grim expression. "Do not feel bad. He'll die with honor and not as a coward who had betrayed his tribe."

"I'm going to do my best so he doesn't," Emery said sourly and left the family alone with Lach.

She found Konrad and Thomas inspecting and counting the weapons and tablets they had taken off the dead Minders. Konrad looked up at her. "We need to keep going. They will know their last location. Ask them if there is a different way to get where they are going."

"Okay. I will ask them," she said, and turned around to leave, but stopped. "How do they work?"

"What?"

"The guns. How do you load them? How do you recharge them?"

"Recharge? I don't know what you mean."

"They obviously can't work forever. They need a power source or something. Do they have bullets?" Emery asked, but seeing his blank expression, she waved her hands. "Never mind."

Emery gathered everyone and relayed what Konrad had just told her. "Is there another way we could go?" she asked them.

"Yes. There is another way, but it's much more difficult," Urus said.

"We must take it. Going slower is better than getting into another ambush. Let's gather everyone and head out," Emery said. "Urus, see to that, will you?"

He nodded and started giving commands while Emery returned to Lach's side. "How is he?"

"The same. Is there anything else we could do?" Visla asked.

"I don't know. But we must get him ready. We are leaving now."

"Leaving now? He is in no condition to go."

"We must go now, Visla. They'll be coming after us, and with more people. We'll carry him."

Lannea got up and extended her arms toward Visla. "Come on, daughter."

Reluctantly, the girl got up and went with her mother, glancing back at Lach.

The group switched course and headed directly north, walking on steeper and treacherous switchbacks but well hidden by the thick vegetation. The birds couldn't see them from above.

They walked until the first stars dotted the night sky. Konrad, accompanied by Urus and Thomas, kept watch on the three exposed sides of the camp. The fourth side rested against a rock face. Emery sat by Visla near Lach's bed of blankets, on which he lay, taking short, gurgling breaths. Emery remembered that lung cancer survivors lived with just one lung after tumor and lung removal operations. There was still a chance he might survive. "Let's turn him over," Emery said. Blood spilled out of his mouth as soon as they turned him.

Visla glanced at Emery with gloomy eyes. "What's happening?"

"He has blood in his lungs. I'm hoping to drain the pus so he can breathe," Emery said, trying to sound confident when, in fact, she had little hope.

"I'm proud of him and grateful he saved you. If he dies, he dies a hero."

"You sound just like your grandfather. There is nothing heroic in dying. He should not have done it. I would have had a much better chance of surviving if I were hit—"

"You just got hurt and barely survived. You're still hurt. I can see you wincing in pain when you strain yourself. But you are too proud and stubborn to show it. This is what he would have wanted. To die with honor, saving someone's life."

"We won't let him die, Visla," Emery said. "You remember when we were fighting with the Minders after we had left Marianne's apartment?"

Visla nodded.

"I think I dodged a bullet?"

"You did what? What's a bullet?"

"It's the thing inside the guns that Minders kill people with. Or at least I think they have bullets or something like that. When the Minder pointed his gun at me, I … moved so fast, I dodged the gun. I don't know how it happened. It was something my body did instinctively. I don't know if I could do it again. But I will try when I'm alone not to spook anyone. Maybe you could do it too?"

Visla gazed into Emery's eyes with admiration and squeezed her hand.

"I'm sure you can."

Emery rested her head on Visla's shoulder. And they soon fell asleep, almost in each other's arms, as their tired bodies slumped on the blankets next to the sleeping Lach. They didn't know that he woke up in the darkest hour of the night, gasping for air, and searching for his daughter. Seeing them asleep, curled together like sisters, he stared at them for as long as his eyes would stay open, smiled, and then fell asleep again. The smile stayed glued to his lips even after he was sound asleep.

The following morning, Emery awoke to Lach's gurgling attempts to breathe. During the night, he'd fallen onto his back and was struggling to get enough air. Emery jumped up and turned him sideways. She supported his head to open the airway. His eyes were wide open and bulging out of their sockets as he gasped for air. More blood and pus came out of his mouth, and then he started breathing again. He closed his eyes again, breathing with more ease than before.

"You are okay now. Just rest."

Visla woke up and rushed to her father's side. "What's wrong?"

"He's fine."

Visla looked up at Emery, questioning what she had said.

"He is fine, Visla. I think the worst is over. I think he'll be fine. He's breathing much better now."

"His eyes?"

"They are still brown."

Emery left in search of Konrad, whom she hadn't seen in several hours; she missed him. She found him sitting with Urus and Thomas. They were learning the names of their weapons in their languages.

The boys are bonding. Funny, the first thing the men want to learn is about weapons, not food, sky, or trees, Emery wondered, surprised Thomas was with them.

Konrad saw Emery approaching, and his face lit up with a smile. The first time she'd seen him smile. She held her breath and then returned a smile infused with the warmth of the morning sun. Her unbraided hair fell on her shoulders in long golden waves, bathed in a soft morning glow. And at that moment, Konrad stopped breathing, watching her. Urus looked at him and murmured to himself, grinning. Konrad didn't hear it and didn't care. His eyes were fixed on Emery, walking toward him, until the noises of the waking camp and children running and playing in front of him broke his gaze.

Konrad realized he had been holding his breath. He exhaled and slowly rose.

She got close and took his hand in hers. "We must leave now," she said softly.

Konrad looked at everyone gathering supplies and packing, knowing he should do the same, but he felt as if his head had suddenly reached the skies and gotten lost in the clouds. Emery left to pack, and he sighed, not knowing why.

That day was the hardest yet. The steepness, the snow, and the cold increased, making the journey slower and more arduous for the young and the old. But the mood improved. Because they knew they were close to leaving the mountains. Tomorrow they'd be on their way down a much gentler slope, yet still protected by trees. Konrad and Thomas divided the tablets and guns between themselves. Lach was asleep most of the day, but he woke up a few times to catch a deeper, gurgling breath. Each time he did that, Visla grimaced, and Lannea, noticing it, took her hand.

In the evening, they made a small fire for the children as the temperature dropped after sundown. The tribe settled by the fire, munching on a quick and simple meal of cakes, dried fruit, and nuts. Emery sat by Konrad when everyone suddenly stopped talking and watched Omana expectantly. The medicine woman, sensing stares, sat by the fire and sang in a soft, melodic voice. That was the first time Emery had heard her sing this song. She sang about a golden goddess waking up from her long sleep. "Shine your golden light on us. Guide us. Bring us back what was taken from us, golden goddess ..." When she finished her song, she fixed her gaze on Emery and mouthed something Emery couldn't hear.

As the walking grew easier every day, the moods improved. Children threw snowballs at each other. Snow fell, covering everything in white fluff. Elena couldn't get enough of it. She watched the children play in the snow with envy and finally couldn't contain herself, and joined them. At first, the children were uncertain, but as she skillfully planted the first icy ball on a boy's head, they all giggled and welcomed her to play with them. They didn't go easy on her, throwing ball after ball at her. She soon looked like a snow girl, making the children point and laugh at her. Their laugh had no prejudice or malice, only pure joy, perhaps peppered lightly with a little mischief.

Lach started recovering, much to Emery's relief and Visla's joy. Omana kept bringing him her herbal concoctions, sweetened with honey, and would not leave his side until the wooden cup was empty. She said little to him, and, catching her glancing at him sideways, Emery guessed she was still cross with him, despite his heroic act. Emery held her breath while glancing at his eyes, but to her relief, they remained brown, making her wonder why Visla was changed with her blood and not Lach.

Once Emery noticed his gurgling subsiding and breathing becoming easier, she stayed away, letting Visla and Lannea spend more time with him. She noticed Lannea's frequent glances at Lach and her sudden desire to be with him, and hoped that she finally had started remembering him and her life before the change. Or maybe she just followed Visla's unspoken cues.

Emery looked at Konrad, wondering if he remembered her. It would have been so much easier if he had. She noticed a change in the way he looked at her. More intensely, searchingly, longingly. She didn't ask him whether he remembered more. She didn't press. For the time being, his closeness was enough to make her feel alive again. Everything around her seemed brighter and more colorful, smells were more intense, and her lungs held more air as if a tormenting haze lifted off her.

After they had descended from the mountains to a more even terrain, Lach started walking again. Visla, delighted, babbled happily, walking by his side and playing with the children and Elena. Elena had found her calling. Ever since she threw snowballs with the children, she has taken every opportunity to spend time with them and mimic their play. They started teaching her their language, and she taught them English, which they caught on to almost as quickly as Visla had, and then they scattered around laughing and shouting a new word they'd just learned.

Curious Thomas took an interest in everything and everyone. He easily mingled with women and men of all ages. Omana adored him, as he'd proven skillful in making potions and the healing paste.

Emery was delighted at how they integrated into the tribe's life, lessening the guilt she experienced at the thought of leaving them in this unfamiliar land. It seemed that spending time together lessened the differences between the tribe and changed people. Although their bodies were very different, their minds were becoming more human every day as they remembered more from before the change.

Her heart filled with heavy sorrow whenever she looked at Visla, wondering if she'd be able to leave her. Maybe forever? It would be so easy to stay with them. To love Konrad for as long as she could.

Watch Visla grow, fall in love, and have children. Forget about the thousands of people in the city below. After all, they chose this path for themselves. Why was she always playing a heroine? She wished she could forget about the lab and her mother. The more she tried to forget, the more she realized she had to go back into the dark world, solve the mystery, and vindicate her mother in her own mind. Find the ones responsible for this mess and fix it.

26

WHY YOU?

She felt stronger every day; her wound had already scarred into a thin line. As she traced her finger over her scar, she shivered, remembering the hatred and sadistic tendencies the father-son duo embodied. Never had she met a human capable of such immense coldness and brutality. She considered the possibility that the change had turned them into a different species—non-human monsters. Was it their choice or the result of the change? Were the other Masters monsters as well? The siblings, as well as Konrad and Lannea, were changed and yet kept some humanity, hidden and suppressed by drugs.

Visla noticed Emery's silent brooding. One evening, she confronted her, sensing something ominous brewing behind Emery's sudden silence and avoidance. She went at her with full force, hoping her aggression would dislodge and scatter whatever was developing in Emery's head. "What is it? Are you sick? Are you feeling worse? Show me your belly."

Emery showed her the scar. "I'm all right. Completely healed now."

"So what is it? You are planning something stupid. I know that look."

"Sit down, Visla. You are just too damn perceptive. I can't hide anything from you." Emery paused, breathed in, and blurted out. "I must go back."

"Go back where?" Seeing Emery's face, Visla's face paled. "Back down? No! You are crazy. There is no reason for you to go back. You rescued everyone. Everyone is safe now. No! I won't let you. You are not leaving me! No, no, no, no—"

"Shush, Visla, don't shout. I don't want anyone to know yet. I want to make sure you get back to your northern cousins."

"No, I won't shush. You have no reason to go. It's a stupid idea."

"Look at your mother. Look at Elena and Thomas. Do you see the change in them? Can't you see how alive and happy they look now?"

"Yeah, so?"

"There are tens of thousands of people like them in the dark city below. Don't you think they'd like to experience this? To be free and to feel? They've been robbed of it and lied to. They are being kept in that dark city, believing the Masters' lies that the world is uninhabitable. Someone must help them."

"Why does this someone have to be you, Emery? You've already helped. Let someone else help them."

"Who?"

"I don't know. Anyone."

"There isn't anyone else who could help. And I feel responsible."

"Responsible? Why? You did nothing wrong."

Emery told Visla about her suspicions that her mother could have been responsible for discovering the mechanism leading to the development of the change and might have inadvertently caused all this.

"I love my mother, Visla, and want to believe she didn't know how it was going to be used and how it would affect humanity. I hope she didn't. But I must know for certain, and I must fix it."

Visla quieted, staring at the ground. "I understand, but I don't want you to go."

"I don't want to go either. I want to stay with you and your tribe. But if I don't fix it, more people will be changed, and more people will die. Humanity will die. How would I ever be able to love someone knowing that?"

"I'll go with you."

"You can't because you must lead your clan. You might not know it yet, but you are a natural leader. Lead them north and stay there. Never come back here."

"They come north, too."

"Who?"

"The black birds and the 'bad people'. They come during the summer. Kidnap and kill."

"You can't hide from them?"

"We can, and we do. But they are clever, and their birds often find us. Not all of us. There are more places to hide there."

Emery fell silent. She had been wrong, thinking Visla would be safe if she went north. Now she knew with absolute certainty that she had to go back. She embraced Visla, who immediately started sobbing. "I don't want you to go …"

"I'll be okay. I am a superwoman."

"A what?"

"A woman with superpowers who can fight an entire army of 'bad people' and who always wins. Where I came from, there are stories about people with superpowers who fight bad people."

The time to say goodbye had come. Everyone knew where and why Emery was going. They admired her bravery but shook their heads at her stupidity in returning to the place from which she had barely escaped with her life. Before they left, Konrad taught everyone how to use the guns, leaving most of them with the tribe, only taking four. Emery watched him with surprise as he packed all the tablets to take with them and asked why he wanted to carry them. "I have a plan," he said, and that was all he said.

Emery cried. Everyone cried. Even Lach cried when embracing her one last time.

Elena's eyes widened when she heard the news. "They'll kill you. Is knowing worth losing your life?"

"It's not only about knowing. I must go back to the time before it all started and fix it. There is a time travel capsule under the Silver House, which I hope still works."

"But you can't go back in time. It's not possible."

"How do you know? Who told you that? The Masters? They lied about everything. I must at least try."

"What about the predestination paradox? Even if you succeed and go back in time, you not only won't be able to fix anything, but you might cause the very thing you want to prevent."

"I must try. You know, I came here thinking I would find the black shards and bring them back as a gift for humanity. And now, I am going back without having accomplished anything and having learned that I was cheated out of my life. I'm going back defeated."

Elena fell silent, observing Emery with her deep, wise eyes. "Emery, you're wrong about not accomplishing anything. You've accomplished something incredible."

"Huh?"

"You gave us the gift of love, Emery. A glimpse of life with feelings and emotions, and without deception. Because of you, we can remember who we were and the people we loved. Each day, I remember more and grow more aware of who I am. I can love other people and all this," Elena said and made a sweeping movement with her arm, pointing to the mountains and the trees. "There is no better gift you could have given to humanity than to return us to our true nature," she said and embraced Emery in a hug that felt natural and warm. An embrace a loving friend would give, not a non-human.

Elena blinked rapidly as if her body remembered the act of crying.

Omana waited for Elena to finish her goodbyes before she approached Emery. "Be careful and keep your eyes open, my golden child. I know that man of yours would give his life to save yours. He is a good one. You'd better keep him." Omana hugged Emery in a tight embrace and kissed her cheeks, standing on her toes to reach them.

"I need to ask you something important. Something that has been on my mind since I came back from the underground city. How did you survive when the land became dry and didn't produce any food?"

"Hmm. When I was a little girl, I remember my great-grandmother talked about the Big Dry, but I don't remember the story itself."

"Thank you. Watch over Visla."

Visla was the last to say goodbye. She couldn't say anything, just hugged her friend with her slender body shaking with sobs.

"You'll be in my heart forever, my little sister. My best friend. Stay safe," Emery said and embraced her for a long time. Then she held her chin and looked her in the eye, smiling through tears. "Maybe I'll see you in another life. I'd lost him in another life and found him in this life," she added, pointing at Konrad. Visla nodded and smiled through her tears. Brave and selfless.

Then, Konrad and Emery left. Emery turned around and, through her tears, saw an ocean of waving hands. She shuffled forward. Her gait was erratic as she fought the desire to turn back and walk with the tribe in the other direction.

27

ON THE WAY

They walked in silence. Emery's sullen face wasn't inviting. As soon as they left the tribe, she started having doubts. She kept her eyes on the ground, fighting the itch to look back. She suddenly felt like a child who wanted to throw a fit, cry, and stomp her feet in protest. But the adult Emery pushed forward, one foot ahead of the other.

Konrad, watchful, scanned their surroundings as they walked while watching Emery. "We can go back to the tribe. Everyone would be happy to see you. Nobody would hold it against you."

"Nobody but me. I can't."

They kept up a fast pace, having more than a week of travel ahead of them. But that wasn't the only reason they moved so fast. Hiking all day, only stopping for a few minutes, left Emery exhausted. She had no strength left to think about her decision or imagine running back and falling into her little sister's arms. Konrad kept watch for the first two nights, but on the third night, Emery insisted he should sleep. While Konrad slept, Emery kept watch, thinking about her mother and hoping, hoping against reason, she was wrong about her suspicions.

"What's your big plan with all the tablets you are carrying with you?" Emery asked when Konrad woke up.

"I want to create a diversion and scramble their surveillance system before we go back inside."

"You know how to do that?"

Konrad's lips twitched in a mischievous smile. Seeing the smile, Emery's heart quivered, and she silently wept. *I love you so much. Just wish you remembered us. I miss your love.*

"I do," he said. "You know, I'm more than pure muscle and strength. I have half a brain."

Was that an attempt at a joke? "You have more than half a brain. Just a little, tiny bit more," Emery said, showing him the tip of her finger. And he smiled in response. Again. His ability to smile was still in its infancy. His lips didn't quite unfold completely but twitched from side to side like a broken doll.

During the sixth night of their journey and the last night before they would reach the dark city, Emery insisted on keeping guard during the first part of the night. Konrad slept like a baby, curled into a ball by her side. Suddenly, he moaned, cried out, and sat up abruptly.

"What's wrong?"

"I saw things while I slept. I saw myself, and I saw you. It was so vivid, as if it were real."

"And that has never happened to you before? Seeing things while you sleep?"

"No. Does it happen to you?"

"All the time. You were dreaming." Emery smiled and reached for his hand. "Do you remember your dream?"

"You. I dreamed of you. I remember you. I remember us. I remember you going into the chamber, and the pain I felt for not being able to go with you. Oh, Emery," he cried out again, and wrapped his arms around her in an embrace that had gained a new level of tenderness. "Emery. My Emery."

Emery folded into his arms. *Finally. You're back.*

"I remember everything. It is as if a curtain had lifted. I

remember seeing you for the very first time. You were such a bad snoop," he said, inhaling the scent of her hair. "I spotted you when you first pulled up and parked across from the building. When I saw you in the car, my world changed, and my life began again. And then it collapsed again after you disappeared into the chamber."

"What happened to you? You look so much younger."

Konrad sighed deeply and rubbed his forehead. "A year after you left, Sebastian came to me, asking to see Regis. He said he missed him. I didn't think much about it. After all, the dog had spent his life with him and Zoe. I thought maybe he was missing Zoe, and seeing the dog would help, so I let him in. Besides, I would not live forever, and Regis would. I was hoping yet dreading he would take Regis with him."

"Sebastian ..." Emery whispered, remembering what Elena had told her about him.

"I offered him a beer. I went to the kitchen to get it, but I never got there. Instead, I woke up sitting in the capsule with my hands tied behind my back and Sebastian staring at me. To this day, I don't know how he did that. But I should have known not to turn my back on him, especially seeing the wretched expression on his face. He was hurting and hating."

"Why would he hate you? You've done nothing to him."

"I don't know if he hated me in particular. I think he hated the entire world. He went back to the chamber and listened to the holograms your mother had created as her journals and manuals. I have not heard them either. Only what Sebastian told me. I don't know how much of it was true, how much was a lie. But what he told me shook me to my core."

"What? What did he tell you?"

"Olesya designed the chambers."

Emery's face went pale. She stood up abruptly and left. She paced for a moment, then returned and joined him on the ground, wrapping her hands over her ears so she could hear no more. Konrad stood up and started packing the camp, guessing she needed time to process what he had told her. He returned to her side after finishing packing and sat beside her. "Are you okay?"

"In the letter, she said she didn't know what the chambers were. I don't understand. Why would she lie to me?"

"She probably didn't remember it. She invented them in a different world, a different dimension."

"Are you serious?"

Konrad winced and rubbed his forehead. He looked at her sheepishly and gently touched her hand. "We are not in the same dimension you left. Sebastian and I traveled through the dark dimension and the light because Sebastian assured me I'd find you there—"

"You trusted him after he drugged and kidnapped you?"

"I was pissed, sure. But when he told me we could find you, I didn't care. Besides, he didn't give me much choice. I was already in the capsule."

Konrad shared what Sebastian had told him. According to him, Olesya designed the chambers to travel back in time and release dark matter. But she failed to go back in time, only into the future or into the dark dimension.

Emery got up and started pacing, pondering what Konrad had told her. More secrets to uncover. More uncertainties. When would it ever end? She paced for a while, then returned to Konrad, who sat quietly with his back against a boulder, watching her.

"What happened to Regis?"

"Sebastian told me Mary and Henry would take care of him."

Emery gazed at Konrad with tears in her eyes. "You fool," she said, stroking his cheek. "You risked your life for a slight chance of finding me."

"Even if it was a shadow of a chance, it wouldn't have mattered. I'd still have gone."

He kissed her hand and continued. "We arrived at a world that was falling apart. The thirstwaves caused by the warming of the planet had ravaged the crops. The famine, the unrest, and the ensuing wars for resources made for a terrifying reality. Yet, that wasn't the worst. I didn't remember you or my life before, and never searched for you. Sebastian never told me I would remember nothing from my previous life. I don't know whether he lied to me or he didn't know what awaited us in different worlds.

"I was reborn into a family with a strong military background and was brought up by strict parents. I knew nothing else; I became a soldier and rose high in the ranks. When the change came, they offered it to me if I agreed to serve and protect. I accepted, pressed by my parents. We weren't told the details, only that the change was the only solution to save the planet and our species ..."

"How so?"

"We wouldn't have to use any resources. No food, no water. Only oxygen. We would help the drying planet by not depleting it even more. I imagine some people signed up believing they were doing the right thing..."

"The right thing? They used their trillions of dollars to buy into a change and let the planet go to shit. And who was behind the change and took the money that people paid for it? Who benefited most from all this? Master E?"

"I don't know. Maybe."

"What about the resistance? Elena told me about them. That they were protesting the change, demanding the rich fucks fix the planet instead of funneling all their money into the change to save their own asses. The resistance was not powerful enough to stop this?"

"Yes, I remember the resistance. The Emerites." Konrad paused, realizing what he had said.

"The what?"

Konrad looked at Emery as if he had seen her for the first time. "The Emerites. That's what they were known as."

"Why would they call them that?" Emery asked. Her face stiffened and paled.

"I don't know. I don't remember much from that time. I felt lost and not whole, as if an essential part of me was missing. The military helped fill the void and suppress doubts. The repetition, the intense and brutal training, and blind obedience left no room for guessing what was missing from my life. Who was missing from my life. If I had only tried harder to remember ..."

"Then what? Nothing would have changed, and you might have been dead. At least you are alive, and I have you now." Emery bent down to embrace him, and the coin fell out of her pocket.

Konrad picked it up from the ground, glanced at it, and his jaws clamped, tightening his face. "It's you ... your face."

She'd forgotten about the coin. Now, she inspected it more carefully and with mixed feelings. When she first saw the coin, she thought the face resembled her mother's. But she later dismissed it, doubting her mother would have had anything to do with the resistance. "It can't be me. How could it?"

"Your mother was here. It's quite possible that ... you existed here."

"If I did ... exist here. Who was I? What was I?"

She took the photo out and looked at it again. Her mother and father's faces looked crisper in the sun, but the face of the girl in the middle was even fainter than before. Countless scenarios crossed her mind, but none made any sense.

Emery sat next to Konrad, feeling disheartened. She rested her head on his shoulder, and he stroked her hair. "We'll figure this out. Whatever it is, we'll figure this out together, and we'll do what we need to do."

"I'm scared, Konrad."

"Call me Peter. Don't be scared. Your mother couldn't have done anything evil. Not knowingly."

"How do you know?"

"Just my intuition. Her eyes. They bore no evil. She was pure, just like you are."

Emery rested her head on his chest. He stroked her head. "It'll be okay."

In response, she searched his eyes and then his lips. They kissed, but they could never make love the way they used to, as they had taken that away from him. Emery loved him even more.

28

THE QUEST

At dawn, Emery got up before Konrad and squatted behind a low-growing bush to pee. When she got up and started walking away, she tripped on a piece of wood that was sticking out of the ground. She fell, and when her eyes landed on what had tripped her, her mouth dropped. "What the…"

Four black letters—"NESS"—boldly stared at her from the weathered piece of wood. She flopped on the ground, speechless, gazing at her find. As she stared at them, the letters started spinning while her dry mouth tried to produce a sound. After a while, she reached for it and dragged it out of the sand. She gasped, seeing an old, blackened, and partially broken sign. The bottom part was mostly intact, while the letters on the top were mostly either broken off or weathered out. But the bottom part spelled clearly, "WILDERNESS".

Peter found her holding the sign with both hands, staring at it. Her face was pale. He dropped beside her and looked over her shoulder. Emery regarded him with eyes pleading for an explanation other than what stared her right in the face. "Where are we?" she finally asked. "Do you know?"

"Idaho," he whispered. "Diamond Eldorado was built under the Frank Church—River of No Return Wilderness."

Another confirmation that Elena had spoken the truth. This was the future.

The next morning, Emery woke up early, finding herself bound tightly to Peter in an embrace. She remained still for a long time, watching his chest move in deep breaths, certain he was still asleep, praying the moment they had to be on their way would never come. But just like her, he was awake and resisted the slightest move. A flock of sparrows, flying bizarrely close to the ground, cast a shadow and a gust of air as they fluttered their hundreds of wings.

Emery and Peter's faces were somber as they prepared to break into the fortress, now guarded by Minders who would most likely be more vigilant. But Peter had a plan. Once they reached the area where they could access the Moonlight, the elevator that would take them down closer to the Silver House, he went to work. Emery watched intently as he set up each tablet with a code that would activate an alarm in the headquarters, each a few minutes apart. He set one up to go off momentarily and buried it in the ground, and then they waited for the first group of Minders to scramble out of the elevator and scatter around, looking for the signal.

Once they disappeared from view, Emery and Peter entered the elevator and used the earpieces they had previously taken from the dead Minders. The elevator was empty, and so was the hallway leading to the Silver Palace. That is where Emery wanted to go first to listen to her mother's hologram recordings, if they were still there. Unnoticed, they tiptoed past a room where two Minders were leaning against a wall, engaged in a quiet conversation.

Peter set up another tablet inside the elevator and sent the elevator up. Then he opened a passage in the floor behind a masterfully carved marble statue of a naked man. Emery recognized the strange lock on the back of the statue's head. *This must be Master E. He made himself look like a Greek god. Naked evil. Yikes.*

They climbed down the steps, which materialized as soon as the floor opened. The narrow and dark hallway led them to a black metal door reinforced with bars extending from the ceiling to the floor.

"How are we getting in?"

Peter pulled out a tablet and touched it. The bars went up smoothly and disappeared into the ceiling. Emery wondered how many more surprises he'd pull out of his sleeve, this new Peter of hers. He opened the door, and they found themselves in the chamber. The lights came on as they entered, and Emery gasped, recognizing the familiar-looking console and the crystal capsule.

"But there is no weightlessness in here," she observed. "Does that mean it's not working? There is no blue light on the console's triangle." Emery's face showed disappointment as she walked around the console and the capsule, inspecting them. "Oh, I forgot," she said. "I must have the black shard for the capsule to open and work. Maybe the console needs the black shard to work, too?"

"I don't know."

"Have you ever seen the black shards here in this city?"

Peter looked at her, trying to remember.

"When you arrived in this dimension, did you remember Sebastian?"

"No. I didn't remember him or anyone else."

"So when Sebastian threatened to destroy Italy, you didn't know who he was?"

"No, I thought he was some demented wacko."

"Hmm." Emery fell silent, pondering. "He must have remembered his past, or at least some of it, because he was shouting Zoe's name before he died—"

"Died? What makes you think he died?"

"Elena told me he was shot by the resistance."

"That wasn't Sebastian."

"No? Who was it?" Emery's eyes widened in shock.

"Jonah Watson was his name. He resembled Sebastian. I had the feeling this was all staged to make people think he was dead. The corrupt media propagated the deception."

"Why?"

"To get the target off his back."

"If it wasn't Sebastian but that Jonah guy, why would he shout Zoe's name?"

"I don't know, but I know for sure it wasn't Sebastian."

"How can you be so sure?"

"Because I disposed of his body."

"Disposed?" she asked, raising her eyebrows.

"Cremated it. I transferred him to the crematorium."

"Fuck! I still know nothing. It's even murkier now. Elena said he invented the change. Did he really?"

Peter scratched his head, trying to recall. "He and Master E were behind the planning and executing it, but I don't know who actually invented it."

"Is he still alive?"

"I don't know. I never saw him after that."

Peter took out one of the Minders' tablets and hid it behind the console. "We must get out of here now. The tablet will go off in a few minutes."

"What if we have to come back here again?"

"They'll be long gone, searching for us elsewhere."

"Is Master E the highest ranking?"

"I always thought so..."

"But what?" Emery impatiently watched Peter scratch his head.

"I don't know, it's just a—"

"A hunch?" Emery asked and reached for his hand. He grabbed it moved it to his mouth and kissed it. She smiled, despite the disquieting suspicions about Sebastian's role in the change. She had only met him once but got good vibes from him, and part of her refused to believe he was guilty of such atrocities to humankind.

"Yeah," he answered and smiled with his new crooked smile while pointing to the exit. Emery obediently went up the stairs and emerged back into the Silver House. Peter climbed up and pointed toward a small corridor at the far end of the enormous room. "We must go," he urged.

"Why do you think there may be someone above him?"

"I noticed occasionally that he waited to decide on a few important issues until the next day or even longer. He is hot-headed, and yet he waited."

"I see. Where are we going now?"

"Under."

"Under what?"

"We are going under the Masters' ceremonial headquarters."

"Ceremonial headquarters? What's that?"

"It's exactly what it sounds like. It's where they conduct ceremonies and celebrations."

"What type of ceremonies?"

Peter didn't answer. Emery looked at him expectantly. He appeared slightly embarrassed.

"You don't know," she whispered. "How can you not know? You were not invited to the ceremonies?"

Peter shook his head, looking ashamed. Emery regretted her sarcastic tone. "It's not your fault. Let's go."

Peter took out the earpiece, smashed it with his foot, and turned off his tablet. Next, he led them through the corridor, which, in contrast to the opulence of the Silver House, appeared rather drab. With a low ceiling and dim light, the corridor had a slight downhill slope. When they reached a "T" at the end of the corridor, Peter, to her surprise, went neither left nor right. Instead, he took out his wand gadget, which served both as a knife and a glue gun, and cut a hole in the wall's bottom. Just big enough for them to get through.

After they came through to the other side, Peter glued the wall back, closing off the sliver of light and immersing them in complete darkness. Emery fumbled with her gun and turned the flashlight on. She tried to get up and hit her head on the low ceiling.

"Where are we?"

"We are in the building's skeleton—its structural framework. This is where the construction of all the buildings began. These shafts go under the entire Silver House, the Masters' quarters, and the various administrative bureaus. We'll have to crawl for the first part. Then the shafts get slightly bigger. Big enough for us to stand and walk."

"How did you know about this shaft?"

"I had a ... I knew someone who built this. I spent some time there when it was being constructed. It wasn't part of my duties to monitor construction, but back then, I had more time to explore."

"Before they made you the special Minder, the Sage." Emery tried hard not to sound cynical, but her tone was harsher than she intended. She was glad she couldn't see his eyes in the dark.

They continued crawling for some time. Peter navigated through the maze without problems most of the time. Twice, they had to retrace their steps and take a different route. Emery noticed the shaft was made of a different material from the building. It was stiffer, harder, and cold to the touch, but still seamless.

"How did they build all those structures with no visible seams? I don't see any nails, bolts, or support structures anywhere. How can the buildings just hover in space, not attached to anything?" Emery wondered aloud, not expecting an answer.

"It was part of the change."

"How?"

"It all resulted from a new revolutionary technology. Something about the charge and energy of the smallest existing particles that, if manipulated in certain ways, would push them into countless unique states, producing new materials with extraordinary properties."

"What was the technology called?" Emery whispered and stopped crawling.

"I believe it was preontechnology," Peter said, and realizing she wasn't following him, turned around and glanced at her. Her gun flashlight lay on the ground, illuminating her pale face and trembling lips. She stared at the ground blankly, swallowing hard.

"What's wrong?"

"Olesya Solensky, my mother, received a Nobel Prize for preontechnology, Peter. My mother was responsible for the change ..."

"No, she wasn't, Emery. When did she get it?"

"In 2224."

"The change happened a hundred and fifty years later. She had nothing to do with it. I don't remember her name being mentioned in association with the change. If I had, it could have triggered a memory."

"Oh," Emery whispered and looked up at him. "Inadvertently, she was."

"You can't think this way. We'd still be in the Stone Age if we'd been afraid to use new technologies ..."

Emery nodded slowly. "Yeah. This is exactly what happened here. Don't you see? Whoever is behind all this is a very sick man ... or a woman. Is there anyone who can explain this technology? How does it work? The floating buildings, the change?"

"I don't know anyone. But I am not the right person to ask. I don't know much about science and technology."

"Is there a university or a—"

"We'll find out. I promise," Peter said, touching her hand. "We must go now. We must keep moving. Just in case someone remembers the existence of this shaft."

Soon, they reached a section of the labyrinth with higher ceilings, which allowed them to stretch their limbs and walk instead of crawling. The maze attained a new level of complexity, with multiple levels crisscrossing each other in intricate patterns. Peter had to stop frequently and retrace his steps. At one point, he stopped, looking up.

"Are we there? Below the ceremonial headquarters?" Emery asked and moved closer to look at the tablet.

"Not yet."

"What's that?" Emery asked, pointing at the screen.

"That's an aviary."

"Is this the place where they store the birds? The birds that spy on people?"

"Yeah," Peter said and, glancing at Emery's face, shook his head. "No, it's too dangerous. This place is right next to the Regulatory Headquarters, which is full of Directing Minders at all times."

"What's Regulatory Headquarters?"

"It's where they monitor and control the city."

"Oh," Emery breathed, and her eyes betrayed her excitement. She tried to hide her smile, but Peter noticed it.

"No, out of the question. We'll never get through."

"Peter, this could save thousands of lives. It could save Visla. Think. Is there another way to the aviary?" She sounded troubled but her stubborn posture suggested that she would not take "no" for an answer.

Peter opened his mouth to speak. To object vehemently. To tell her with absolute certainty, he would not risk her life. But then he remembered something, and Emery noticed it. "What is it?"

"You're not going to give up, are you?"

Emery shook her head and looked at him, cocking her head.

"There might be another way to the aviary."

"Great, let's go."

"Don't get your hopes up. I said there might be another way. If it's still there," Peter said and fiddled with his tablet, then started walking ahead, still looking at the glowing gadget in his hand. Emery grinned and followed, almost skipping. "Can you just imagine if we could somehow disable them?"

Peter didn't answer, looking at the tablet and glancing left and right, trying to decide which way to go. "That way, I think," he said, turning left at a "T".

They walked for a while down a long corridor, which narrowed and descended as they went further into it. Peter stopped suddenly, and Emery, not paying attention, bumped into him.

He pointed his flashlight at the ceiling. "I think this is where the old access was. If I am right, I'll be able to cut a hole in the ceiling."

"Great. Cut the hole."

Peter cut the hole with his gadget, nodding his head. "Yes, this is it."

The ceiling opened, unveiling a brightly lit room above. Peter looked at Emery. "I'll go first," he said sternly. "No," he added, seeing Emery was getting ready to jump up and grab the edge of the hole. "Please, Emery. Wait here for me."

"Okay," she relented. "Just be quick."

Peter jumped up, grabbed the edge, and pulled himself up. A few seconds passed, and his face appeared in the hole. "Come on, up. There is nobody here at the moment."

Peter helped Emery up to the aviary. There were thousands of birds in the gigantic room. Even though the room was dazzling with invisible lights, the sheer number of birds made it appear darker. Stacked on shelves and tables, the rows of mechanical creatures melted into the murky abyss of the room. The unnerving blank stares sent goosebumps along Emery's arms. "So creepy. Why so many?" she sighed.

Peter wrapped his arms around her. "Are you all right?"

"Yeah," she said and fell silent for a long, breathless moment. "Can we disable them all somehow? Destroying them one by one would take forever."

"From the control room, we could. I could."

"No! You said the room is heavily guarded. They'll kill you."

"Well, I've thought about it and reconsidered it. Nobody. I mean, nobody, would expect me here. I could easily blend in with the rest of the Minders, get to the aviary control panel, and scramble their programming."

"And you know how to do that? Huh?"

"Yup," he said, smiling. "I can do that. I really can. Safely. I promise. I'll be back in no time," he added, thumping his chest to add sincerity and weight to his promise.

"Fine." Her response felt rather weak. "Let me clean you up a bit. You have some dirt on your pants. They might notice it," she said, and bent down to help him clean the bottom of his pants.

Peter noticed her voice breaking and raised her chin with his hand. "I'll be back. I promise. I wouldn't have risked it if I weren't sure I'd come back to you. While I am gone, open the hatches."

"Open what?" Emery asked, looking around.

"There are at least fifty hatches in this room. Normally, they open automatically when a group of birds is scheduled to fly off on an exploratory mission. I can't do that while scrambling their brains.

Can you open them?" Peter asked, pointing at a hatch between the shelves. "Just press on the indentations in the middle of each one."

"Are you going to send them through the hatches?" Emery asked, worried.

"No, I'll tell you later. Trust me."

"Of course, I trust you. Go. I'll open all of them," Emery said and headed for the closest hatch. He smiled, with pride laced with sorrow.

For the next twenty minutes, Emery opened forty-eight hatches. When she opened the last one by pressing the indentation, Peter came back running. "All set. Let's go back down."

They climbed down to the corridor and returned to where they had set out. Peter led them through more corridors, verifying the direction with his tablet.

"The guns and flashlights are part of that technology, aren't they?" Emery marveled at her gun flashlight, still giving out bright light. "They need no recharging?"

"That's right."

"No wonder she got the Nobel Prize for it," Emery murmured. "She invented a perpetual world. And I didn't inherit even the smallest part of her brilliance."

"You inherited more than that, Emery. Yours lies in the transformation you bring in people. You produce some sort of magic waves around you that bring out the best in people—"

Peter was interrupted by a sudden noise. Multiple explosions and whistling sounds reverberated through the labyrinth, bouncing and echoing off the sleek walls and creating an odd cacophony of unearthly sounds. With that, a slightly burned and pungent smell filled the shaft.

"What's that?"

"I don't know, but I think we've reached the ceremonial headquarters. We are directly underneath them now."

"What's going on? Is someone attacking them?"

Peter didn't answer, looking up and listening to the noises. "Sounds like ... fireworks."

"Fireworks? Inside a building?"

"Yeah, it's strange, but it sounds like it."

"How do we get up there?"

"We? We don't. You stay here while I go up and kidnap one of the Masters and bring him back to you, so we can question him together."

"No, you're not. No fucking way I'm going to let you go up there by yourself," Emery said, crossing her arms in front of her with defiance.

"I can blend in. You can't. Your blonde hair and blue eyes would draw everyone's attention right away."

Emery glared at him. "You're right," she conceded with a deep sigh. "But you are not going alone. Was that your plan all along?"

"I'll be fine. I'll go up quickly and see what's going on."

"I just found you again. I don't want to lose you, Peter."

"You won't. Be right back," Peter said and motioned for Emery to follow him. He led her up a steep ramp-like structure and then through a narrow shaft. Then he stopped and pressed his knife to the ceiling. "Stay here."

"Don't you dare not come back."

"I'd never leave you, Emery," he said while cutting a small opening. "This leads to a storage room, if I remember correctly."

"What if you are wrong, and you end up in the middle of a room filled with Masters?" Emery said, grabbing his hand to stop him.

"I'm not. Hear it? The sound is not as loud here. I am right," Peter said, and gently removed his hand from Emery's clutches. "The sooner I do it, the faster I'll return."

He cut the hole and disappeared through it. Then, his smiling face reappeared in the hole just a few seconds later. "I was right. This is a storage room."

"Then I'm going up, and I'll wait for you there," Emery said and pushed on the top of his head to get inside.

"No, Emery. It is not a good idea."

"It is too. Move," Emery hissed. "I am not staying down here."

"Fine." He sighed with exasperation, but the corners of his lips twitched. "I have no authority over you."

"Would you like to have authority over me?"

He gave her a sidelong glance and a crooked grin.

"I thought so ... What do we do now?"

"You wait here and I'll be right back," Peter said and turned to leave, but Emery stopped him. "Master E's girlfriend is blonde and blue-eyed."

"What? Are you sure?"

"I saw her with my own eyes. She looked strange, though. Reminded me of an animated doll."

"Really?"

"Yeah. You've never been up there, have you?" Emery asked, seeing his surprise. "You've never been in the Masters' quarters?"

"No. I didn't need to go up there. I was never involved in the direct protection of the Masters."

"Then you have to be very careful, Peter. Promise me."

"I promise," he said and left the room.

Emery looked around the room and, recognizing the same hidden cupboards she'd seen in other places, she pushed one open. Her mouth dropped in disbelief, seeing a closet spanning the entire wall of the spacious storage room. It was full of clothes, shoes, and masks. The clothes were from different historical periods. Starting with tunics dating back to the Roman Empire, through various momentous epochs in human history. Stunned, Emery leafed through the clothes, trying to guess what they were for. Remembering the strange, archaic words the boats and the robots used, she speculated the Masters held a special veneration for certain conventions meant to maintain societal status and divisions, holding themselves above everyone else. She remembered the evil eyes of Master E and shuddered. She wasn't looking forward to questioning him, and yet couldn't wait.

The door opened, and Peter returned. Emery ran to him and embraced him with such strength that Peter wheezed.

"You will not believe it. They are having a masquerade party," Peter said after Emery released him from the hug. "They retracted the cover on the roof and are firing all kinds of fireworks."

"Masquerade party?" Emery gasped and waved at the closet.

Peter's jaw dropped when he saw the clothes. "What the hell?"

"Seems to me like the masquerade parties are a recurring theme," Emery said and walked back to the clothes, rummaging through them. Peter noticed with surprise that she was smiling to herself.

She caught his look. "What? I've always wanted to be at a masquerade party."

Emery picked a costume dating back to the nineteen twenties—the era of the flappers. Her blue eyes glistened when she gawked at the dress, enthralled by it. She didn't waste time putting the dress on. The simple, straight dress was made of very light, shiny blue material, studded with gold sequins and hanging lappets with silver beads that fit Emery's body perfectly. She slid her feet into T-shaped sandals and turned around a few times, sending the silver lappets into a shiny frenzy. Captivated by the magical phantom before him, Peter watched in silence. Emery, enthralled by her outfit, didn't notice Peter's solemn face. She didn't see the yearning, the sorrow, and the love on his face, contorted by tears that would never come.

"What should I wear?" he finally asked, straining to keep his voice steady.

"Oh, I should have asked before putting this dress on," Emery said shyly, as if realizing she'd been acting like a girl who hadn't seen a dress in a long time. "How were they dressed? Was there a theme?"

"Not that I'd noticed. They are wearing all sorts of costumes. And masks."

"Masks? That's great," she said and went on a clothes hunt again. "Put this on," Emery said, handing Peter a red felt cloak embroidered with silver thread and braid borders. She completed his outfit with a large, plain bicorne hat with a red, white, and blue cockade.

"Perfect," she said, grinning when he put the costume on. "Don't look so grim. You look very handsome, my Napoleon."

Emery ran back into the closet and found a black wig—a short black bob. She put it on and added a gold band on top of her head. "We are ready. Let's go mingle," she said, drawing a deep breath as she slid her hand into Peter's arm, bent at the elbow.

29

GOING BACK IN TIME

The hallway led to a gigantic room and a spectacular view. If she wasn't here to capture and question one of the Masters, Emery would have had a blast. The décor and lavishness of this enormous place surpassed the Silver House. Diamonds, precious metals, emeralds, and rubies studded the walls and the ceilings. The crystal stairs, with complex glass and silver banisters, led to the balconies overlooking the immense area. There were small and large rooms, nooks and crannies partially hidden by Doric columns and cloudy curtains, behind which people hid in pairs or small groups. Colorful, flowery, seventeenth-century-style furniture was adorned with gems, gold, and silver, and flanked by what seemed like real palms. Emery gasped, seeing diamond chandeliers floating in the air, unsupported. The spectacular fireworks show went on above as if the fake black sky was speckled with exploding gems.

They strolled through the room, ignored by the Masters. Emery, slightly shorter than the other women, was glad she'd worn the high-heeled sandals that boosted her height. They walked through the colorful crowds boasting flamboyant costumes and even gaudier masks. There were giant beaks and silvery feathers, gold manes, and objects defying description moving through the mob of socialites.

In a circular area, a group of people was engaged in an intricate dance. Their colorful costumes and extravagant masks twirled in a multitude of colors and shapes. Emery felt secure in her costume, wig, and mask, large enough to hide her blue eyes behind its shadow.

A translucent sign floated above, meandering between the chandeliers. "700 YEARS OF BRILLIANT GENESIA!" the sign announced.

They are celebrating the change. Sick!

The beauty, gaudiness, and outlandishness of this remarkable celebration made Emery forget where she was, and she simply admired the spectacle, thrilled to have witnessed it. But once she recovered from her initial wonder at her surroundings, she noticed with astonishment that hundreds of people attended this party and deduced there were more than the twenty Masters she'd originally presumed there were in this city.

"Peter," she whispered. "Do normal people like Elena attend these parties?"

"I don't believe so. They don't ... No, I would have known. I was in charge of overseeing all the comings and goings of ..." Peter's voice trailed as he failed to find the right word to describe people like Elena and Thomas.

"The rest of the people remain in their small apartments, staring at fake mountains for years. For centuries. How cruel. Callous," Emery spat. She felt her face get hot as her anger soared.

Peter scanned the people's faces, searching for the one, but he quickly realized finding Master E in this stirring soup of costumes and masks would be impossible. Holding her elbow, he steered Emery into a small, empty alcove. "We won't be able to find Master E in this mess," he whispered.

"I know," Emery whispered back. "He might not even be here celebrating whatever they are celebrating after losing his son. What are we going to do? Grab someone else?"

"That or we could go to Masters' quarters and search for stragglers."

Emery looked at him, and the golden dots in her eyes shone. "Where would they keep the black shards if they had them?"

"I don't know. Most likely in some protected vault."

"Do you know where that vault would be? Is there such a vault around here?"

"There is a Treasury Chamber, where they keep the diamonds, gems, paintings, and sculptures."

"There is? Where?"

"We can't just go there. It's not only heavily guarded, but it requires their bio scan in the form of a special badge."

"So we must get one to open it for us."

Peter got quiet, looking at her with profound sorrow.

"What, Peter?"

"You still want to travel in time?"

"Do you have a better idea?"

He didn't answer, but she guessed what he was thinking.

"I need to fix this. Stop this. But first, I need to understand it. If I can't find anyone to tell me how this works, then I must go back. I'm even more certain now. I must, Peter."

He said nothing, and the sadness burrowed deeper into his eyes. He sighed and turned around, scanning the crowd behind him. "I'm not sure if all Masters have access to the chamber."

"Okay, let's just grab a man," she said, looking at the people passing by. "I have a feeling this is a chauvinistic society and that men play more important roles than women here. That's just my hunch."

"I think you're right. There is a difference between the roles of men and women," he said, and paused. "Here's what we are going to do," he added and described his plan.

Emery and Peter pushed through the celebrating crowds, heading toward an exit. Emery turned her attention to a woman who was laughing behind them. The woman's white teeth gleamed under a black crow mask, covering her eyes.

"They laugh, Peter. I heard them laugh. They must have undergone a different change than you, Elena, or Thomas, and other lesser members of their society."

Peter nodded somberly and, keeping his eyes on the exit, grabbed Emery's hand and pushed forward. She kept looking around, growing more incensed at the inequity of how the Masters lived compared to the lower-ranking people.

"Did you see that vase over there? I think they are real flowers. They have real flowers here, Peter. Fucking scumbags." Emery shouted the last two words, and many cold eyes landed on her, evaluating her with venomous interest.

Peter increased the pressure on Emery's elbow and pointed at the exit with his eyes. Emery followed his lead, but the anger heating inside her was close to boiling over. One more Thin Mint and she'd explode. "Do you want to die here?" he hissed.

"I don't see any Minders. They are probably not allowed here."

"They are probably guarding the outside of the building, so nobody gets in. But there are too many to fight. Let's go," Peter said and started heading for the exit, but stopped suddenly and looked at Emery with the strangest expression.

"What is it?"

"Wait. Before we go, we need to do something."

"What?"

"Do you hear that? The song?"

"Yes. I know it. My grandpa hummed it often. 'Can't Help Falling in Love' by Elvis," she said hesitantly, surprised. Her surprise faded as she saw Peter's smiling eyes. "Really?" She asked, smiling back, and eased her hand into Peter's bent elbow.

"Really. We shall dance before we leave here. Emery, would you dance with me?"

The next few minutes were the most magical moments she'd ever experienced. She felt as though Peter's eyes had wrapped a string around her chest, constricting it. They moved together to the music as if they had danced to this song a thousand times. There were no mistakes in their movements, no hesitations; their bodies moved in unison as one. Nearing the song's end, Peter started edging toward the exit. Emery sighed, not wanting this moment to end.

Once they reached an area close to the exit, they stopped and pretended to engage in a conversation while gawking at people around them, searching for a male without a companion. When they saw a man walking toward them, Emery stepped in front of him and feigned to stumble. The man caught Emery's arm to steady her while Peter, pretending to help him, rendered him unconscious with a quick and accurate blow to his temple. Then they each held him from opposite sides, faking a conversation, but before they headed for the exit, a scream cut through the air behind them. Everyone looked in the direction of the scream. With his head, Peter pointed toward the exit, not bothering to look back.

"What's happening?"

Peter gave her a quick, crooked smile. "The birds showed up to the party."

"You made the birds come here?" Emery asked, looking back. She saw a dark shadow swoop over the crowd. And then another. She noticed that Peter was not a bit worried, but grinning mysteriously.

"Yup. They'll have fun for a while." As Peter said that, another scream sounded nearby. "We must go now."

"How far is this chamber?"

"Not far, but we have to take an elevator."

Using the man's tablet, Peter called the elevator, and they descended. Emery saw many floors whoosh by as it carried them down. Too many to count.

"What did you do to the birds?" Emery asked, taking his mask off his eyes.

Peter looked at her and chuckled. "I programmed them to attack the Masters. It's going to take a while to immobilize them. They will have to destroy them all because I scrambled them so good, they'll be useless afterward."

"You are some kind of electronic genius, Peter?"

"No. But I've been around."

Emery stared into his smiling eyes, suppressing tears of love. She ached, wanting to touch and kiss him. And she did, but only in her mind.

Once outside the elevator, Peter picked up the unconscious man and carried him through a maze of corridors. He stopped just before a bend. "Stay here with him. I'll be back," he whispered.

"Where are you going?"

"There are Minders ahead guarding the entrance to the vault. I must take care of them first."

"No, it's a dumb idea. Stop trying to protect me. I am the one with the power, remember? Let's go together, and we can both attack them. It'll be safer that way," Emery said decisively.

"Fine," he said between gritted teeth. "Be careful."

"Let's leave him here for a moment," Emery said.

Peter carefully placed the man on the floor, and they moved toward the chamber. Four Minders stood guarding huge double doors fronted by enormous bars embedded in the floor and the ceiling, like the ones guarding the chamber holding the time capsule. When they saw them approach, they straightened their already straight backs and scrutinized them.

"We must get into the chamber to retrieve something," Peter said to them.

"Show us the purple badge, sir," one Minder said.

Peter yanked the gun from his pocket, but didn't have time to fire. Emery thrust her hands forward, and all four guards fell.

"Go get the guy; I'll wait here," Emery said, staring at the fallen Minders.

Peter carried the man and then searched his costume for the purple badge. The man had nothing resembling a badge of any color. Peter sat beside him, pondering.

"Can't you just open it, like you did before?" Emery asked impatiently.

"I can't. I don't have the clearance."

"What are you not telling me, Peter?" she asked, noticing his troubled expression. The gut-wrenching feeling that something was seriously wrong returned and settled deep in her stomach.

The Master woke up. Peter and Emery left the unanswered question lingering in the air while they shifted their attention to him. Emery took the black mask off his face and stared at him for longer than she intended. He looked somehow familiar, but she couldn't put a name to his face. Young and handsome, despite his gray complexion, the man looked at them without the malice Emery expected to see, but with interest mixed with shock. "Who are you?" he asked Emery.

She took her mask off, revealing her sun-kissed face and blue eyes. "Do you have a purple badge?" she asked him.

"In my quarters."

"Where are your quarters? Can we get there quickly?"

"Why do you need my badge? Don't you have one of your own?"

"I've lost mine. I need to borrow yours."

The man appraised her once again and then looked at Peter, who, without removing his mask, held the man's shoulder while searching his pockets with the other. He found his tablet and quickly figured out who he was and where he lived. "Let's go to your quarters, Ryan," he said, grabbing his shoulder and forcing him to get up.

Ryan tried to free himself, but Peter held him tight in his iron grip. Ryan obediently walked alongside him while glancing curiously at Emery. "Who are you? You look very familiar," Ryan said.

"I could ask you the same. You look familiar."

"He is Ryan Solding, once a famous actor," Peter said.

"Hmm, I don't know him," Emery said and fell silent.

In the elevator, she looked Ryan in the eye and asked. "Do you know any universities in this city?"

"University? Why would you want something so absurdly unnecessary and antiquated?"

"Unnecessary? Antiquated? Ugh." She wanted to yell in his face, tell him how wrong he was, but seeing his stupefied expression, her anger shrank. "Can you laugh?"

"That's a strange question. Can't you?"

"Just answer the fucking question. Can you laugh? Can you feel?"

"Yes, of course I can. Why wouldn't I?" Ryan answered. His

curiosity prevailed over his concern about his abduction. "What's this? You are not one of us. Are you new?"

"Yes, I'm new. I'm Mister E's new girlfriend. Melinda is my name."

"Oh," Ryan said and moved further away from her, pressing his body into the elevator's wall. *He's scared of me*, Emery noticed with amusement, and glanced at Peter, who smiled at her with his eyes.

His quarters were richly decorated with gold and emeralds and carpets so soft, it felt as if she was walking on clouds. Emery was particularly enthralled by the floating blue chandeliers with long, intricate crystal icicles so thin they almost looked like human hair that gently swayed as they moved. Blue sofas embroidered with gold spun around the room in slow motion.

"Where is it?" Peter asked.

"In my bedroom. I'll go get it."

"We'll go together," Peter said.

Emery waited for them to return, enjoying the living room. Here, Picasso's Blue Period pieces occupied the entire wall. Ryan had a thing for blue. Peter returned alone.

"Where is he?"

"Sleeping."

"I wanted to ask him questions."

"He knows nothing, Emery. He is just a pawn, not the mastermind. Several famous and interesting actors, singers, and other performers were hand-selected to add sophistication and class to the change. And entertainment."

Emery and Peter returned to the chamber, still guarded by the four dead Minders. Peter placed the thin glass badge, resembling a purple leaf, on the door. The bars went up into the ceiling, and the door opened. They walked through rooms filled with marble, gold statues, paintings, and gems in glass cases stacked floor to ceiling. In the center of the last room, a glass case displayed very different gems. Behind the thick glass, several black shards were displayed on red velvet that was embroidered with delicate gold and silver threads. Emery reached out to touch the glass case, but Peter stopped her, pointing at the sign on top of the case.

"Property of Master E."

"So what?"

"If we take it, he'll be alerted."

"So let him. He'll have to come down here, and we'll interrogate him."

"He won't come. Minders will. Once we open it and take the shards, we must run."

Emery looked at him, pondering, deciding what to do. And she saw the look on his face, the sorrowful look that forecast a disaster, a heartbreak.

"What?"

"I can't go with you to the chamber. Well, I can, but I'll disintegrate instantaneously. The chamber cannot be used by changed people. It was designed for humans before the change, and it was never adjusted because time travel has been prohibited."

"You knew this all along?" Emery said through her teeth. Her face paled, quivering lips curved downward, and her body trembled in shock, anger, and despair. "Why, Peter? Why didn't you tell me that before?"

"I didn't want to influence your decision. I don't want you to go, but I will not stop you because I love you. Besides, would it have mattered?"

"That's a load of crap," she whispered. Her legs gave out under her. Her arms flopped as her body collapsed, suddenly too heavy for her unsteady legs. Emery wanted to cry, but couldn't. She couldn't bear to look at him and stared at the ground while her world crumbled. She'd just found him, and he'd just remembered her. They could be together and be happy. Instead, they got a few crumbs of a life together. Fate was mocking them and their misery.

Peter sat facing her and took her hands in his. "Emery, listen to me. You are the love of my life. I believe we were together in other lives, other dimensions, and I believe we will still be. Maybe not in this world, not in this dimension, but in a different one. A better one. I'm sure of it. Even though my heart is breaking, I have this profound, overwhelming feeling that our story is only just beginning and we only glimpsed a small part of it. And that small part is big enough to fill the entire universe and all of its dimensions with our love. Look at me. Don't you feel the same?"

She looked at him, and in his eyes, she found an overpowering oath of love, assurance, and courage to continue. She saw what he saw, and she knew he was right.

"What will happen to you if I leave?"

"You can't worry about it. I'll be okay. I'll see you again. We must decide. Ryan will eventually wake up. I didn't kill him."

Emery got up and looked at the glass case.

You could still change your mind. Change your destiny.

She thrust her hands out, and the glass burst into a million pieces, scattering on the floor. Emery took all the black shards and stuffed them in her pockets.

You could still change your mind and leave with Peter. Go back to Visla.

"Back to Silver House?" Peter asked.

She swallowed and nodded.

Go back with Peter.

They ran in silence, back through the ceremonial headquarters, now abandoned and in disarray, and back under the building, where they crawled back through the labyrinth until they reached the Silver House and the stairs leading to the chamber.

You don't even know if this is going to work. You are risking your life and his. Go back. It's not too late. I beg you. Go back with Peter. Someone else can save the world.

Peter opened the door of the chamber. Emery could barely walk —the anguish of having to say goodbye to him again made her feet too heavy to lift. She could hardly breathe as the grief clamped her chest, robbing her of her breath.

The room brightened when they entered. The console came to life with the familiar blue triangle. She pressed it with her trembling hands, her whole body shaking. Peter stood by the door, listening. Ready for intruders, and yet looked at her with an encouraging smile. The love in his eyes, beautiful and tragic, stabbed her in the heart.

Her eyes shifted to the console as her mother's face appeared in the hologram in front of her. Emery whimpered, seeing her face. She looked different from how she remembered her; her hair was cut short, and she appeared a little older. But it was her mother. Her heart recognized her.

"I don't have much time. Emery, if it is you watching this, I've accomplished what I needed to accomplish. You are the only one who can travel back in time. Possessing the black and golden fragments allows you to get through the time barrier. There is a hidden compartment at the bottom of the capsule. Open it with the black shard and—"

Peter tapped her on the shoulder, grabbed her, kissed her, and then backed away, shouting. "I love you. You must go now. They're coming. See you in the next dimension, my Aphrodite."

And he was gone. Go after him. Run after him. Stop this nonsense.

Emery looked at the hologram again and caught the last words.

"... Grandma used to call me."

The hologram ended, and shots sounded in the corridor. She felt each shot in her heart, imagining Peter falling. The door opened, and two Minders came running. Emery ran to the capsule, which opened when she approached it. She took the shard out and fumbled to find and open a small panel on the bottom, pressing a barely visible triangle while two Minders were just a few feet away, pointing their guns at her. That meant Peter was dead. Her hands shook even more. The panel opened, revealing a glass pad with letters.

She remembered the last words of the hologram, "... Grandma used to call me," but she couldn't think of what Sasha used to call her mother. Her heart pounded while her mind was racing, trying to find that word in her blank mind. Sweat covered her face despite the coldness of the capsule.

Then, the word suddenly materialized in her mind, and she typed "Malenka" into the pad. The capsule lit in a brilliant blue light just as the Minders began pounding on the crystal walls, trying to open it.

One shot at the capsule. But he was too late—Emery was already on her way to her new destination, going back in time.

At last, she could weep, grieving Peter and the life she left behind. Again. As she descended at an incredible speed, grief gave way to hope of a new beginning. Going back and discovering that her mother was not to blame for the change. She'd find Peter again and Visla. She'll find them all in another dimension.

OTHER BOOKS

THE DARK WORLD SERIES
BOOK I
UNBORN

Unborn tells a tale that feels like a dreamy collision of family bonds, mystery, and the tug of destiny. It opens with the discovery of a mysterious infant in the forest, devoid of a belly button, by a couple in rural Russia. Sasha and Lev, battling their own heartbreak over childlessness, decide to keep the child despite its otherworldly origins. What unfolds is an exploration of the girl Olesya's extraordinary nature, her struggles with identity, and the looming forces seeking to claim her.

Unborn is an atmospheric and thought-provoking read for anyone who enjoys stories about family, identity, and the intersection of science and the fantastical. Fans of speculative fiction with a strong emotional core, think *The Midnight Library* meets *The Giver*, will find much to love here.

-Literary Titan Book Review

THE DARK WORLD SERIES
BOOK III
BRILLIANT GENESIA

In a society that cages women's minds, a young girl's disturbing visions lead her to Dr. Michell, a psychiatrist who helps her escape a predestined existence. Zara must now hide her true identity to follow her dreams of becoming a scientist. But when a tragic explosion shatters her world, she must flee to a new continent with her secret lover and their unborn child.

Years later, her daughter emerges from a different dimension with amnesia, forced to piece together her mother's fractured legacy to rediscover her own identity and power. Haunted by figures from the past, she must confront a multi-generational conspiracy that threatens to alter reality itself.

MISUNDERSTANDING

Psychological Thriller

Eva Barber's *Misunderstanding* is a gut-wrenching, beautifully layered novel that fearlessly explores trauma, friendship, betrayal, and the long, painful road to healing. At the center of it is Alice Williams—a girl raised in poverty and brutality, whose fight for survival becomes both physical and emotional. This isn't just a story about abuse. It's a story about what happens after—the aftermath, the unearthing of dark truths, and the question of who you become when the world breaks you and expects you to stay broken.

Barber writes with fearless clarity and emotional depth. Her prose is sharp, poetic, and unflinching. *Misunderstanding* doesn't offer easy redemption or tidy closure. Instead, it offers something more powerful: truth. Hard-won, painful truth—and the strength to face it.

Alice grows up in a suffocating trailer with her alcoholic, violent father and a mother who is more ghost than guardian. The trauma begins early and leaves no part of her untouched. Her only escape is her imagination—turning old playing cards into characters and narratives to distract from the chaos—and eventually, a friendship that will define her life: Lilly Labarre.

Lilly lives in a different kind of prison. Outwardly wealthy, stylish, and picture-perfect, her world is one of emotional starvation and cold neglect. Her mother, Chloe, is obsessed with appearances and perfection. Her father is passive, always caving to Chloe's icy authority. But in Alice, Lilly finds not just a friend, but someone who sees her. And in Lilly, Alice discovers safety and joy for the first time.

Their bond is immediate, intense, and unwavering. Despite coming from opposite worlds, they recognize each other's pain and fill the gaps their families have carved into them. This friendship is the emotional center of the novel—and the compass by which Alice navigates everything that follows.

Misunderstanding is not just a great story—it's a roar!

-Book Viral Review

www.ingramcontent.com/pod-product-compliance
Lightning Source LLC
Chambersburg PA
CBHW070051120726
47909CB00002B/353